PRAISE FOR THE NOVELS OF SHAYLA BLACK

"Scorching, wrenching, suspenseful, Shayla Black's books are a must-read."
—Lora Leigh, #1 *New York Times* bestselling author

"Wickedly seductive from start to finish."
—Jaci Burton, *New York Times* bestselling author

"[Black] always delivers strong characters, great stories, and plenty of heat."
—*USA Today*

"Absolutely fabulous."
—Fiction Vixen

"The perfect combination of excitement, adventure, romance, and really hot sex . . . This book has it all!"
—Smexy Books

"To die for. [A] fabulous read!"
—Fresh Fiction

"This one is a scorcher."
—The Romance Readers Connection

Falling in Deeper

SHAYLA BLACK

BERKLEY BOOKS, NEW YORK

BERKLEY

**An imprint of Penguin Random House LLC
375 Hudson Street, New York, New York 10014**

This book is an original publication of Penguin Random House LLC.

Copyright © 2016 by Shelley Bradley LLC.
Penguin supports copyright. Copyright fuels creativity, encourages diverse voices, promotes free speech, and creates a vibrant culture. Thank you for buying an authorized edition of this book and for complying with copyright laws by not reproducing, scanning, or distributing any part of it in any form without permission. You are supporting writers and allowing Penguin to continue to publish books for every reader.

BERKLEY® and the "B" design are registered trademarks of Penguin Random House LLC.
For more information, visit penguin.com.

Library of Congress Cataloging-in-Publication Data
Names: Black, Shayla, author.
Title: Falling in deeper/Shayla Black.
Description: Berkley trade paperback edition. I New York: Berkley Books, 2016.
Identifiers: LCCN 2016002069 (print) I LCCN 2016009632 (ebook) I
ISBN 9780425275474 (paperback) I ISBN 9780698164000 (ebook)
Subjects: I BISAC: FICTION / Romance / Contemporary. I FICTION / Contemporary
Women. I FICTION / Romance / General. I GSAFD: Romance suspense fiction. I
Erotic fiction.
Classification: LCC PS3602.L325245 F35 2016 (print) I LCC PS3602.L325245
(ebook) I DDC 813/.6—dc23
LC record available at http://lccn.loc.gov/2016002069

PUBLISHING HISTORY
Berkley trade paperback edition / July 2016

PRINTED IN THE UNITED STATES OF AMERICA

10 9 8 7 6 5 4 3 2 1

Cover photographs: man © vuk8691/Getty Images; smoke © Ambient Ideas/Shutterstock Images;
tattoos © phugunfire/Shutterstock Images
Cover design by Alana Colucci.

Penguin
Random
House

Acknowledgments

To my wonderful assistant and friend, Rachel Connolly, for holding my hand and juggling so many tasks during this crazy time, and for your amazingly kind words about how much you love this book. I cannot tell you how grateful I am.

To Shayla Fereshetian for beta-reading this book for me in what has to be one of the most comical, entertaining, and extremely helpful fashions ever. Thanks so much, doll!!! When I met you and realized we had a shared love of snark, I knew we had more than a name in common.

Last (but never least), to my husband of nearly twenty-five years. You may think you're only throwing together a meal or making me a cup of tea or starting me a fire or getting me a blanket when I'm working. But you're wrong. You may think that I don't notice the way you take care of my website or shipping or any of the other million and one tasks you do so I can keep writing. That's not true. I'm blessed and humbled every day to be married to the one man on the planet who loves me, respects what I do, takes care of me when I forget, plays a video game with me when I'm tired, is the best dad in history, and still makes me laugh. Love you forever! Happy silver wedding anniversary, babe!

Falling in Deeper

Chapter One

STONE Sutter squinted against the glare of the rising sun as he watched the increasingly familiar sights of Lafayette, Louisiana, zip past the windows of his black pickup. The early hours were almost bearable, but he knew the morning would become a hot, wet blanket by nine a.m. Every August day in the South felt like a special level of hell.

When his phone chimed, he glanced at the display: UNKNOWN NUMBER.

His fucking persistent fed. Just fabulous. "What?"

"Good morning, Sutter."

As far as he was concerned, anything good about the day had just swirled down the toilet. "What do you want, Bankhead? I'm still working on it."

"Too slowly."

"I don't move any faster with you breathing down my neck."

"Election deadlines are coming up. If we're going to stop Timothy Canton before he throws his hat into the ring for governor of California, we need to sew up our case now. Otherwise, he's got enough money and financial backing to plow over the competition. We need everything ready to indict him as he's declaring his candidacy so we can cuff him while we start spilling juicy details."

"You've explained this," Stone snapped. "I've got it. Give it a rest."

FBI Special Agent Bob Bankhead—or Blockhead, as Stone preferred—huffed into the phone. "Lily Taylor bought a gun this morning under her Misty Smith alias and registered for a comprehensive gun-safety class this afternoon. Her Internet searches suggest she intends to run."

Given Lily's sudden and fervent interest in the Florida Keys, Stone had thought the same thing. Why, after all these years? Because her previous boyfriend, Axel Dillon, had fallen in love with someone else? Was the shy beauty stuck on a nearly married man?

"Not so cocky now, are you?" Blockhead barked. "You know how many years it took us to track down Ms. Taylor, and the political capital it cost isn't something my boss would like to expend again. Don't let her slip away or . . ."

The fed didn't bother finishing his sentence. Stone knew the "or" well. He'd already spent enough time behind bars, watching his back, proving his toughness, and sidestepping inmate politics. That shit still made him break out in a cold sweat.

"I'm on it," he swore.

"You've had three months. You haven't produced a single result."

Stone really wished he could tell the FBI to fuck off because he wasn't a snitch and Lily wasn't a pawn. But he didn't have that option if he wanted to avoid another extended stay at the lovely Federal Correctional Institute in Beaumont.

"My first contact left the country before I could even approach him with the deal." Axel certainly hadn't stayed around long enough to see him meet his target, Lily Taylor, aka Sweet Pea. "And subsequent contacts have been . . ." *Pains in my ass.* "Reluctant to let me see her."

"None of that is my problem. Do whatever you have to. Just get me a fucking witness, or you'll be heading back to prison. You have two weeks."

Blockhead hung up. Stone resisted the urge to pound his phone against the dashboard. It wouldn't help his situation. Instead, he mentally reviewed his options.

Just yesterday he'd tried to move forward—and he'd been shut down again by Lily's two staunchest guardians: Mitchell Thorpe and Sean Mackenzie. If they didn't each already have a beautiful wife between them expecting their first baby, Stone would suspect ulterior motives. But they simply wanted Sweet Pea happy and safe.

They weren't his only obstacles. Stone had keepers of his own. Jack Cole and Logan Edgington were supposed to ensure that he could close the deal with Lily Taylor when the time was right.

As far as Stone was concerned, the time had to be right now.

He pulled over into a nearby parking lot, empty just before eight a.m., and opened his laptop. After connecting it to his hot spot, he opened a file with a string of code he'd written and embedded it in a jpeg of a funny comic strip before he e-mailed it. Then he waited. It wouldn't take long.

Fifteen minutes later, Jack Cole, his "boss" at Oracle, a firm that specialized in personal security and military consulting, called. Stone wasn't a trained operative, just the technical help. And since Jack wasn't a social creature, he knew the guy hadn't dialed him to shoot the shit.

Here we go . . . Stone pressed the button and accepted the call. "What's up, man? I'm on my way into the office."

"I need a favor first."

Jack had a superhot wife, a cute little boy, another kid on the way, and plenty of buddies, so Stone surmised this favor required his particular skill set. If most anyone else he knew had called for help, it probably wouldn't have been legal. But Jack didn't have a criminal bone in his body.

"Sure." Stone sat back, feeling pretty damn optimistic. "What do you need?"

"Deke just got off the phone," Jack said of his business partner. "His brothers-in-law could use a hand with a problem they're having."

"Computer-related?"

"Yep. Do you mind?"

Mind? Stone smiled. If he had minded, he wouldn't have infected their servers in the first place.

Deke's wife, Kimber, had two brothers, Hunter and Logan. The Edgington men were tough guys. Former Navy SEALs. Fucking heroes all the way. But more important, they weren't tech experts, and Stone now had a way to grease the wheels and get this train moving so he could reach Lily sooner.

"Sure. Should I head to their office?"

"Yeah. Joaquin is waiting for you." Jack referenced the Edgingtons' stepbrother. "He'll walk you through the issue."

That wasn't what Stone wanted to hear. "Will Logan be around?"

Because Stone really needed to make one of these overprotective hens understand, and Logan seemed the most likely one to see reason.

"Probably. Why? You got a man crush?" Jack teased.

Stone hadn't expected to like the guys he now worked with, but they were damn good at what they did and had wicked senses of humor.

"No more than you're jonesing over that dude who makes those custom knives."

"Keith?" Jack scoffed. "He's a freak." After a pause, he went on. "And Logan might be, too. Good point." After they both had a laugh, Jack instructed, "Keep me posted about the scope of their problem."

"You got it."

He arrived at their office less than five minutes later. Joaquin Muñoz met him at the door. He was a somber sort who only seemed to smile when he looked at or talked about his fiancée, Bailey. The guy was head over heels for his ballerina, who appeared equally into her big bruiser of a security specialist. In fact, the Latino lover probably could have made a big splash in Hollywood if he'd been less surly.

As usual, the man was all business. Probably because he owned a third of what had become EM Security Management, the personal security company he, Hunter, and Logan had taken over when Caleb Edgington retired.

"What's up?" Stone called as he climbed from his pickup.

"This fucking virus. It hit suddenly this morning. God, I hate computers sometimes."

Stone had no doubt that work for everyone in the office would be at a standstill until he purged the particularly nasty code he'd planted on their server. "I can fix that, no sweat."

"Thanks. I appreciate you coming on such short notice."

The pleasure was all his. "No problem."

"You're saving our ass." Joaquin thrust out his hand.

No, Logan was going to save his—and Lily's. Stone liked it when a plan came together.

After he shook Joaquin's hand, they headed for the door. Stone turned to the big guy. "So what are the symptoms? What have you tried?"

Joaquin scowled and launched into an explanation that Stone zoned through. "All the usual tricks aren't working on this virus. I can't seem to get rid of it."

Because Stone had written it for just this occasion, and he'd known exactly what they would do to eradicate it. He couldn't lie; pride beamed. Good to know he hadn't lost all his skills while languishing behind bars. "I'll fix it."

"Quickly, I hope." The other man went on, frustration visible on his face. "We've disconnected everything we can from the servers in the hopes it won't spread, but it's brought our operation to a grinding halt."

"Got it. Lead the way."

As Stone wound through the building that had once been a factory, its stark concrete walls didn't provide an ounce of visual interest. Down a flight of stairs they reached a room so chilly it could have passed for cold storage. Inside sat a bank of servers all twinkling like Christmas trees in straight, symmetrical lines. Ah, he felt at home here. People often pissed him off. Computers were far more straightforward. They didn't lie and weren't hard to figure out. They didn't betray him, and he never had to guess where he stood with a machine. Every encounter with one was simply a matter of determining who was more clever, and Stone made it his business to win.

Joaquin set him behind a desk with a computer. "Let me know if you need anything else."

"Can I grab a cup of coffee first?" he asked, mainly because he knew Logan kept his desk as close to the coffee machine as humanly possible.

"Yeah, you know where it is. I have to get back to another situation. If you have any other questions, Logan is back there."

"Hunter?" Just in case his younger brother needed further convincing.

Joaquin shook his head. "Baby Phoenix had a rough night. He has a cold, so Hunter and Kata stayed up with him. I can call him for emergencies."

He hoped it wouldn't come to that. "Thanks. I'll do my best to take care of the problem without involving him."

With a nod, Joaquin wandered off. Stone followed slowly until the other man disappeared into his cubicle area and started barking into the phone. Then he crept toward the coffeemaker and brewed a cup. With a steaming mug in hand, Stone poked his head around the corner and found Logan swearing over a map spread across his desk.

"Hey," he called.

The younger Edgington seemed like the friendly sort, at least until someone pissed him off.

Logan lifted his head, piercing him with blue eyes. "Thank fuck you're here to fix this virus. We're so careful. I have no idea how this happened."

"The writers of malicious code delight in being more under-handed than you." He smiled at the irony.

"Yeah? They can go fuck themselves. They could be putting lives at risk."

Stone had thought of that and felt vaguely guilty. The good news was that he would disinfect all their machines quickly. He'd even install a few extra goodies to keep them secure from potential out-side threats in the future . . . as soon as he'd secured Logan's assistance.

"Asshats," he muttered in vague agreement. "But as long as I'm here, I want to talk to you about Sweet Pea."

Even speaking her nickname made Stone unbearably hard.

Shortly after he'd walked out of the pen, he'd tested his pick-up skills and realized that he still had game. Hell, if anything, getting ass had become easier since women apparently liked a bad boy. Every woman except Sweet Pea aka Misty Smith—both bullshit aliases for Lily Taylor.

Stone didn't want anyone but her, and that was inconvenient as hell. But after spending his first thirty seconds with her, the chemical zing between them had left him beyond intrigued. He wasn't even sure why he'd so totally fixated on her shy sexiness, but he burned to know what sort of woman spoke that softly yet wore siren-red lip-stick. What was she trying to hide with all that vampy black lining such vulnerable chocolate eyes? If he could pry open her defenses and her thighs, not only would they be combustible together, Stone knew he could help save her.

Too bad that, after their promising first meet, she'd begun avoid-ing him as if she'd rather have the plague.

Logan's stare turned somewhere between grim and inhospitable. "Dude, you asked yesterday. The answer is no."

"Bankhead called this morning. I have two weeks. We've run out of time."

The former frogman hissed a curse. "Son of a bitch. I don't like this."

"Not my first choice, either."

"The plan would work better if you two had been seeing each other all summer."

True that. But she wouldn't take his calls. Stone suspected she was dodging the heat between them, but that wasn't all. Something else had spooked her.

For the hundredth time, he wondered what she was thinking. Why was she afraid of him? How could he persuade her to testify against Canton before the guy decided to snuff out all the skeletons in his closet prior to the election?

What would Lily feel like under him, whimpering and calling his name, when he thrust deep inside her?

"But I'm still not sure you roll hard enough to give Sweet Pea what she needs." Logan scowled.

Maybe, maybe not. Logan and Jack had spent the better part of three months trying to teach him. He hadn't trekked down the Dominant path in the past. But he'd be whatever Lily needed in order to make her happy and secure her help.

Then he would be a free man.

The luscious pinup beauty was his get-out-of-jail-free card—literally. If she agreed to play nicely with the feds about the rape and murder of Erin Gutierrez, he could put the past behind him and try to forget how badly he'd fucked up his life. While he'd been away, he'd inherited enough money from his late uncle Vince to live somewhere between frugally and comfortably until he found a new city to call home and a corresponding job.

But right now, it was damn inconvenient that he couldn't seem to focus on Lily Taylor as a witness, rather than a woman.

"I'd like to find out," he told Logan. Hell, he'd welcome any chance to be near her. "Get me face time with her and I'll do my best."

"Tell you what. You fix this problem in less than an hour, and I'll call the others on your behalf. If not . . ." The mock regret in Logan's expression was all "too bad, so sad."

It was Stone's turn to smile because the joke was on Logan. "You've got a deal."

Sipping his cup of joe, Stone turned to make his way to the bank of servers and bumped into an unfamiliar guy. Dark hair, midnight eyes, all the levity of an undertaker. Stone met his gaze straight on and realized that even at point-blank distance, the guy hid everything behind a steely stare.

"Stone, this is Pierce." Logan introduced them.

First name or last?

"One-Mile," the dude corrected, still taking Stone's measure with dead eyes.

Logan sighed. "One-Mile. He's our resident sniper. Rather than his given name, he'd prefer to be known by his longest kill shot. God save me from big egos."

Holy shit. Stone tried not to look impressed. He doubted this dude wanted any admiration. He'd bet One-Mile had come from the army and probably done a few tours in Afghanistan. Despite his insistence that everyone use his moniker, he was the type who never wanted anyone fawning over him for performing his duty to his country.

Stone stuck out his hand. "Hey."

One-Mile shook it with an absent nod, focused instead on Logan. "I'd like to speak to you."

"What's up?"

"I quit." After he'd delivered his news, the lean whip of a man turned away as if he'd fulfilled his duty and began to walk off.

"Nope," Logan called after him. "You can't. I've got a contract. You signed. We paid the bonus, and you cashed the check. End of conversation."

One-Mile stopped in his tracks.

Another man appeared in the hall and sidled past him, glaring daggers. "Fucking douche."

"The feeling is mutual."

"Give it a rest, you two." Logan rolled his eyes. "If I can work with my older brother, you can tolerate each other long enough to get your shit done."

Before Stone could even wonder what beef they had, the newcomer raked a hand over his military-short blond hair. "I will never trust him enough to be on an operational team with him. If he wants to quit, I say good riddance."

Logan slammed a fist on his desk. "Cutter, I don't give a shit if Pierce slept with your best friend."

"One-Mile," the guy corrected.

"Whatever." Logan waved a hand through the air.

"No! It's not whatever," Cutter insisted. "I can't work with Brea's rapist."

"I had her consent," One-Mile snarled, his eyes finally coming alive with hate.

"You manipulated her so that she had no choice but to say yes." Cutter clenched his fists.

"She had a choice." One-Mile crossed his arms over his chest. "If you want her that badly, you should have claimed her sometime between junior high and this July. You had plenty of time. But it took you that long to find your dick, and that's not my problem. She's mine now."

Cutter narrowed fierce eyes at One-Mile, as if he'd lost his mind. "She's not even speaking to you, asshat."

"Misunderstanding."

"No, reality. Something you're obviously not familiar with. If she winds up pregnant—"

"That's enough," Logan shouted. "I don't care if you beat the hell out of one another after hours, but stop bringing your personal shit to work. If you can't, I'll lock you in a room together until you learn to get along or one of you kills the other. I don't care which at this point. Be professional and do your damn jobs."

Silence fell in the wake of Logan's verbal beatdown. Cutter swore and stomped away.

One-Mile cocked his head and regarded Logan with a solemn expression. "I didn't rape her."

"Since she had to choose between saving her best friend's life and sleeping with you, I'd say you coerced her. It doesn't get much lower than that in my book."

Yeah, Stone didn't doubt that's how Logan saw that situation. All of Jack Cole's pals had Captain America complexes. They were heroes through and through. They refused to bend their values for a dog-eat-dog world. They figured out how to make the world bow to them. A vague shame clogged Stone's veins. Every time he thought he liked these guys, he remembered that he didn't belong.

Logan rubbed at the back of his neck and glared at One-Mile. "Get the fuck out of my face."

"Roger that." Pierce gave him a mock salute and marched away.

Once the guy was out of sight, Logan let out a long, low curse. "I swear, some days I get why my father retired and dumped this shit in our laps. Hunter, Joaquin, and I inherited those two when the colonel stepped down. They're exhausting, and with twin girls toddling around my house, peace is already at a premium."

Stone smiled faintly. "Those dudes look like a pain in the ass."

"Too bad shooting them would be illegal. I think I'd be doing the world a favor." He glanced at the clock on his computer. "You've only got fifty-one minutes left to fix my problem if you want me to talk to Thorpe and Sean about arranging time for you with Sweet Pea."

"Bastard," he poked, not worried. "I'm on it."

Stone pivoted away, back to the chilly room with the gleaming row of hardware—and, he hoped, his future.

* * *

"I don't like it." Sean Mackenzie glared across the table from Stone that evening.

As always, Thorpe was in lockstep with his buddy. "She's not ready."

"Why?" Stone demanded, sitting with them around the kitchen table at Dominion, the exclusive BDSM club Thorpe owned.

Granted, he hadn't seen Lily in months, but when he'd met her she hadn't looked ready to fall apart at Axel's imminent departure. Supposedly, she'd completely imploded once the man had gone. Stone wanted to know the reason, so he could devise a plan to help her.

"We've been over this." Thorpe scowled. "Axel was her pillar. He propped her up and gave her boundaries and—"

"I can do that," Stone insisted. "Logan and Jack have spent the last three fucking months preparing me to be whatever she needs. Let me do it."

"All theoretical knowledge." Sean shook his head, then glanced Thorpe's way. "But Stone is right. Bankhead called me today, too. So did a couple of my former colleagues from the Bureau. He's getting the squeeze, so it's now or never. Axel isn't coming back anytime soon?"

Thorpe shook his head. "Not for another month at least. I talked to him this morning. He and Mystery have decided to stay in the UK until her father has to fly to the States to start filming a new movie."

A familiar Cajun curse sounded over the speakerphone. Jack Cole couldn't be in Dallas today so he'd called. "Maybe if you let Axel in on our plan and asked him to contact Sweet Pea—"

"He'd object like a motherfucker." Thorpe grimaced. "Besides, if Lily is going to start relying on Stone for guidance, then we can't ask Axel to provide it."

"Exactly," Stone insisted. "Axel left you in charge of Lily's well-being, Thorpe. Let me see her again so I can start building trust between us. But I need every minute of these two weeks to convince her to testify." Still, the trio said nothing, and Stone's frustration mounted. "We agreed months ago that she won't have a future until she faces her past, right? Axel can't help her do that. Only I can."

Despite their grumbling, they all reluctantly agreed.

"Then stop dicking around. You're keeping her in limbo." Stone looked Sean's way. "Look, I get why you refused when the feds asked you to talk Lily into testifying. We all do. Canton is a psycho with a trail of dead bodies in his wake, and Callie is pregnant."

Sean nodded grimly. He clearly hated shirking anything that resembled his duty. "Thorpe and I can't risk our wife."

Not long after the FBI approached Sean, a former agent who knew Lily Taylor well, Jack had needed a hacker with Stone's skill set and pulled strings to have him released from prison temporarily to assist with a client's nasty cybersecurity problem. While working in Dallas one night, Stone had taken a single look at Sweet Pea and he'd wanted that petite bunch of curls and frills fiercely. Determined to do whatever it took, he finagled a meet and greet. Based on their instant—and mutual—attraction, Sean and the feds had concocted a plot to task him with persuading Lily to testify.

Admittedly, the idea was brilliant. By strong-arming Stone to soften Lily up for the stand, the FBI wasn't risking the life of a former agent or his loved ones if Canton caught wind of the scheme. It only took a single threat to control Stone, whom the feds no doubt saw as a thoroughly expendable resource. Best of all, if Stone succeeded, his sentence would be commuted. A win-win for everyone.

"And if the feds drag Lily in on a warrant as a material witness, it doesn't matter if she saw Canton participate in the gang rape and murder of her best friend at sixteen. They can't force her to testify," Stone added. "Convincing her to tell a jury what she knows will be one hell of a hard sell because the last time she agreed to do the right thing and be the prosecution's star witness, Canton had her mom and little brother slaughtered. You and the FBI didn't send me back to prison so I could have the opportunity to convince her. Let me do it. Use me. If you want her safe in the long run as much as I do, then we've got to help her put this asshole away before he gains more power."

"Don't pretend for one second this isn't about you." Thorpe glared his way. "You don't want to go back to prison."

"Who does? Most people aren't eager for incarceration. But we've all agreed that Lily has been living a half life since she came here, and you've let her."

All three men fell quiet, the guilt of their silence heavy.

"He's right. You need to act soon." Callie poked her head into the room. "Hi. Sorry. I know you didn't ask for my opinion, but Stone has a good point."

"Pet . . ." Thorpe warned as he spun around to the pretty brunette.

She ventured closer, absently rubbing her expanding belly as she dropped a kiss on both Thorpe's and Sean's cheeks. "Don't 'pet' me. Earlier, I talked with Sweet Pea—I mean, Lily. I still can't believe that's her real name. She's withdrawing further into herself. You two know she doesn't want to lean on either of you and divert your attention from me."

Given the sweetness Lily had exhibited in that one precious hour he'd spent with her, that didn't surprise Stone at all.

"But she needs someone," Callie went on. "She's not sleeping, and she admitted that her nightmares are getting worse."

Stone sat up straighter. "Nightmares? About what?"

Callie gave him an apologetic grimace. "She won't say. I don't think even Axel knew."

That gave Stone pause, then a little bit of hope. If she'd loved the big bastard, wouldn't she have shared her nocturnal fears with him?

Stone wanted to be more important to Lily. He wanted to be the man she trusted with all her secrets.

His future depended on it, too.

"C'mon, you guys," he urged. "We've talked about a dozen reasons why we should proceed. You've prepared me. I've got this. The only reason not to is because you don't have any faith in her ability to come out of her shell. She's not broken beyond repair."

Thorpe and Sean exchanged a glance and seemed to get on the same page without a word. Then Thorpe leaned toward the speakerphone. "Jack?"

"Yeah. As much as I hate the thought of throwing Sweet Pea to the wolf—no offense, Sutter—or putting her in danger, I don't think we can wait any longer."

Sean pulled out his own phone, sent a text or two, then looked back his way. "All right. We're a go. Contact Bankhead as soon as she says yes."

"What's your plan?" Thorpe asked.

"I've got some ideas," Stone answered vaguely. "Leave everything to me."

No one at the table looked as if they liked the sound of that, but the feds had tapped him for this task. And Stone relished it. Yes, he could avoid going back to prison, but he also fucking wanted to get his hands on pretty little Lily, explore the sparks between them.

"Look," Jack began, only to be interrupted by a pounding noise. "Someone's at my office door. For fuck's sake . . . Hang on." Footsteps retreated, and the sound of a door opening followed. "Logan?"

"Are you on the phone with that fucker?" Logan barked.

Stone tried not to smile. "Hi, Logan."

"You planted that virus in our network. I slaved all fucking morning to make sure that nothing was affected, and you did that shit on purpose. Last time I'm opening an e-mail from you."

"I knew you couldn't resist Dilbert," he teased.

Around the table, everyone else laughed.

"You suck," Logan growled.

"I had to do something to make you guys reevaluate the situation. Sorry. Desperate times, desperate measures and all that shit. But we're on the same page now?" A pair of nods, a sighed yes, and an assenting grumble later, Stone stood. "Good. I want to see Lily. Now."

Chapter Two

THE moment Lily Taylor had been dreading for nine months had finally arrived. Around her, the emergency room buzzed. People in white coats and scrubs scurried around the freezing, sterile space wearing grim expressions. Because they knew how much she was giving up?

The pain wracking her body barely penetrated her head. They'd injected something in her IV finally. Now she felt as if she were floating off the table. Vaguely, she wondered if her mother would come or if she'd decided to wash her hands of her teenage daughter after all.

Normally, it wouldn't matter. She had her bestie. Erin had agreed to hold her hand. Her friend's brother, Corey, had sworn he'd back her up, too.

In one terrible afternoon, everything had changed.

"Push!" a woman in bloodstained blue scrubs shouted at her.

Where was the doctor?

Still, the urge wouldn't be denied. She bore down, one push flowing into the next until time had no meaning beyond the pain gripping and the sweat drenching her. Pressure pulled and tugged at her middle, nearly crushing her. She screamed, then clenched her teeth as she struggled up and gave a mighty push.

At once, the agony and the stress ended. Lily wilted back but stayed awake to savor the very few moments she would get with the most precious person in her life.

A nurse bent to her, filling her line of vision with a clinical expression, but her eyes held pity. Around Lily, machines beeped. Everyone else bustled to cluster around a table a few feet away, shouting at one another. Stress charged the room.

Anxiety filled Lily, replacing the languid feeling of accomplishment. "What's going on?"

She didn't hear the sounds of a baby crying.

Panicked, she tried to climb off the table, but the nurse who wouldn't answer her shoved another needle in her IV. Then nothing . . .

With a gasp, Lily opened her eyes and sat up in the dark, empty room, tangled in the damp sheets. Her heart raced. She looked around the shadowed room and heaved a sigh of relief. Present. Dallas. Dominion. Another time, another place. After seven years, she wished the goddamn nightmares would stop.

Tears welled in her eyes—pooling in the corners—but she couldn't quite spill them. She trembled, fought for air. Would she ever have a normal life? Lily needed to bury her past and stop being afraid of the future. Stand on her own two feet.

Her head acknowledged all that. That scared girl who'd lost everyone she'd ever loved had no idea how to make that happen.

Hating herself for her weakness, she reached for her cell phone and started to dial her friend and former protector, Axel. Before she completed the call, she remembered that he was in London with his new fiancée. Eventually they would return, but he had his own life and a future he couldn't wait to begin.

He deserved more than to keep dealing with her broken past.

With a sniffle, she climbed out of bed, a bit embarrassed that she'd fallen asleep on the job. But she couldn't seem to drop into slumber in her solitary apartment these days, so she came to work exhausted.

Lily rose and smoothed out her clothes, then patted her hair back into place. For years, she'd felt almost secure here at Dominion. Until recently, she'd stopped looking over her shoulder quite so much. Yes, she'd always known her past hovered there, breathing down her neck. But now she feared it had come back to haunt her.

Maybe she was being paranoid, but she would swear she'd seen a guy watching her at the grocery store one day, then bumped into him at a fast food joint the next. Another girl might write it off as mere coincidence or think he was following her because he was interested. But she didn't believe in coincidence, and he hadn't flirted with her at all. In fact, he had watched her with a dissecting stare that made her anxious and afraid. He certainly hadn't ogled her as if he couldn't wait to strip her bare the way Stone Sutter had.

Maybe it was time to pack up, move on . . . just in case. She'd been in Dallas for years now—plenty of time for Canton to have caught on.

According to Axel, when she was feeling scared or overwhelmed like this, she was supposed to call Thorpe. But her employer had his hands full with Sean, Callie, and their coming baby. Lily refused to dump her personal problems in Thorpe's lap. Hell, he still called her Sweet Pea or Misty—just like Axel—because she'd never told any of them her real name or her real truth. Setting him straight would be an uncomfortable conversation after all these years. Not that she'd put him or any of her friends at risk.

The only person she might have told what she was feeling? Stone. He'd sucked her in with a single burning stare and made her tremble. His seemingly devil-may-care attitude and the rocking tats on his bulging biceps had intrigued her. He was quick with a smile or a quip. He seemed gentle on the surface. He came across like someone who might understand. She'd been so damn giddy to spend time with him.

Lily bit her lip against the ache that bloomed in her belly. What a fool she'd been.

She hated walks down memory lane, but her mind trekked the path anyway, taking her back three months, to the night they'd met.

Zeb had led her to a well-lit playroom. Stone had been waiting inside. He'd zipped his gaze around to zero in on her as Zeb ushered her through the door. Dark eyes narrowed, body coiled, Stone had given Lily the impression of a male animal on high alert as he sized up his prey.

After quick introductions, Zeb had smoothed a hand across the small of her back and bent to her ear. "He asked to meet you."

Lily had no idea why. As she looked into Stone's face, she'd seen hunger, the kind that made both uncertainty and excitement jet through her blood. She'd blushed because despite being twenty-three, she'd had sex with exactly two men in her life, and neither had really made her breath catch or her heart race. With just a glance, Stone made it clear that he intended to seduce her and give her pleasure until she screamed. In that moment, knowing Axel was in love with Mystery and that she had to start looking forward, not back, she'd met Stone's hot stare.

"Hi, there."

Even his husky voice sent tingles of excitement racing across her skin. Lily's chest tightened as if she couldn't breathe properly.

"Hi." The word had come out barely a whisper, but he gave her an encouraging smile.

"She's a little shy, our Sweet Pea," Zeb supplied with the sort of watchful glare she'd expect from an older brother. "Talk to her about pop culture and she'll relax."

Lily blushed again, this time in embarrassment. Most men didn't care about celebrity crushes and breakups. She loved keeping up. Their lives seemed so bright and interesting. Taylor Swift didn't hide in the shadows. Jennifer Lawrence wasn't worrying about her past.

They had so much confidence, and Lily hoped that someday some of that would rub off on her.

"I don't know much about it," Stone said, that voice of his like a caress. "But I want to hear about everything that interests you."

"We can talk about something else."

"Remember, no sudden moves and nothing sexual," Zeb warned as he backed away, hovering at the door.

She tried not to roll her eyes at his overprotective spiel. Thankfully, Stone ignored him and approached her slowly, towering so she had to crane back her head to study his hard, chiseled face.

Then he cupped her shoulder and she barely managed to bite back a gasp. Hot, sure, electric, his touch wasn't like anything she'd ever felt. Zeb had laid his palm on the small of her back just moments ago and she'd felt nothing. Why did Stone affect her so differently?

Lily peered into his dark eyes. She didn't have to ask if he felt the pull between them. He made no attempt to hide his desire to get her naked and put his hands on her.

Was being romantically interested in someone supposed to feel like this? She really wouldn't know.

He walked her across the room, to a bench usually used for sub restraint. Long and somewhat narrow, it wasn't the most comfortable but still one of the few places in the room to sit.

After Stone helped her down, he perched beside her, his thigh nearly pressed to hers. She experienced that difficulty breathing again. As if her body were a divining rod, all her senses seemed attuned to him. Her stomach knotted into a nervous ball.

"You okay here?" he asked softly. "Do you need me to put more space between us?"

Mentally, she probably did. But she answered him instinctively. "No. Tell me about you."

He shrugged. "Not much to say. I've been living in South Texas for a while but I'm working with Jack Cole on a technical project now. I'm a computer guy. I saw you a few weeks ago, the night of Thorpe's birthday, and I thought you were one of the prettiest women I've ever seen."

Heat crept up her face again. The curse of having a fair complexion. She had to get control of her reactions and start acting more like a normal woman if she ever wanted to have a normal life. Stone might not be a forever guy—who knew?—but maybe they could try dating or something.

"I remember seeing you that night, too," she admitted, not quite meeting his intense, dark stare.

He curled a finger under her chin. "Look at me."

Once she complied, he smiled. And Lily wasn't sure she'd ever felt more connected to another human being. Her skin sizzled, her body trembled—and she didn't even want to think about what his mere gaze did to her girl parts.

"Tell me about you," he murmured.

"I've been Dominion's receptionist for the last few years." And . . . what? She couldn't tell the man her past. She had no idea what to say about her future plans or aspirations since she couldn't look ahead knowing Canton might catch up to her. "Like Zeb said, I follow pop culture. I also like to read." She rolled her eyes, tried to poke fun at herself, and not think about the fact that she felt like a high school girl with her first crush. "I'm shy."

"You're doing great," he praised. "Do you have a favorite sport or hobby?"

"I'm not so good at anything that requires a ball, but I sew a lot of my own dresses." She fluffed the full red skirt of her swing dress; then she realized how many men didn't care about sewing. "You must think that's boring."

"No. I wouldn't be any good at it." He shrugged. "But I find it interesting that you can measure out cloth and put pieces together to make something to wear."

"No, you don't."

"Seriously," he vowed. "It's probably like me telling you about the web codes I unravel."

He had a point. "Yeah, I don't know how you do it, but it would be cool to watch."

Stone smiled wide. "Exactly. So . . . what would be a perfect date for you?"

"I have no idea." To be honest or not? Lily gnawed on her lip. If she ever saw him again, she would already have to lie about so many other things. She'd rather tell him the truth where she could. If he thought she was a freak, then he was never going to like her for her anyway. "I've never been on one."

That took him aback. "Never? Baby, why not? Have all the men in your life been blind?"

She laughed. "I left home young, and at first I was just figuring out how to make ends meet. When I came to work here, the environment was a little intimidating at first, you know?"

He grinned. "I have to admit my first trek through the doors was more than I bargained for."

"You don't . . ." How did she ask a virtual stranger who seemed to give off a Dom vibe if he'd ever topped anyone?

"I'm intrigued and I'd be willing to look into it, but so far, no." He took her hand, his thumb grazing her fingers. "What's the deal with you and Axel?"

She squelched her grief that Axel was no longer her protector. It conflicted with the excitement she felt around Stone. Which confused her. Besides, Axel needed to move on with his life and embrace the woman he loved. "We're not together anymore. And we didn't really date, per se."

Stone frowned as if he didn't quite understand. Truthfully, her relationship with Axel wouldn't make sense to most people. And it didn't matter now. He had his future. Maybe Stone could be a part of hers in some small way, even if only in her fantasies.

"Um . . . What else? Until a few months ago, I had a cat. A male.

I took him in as a stray but he got cancer and I had to put him down. I named him Bongo because he liked to bounce around the house like a drum," she added, then shook her head. "Do you have a pet? Sorry I'm babbling. You make me nervous."

"Sorry to hear he died." He squeezed her hand. "No pets. And I'll be honest. You make me a little nervous, too."

Lily couldn't help the smile that widened her lips. "You're just saying that."

"No. Here." He lifted her hand to his chest and placed it over his racing heart. The hard, rapid thump under her palm made her insides jump with delight. "You feel that?"

She nodded earnestly. And as if she couldn't control herself, her gaze dropped to his lap. His heart wasn't the only thing filling with blood. Lily closed her eyes and stifled a grin.

"I do." She bit her lip as she withdrew her palm. "My heart is beating fast, too."

Was that admitting too much? She looked down at the hands she wrung in her lap and realized that her skirt had ridden up on the side and exposed her black thigh highs.

Lily yanked the skimpy fabric down and looked up in time to see Stone's stare glued to the sight. "That's embarrassing."

His face tightened as he swallowed. "Not at all, baby. You're sexy." He gave her a deep rumble of masculine laughter. "Forget I said that. I asked Axel to set up this meeting so I could get to know you, not so I could talk you out of your clothes. At least not yet." He winked. "So you work for Thorpe?"

She accepted the subject change but couldn't wipe the pleased little smile off her face. Big, attractive Stone thought she was sexy. He didn't seem to care that she didn't know what to say and fumbled over her words. "I do. I don't think he really needs a receptionist, and I try to help with inventory, organization . . . whatever he can't get to. I've also pitched in with the tasks Callie used to complete. She's had a tough pregnancy at times." Lily smiled fondly. "But every time she's sick or tired, Thorpe and Sean are both so attentive, I can't decide who's more over the top in taking care of her. She's had a terrible past, so I'm happy for her."

"That's thoughtful. They're lucky to have you."

"I like to help. Thorpe has given me so much . . ." She shook her head. Stone didn't care about that, either. "So you do technical things for Jack?"

He shrugged. "I've been helping him with a case. It's been complicated but successful."

"Jack is great. All the guys here are. Thorpe only grants membership to people who have a really positive vibe. He and the Edgington brothers are some of my favorite people."

"But you never dated any of the members?"

Lily wasn't sure how to answer that. She came with a lot of baggage, and even if the men of Dominion didn't precisely understand, they knew it was heavy. Of course, they'd chosen women who could give them their hearts, souls, and bodies.

Because she probably couldn't, she should stop wasting Stone's time.

"No. I should go." She stood and fluffed out her skirt, then held out her hand. "I enjoyed meeting you."

"Why are you leaving?" He wrapped hot fingers around her wrist. She could have escaped if she wanted but the second he put his hand on her, Lily ached to ease closer. "I drove over five hours just to meet you. Don't go."

She bit her lip. The excited girl inside her wanted to cave immediately. She was flattered and she liked him, probably more than was smart. On the other hand, she'd never felt this way about a man and he scared the heck out of her.

"If no one told you, I'm not typical."

"I'm not, either. So maybe that makes us a good match. Is there anything wrong with seeing if we are?"

When he put it like that, no. But . . . "I'm a project."

He seemed to mull that over as his grip around her wrist tightened ever so slightly. "That term indicates you think there's something wrong with you. Maybe there's just something wrong with the people you've been with in the past. Maybe they simply weren't right for you."

"You think you are?" she asked, more breathless than she'd like.

He shrugged. "How do we know if we don't try?"

Another good point.

"It takes a long time for me to trust." After this confession and admitting that she'd never dated, she didn't want to go for the trifecta and blurt out that she was afraid of sex. Lily wanted to be at least somewhat honest with him, but that was more than she could make herself say just now.

"Let's take it one day at a time. I'm attracted to you. I think it must be mutual because you keep eating me up with those pretty eyes."

Oh god. She probably was. Lily felt heat scorch her cheeks.

When she tried to tug from his grasp, he held firm but his expression gentled. "That's nothing to be embarrassed about. I like you. I'm hoping you could like me, too. It doesn't have to be more complicated than that right now."

Lily thought of a hundred objections, mostly centered around her insecurities. She didn't want to seem like a head case, and she liked the way he made her feel both beautiful and adored with just a glance. "I guess not."

Just then, the lights in the room went black. The hum of the air conditioner ceased. For a moment, her heart stopped. It was probably paranoia, wondering every time something out of the ordinary happened if Canton had found her.

"Sweet Pea?" Stone called as his firm grip on her wrist turned reassuring. He wound his other arm around her and anchored his hand protectively on her hip. "You okay, baby?"

"A little scared of the dark." She squeezed her eyes shut, not wanting to remember why.

Stone's voice and presence was a balm. Surprisingly, instead of fearing the big man, she had the sense that he'd protect her, and she edged closer.

"That's it. Come here." Gently, he guided her down onto his lap and nestled her against his chest before he wrapped his beefy arms around her. "I'm sure it's nothing. But I won't let anything happen to you."

Across the room, Lily heard Zeb opening the door. Not a sliver of light entered the room from the normally bright hall.

"Thorpe?" the Dungeon Monitor called out.

"The power probably surged or something." Stone soothed her as he caressed her hair and eased her head onto his shoulder. "Breathe. I've got you."

She almost felt safe. Maybe his words or voice had calmed her. Maybe it was the way he'd brought her close as he'd reassured her. This felt like being with Axel . . . but different. His nearness didn't merely comfort her. For the first time, being close to a man excited her, too. Lily let herself melt against him.

Zeb apparently stepped into the hall but left the door open. She could hear him and Thorpe calling back to each other. The breaker had tripped. They'd be able to restore power in a minute.

Problem solved, Lily let out a huge sigh of relief and drank in the moment of feeling like a normal woman enjoying alone time with an interesting guy.

Then Stone cupped her cheek and led her face down, her mouth close to his own. His warm breath feathered over her lips. She froze and fought the impulse to lunge forward and close the distance between them.

"I don't think I can wait another second, but stop me if you're not ready for me to kiss you," he whispered.

Lily didn't have the will to resist him in that moment. As a freshman in high school, she'd first kissed Rick Mensell because he'd been the cutest boy and every girl had wanted him. As a grown woman, she'd first asked Axel to kiss her because she'd needed to know if she could bear a man's touch again. Neither guy had made her feel a tenth of the thrill that having Stone Sutter's mouth hovering over hers, teasing her with his almost-kiss, did.

She didn't think she could speak, so she tilted her head instead, positioning her mouth perfectly against his, and dropped a brush of fingers on his shoulder. That was all the encouragement he needed.

A heartbeat later, he settled his lips on hers. He didn't experiment or bother to test their fit. He kissed her as if he already knew how thoroughly he intended to take her mouth and how good it would feel. For a delicious eternity, Stone cupped her jaw and held her exactly where he wanted her. She couldn't misinterpret his touch, which said he intended to take every bit of her that she'd surrender.

He nudged her lips apart. Something shockingly alive dashed down her spine. A dizzy euphoria filled her head. Lily clenched her legs together, feeling an ache tighten there that could only be desire.

With the tender press of his fingers against her face, he guided her as he dove deeper into the kiss and slid his tongue against her own. She'd kissed Axel this way before. But it had never made her feel antsy and hot, like she wanted to writhe against him, strip her clothes off, and beg him to touch her.

She barely knew Stone. They had no history. Why did she ache for him so desperately?

Suddenly, the lights flicked on, glinting behind her eyelids. Lily tried to ease away and survey the situation. Stone only held firm, stroking her jaw with his thumb, and kissed her with more urgency.

She let him. As he possessed her mouth, the world and all its problems melted away. She forgot to be scared or worry that he would want more than she could give. She didn't even think about the fact that they were virtual strangers. Instead, she sank against the warmth of his substantial body and into the fantasy of being normal enough to interest a man who seemed both incredibly masculine and kind. And god, he smelled good.

Lily gathered her nerve and slid her hand down his shoulder, over the defined muscles covered in ink. He must have a high threshold for pain. She'd screamed and held in sobs through the first twenty minutes of her lone tattoo.

Pushing that memory away, she focused on his kiss. On him.

She wrapped her hands around the mind-boggling girth of his biceps and trembled, pressing closer. He grabbed her tighter, his fingers sliding down her nape as he gave her lip a playful nip, pressed a kiss just under her jaw, and smoothed a palm around the curve of her hip.

She wanted to ask him to peel his shirt off just so she could drink him in. She'd bet the sight would make her daydreamy and tingly. He certainly knew how to kiss. With a simple press of his fingers, he guided her head back, then shifted the angle of the kiss, maneuvering her into opening completely to him. Little by little, Lily found herself willing to cede her control.

"That's enough." Zeb's hard voice from the doorway broke their cocoon. The lights had returned, illuminating his scowl. "Axel promised you a meeting, not a gropefest. Let her go."

Stone stiffened but pulled back, looking into her eyes as he pushed one of her chestnut and fuchsia curls from her face. "You okay?"

A half-drunk smile wobbled across her mouth. "Yeah."

She slid to her feet, but he wrapped an arm around her as if he didn't trust her legs to hold her upright. Good instinct. The second she tried to stand, her shaking thighs wobbled. A druglike weakness still pumped through her veins, infecting her muscles. And when she looked at him, she could hardly catch her breath.

He sent a megawatt smile down at her. "You look pretty with your cheeks flushed and your lips swollen."

Lily felt pretty, too. She felt like a woman, not a broken responsibility someone always had to pick up and care for.

"I don't know what you did to me but . . ." She sighed, unable to put this feeling into words. It felt like those times as a girl she'd gone to the park and put her arms out, spinning around and around until she'd fallen down, giggling and happy.

"Something I can't wait to do again, baby. Let me take you to dinner."

That sobered her up a bit. She blinked. "I-I'm supposed to be working. I came in to see Axel tonight but when we decided he should move on, I asked Thorpe if he needed me. I have a few tasks to complete. Sorry."

Stone didn't say anything for a long minute, just brought her closer to him and drilled down into her with a dark stare that made her knees threaten to give way. "How about this weekend? I'll drive out. We can eat and talk. Or we can stay here and talk. Whatever makes you feel more comfortable."

"I'd like that." She tried not to let her giddiness show too much. Maybe he'd even kiss her again.

"I want to see you more, Sweet Pea. Tell me what will set you most at ease."

"I'm not really sure. I mostly saw Axel here."

"Since you two didn't date. Got it." When she nodded her agreement, he slanted a speculative glance her way. "But he was your Dom?"

She swallowed. Would that turn Stone off? "And my protector. He helped me feel safe."

"Didn't you say he just left you?" He sounded annoyed on her behalf.

She'd let Axel go with a heavy heart, knowing she had to stop dragging him down. "It was time. I'm fine."

Lily knew she might be lying. She wouldn't pine for Axel as a lover. But she would very much miss her friend.

"I should be a good guy and tell you I can wait until you're sure. But after that kiss, I don't even know if I can wait three days to see you again. I don't know if I'll stop thinking about you between now and then."

She didn't think she would stop thinking about him either but hearing him say that made her feel so coveted.

"Here." Lily plucked out a pen from the deep pocket of her full skirt and reached for his hand. She dragged the ballpoint across his palm and wrote her number in purple ink. "Call me if you feel like it. Okay?"

"I will." And despite Zeb's glare, Stone leaned in and brushed a lingering kiss on her lips. "Be thinking about what you want to do Saturday because I *will* come for you."

She merely smiled his way. He gave her one last heated glance and turned, heading for the exit. Zeb watched him leave and shut the door behind Stone with a shake of his head.

"What's with the disapproving-brother bit?" Lily frowned at Zeb, fists on her hips. "I know you and Axel are friends, but I'm not cheating on him or anything. We were never exclusive." Axel had merely watched over her and kept away any man who came on too aggressively or clearly had a booty-call agenda.

"That guy, Sutter? He isn't good for you." Zeb scowled, his mouth twisting under that infamous dark beard of his.

"Why would you say that? He seemed nice."

"He buttered you up with compliments."

Was Zeb saying she didn't deserve them and had been dumb enough to fall for his lies? "He came all the way from Lafayette to see me."

"And he damn near peeled your clothes off, too. He knows you aren't with Ax anymore. I don't want him thinking that means you're not surrounded by people who will step in if he crosses the line."

Now Zeb was being beyond overprotective. Stone would have stopped with just a word from her. "What do you think he'd do to me?"

"With his kind, you never know. But I'm watching him. I'll make sure Thorpe does, too."

Lily reared back. "This is the first time I've liked a guy. Romantically liked. And you're trying to scare me away from him?"

He shrugged. "You're better off without that dude. Since he just came from the big house, I assume that means he plays in the big leagues. I don't think you're ready for that."

"The big house?" He couldn't have meant what Lily thought he had.

"Yeah. He's a fucking felon fresh out of prison. Some of the guys around here might pull a prank now and then or party a little harder than they should, but no one breaks laws. I heard he beat the shit out of some guy while he was away and got put in solitary for a month. He's bad news."

Stone was an ex-con? A criminal?

Lily gaped, trying to reconcile the man she'd just kissed, the one who'd made her feel special, with a violent thug who'd spent time behind bars.

Canton was the worst sort of offender. He'd just been smart enough never to be convicted. And he surrounded himself with the violent gang-bangers who liked a side of rape with their murder. Was Zeb saying Stone was the same?

Her entire body iced over. She stumbled, falling onto the bench.

In her pocket, her phone began to vibrate. Lily pulled it free and glanced at the display. A number she didn't recognize, area code 337. Lafayette. Most everyone who lived there and would call her she'd programmed into her contact list so their name would pop up on her display. This was just a number, and her spine tingled, telling her that Stone was already ringing.

A criminal. A felon. A man who, under that smiling facade and polite demeanor, might be capable of terrible, heinous acts that would give her nightmares for another half dozen years to come.

Trembling and holding in a cry, she declined his call.

Chapter Three

M ISTY?" Thorpe stood in the doorway later that morning, yanking her from the bittersweet memories of her one meeting with Stone
and bringing her back to the present.

When she heard the name that it had become almost second nature
to answer to, she spun around. Years ago, Lily had picked it because
that's what she'd called her cat and she'd hoped she would remember
to answer to something familiar.

Thorpe looked every inch the imposing authority figure in a perfectly tailored navy suit, with a well-groomed dark beard framing his
hard jaw, and gray eyes that saw everything. From the beginning,
Lily had almost regarded Thorpe as a father figure. And the expression on his face now told her that he had something serious to say.

She tensed. "Yes, Sir."

He raised a brow at her sudden formality but didn't otherwise
mention it. He simply shut the door behind him and entered the
playroom. "Callie says you haven't been sleeping at home?"

She should have guessed that her concerned friend would say

something to her Dom and Lily's boss. "I'm sure it will pass. I'm sorry for napping on the job."

Unless she saw that guy who seemed to be following her again or anything else suspicious. If that happened, she probably wouldn't close her eyes for a week. She would also need to disappear from Dallas. Better safe than dead.

Thorpe sighed as he came closer. "I'm not angry that you slept, Sweet Pea. I'm worried about the reasons you're not sleeping in the first place. Is there anything you want to talk about?"

And potentially bring the violent wrath of Timothy Canton down on his head? "No."

She could probably tell him that she feared she'd been followed, but then she'd have to tell him why that possibility terrified her. And they'd be right back to talking about Timothy Canton. Besides, she'd bought a gun this morning. In an hour she'd be starting the gun-safety class she'd registered for. She damn well intended to become self-sufficient.

"You've struggled since Axel paired off with Mystery. He didn't want to leave you for this long. Was I wrong to encourage him to spend time away with his fiancée?"

"Not at all. I'm no longer his responsibility."

"No," he agreed. "You're mine now, and I've done a poor job of understanding your needs. Talk to me."

She was not a child and shouldn't need his guidance. He didn't have the time or energy for her. Most of all, she didn't want to spill her guts to someone who wouldn't be a permanent fixture in her life. The part that involved Canton was too dangerous. The rest was simply too painful.

"Thorpe, Sir . . . I appreciate your help but it's just a patch of insomnia."

"So the perpetually long face, the avoiding outings with the others at the club, the episode with the half bottle of vodka last week . . . That was all you being perfectly happy and well-adjusted?"

Lily hated that even when she thought she'd slipped something past Thorpe, he still saw. Axel had asked him to watch over her because sometimes she felt overwhelmed. And god knew she'd made some terrible decisions in the past.

She sighed. "I'm a little lonely but otherwise fine. I want Axel to be happy. I've missed him but he's better off, and I'm thrilled he's found someone."

"So you're lonely?" Thorpe appeared to mull that over.

Slowly, she nodded. Why did she feel as if she'd just walked into a trap?

"Since you've eschewed all the girl time Callie has tried to talk you into this summer, I'm going to guess it's not female companionship you're missing. Before his departure, Axel asked me to be responsible for your physical safety and emotional welfare."

Oh, this couldn't be good. "You don't have to take care of me. I'm a grown woman."

"But Axel provided you with guidance and helped you out with whatever you needed. That's what you've been missing this summer. So I've been thinking these last few days about a new protector for you, one who can mentor you and devote far more time to you than I'm able."

Her heart froze. Lily wasn't sure how she felt about that when she couldn't be honest with him about virtually anything . . . and she couldn't exorcise Stone Sutter from her thoughts. He'd been the cause of her summer malaise. Sure, she missed Axel . . . but she'd never stopped thinking about that kiss Stone had given her or wondering what could have been between them if she weren't so afraid of his violent past.

Someone new might be good for her but . . . "I don't know if I'm ready for that."

Maybe she could play the fragile card and put Thorpe off. But for how long? And how could she move on with her life if she didn't change anything in it? She and Axel had both needed their time together to be over for different reasons. Granted, she wasn't doing well alone. When she made emotional decisions, they usually turned out the worst. Maybe Thorpe was right and she needed a distraction so she could finally purge Stone from her yearnings.

"I think you are. I know a man who could be good for you. Why don't you meet him, spend time with him? Maybe you could try opening up. He might make you happy. If not . . ." He shrugged. "We'll reevaluate. But give him a couple weeks and genuinely try before you walk away."

Lily sighed. Thorpe's interference made her bristle, but he—and Axel—only wanted what was best for her. And she had been desperately lonely, even before his departure. If she considered Thorpe's proposition like a blind date, it might work. If it didn't, she'd have a funny story to tell. "All right. I'll try."

"Good. Remember, he can only help you as much as you let him."

Every word Thorpe said was true. Axel had proven that. He had been extremely patient and dragged information out of her over time. As she'd come to trust him, her sense of security had grown. Over and over, he'd proven himself to be solid. Some of her evenings with Axel had been her happiest, even if they hadn't been romantic and she hadn't been emotionally fulfilled. She'd felt safe. To Lily, that meant the world.

Though she wasn't sure she wanted a new mentor and protector, she probably needed one.

"You're right, Sir." She stared at the decorative concrete beneath her feet and wondered who Thorpe thought would be good for her. Zeb? That new guy whose name she couldn't remember? Someone else entirely?

Thorpe held out his hand. "Come with me."

Now? She blinked up. Resolution firmed Thorpe's features. He wasn't the sort to put off until tomorrow what he could accomplish today. She should have realized that if he'd bothered with a speech, he was ready to execute his plan.

With a wry smile, Lily slid her palm into his and savored the moments of comfort. Being with the big club owner really did feel like having a father figure she could trust. Since her own dad had run out when she was four, it was nice.

Together, they walked down the hall to Thorpe's office. Inside, she spotted Sean leaning against the wall beside Thorpe's empty leather "throne" on the far side of the room. In a chair facing the desk, she saw another man from the back, one with buzzed dark hair and strong, wide shoulders.

He began to spin around in his chair. Combat boots and long legs encased in faded jeans came into view first. A solid torso wrapped in a gray T-shirt appeared, rippling with every move. Inked biceps caught her gaze, along with veined forearms and big hands. He radiated formidable power.

Without even seeing his face, Lily knew exactly who'd come.

Stone Sutter.

His nearness sent a hot flush rushing from her toes to her cheeks.

She jerked a stunned glance up at Thorpe and yanked her hand away. The man almost never made mistakes, because he considered everything carefully before he acted. But he couldn't possibly have thought this through. If he had, he would never have paired her off with a felon who made no secret of the fact that he wanted inside her panties.

"No." She shook her head.

Stone swiveled to face her, and their eyes met for an electric moment. She felt dizzy and overwhelmed. Her knees weakened. Even being this close to him messed with her head.

Thorpe's face hardened. "Why not?"

A mere six feet away, Stone stood, his stare fused to her. He nodded in greeting. "Sweet Pea."

She didn't acknowledge him, just backed away, unable to tear her gaze free. "I can't."

Felons weren't good guys. They raped and murdered and laughed as they disposed of a girl's body like the contents of the kitchen garbage.

"Not two minutes ago, you promised that you would try," Thorpe reminded her with a raised brow. "Now that you know who's agreed to take you in hand, you're refusing? Explain."

"We don't suit." For so many reasons. She needed a friend who would be by her side and provide a willing ear when needed, not a man who complicated everything. Stone's past aside, the man lit up every cell in her body in a way she didn't know how to process or fight.

"That wasn't the impression I got when I kissed you." Stone prowled closer.

Lily couldn't decide if she wanted to blush furiously or punch him. Instead, she ignored him altogether and sent an imploring glance to Sean before whirling back to Thorpe. "He scares me."

"Why?" Stone asked. "Did I do more than kiss you when we met?"

Lily pressed her lips together. Thorpe didn't object to Stone's line of questioning, merely looked at her as if he was damn interested in her answer, too.

"No," she admitted.

"Did I force you to kiss me?"

"No. But I—"

"Felt like a woman when you were with me and wanted more, which made you run scared?" he challenged. "Lie to me and tell me I'm wrong."

A vague shame sliced through her composure. While he wasn't far off the mark, it wasn't the whole truth. He couldn't possibly understand that.

"Can I talk to you for a moment alone?" she asked Thorpe.

If she could explain his criminal past, surely Thorpe would understand.

He didn't say anything at first, merely glanced at her and Stone, then peered over to Sean in silent question. Callie's other man apparently answered in that wordless dude language Lily couldn't grasp.

"No," Thorpe finally said. "You swore earlier that you'd give someone new a couple of weeks. You haven't even given him a couple of minutes."

She couldn't deny that but . . . "Please. Don't."

Was it possible he already knew Stone's past? It wasn't like Thorpe not to perform his due diligence. Lily sighed. Maybe she was overreacting. Or maybe Zeb had been mistaken.

Maybe she should give Stone another try.

"Two questions. That's all I want to ask you," she promised.

Thorpe shook his head. "Ask him first. If you don't get satisfactory answers, then I'll see you. But don't come to me if you're not trying. I'm giving you tough love because I care."

He headed for his office door.

Sean followed, pausing just before he crossed the threshold. "If you want more in life, you have to take chances, Misty. Happiness isn't easy and it doesn't fall in your lap. You have to grab it, take it down, and make it yours. It's time you did that."

Lily didn't have firsthand knowledge but she suspected they were right, which only made Stone's presence more confusing. Maybe he would be the best thing ever for her. It was also possible he could finally be the one who put her six feet under.

They both turned their backs on her, and Stone trailed the men, shutting the door behind them, cutting her off from her friends and only possible escape route.

She and the only man she'd ever actually desired were alone.

Tough love was scary.

Her heart thundered. Even her breath trembled in and out of her lungs. "Let me out."

"Not until you explain why you've been dodging me for three months. I kissed you and asked you on a date. You agreed. Ten minutes later, you acted as if I wasn't even on the same planet. What happened?" He glared, and it felt like the worst of Axel's displeasure but with far more censure and impact.

"You're not my Dom. You're not even a Dom at all, so don't use that expression on me."

"See, that's where you're wrong, baby. For the last three months, I've been training with Jack Cole and Logan Edgington. Yeah, *your* friends. They both think I'd be good for you. Thorpe and Sean obviously do as well, which is why they've asked me to watch over you, give you friendship, support, advice, and . . . whatever else you need. Knowing all that, are you really going to keep fighting the pull between us? Can you truly say you're happy with the status quo?"

No, but she didn't need his questions confusing her right now. May as well go for the truth, get it out in the open, and call him on it. If he did something violent, hopefully Thorpe and Sean weren't too far away to hear her scream. "I'm not too afraid of whatever pull you think we have. It's why I let you kiss me. Then I found out about your past. I know you came from prison."

Understanding lit his face. "You're right. Let's talk about it."

"I've seen enough violence to last me a lifetime. I don't need someone who lives by it."

"I'm not a violent man, unless provoked." He cocked his head. "You have no idea why I went to prison, do you?"

"You're a felon. You beat the crap out of someone so badly they gave you solitary confinement."

"That's true."

He didn't even try to deny it. Lily was shocked.

"But you've also got some very selective information. I went down for a computer-related crime. I played a college prank on an asshole who'd stolen money from my widowed grandmother and bragged about it. So, with the help of a couple of friends, I set up an e-mail scam until he coughed up the same amount of money he'd taken. Then I returned it to her."

"That doesn't sound like a felony," she accused with narrowed eyes.

"It wasn't until the buddies who helped me set up the scheme and I all decided it might be an easy way to make some cash and get out from under our student loans. One of my frat brothers worked at a bank and figured out how to get the account numbers and e-mail addresses of multimillionaires, as well as open temporary accounts. I was the technical guy who created the false messages to bilk them out of money, intercepted the funds as they were being transferred, and diverted them to temporary accounts. Then another pal figured out how to siphon the funds out and turn them into clean, liquid cash through some of his connections. Collectively, we needed to raise about half a million dollars to be debt-free, which we did by the start of our senior year. We successfully laundered money and were set to graduate without owing anyone anything. But we got greedy and decided to pull one more cycle to start our futures with a cushion." He shrugged. "I'm not proud of what I did. My only defense is that I was young and stupid and entitled. I paid for it. I did twenty-two months of hard time. I learned my lesson. As for the guy I beat the shit out of? That was purely for my pleasure. He was a child pornographer."

Lily blinked at his explanation. If that was all true . . . She didn't know how to feel. He really wasn't violent? He wasn't like Canton?

"I would have beat the shit out of the child pornographer, too." The words slipped from her lips.

He smiled and let out a breath, relaxing a bit. "I would never hurt you."

Those words raised her red flags. Where had she heard that before? Oh, yeah. Canton. And maybe she was being too suspicious by throwing Stone in the same realm as her tormentor from her teenage years. On the other hand, if she'd been more cautious seven years ago, her mom and brother, Brady, would still be alive. So would Erin. Being too trusting once had cost her everything.

She had no way of corroborating Stone's story without talking to Thorpe. And did he know anything beyond what Stone had told him?

On the other hand, would Axel have condoned their initial meeting back in May if he'd thought for an instant that Stone would hurt her?

Never. At least he wouldn't have if he'd known better . . .

Damn it, she was confusing herself. She didn't really like making snap decisions without time to think things through. She liked to doodle and do yoga to sort through her thoughts and feelings before she acted. She did not do her best ruminating when she was being pressured and a six-foot-plus mountain of man stared at her as if he expected a response.

"I need to go. I have an appointment I can't miss." It wasn't a lie . . . just not the whole truth.

"We're not done talking." He sidled closer. "Give me a chance to prove I'm exactly who and what I say. Let me show you that I have your best interests at heart."

Even if he was "only" a thief, that didn't make him necessarily safe. She feared that, if she let him, he could steal her heart.

But what if she were letting the best thing that ever happened to her pass her by?

Lily bit her lip. "How about if I promise to call you tonight when I'm done with my appointment?"

He eased closer still, now disconcertingly close, and brushed a curl from her face. Even that light caress made her tingle. "I'd rather be waiting here when you get back. We need to talk this out, baby."

By then, she might have spoken to Thorpe and heard something that would give her peace of mind. Didn't she owe it to everyone who'd been trying to help her for years to at least try a new path?

She grimaced. "If you want what's best for me, why are you rushing me?"

"Because I know what's between us isn't something you find every day. The attraction I feel for you is not like anything I've ever experienced. I like you. You're sweet and sexy. I know you called yourself a project. I like a challenge. We'll take anything physical as slow as you want, but I won't accept you refusing to talk to me. If it makes you feel safer, we'll only see one another here. But we *will* get to know each other. You will do your best to open up to me."

"All right." Lily couldn't effectively argue when he made some really good points. "When I come back, we'll talk."

He let out another breath he'd been holding. "Tell me about your appointment."

She thought about lying but realized she'd already told Thorpe the truth. If they compared notes and discovered she was already being dishonest, it wouldn't go well. "Gun-safety class."

"When did you buy a gun?"

"This morning."

His eyes narrowed. "Why?"

"A girl can never be too careful," she said flippantly because the truth was too dangerous for him and everyone else.

"Why don't I go with you?" he suggested.

Lily didn't think she could successfully fire a gun at a target fifty yards away with him breathing down her neck. "You promised we would only see each other here at Dominion so I would feel safe."

He gnashed his teeth, clearly not thrilled that she'd used his own logic against him. "At least let me walk you to your car."

Even though being near him made her nervous, she had no graceful way to refuse, so she nodded.

When Stone opened the office door, Lily had to brush past him. She couldn't bring herself to meet his gaze. Her stomach knotted as she all but dashed down the hall. She felt him right behind her, hovering and possessive. Desire poured off him, burning her skin, making her body tremble and her breath catch.

Somehow, she had to put distance between them. Otherwise, she feared he would rattle her enough to turn her upside down and inside out. Then, in five minutes flat, she might be on her back, legs spread, and desperately infatuated with someone way more underhanded and worldly than she would ever be.

Lily hightailed it to the parking lot, blanketed by the worst of the August heat, and sprinted for her little yellow Volkswagen. When she neared the driver's-side door, she clicked the fob to unlock it and prepared to duck inside.

His voice stopped her where she stood. "What time will you be back?"

Lily closed her eyes, overwhelmed by another wave of uncertainty. When would she stop distrusting people and figure out how to embrace something that looked like a future? "I still don't think this is a good idea."

Stone stalked toward her, the gentle concern on his face nearly buckling her knees. "We discussed this. I won't ever force you to do anything but talk to me. I'll always hope you want to give me more, but I intend to get inside your head and give you what you need."

Damn it, his deep voice did something to her. She shouldn't want him. Too dangerous. She shouldn't get tangled up with him. Too problematic.

"I can't even tell you how much I think you'll be hurting me."

Those dark eyes of his seemed to take her apart without a word. Before she could stop him, he brushed his thumb over her bottom lip. "I can't even tell you how much I think you're wrong."

For a wild moment, her heart stopped, then began drumming in a frenzied beat. The fluttery, feminine part of her wanted to throw her arms around him, rub up against him, and take the passion he so obviously burned to give her. But as much as he made her ache in places she tried to ignore, she feared wanting him. Even if he wasn't a criminal in the violent sense of the word, she wouldn't know what to do with a man like Stone Sutter.

"I've explained my past," he went on. "You didn't seem opposed to spending time with me when Axel arranged our introduction a few months back. What's changed?"

Maybe she just needed to give him a bit of honesty to make him leave.

"I think you're too much for me to handle." Lily jerked away and wrenched her car door open. She leaned in to toss her purse on the passenger's seat and hop inside.

She opened her mouth to say more, but a bouquet of flowers on the driver's seat stopped her cold. The familiar, pungent scent of its blossoms overpowered her nostrils.

Every last bloom was some sort of lily.

As if she'd seen a snake coiled on the seat, she gasped and jumped back, heart pounding. She sent a terrified stare Stone's way. "Did you leave these?"

That would be the simplest explanation, the one that wouldn't freak her out so much. Whether he had come here to take her under his wing or simply to sweet-talk her into bed, maybe he'd brought this bouquet to ease his way.

But the flowers most associated with funerals? The flowers for which she was actually named?

He peeked inside the vehicle and plucked at the colorful arrangement wrapped in plastic. His expression changed, and he looked ready to beat the hell out of someone. "No. Do you have another man in your life?"

"I don't have *any* man in my life."

"That's no longer true." Stone pulled her into his arms. "Who would leave you a message that he wants to bury the past?"

When their bodies made contact, Lily realized she trembled from head to toe. As afraid as she'd been of Stone just minutes ago, now he made her feel infinitely safer. But she forced herself to pull away and tried to tamp down the panic. She had to think logically. Whoever had broken into her car to leave the flowers had done so in the past few hours. Had that person been the one watching her lately?

"What did you say?" she asked.

He held a little card between two fingers. In neat black pen, someone had written LET'S BURY THE PAST FOR GOOD.

Lily slapped a hand over her mouth. The note hadn't been signed, but the only person she shared a terrible past with was a killer, and he wasn't the sort to extend an olive branch. No amount of time would change the fact that his definition of burying the past would be to put her in the cold, hard ground.

Oh god, Timothy Canton had found her.

What if he or one of his hired goons had been watching her lately, waiting for the chance to off her?

"I-I don't want to be late. I need to leave," she told Stone.

But where should she go? To her gun-safety class? Or, better yet, the freeway heading eastbound? If she drove all afternoon and through the night, she could be more than halfway to Florida. According to her Internet searches, the Keys were a good place to disappear.

"Talk to me." Stone burst in on her thoughts. "You're obviously afraid of something."

So many things, it would probably make him laugh.

"I'm fine," Lily lied. Yes, he might protect her from her past—for a price—but who would protect her from him? Even if he meant her no harm, a man as capable and masculine as Stone wouldn't want a woman who jumped at every shadow and wasn't good in bed. Besides, she refused to put him—or anyone—in danger again.

She managed to fumble halfway into the little car and set her purse down. The cloying odor of the flowers made her stomach heave. It reminded her of everything she'd lost and would never have again. It underscored the fact that someone wanted to kill her.

Stone grabbed her by the waist and pulled her out, turning her to face him. "You're not fine, and lying to me doesn't help either of us. You're afraid of the flowers. Why? Who sent them?"

"You have to let me go."

His face darkened. "Maybe Axel leaving made you believe that you're alone or you have no one to turn to, but I'm here. If you'll explain why the flowers scare you, I'll fix it."

God, if only it were that easy. She would have laughed if she weren't so terrified. "You can't."

"Try me." That deep voice sounded so serious, grave.

"Sorry."

Lily broke free and tried to dash into her car again. He slammed the door and stood squarely in her path, obviously not intending to let her leave.

She gripped her keys tighter. "I've got to go or I'll miss my appointment."

"Perfect. Then you'll have time to explain what's frightening you enough to make you shake."

Why couldn't he be like every other man and ignore her? "Don't worry about me."

Stone snorted. "If you think that's possible, you don't know me very well. But we'll fix that."

No, they wouldn't. Lily couldn't live with herself if Stone became another one of Timothy's victims because of her. It would hurt every bit as bad if he turned out to be one of Canton's goons come to do her in. Oh god. Could it be a coincidence that he and the flowers had appeared within a few minutes of each other?

God, she didn't know what to think.

Stone crossed his arms over his chest and raised a challenging brow. The stare of a displeased Dom.

"Get out of my way," she insisted.

"Not happening."

"If you're too arrogant to hear the word 'no,' that's your problem." Lily turned her back on him, locking the car with a press of a button. She darted around the far side of the vehicle and across the nearly empty parking lot, hauling ass toward Dominion.

She'd probably never see him again, and while that distressed her way more than it should, separating now would be better for

them both, especially if he meant her harm. Even if he didn't, he'd
be all right. Eventually, he'd pair off with another woman. But that
was better for him, too. And Lily would have some peace of mind
that her heart would remain intact.

When she reached Dominion's door, she used her key card to
open the lock and rushed inside, slamming the door behind her.
Thorpe stood there with a watchful glower.

"What was that about?" He frowned her way.

"Can someone fill in for me for a few days? I'm taking a vacation," Lily lied.

Once she knew her few job responsibilities were fulfilled, she could
be gone in less than an hour. She didn't have much to pack back at her
little apartment, just her clothes and a few treasured mementos. Then
she'd start all over again. New identity, new place, new faces.

Thorpe scowled. "Not if what you're saying is that you'd like to
avoid the protector I've chosen for you without giving him a try."

A rattling at the door startled her. It could only be Stone.

When Thorpe reached for the handle to let him in, she shook her
head frantically. "Don't open it. Stone scares me."

"Any particular reason?"

"He knows why." Mostly. Kind of. Enough to keep them busy
hashing it out while she disappeared.

The imposing owner of the club stared at her with shrewd eyes.
"Wait in Axel's room. I'll talk to him. If I'm satisfied with his explanation, I'll stand right beside you until you two work it out."

Not on your life. "All right."

Now that Canton knew where she worked, Lily couldn't put any
of her friends at Dominion at risk, especially not Thorpe, Sean, and
Callie. They were expecting a baby in a few months. She would just
die if anything happened to them. She didn't want to lie to Thorpe,
but if she didn't he'd only insist on solving her problem.

As Lily headed down the hall, she heard Thorpe open the door to
Stone. The club owner spoke. Stone's voice rumbled in return. They

were both straight shooters. It wouldn't take them long to compare notes. If Stone truly sought to help her, then he, like Thorpe, would be concerned and want answers.

Lily intended to be gone by then.

She crept toward the back door and let herself out. The humid afternoon nearly smothered her with heat as she crept around the building and sprinted for her car. She'd give herself five minutes at her apartment to gather up what she could and hope that decision wasn't fatal. If it was . . . well, she'd more than earned her death sentence. If she managed to make it out alive, she'd have to learn to start all over again, more alone than ever.

Chapter Four

W HAT the fuck is going on?" Thorpe crossed his arms over his wide chest. "Sweet Pea seemed more angry and nervous than scared when I left her in my office with you. Now she looks terrified."

"I think we can guess what this means." Stone didn't have time for Twenty Questions. He held up the card he'd fished out of the bouquet. "And exactly who would leave flowers in her car. Not just any flowers, lilies. She found them and her entire demeanor changed. She seems beyond scared and she won't let me help her."

Thorpe glanced at the oblong white card. "So you didn't leave them?"

Stone shook his head. "And no one besides you, me, Sean, Jack, and the Edgington brothers know her real identity?"

"No one. I have no idea how Canton suddenly found her. We have to move fast and get her into hiding. Damn it, I'd rather send her with you, but she doesn't know you," Thorpe pointed out. "She obviously doesn't trust you and your past."

Stone stifled his disappointment and held in a curse. Somehow, he had to get past her fears.

Lily Taylor had been dealt some tough breaks in life and she needed help. He could help her. She definitely pressed all his buttons as a female. With petite curves, she looked like a wet dream of a pinup girl. Her swing dresses, fishnets, and stilettos never failed to make him hard. Today, she'd worn her bangs in a soft twist away from her delicate face. She'd changed her hair color, and now long platinum ringlets bounced down her back, the sides held together at her crown with a bright red bow that matched her lush mouth.

"That's why the next two weeks are critical." *For both her and me.* "You have to let me watch over her. I can keep her safe and convince her to testify."

Thorpe scowled like a disapproving father. "No. Until she accepts you, she's my responsibility. I'll handle it."

"She's kept all the same dark, ugly secrets from you, too. Clearly, she doesn't trust either of us."

Thorpe paused, then gritted his teeth. "Until the FBI came to Sean a few months ago and asked him to get involved, I didn't know anything about her past. I never wanted to pry. Sweet Pea—Lily—always seemed too delicate."

"Or just very good at hiding her issues. I'll get to the bottom of everything and make sure Canton doesn't get to her. You have Callie to think about. That monster would absolutely use your woman to get what he wants."

Thorpe mulled that over for a long, uncomfortable moment. "He's manipulated her using the people in her life before. Let me talk to Sweet Pea for a minute. Wait here."

Before he could respond, Thorpe was gone. Stone cursed. And paced. He didn't want to be at any man's mercy, but Thorpe could prove a formidable ally if Lily continued to be difficult. She might not have shared the details of her past with her boss, but that could be Lily's desire to keep him safe as much as distrust. Though it chafed, Stone had to let this play out.

He'd anticipated waiting for a while, but Thorpe charged back down the hall almost immediately. "She left, damn it. Come with me."

The man didn't wait to see if he would follow, just shoved open the club's front door and pushed his way outside. Stone barged out behind him, worried for the girl. They both stopped short at the absence of Lily's cute little car in the lot. She'd hurled the flowers out of her vehicle, and petals of white, pink, yellow, orange, and purple dotted the blacktop like forgotten confetti.

Thorpe shook his head. "Axel deserves his peace, but I worry that no man can reach Lily except him."

"I can. She's running scared and she needs reassurance. She also needs to understand there are consequences for acting alone when she's in danger. I'll make myself loud and clear."

Just then an electronic ding filled the air. Thorpe dug his phone from his pocket. He cursed again.

"Damn it. That's my reminder that Callie has an appointment with the obstetrician in thirty minutes." He furrowed his brow.

Personally, Stone couldn't picture Thorpe in an office filled with pregnant women. He'd give "bull in a china shop" an all-new meaning.

"With Canton or one of his thugs nearby, I don't think you should leave her alone."

"She's got Sean." But Thorpe didn't sound completely assured.

Stone pressed him. "Do you want to take a chance with Callie's safety?"

"You're right. I need to find her and stay by her side."

"I'll track Lily down and text you," Stone vowed. "I'm the one who has to convince her to testify, so you need to let me handle her from here on out. But I have to find her before she disappears."

"All right." Thorpe cocked his head. "But this doesn't give you free license to do whatever you want to Lily. If you hurt her in any way, everyone who knows and loves that girl will be so far up your ass, we'll disembowel you with a straight pin. Got it?"

Hurting her was the last thing he'd ever do, but no convincing Thorpe of that now. He'd just have to figure it out for himself. "As blunt as you are, there's no way I can misunderstand."

"Good. I'll expect a text soon." The man sent him an acid smile as he straightened his suit coat. "Don't make me hunt you down."

Then Thorpe was gone.

Stone grimaced. It wasn't as if he'd been convicted of anything close to rape or murder. In fact, if he convinced Lily to testify, he might be able to help her move beyond her past wrongs and live a full life.

But he couldn't lie. Those flowers—and what they implied—worried him like hell.

Stone jerked his keys from his pocket. Where to? The gun range? Gut instinct told him no. She had her gun. Even if she wasn't confident with it, if she believed the past was coming back to haunt her, she could well decide to flee and find safer ground. The only thing she might do before leaving town was grab some things out of her apartment. He figured he had a few minutes—tops—to catch up to her before she would be gone forever.

He sprinted to his truck and tore out of the parking lot, running red lights and dodging cars to make it to Lily's place. When he turned into her complex, he pulled into a well-manicured semicircular drive, then sped toward her building. As he approached, gardeners paused. A man wearing a Dodgers cap sat in a rocker on his balcony and watched, diverting his attention from his iPad to peek at the unfolding drama. Stone ignored them.

He had to find her apartment and—without letting on that he knew her identity, which would scare the crap out of her even more— he had to win her trust enough to convince her to rely on him starting now.

Unfortunately, he had no idea how to do that, but he'd better figure it out fast.

* * *

FIGHTING down panic, Lily dashed to the closet in her little efficiency. She reached for her luggage, throwing both pieces on her bed. One by one, she yanked her clothes from their hangers and snagged them from drawers, shoving them into a beat-up duffel and her small brown suitcase. She glanced at her phone. Her five minutes was nearly up. She had to grab her jewelry, shove as many of her toiletries as she could into the tote she kept in the bathroom, and flee.

Panting, she managed all that, then scooped up her laptop, phone charger, and tablet, too. With a frantic gaze, she glanced around the little unit. What couldn't she live without?

She'd better take it now because she wasn't coming back.

After grabbing a few extra bucks she'd tucked away in a tin she kept on the kitchen counter and hoping it would be enough to see her through until she found work, she spun in a circle, searching for her purse. Finding it on the bed next to her suitcase, she stuffed the money in her wallet, then scanned the little place she'd called home since she'd moved to Dallas. She knew she was forgetting something . . .

Kneeling, she glanced under the bed and found a box of keepsakes she'd brought from her former life. There wasn't much: an old birthday card from her mom, a pressed corsage Erin had given her before they'd gone to the homecoming dance together since neither of them had a date, and the hospital bracelet she'd worn on one of the saddest days of her life.

Under all that, she found a heavy book she knew as well as her own face. It slipped into her palm as if it had been made to fit there. She caressed the black velvet cover of her Vista Rio High School yearbook, fingers trailing over her name embossed on the front. That extra had been a frivolous splurge but totally worth it at the time. All her best—and worst—memories lay on these pages.

When she flipped the tome open, the front cover creaked. She skimmed the pages of candid shots and organized activities, seeing a collection of people and places she'd once known so well. Realizing she shouldn't but unable to resist, Lily thumbed her way through until she found a picture of Erin and her hamming it up for a pep rally. With big smiles and cheerleading skirts, she and her bestie hugged tightly, cheeks pressed together. Behind them, her friend's big brother, Corey, photobombed them with his fingers up and his tongue out, his expression pure rock.

Little did they know that in a few short months she would betray them terribly.

With a frown, she slammed the book shut and shoved it in the box again. She didn't have time to run back to her bed and curl into the fetal position. She definitely didn't have time for this eviscerating walk down memory lane. She simply had to get the hell out.

Lily closed all her luggage up, tugged down the blinds, and left the light on in the living room. It was only a matter of time before Canton figured out where she lived. Maybe the little table lamp would fool him or anyone he sent here to kill her that she was cozied up on the couch with a glass of chardonnay, zoned out on TV. Maybe it would buy her enough extra time to make a clean getaway.

As she stacked up her stuff and headed for the door, she glanced out the kitchen window, which overlooked a corner of the parking lot. A black pickup she'd never seen here skidded into view, engine revving. Her heart stopped.

Stone.

Her time was up. If she didn't hurry, she would be too late to make her escape.

And they would both be dead.

Chapter Five

STONE sped through the parking lot, looking for Lily's unit. The big, multibuilding complex was spread out over a wide area with a meandering road in the middle. Damn it, where was she? He didn't see her car, either.

After driving to the exit, he turned around and trolled the parking lot again, this time checking down all the side paths for her car. If she had come here to pack up, she wouldn't be far from that little yellow vehicle.

Craning his head to see down a smaller lane to the right, he caught sight of a bright, sunny color. He burned rubber and hauled ass to get there.

"C'mon. C'mon . . ." He prayed it was Lily's car. Because if he couldn't find her, he'd have to hunt her down, which probably meant heading for the Keys and hoping he could figure out which of the seventeen hundred islands she might have fled to. What a fucking nightmare.

As he skidded around the corner, he saw her hustling toward the little Bug, rolling a suitcase. She also carried a duffel on one shoulder and another big tote on the other. In her hands, she struggled to hold a clearly heavy box.

Suddenly, as she stepped over a curb she couldn't see, she tripped. The box tumbled out of her hands and clattered to the concrete. She fell to her knees. The tote slid down her left arm. The duffel cut into her right. The keys fell from her fingers and skittered across the lot.

She leapt to her feet and started gathering everything again. The fear and defeat on her face stabbed Stone square in the chest. But he gave Lily credit. She swallowed back her tears, then shoved the contents of the box back inside and rearranged her luggage, refusing to let the setback stop her.

Stone was even more determined not to give her a second opportunity to flee from him.

As she finally reclaimed everything she'd dropped, he jerked to a stop sideways behind her Volkswagen, blocking her exit. He shoved his extended cab into park and hopped out. She caught sight of him, then started racing for her car.

He dove for her keys, but Lily realized what he intended and dropped everything again. Because she was closer, she managed to scoop them up first. He could have taken them from her but that wasn't going to build her trust.

"No." She shook her head adamantly. "Let me go."

"Don't leave."

"I have to."

"I know you think you're in danger. Someone from your past, right? You don't want him to catch you or put anyone you care about at risk."

Her big eyes widened with surprise. "How did you—"

"I was born but it wasn't yesterday, baby. Let me help you." He reached for her.

"How do I know you're not involved? You seem to understand this situation pretty well and you just got out of prison." She stood and gripped her tote, then began backing away. "Don't come near me."

Stone sent her a reassuring stare. "I have nothing to do with anyone trying to scare you. Hell, Jack Cole got me out of prison to help solve a cybercrime."

"Did Axel know that?"

"No.

"Then I don't trust you."

Clearly she'd been deeply attached to Axel, and that made Stone jealous as hell. "If you don't believe anything else, then believe I'm here to help you."

Lily shook her head and gathered her scattered belongings again. "It's not that simple. You don't understand how ruthless this monster is. It's better if I go. Tell Thorpe and Axel I said good-bye," she choked out. "Thank them for everything."

When she tried to dash past him, he snagged her arm, holding her just tight enough to make her stay. "Baby, let me help you."

"You can't. Besides, you look at me like you'd ultimately want sex in return. I don't like it and I'm no good at it."

"Whoa." He held up his hands. "I never said anything about an exchange of protection for sex."

She kept on as if he hadn't spoken. "Sometimes in bed I freak out or cry or . . . God, I need to stop babbling and get out of town."

As Lily darted for her car, Stone filed away that assessment of her sexual prowess and blocked her path. "Don't run. No strings. I promise."

"Then why would you bother?"

Stone tried to think through his answer fast. The truth—that he needed her to testify—would scare the hell out of her right now. He certainly couldn't tell her that he wanted her so badly it was fucking with his brainpan because that would freak her out, too. Unfortunately, that didn't leave him with much. "I can't stand to see you terrified, and I promised Thorpe I'd keep you safe."

"If you don't want sex, you feel sorry for me, and I can't handle that. Just let me go before this guy finds you with me. He'll kill you. He'll kill us both." She looked ready to beg. "Please move your truck. Otherwise I'll jump the curb and drive over the grass to get away."

Her little car wouldn't make it, but Stone would bet she'd give it a hell of a try. And he was running out of options. The last one he had up his sleeve pissed him off but if it worked, he'd get over himself.

"Be logical. The person who left those flowers isn't a nice guy, right?"

If anything, she paled more as she shook her head. "No."

"I'm going to venture that he might even be some sort of criminal."

Lily pressed her lips together. Her chin trembled as she fought her fear. "The worst."

From everything he'd been told, Canton was a sociopathic prick who deserved a place of honor in the ninth circle of hell. "You don't know anything about being a criminal."

"I know about running from one."

He'd give her that. She'd managed to keep herself alive for the past seven years. "But do you want to keep running for the rest of your life? How long before it wears you down? How much longer do you want to keep leaving family and friends to start over, all alone?"

His words seemed to slice at her heart, and he hated the way tears filled her eyes. "I don't have a choice."

"You do. Maybe it takes a criminal to think like one."

She glanced up at him in surprise, as if that thought had never occurred to her. Then she frowned. "You said you're not a violent person."

"Prison teaches a man a lot about the lengths he'll go to in order to stay alive."

"You can't kill him." Her voice trembled.

If Canton had frightened Lily this much, then it would be Stone's pleasure. "I can outsmart him, find other ways to make him disappear. Let me handle this."

"Why would you want to?"

"Do you want to have this conversation again or start making a dent in the problem? You don't owe me sex, and I don't pity you. Can we leave it there for now?"

Lily paused, looking torn, like she wanted to say yes but didn't want to drag him into her nightmare.

"Baby," he crooned. "Don't worry about me. Whoever he is—and you can tell me about him later—I got this. I'll keep you safe."

She still didn't jump on his offer. Normally, Stone would appreciate that she was thoughtful and logical and wasn't about to let him bulldoze her. Today, it was damn inconvenient.

"It's my problem," she murmured.

And she didn't want to be a burden. He understood. All too often, he had a bitch of a time asking for help himself. "You're in over your head."

Lily let out a breath as if she couldn't deny that. "I don't know how long this will take. You can't put your life on hold—"

"Let me worry about that. It's handy that the men I work for refuse to leave a woman in danger when they can help. I agree with them. Call me old-fashioned. Or a caveman. They're both true. Let's go." He retrieved the bulky box she'd dropped earlier and dragged the duffel off her shoulder. "Bring your tote and get in the truck."

Finally, reluctantly, she nodded. "Thanks. I don't have much, but I'll pay—"

"You don't owe me a dime." Ire surged. He felt his face tense, his jaw firm into a hard line. "And I don't want to argue about it."

This time when he gestured her to the truck, she nodded. "Thanks." As he set the items he'd taken from her into the covered bed, she set the tote on the floorboard of the passenger's seat. "Can you back your truck up a few feet? I need to move my car or it will get towed. I'd rather make sure Thorpe gets it in case the next sad sack he takes in needs wheels."

Stone saw the sign that proclaimed her car sat in a fifteen-minute spot. "Yeah, but if you run, I'll hunt you down. Think long and hard about how that will end."

Lily scowled. "I'm going with you because it makes sense and you're right about being in over my head. You're supposedly with the good guys. You say you don't want sex and you don't pity me. That's great. You also don't own me."

Not yet, but the day wasn't over.

"In order for me to protect you, you're going to have to listen to me and follow directions without question. You know how to do that." He raised a brow at her.

And it burned him that Axel had taught her.

She flushed, then lowered her gaze. Something about the gesture made him hard as hell. His entire body tightened, lungs squeezed. An ache for her that had been coiled deep for months began to unfurl. Stone forced himself to breathe. Now wasn't the time for this.

"I do," she admitted softly.

"Now move your car. I'll follow and watch."

Keys in hand, she headed to her little yellow Bug, skirt swishing with the breeze. He backed away and gave her enough space to move her vehicle from the side of the building, into an assigned spot under an overhang. He frowned when she stepped out of the car, then dashed back to his truck and reached into her tote. "The complex issued new parking tags yesterday. I need to hang it from my rearview mirror or they'll tow me before I can mail my keys to Thorpe." But it wasn't a hangtag she pulled from her bag; it was a shiny new gun. Lily pointed it in his face. "The guy who's after me knows what my car looks like. Get out and give me your keys."

So she could disappear alone? "Not a chance, baby. You won't shoot me."

"You don't know how determined I am," she insisted. "I'll do it. I—"

A deafening explosion rent the air as a ball of orange fire burst and swelled. Heart hammering, he whirled around in time to see the blaze roar and belch while it swallowed Lily's car whole.

Chapter Six

As they sped away from Dallas, Stone dug into his pocket for his cell phone. Beside him, Lily had thankfully stopped trembling and had fallen silent. That fucking bomb had changed everything, and after mentally scrambling for a plan, he'd told her they were headed to Louisiana and he wouldn't hear any more arguments. She'd shoved a pair of buds in her ears, retreating into herself to deal, and stared out the window in silence as the scenery zipped by.

Holding in a sigh, he dialed Jack, who answered on the first ring. "What the fuck is going on? Thorpe called me when you left Dominion. Did you find Lily?"

"At her apartment, yeah. Just barely," Stone admitted. "She pulled a gun on me." And he admired the moxie she had to try that move. "But then her car exploded. If I hadn't followed my instinct that she'd run or if I'd been a few minutes later . . ."

The realization that she could have died made his gut churn.

"Her car exploded? Like a bomb?"

"Exactly like that."

"Merde," Jack swore. "Thank god you got to her before Canton. That's what's important. When we didn't hear from either of you, I worried. You provide technical assistance, not operative intelligence."

"I can hold my own." He'd learned a lot in prison. "Right now, I'm headed back toward Lafayette but I need a place to hide her, somewhere secluded and difficult to trace. You got a safe house? If I can isolate her, I can figure out what to do next."

"I'm already ahead of you. I'll text you directions to someplace Canton will never find, and if he does, the gators will find him first. In the meantime, I'll get with Sean to see if we can track down anyone in the Dallas PD working this case who'd be willing to keep us apprised of their investigation, the type of incendiary device, and how sophisticated it was, any suspects or witnesses. Whatever information might help."

"When we get to your location, I'll see what I can dig up with a little online trolling and hacking. Someone somewhere knows something. She's suffered for too long. This shit is going to stop."

"Testifying will be really damn hard on her, but she'll finally have a future once it's over and she'll thank you. But you don't have very long to persuade her to cooperate."

"Thanks for the reminder," Stone returned flippantly.

"Sorry, just . . ." Jack sighed. "The two of you will be spending all your time alone at my old fishing cabin. It's got the basics. I keep it stocked with groceries because Morgan and I go out there whenever we can. The kitchen mostly runs on propane. Extra tanks are in the shed out back. There's surveillance equipment in the room at the end of the hall. One bedroom . . . but you can make that work in your favor."

"How? I can't fuck her into complying," Stone protested in a low voice. "Couch?"

Lily's words about being both bad at and afraid of sex echoed in his head. Stone didn't believe she could possibly be terrible between the sheets. As gorgeous as she was, as giving as she tried to be, he just couldn't picture that. He didn't know what the deal was between her and Axel and whether the guy had given her a complex about her prowess, but Stone intended to make her feel a whole lot better as soon as she let him.

Her fear of sex was a totally different problem. So that lone bed in Jack's cabin might spook her. Until she was able to start trusting him, they couldn't move forward.

"No on the couch, not if you want to stand upright tomorrow," Jack quipped. "Can I give you some advice?"

"Shoot." Maybe the guy had something helpful to say. As it was, Stone had no idea how he was going to keep Lily calm, much less convince her to be the prosecution's main witness against a man who'd once wiped out everyone she loved and now obviously threatened to do away with her.

"I've been in this situation. With Morgan, actually. We were strangers at the time. I managed to keep a psycho from shooting her in broad daylight. Then I took her out to the cabin to hide. If you want to save Lily—and your own ass—get inside her head fast."

"She has no idea that I know anything about her past or her true identity." He glanced Lily's way. She was still looking out the window, listening to her tunes. Logically, he understood this was her way of keeping space between them while she processed and calmed herself down. But the way she kept him at arm's length grated on his nerves. "I want her to tell me who she is and who's after her. I worry that if I tell her I already know—that we've all known for the last few months—she's never going to trust me or agree to tell a jury what she saw."

Jack sighed. "I'm not being blunt enough. She's a submissive looking for someone with a firm hand to belong to. Learn her backward and forward, then figure out exactly what she needs and give it to her. If you can do that, she'll follow you to the ends of the earth."

"I know that's what you and Logan have been coaching me for during these last three months. I'll give it every fucking thing I've got."

"I have faith in you. After all, you put one over on Joaquin and the Edgington brothers with the Dilbert virus. That was pretty clever. Turn that same shrewd mind on her. And just so you know, the cabin comes with a fully equipped playroom. Have fun."

Jack hung up, and Stone stared at his phone. On the screen a few seconds later, up popped directions to the place, along with a few instructions on how to disable the cabin's security.

Stone tucked away the device and looked across the cab of his truck. He resisted the urge to place a palm on Lily's thigh, still barely covered in a short pink skirt and white thigh highs, now with holes in both knees. Thankfully, she didn't look as if she'd scraped herself too badly or been otherwise hurt in the blast. But she was terribly quiet.

He opted to touch her shoulder and waited until she took out her earbuds and shut off the music blasting from her phone. "You hungry, baby?"

She shook her head. "How did you know where to find my apartment? I never told you where I live."

"I'm a hacker, remember?"

Her frown told him she didn't like that answer. "So where in Louisiana are we going?"

Did she think he would tell her so that she could potentially start planning an exit strategy? "Jack gave me a location where we can hide while we figure out some things. I've never been there, but I'll find it."

Lily gnawed on her lip. "You can't make my problem go away. You'll just ruin your life."

"News flash: It's already pretty screwed up. I don't have a lot to lose except you. Tell me about this dirtbag who's scaring you."

She shook her head. "Don't do this. You can't keep me in hiding forever, and that's probably how long it would take to bring this guy down. If the place you're taking me is safe, great. I'll use that time to regroup and figure out where to go next. When you get bored, I'll have a game plan ready."

"Like heading to the Keys?" he challenged.

That got her attention. She reared back. "H-how did you . . . You're a hacker. Got it."

"Baby, when you wouldn't talk to me, I wanted to know all your secrets. I picked apart your Internet searches and scoured your browsing history."

"Are you sure you're not a stalker?"

"I'm just a man who's worried about you. When you first blew me off, I didn't know if you were still in love with Axel. Then I just wondered what the hell you were up to."

"Why are you helping me? Really. You barely know me."

"Well, ever since your car exploded, Jack Cole and I are on the same page. I'm going to guess Thorpe is, too, especially since he asked me to be your protector even before then. Text him and let him know I've got you and that you're okay. Let me see before you send it."

Lily looked as if she wanted to object but finally sighed and tapped on the keys. With a hint of rebellion, she practically whipped her phone in his face to show him that she was, in fact, texting Thorpe the message Stone had requested.

He nodded. "Send it."

She pressed her finger to the screen. "Done."

Then she blinked back at him. Her lack of expression bothered him. She looked as if she'd crawled into some protective shell where no one could reach her and decided to stay. She also looked exhausted. The dark circles under her eyes didn't give him any doubt that she'd been losing sleep. He would fix that ASAP.

"Good," he praised. "Now put your phone on airplane mode so it can't be tracked, just in case this bad guy has a bead on you."

Lily bit her lip. "I'd feel better if Thorpe could find us."

Stone wished he knew how to reassure her with just a word or a touch, but she didn't trust him enough for that—yet. "Jack will know. But the fewer people who can locate you electronically, the safer you'll be." He gripped the wheel, the glare of the afternoon sun glinting in the rearview mirror.

She clutched the phone in her small hands, her black nail polish nearly blending with the device itself. "What if I need to talk to someone?"

"I've got my phone." He patted his pocket.

Finally she complied. He breathed a sigh of relief.

"Now what?" she asked.

"Trust me."

But she wouldn't until he had earned it.

If she would testify, Canton would probably go away for a long time. She could resume her life, even be Lily Taylor again. But without that option, taking down a gubernatorial candidate wouldn't be a simple feat. And making her disappear from his radar forever . . . This guy had reach and pull, so it wouldn't be easy.

"So let's take this from the top. Who is this guy and what does he want?"

She merely sent him a sidelong glance, shoved her earbuds back in, and cranked up the music.

Stone gritted his teeth. Patience. He wanted to press on and get the answers to his thousand questions about her past, but her day had been harrowing and overwhelming. She hadn't eaten, hadn't slept, hadn't had a moment's peace. Once he took care of those needs . . . Then he'd rip those buds out of her ears and start peeling away the layers of her secrets until she gave him everything he wanted.

* * *

THE late afternoon was hot and harsh as Stone pulled up in front of a small dock area. "We're almost there."

Lily looked around and saw only a rickety vessel floating at the end of the little pier. "We have to take a boat?"

"It's a skiff. The house is meant to be safe, not necessarily convenient."

Around her, the swamp felt alive. Cicadas sung as cypress trees reached for the sky, their branches weighed down by Spanish moss. A fungus-like growth clung to the top of the sludgy brown water. She didn't even want to know what reptiles and other creepy things crawled under the surface. A beady pair of eyes skimming the opposite side of the shoreline suggested gator or whatever else lived out here.

"I don't know about this."

Stone lugged her suitcase, duffel, and box all at once, and she tried not to notice how his arms, shoulders, and chest bulged, rippling with every move. "You'll be a lot safer at the cabin than if you stay here. Cottonmouths live in these parts. I think they're nocturnal creatures." He shrugged. "I know they're venomous. But it's your call."

"You're backing me into a corner."

"I'm trying to save your life," he said as he dumped most of her luggage into the skiff and climbed in.

She grabbed her tote and slammed the car door, tiptoeing carefully to the shore to avoid anything that might bite and kill her. "I've never been to a swamp."

"Hopefully, neither has the guy chasing you." He reached up to grab her duffel, then piled it on top of her other pieces before holding out a hand to help her in.

Once she'd settled into the narrow seat opposite him, he pulled the key fob out of his pocket and hit a button. She heard an electronic beep and the truck's lights flashed, signaling that the vehicle was locked. Lily had a sinking feeling that might be the last modern convenience she saw for a while. God, she was in way over her head. Heck, she'd never even been camping. She certainly didn't understand anything about where she was, only that pretty much everything around her could kill her before Canton even came close.

Beside the boat, movement caught her peripheral vision. The water sloshed. Something moved just under the surface, not five feet from her. She held in a scream.

Stone shook his head as he plucked out his phone and used the flashlight feature, illuminating the bottom of the boat.

"What are you doing?" she asked.

"Making sure nothing crawled into the skiff before we leave the shore."

Though she wondered if he said that merely to yank her chain, Lily was still tempted to crawl onto his lap and beg him to protect her from anything that had more legs or teeth than she did.

"We're clear," he murmured, killing the light and pocketing the phone again.

He grabbed the oars and started to row.

"The boat doesn't have a motor?" That horrified her.

"Skiff, and no. The water is too shallow and the chemical runoff from the engine isn't good for the ecosystem, according to Jack. It's not a long ride. Hang tight. I'll keep you safe."

Lily believed that. For whatever reason, he'd decided to save her from Canton. He'd kept her from exploding in her car. Now he seemed determined to drag her out to the middle of nowhere until . . . what? She had no intention of coughing up her past so that he could learn all her secrets. She wouldn't give anyone that sort of power over her. Nor would she put anyone in that much danger.

The boat ride seemed like the longest five minutes of her life. She waited for a giant reptile to snatch her from the boat and chomp her into a watery grave like a scene out of a horror movie. She shrieked as something heavy bumped the side of the boat but it swam on. Egrets and herons swooped around as orange, gold, and bright pink rays slanted through the clouds, dazzling with the dying daylight. Something else she couldn't identify called into the coming evening as the wind blew hot, humid air over her skin. The mosquito population out here had to way outnumber humans.

Finally, they nudged up against another dock. Stone stood and lifted her things onto the adjacent pier with seemingly little effort. That crap had weighed a ton to her.

He hoisted himself out, every muscle in his back, shoulders, and arms bulging once again until he stood on top. Then he reached a hand out to her.

She blinked up at him. "You're just going to lift me up?"

"You got a better idea?"

Lily looked around. Short of trying to take a giant step over the slimy, life-infested waters and potentially falling, she didn't. Grimacing, she held out her hand.

With a chuckle, he pulled her up, then tied the boat off and turned around. "We're right over there."

She followed suit and saw what appeared to be a small brown cabin with a wraparound porch blending in with its surroundings. It wasn't remarkable. She wasn't even sure it was stable. But anything had to be better than hanging out where some creature might decide that she'd make a good dinner.

"Lead the way," she said finally.

Stone picked up her suitcase and duffel. She retrieved her tote and reached for the box.

"I've got it," he told her, lifting it between big, capable-looking hands.

Why couldn't she stop looking at Stone? Why did she want him this much? Lily already knew that no matter how sexy she found him, she wouldn't enjoy actual sex with the man. She never did, even with someone like Axel, whom she trusted.

At the front door, he shined the light from his phone on a keypad. The shack might appear on the rickety side, but that electronic entry and the cameras tucked under the eaves overhead said otherwise. Once he'd punched in the code, he opened the door and ushered her in, carting her stuff.

Lily groped around the wall for a switch. When she flipped it up, nothing happened. "No power."

"Jack keeps a few of the breakers off when he's not using the place. Let me go flip them."

Stone disappeared out the front door again, leaving her in the shadowed room. With the last of the daylight slanting through the windows, she saw an old blue couch, a beige chair, and a coffee table that had seen better days. Dark hardwood floors felt solid beneath her feet. The space opened to a serviceable kitchen. It wasn't the Ritz, but it wasn't any worse than the childhood home she'd shared with her mother and brother. Bonus, she would bet they didn't see gun violence and gang activity here.

A moment later, bright lights illuminated the cozy little place. She tended to like loud, eclectic decor, but this place had a kitschy, homey vibe. The refrigerator and kitchen table looked like something out of the fifties, and the living room furniture wasn't much newer, but she'd bet everything here was well used and well loved.

Stone stepped back inside a moment later and locked the door behind him. "Have a seat at the kitchen table. I'll put our stuff away and have a look around. Then we'll figure out something that resembles dinner."

Lily kind of wanted to argue because she didn't want him to get the impression that she'd simply comply with whatever he wanted her to. But the truth was, despite her nap earlier, she was still beat. This day had worn her out. And if she was being totally honest, something about the edge of command in his voice incited a zip of excitement down her spine.

He didn't wait to see if she complied, just picked up her crap and headed down the hall. As Lily watched him retreat, she held in a sigh. She almost never noticed a man beyond his eyes, his hands, and his behavior. But she took one look at Stone's ass and thought she might swallow her tongue.

God, she had to get her head together. No doubt he would have a million questions for her once he came back. She'd been trying to decide how to effectively skirt the truth or if she should simply feed him a bunch of lies. She still hadn't reached any conclusion, and now she had only moments to decide.

She heard the thump of her luggage hitting the floor in a nearby room; then his footsteps resounded through the cabin, coming closer. Her stomach knotted into a tangle of nerves.

He appeared in the opening between the kitchen and the hall-way, bracing a big hand on the wall. His biceps flexed, the colored ink there snagging her gaze.

"You hungry, baby?"

To be contrary, she wanted to say no. But she really was famished. "Yes."

With a curt nod, he peeked into the fridge. "What are your kitchen skills? Mine suck."

"Mine are good." She'd been feeding herself and her little brother since she turned nine and her mom had picked up another full-time job in a better part of town, which had been far away from where they could afford to live. But that was Los Angeles. "What's in there?"

"Besides condiments and bottled water, eggs, yogurt, a few veggies . . ." He shut the door and bent to open the freezer beneath. "Looks like we have some chicken and hamburger patties. And lots of frozen crawfish."

Lily shuddered. "Not much of a fish fan."

"By the time folks from Louisiana get done cooking crawfish and putting it into an étouffée, it doesn't really resemble fish anymore."

Still, she shook her head and rose, peeking inside. "If you'll hand me the hamburger patties, I think I have an idea."

He passed her the frozen meat. "Good to hear. I could eat a dozen eggs by myself and still be starving."

Taking a few items she needed out of the fridge, she winced. She needed to remember she wasn't cooking for one now, and Stone could probably eat enough for three of her. "Anything here that resembles booze?"

He narrowed his eyes. "No."

"You didn't even look."

"I don't need to. We're not drinking tonight. I want you completely sober."

That sucked, but she should probably keep a clear head for all the questions he would surely ask her. "Give me about thirty minutes. I'll have food ready."

"I've got nowhere to go." He pulled out a chair. "Except wherever you are. So why don't we start at the top? The man after you is named . . ."

She turned on the gas stove and fished around the cabinets until she found a pan. "Homicidal Maniac. I'm not filling in that blank for you."

Stone clenched his jaw, obviously wishing that she'd stop stone-walling. He simply didn't get that she was doing him a favor.

"In order to defend you, I have to understand what I'm up against. If you don't want to give me a name, I need to know what sort of crimes he committed. What is he capable of?"

"Anything. Everything." She tossed the hamburger patties into the warm pan, trying to focus on the mundane so that images of Erin's last day on earth didn't cripple her. "Drugs, extortion, racketeering, rape, murder. I can't prove it, but I think he once had a ring of sex slaves he sold off to fat, rich men. He denied it, but it was amazing how many young girls disappeared from our neighborhood, seemingly without a trace. He doesn't possess a shred of humanity."

"And you found that out and lived to tell the tale."

She didn't know how to answer that without implicating herself so she just shrugged and listened to the meat begin to sizzle. A moment later, she poked her head in the fridge again. It was a good excuse not to meet Stone's demanding gaze.

"How old were you?"

"Sixteen. And that's the last I'm saying about it." She grabbed what looked like arugula, a bag of thick sandwich rolls, and some shaved Parmesan. If this was Jack's place, he knew how to eat decently.

"Did he hurt you physically?"

Lily hadn't expected that question. Stone sounded on edge, like the answer could really, truly set him off. "Me? No."

Just everyone she'd ever cared about.

"So you witnessed a crime."

She'd witnessed absolute horror.

"I'm done talking." She flipped the first of the burgers, more for something to occupy herself than for any real need.

Stone didn't say anything for a long minute. At first she was happy for the silence. Then it began to worry her. She didn't know him well, but in her experience a silent Stone was a thinking Stone.

Lily looked over her shoulder at him. Sure enough, he'd fixed his stare on her, his eyes full of speculation. But he didn't say a word.

Somehow, that made her more nervous.

"Do you like Parmesan?" she asked inanely, then berated herself. The first tactic of a good interrogator was to leave silence for the witness to fill.

"Sure. Tell me about your family."

"My dad ran out when I was little. The rest are dead." To preclude him from asking the next, obvious question, she countered with a query of her own. "What about you?"

"When I was arrested, the feds decided to make an example of me and my buddies so that other affluent kids would understand they weren't above the law. Around that time, my grandmother fell and suffered some internal bleeding. She passed away. A few months later, shortly after the sentencing, my mother died of a heart attack. We never reconciled. I didn't get to attend her funeral. My father severed all ties after that. I spent a lot of time behind bars reeling from the fact that one decision cost me a future, my family—everything. That answer your question?"

"Yes." It certainly was honest. She let out a breath as she scoured the nearby cabinets for a pair of plates.

"How did the rest of your family die?" he asked.

She should have known he wouldn't simply give up.

"It doesn't really matter because they're gone now."

Stone looked as if he disagreed but didn't say so. "Where are you from?"

She checked the burgers and grabbed the sandwich rolls, slicing them in half while trying to keep her calm. "Not talking about my past."

"How long have you been in Dallas?"

"Longer than I should have apparently."

Lily glanced at Stone. He didn't look thrilled by her answer, but he was far from losing his cool. "I'm not the enemy."

"That remains to be seen. I told you when we first met that it takes me a long time to trust." She plopped the burgers down on the buns, then cracked open two eggs into the hot pan.

"You did," he acknowledged with a nod, then rose. "I'll check to make sure we're locked up tight. Don't want anyone getting in."

Or out.

As the eggs fried, she listened to the air around her. Everything sounded so still, quiet. She wasn't used to it. At Dominion, something always seemed to be going on. People talked and played, often loudly. Even in her apartment building, her neighbors had been young professionals and single parents. She'd always heard voices and televisions or doors slamming.

Now? Absolute silence. It made her uneasy. For the first time, she wished Stone would come back. She'd say she was better off with the devil she knew, but she didn't really know much about him. An ex-con with a sad story, he'd jumped in to save her for reasons only he understood. She bit her lip, uncertain what to make of him.

Frowning, she flipped the eggs, waited a few moments, then finished plating the sandwiches and threw some Parmesan on top, along with a little salt and pepper.

As she set the food on the table, Stone entered again and sat. "Everything smells good."

She scrounged up a couple of paper towels and some silverware. "If you're still hungry after this, I can make you another."

"Thanks." He rose from the table and hunted through a cabinet in the living room, then returned with a bottle. "You object to vodka?"

"You changed your mind?"

He gave her a single sharp nod. "You stop when I say so. Is that clear?"

Lily swallowed. Something in him had changed. He'd morphed from interrogator to Dom. She heard it in the tone of his voice. She risked a glance his way. Yeah, it was all over his face.

Against her will and better judgment, arousal laced her blood, making her tingle in some uncomfortably personal places. A disturbing excitement left her breathless. She couldn't seem to not stare. And that only made her nipples pebble and the ache between her legs coil tighter.

She ripped her gaze away. "Yes."

He looked as if he had something else on his mind. Her lack of protocol? She refused to call him Sir. She was afraid that once she started, she would never stop.

With a defiant glance, she lifted her chin. "Are you pouring?"

"Yep." He produced a shot glass from his big fist and tipped the bottle, filling it. "Go."

"Why are you giving me booze?" To interrogate her while she was under the influence?

He cocked his head and sent her a shrewd stare. "Why did you ask for it? And don't give me some flippant shit that you're thirsty."

No, she knew that wouldn't be smart. "Because I still feel as if I'm shaking all over from the car bomb. I haven't slept in days."

"And you were hoping to escape for a few hours by passing out?"

"Something like that."

"You'll sleep. I'll make sure of it. Drink."

"Are you going to ply me with more questions?" she asked suspiciously.

"Not tonight."

Lily wasn't sure she believed him, but the chance for a little bit of oblivion was too much to pass up. She lifted the glass and sent him a mocking salute. "Cheers."

Without another word, he dug into his sandwich, eschewing

silverware in favor of good old-fashioned eating with his hands. As egg yolk ran down one of his fingers, he licked it off. Instead of being annoyed or disgusted, she found him sexy . . . primal. He moaned and closed his eyes when he ate. His strong jaw worked. His Adam's apple bobbed. She couldn't stop staring.

What was wrong with her?

Lily wasn't sure she wanted the answer to that question, so she tossed the vodka back, relishing the burn of the alcohol down her throat. Then she dug into her sandwich, carefully carving it with her knife and fork.

When she looked up again, she found Stone watching her. "What?"

A glance revealed that his plate was empty. "That was fantastic."

His opinion probably shouldn't matter, but she couldn't help the thin ribbon of pleasure that wound through her at his approval. "Thanks."

He fell silent as she finished what she could of her sandwich. Knowing his eyes were on her, she couldn't eat anymore. With his big presence and intent stare, he rattled her. Tension thickened the air between them. Lily had never felt anything like it, but she understood damn well that it was sexual.

Licking her lips, she shoved the shot glass closer to the vodka. "Another?"

Stone took a long time to answer. "All right. If you'll agree to try to sleep afterward."

As tired as she felt? And to avoid more questions? "Sure."

He poured. She drank and savored the burn. Funny, she felt more relaxed but not unwired. And nothing was going to make the terror of her car blowing up less than twenty yards away from her disappear.

Stone screwed the top back on the bottle of vodka. "I'll do the dishes. You take a shower. The bathroom is the first door on the left. The bedroom is directly across the hall. Meet me there when you're done."

She stiffened. "Why?"

"Not to violate you against your will. I haven't hurt you yet and I'm not planning on it."

Lily had to admit he had a point. "All right."

With a nod, he began clearing the table and washing the dishes. She retreated to the bathroom with her tote and suitcase. After a relaxing bath in the old claw-foot tub that felt like a little slice of heaven, she should feel more relaxed. All she could think about was that Stone would be waiting for her in the bedroom.

Lily dug through her suitcase. She found a blush silk-and-lace number that Callie had given her for her birthday. It was great for luxurious slumber in the summer but way too seductive. Instead, she grabbed one of Axel's old T-shirts, stained with dye from one of her many hair-color experiments. The short sleeves hung down to her elbows. The hem fell to her knees.

She washed her face and took down the victory rolls that swept the long bangs from her face. Then she brushed the curls from her hair, letting the strands fall past her shoulders. After a quick brush of her teeth, she dragged in a deep breath. *Now or never.*

The five steps across the hall were some of the hardest she'd ever taken. When she walked into the bedroom, Stone stood beside a four-poster bed. He'd tugged down the cozy blankets and sheets.

"Get in," he instructed.

When he stepped back to give her room, she climbed into the bed, her gaze never leaving his. She pulled up the covers as if they would protect her. As if some part of her didn't want to strip off everything she wore and try to actually enjoy the touch of a man.

But no, she'd just freeze up. Like she always did.

Stone swept her hair back from her face and bent to her. Lily's heart revved as he came closer, closer . . . But he only kissed her cheek.

"Close your eyes. Rest," he murmured.

"Where are you sleeping?"

"I'll figure it out. I want to check in with Jack and reassure Thorpe before I call it a night."

He didn't say anything else, just shut the door behind him. She felt alone—in a bad way. Usually, she preferred solitude. Tonight, she simply felt lonely.

Lily tossed. Turned. Shaped her pillow. Rolled to her side, then her back. Every time she closed her eyes, she saw terror or sadness or . . . Stone, who confused her. Lily had no idea how long she'd been seeking sleep, only that the sheets had turned warm, the ceiling fan was completely ineffective against the August humidity, and she didn't want to lie there alone anymore.

As if he'd read her thoughts, Stone opened the door a moment later and eased inside, his footfalls nearly silent. "You're not asleep."

Why rehash the obvious? "No."

He watched her, taking her in. Then he reached behind his head, grabbed a handful of his shirt, and peeled it off. His tattoos covered both shoulders and spilled onto his pectorals. He was every bit as powerfully built as she'd imagined, and as she stared, she couldn't breathe.

"Stone?"

He didn't answer, simply kicked off his shoes and shucked his pants. Her breath caught at the sight of him in nothing but a pair of dark briefs. He put underwear models to shame. His body—and his erection—looked beyond hard.

But the expression in his eyes undid her most. Understanding, concern, tenderness. Caring. God, why was he looking at her that way?

He sauntered to the bed and pulled back the sheets on the other side. Lily thought she should object but she didn't. She wanted to know what he intended, was desperate to find out what thoughts bounced around in his head.

When he climbed in bed beside her, he did nothing but open his arms to her. "Yes, I have an erection. I know it, just like I know you saw it. Rest assured, I can control it. Come here. I want to hold you until you fall asleep."

It was a sweet notion. "I won't be able to nod off with someone touching me."

Even the idea made her shudder.

"Humor me." He motioned her closer.

No denying that he scared Lily, but a part of her just couldn't pass up the opportunity to touch him, feel his strength. Besides, he wouldn't leave her in peace until she complied.

With a sigh, she rolled over and laid her head on his chest and listened to the beating of his heart.

Chapter Seven

WHEN Stone woke just after six a.m. with his arms all full of Lily, he wanted so badly to wake her with a kiss, then roll her onto her back and bury himself inside her. For now, he found himself equally content to hold her close.

Through the gray fingers of light filtering through the bedroom's lone window, he watched her sleep. She looked young and so innocent that it hurt. Nestled against his body, she'd relaxed utterly, giving him her trust, even if temporarily and unconsciously. But if he lay with her much longer, he would wake her up in a way guaranteed to freak her out and earn him a kick in the balls. Besides, he had work to do if he wanted them both to be free.

Stone crept from the bed and brewed a cup of coffee. No doubt, he needed the liquid brainpower before starting this day.

He'd barely swallowed his first sip when Jack Cole strode through the door, carrying a few bags, which he set on the kitchen table. "Morning."

"Hey. Lily is still sleeping."

"Perfect. How did you two get on last night?"

Not half as well as he would have liked, but she wasn't ready for any of the million and one sexual thoughts burning behind his retinas. "She's wound tight. Like we suspected, trust is going to be a huge issue. Another woman might soften up enough to tell me something that resembles the truth about her past in the next two weeks, but I'm not sure about this one. I can't afford to chip away at her slowly."

"Nope," Jack agreed, grabbing a cup of coffee for himself.

"I've been devising a plan to cut through her subterfuge about her name and past. I just need to gather more research. Shouldn't be hard. Then we'll get the truth on the table so we can start dealing with it."

"Is this plan going to set you back in the trust department?"

"Probably, but not for long. I just don't see a more expedient way to start talking about the truth."

"You work on that. In the meantime, I have some information for you. The press says that Canton and his wife are headed to an undisclosed location for a lovely vacation off the grid before what's expected to be his announcement to join the race to the governorship." Jack sneered. "That's a tall tale, from what I'm hearing. His wife is in rehab—again—and he's supposedly gone camping with a couple of his aides somewhere in Texas near the coast."

"In August? In the heat?" Stone shook his head as they sat at the kitchen table. "That's bullshit. This time of year, the mosquito population there is in the millions. If he's staying in a tent, they'll eat him alive."

"He would know that since he spent his summers as a kid with his grandparents who lived near Galveston."

"On the other hand, it wouldn't take him too long to drive from Galveston to Dallas . . . or wherever Lily might travel. I assume he brought the aides along to do his dirty work? After all, a guy like that has people."

"Unless Lily is personal enough for him to risk everything, yes." Jack shrugged.

Yeah, they could speculate about the plans of this violent asshole all day and still be wrong. Stone didn't want to waste the time or energy now. "Thanks."

"Everything else good?" At Stone's nod, he went on. "We've finally got decent cell service out here recently, so that should make communicating easy. I've brought you a few more groceries. Holler if you need anything else. I'm going to keep drilling down on Canton's location."

"If that son of a bitch is close, I need to know."

"You do." Jack sighed and looked as if he knew something he didn't want to impart. "I have some other news. Somehow Axel got wind of Lily's exploding car. He's heading home on a flight to Dallas this afternoon."

That was all Stone needed, for Axel to come racing out here and undermine what little progress he'd made with Lily. If she had someone to rely on that she trusted more, Stone knew she'd never look to him. "Fuck."

"Exactly. Thorpe will try to hold him off for a few days. I'll do my best to embroil Axel in something else but . . . I can't make any promises."

"Thorpe still doesn't want to tell Axel that 'Misty' isn't real?"

Jack shook his head. "He thinks it will only suck Axel deeper into the situation. I've known the guy for a long time. He's got a hell of a protective streak. He'll take that girl under his wing again. Probably insist on hiding her, too. And maybe she would let him. I think she'd rather go on pretending that Lily Taylor no longer exists."

"I agree." And Stone intended to absolve her of that notion this morning. "Thanks for everything."

He and Jack worked well together, and it was nice to have an ally in his corner right now. They almost felt like friends. Stupid because Stone knew he was no hero. But that didn't seem to matter to the man who sat across the table, sipping a cup of joe.

"No problem. Oh . . ." Jack stood and fished into his pocket and retrieved a key. "I forgot. If you want to use the playroom, you'll need this."

He dropped the little slice of precisely formed metal into Stone's palm. No one had said that he should begin earning Lily's trust through sex or romance . . . but they clearly weren't against it.

Stone leashed his excitement as he pocketed the key. "Perfect. I'll touch base if there are any developments here. Call me if you've got news."

"Will do."

The second Jack left, Stone headed down the hall toward the locked playroom door. He may not have started his sex life as a Dominant, but he couldn't deny that he liked being in control.

As he passed the bedroom, he spotted Lily's luggage and grimaced. Getting his cover story straight came first, so he shoved the key back in his jeans and dragged the pieces of her luggage into the living room.

One by one, he opened them. Once he found the details he needed and her past was out in the open . . . Well, that key was burning a hole in his pocket. He didn't intend to let it smolder there too long.

For now, he crawled back into bed with her. Within moments, she curled around him. Her softness and scent aroused him as if she'd stroked her hand up his cock. But Stone resolved to savor every moment of the delicious hell until she woke.

* * *

LILY woke cozy-warm and wrapped in Stone's arms. At some point, she'd laid her head on his chest and simply dropped into slumber. In the past, she'd only ever done that with Axel, and it had taken him months to coax the necessary trust from her. Stone had broken down that barrier in next to no time.

Oh my god.

She jerked out of his arms and jackknifed up, staring out the window that was covered in gauzy black drapes. Sunlight streamed from high in the sky. She hadn't just slept through the night; she'd conked out and snoozed through most of the morning, too.

Staring down at the muscled, mostly naked ex-con, Lily wasn't sure she wanted to know why she'd trusted him on any level so readily and easily.

"You don't have to jump up. We have nowhere to go," he said lazily, his eyes still closed.

She swallowed hard and tried to breathe. So much intimacy . . . Their bodies were nearly plastered together. The sheets smelled like him, woodsy, musky. Intoxicating.

Detrimental to her mental health.

"I-I should get up."

When Lily tried to crawl from the bed, Stone clamped a hand around her wrist, not hard enough to hurt her but tight enough to make certain she knew he didn't want her to leave. "We're going to talk."

Meaning he planned to ask her all the questions she'd refused to answer last night.

"I've already talked as much as I intend to." She yanked her arm, but he didn't give an inch. "Let go."

He cracked his eyes open, and his dark expression told her that he wasn't in the mood for pushback. "Here's what's going to happen: You have ten minutes in the bathroom. Brush your teeth, wash your face, change your clothes—whatever you need to do. Then you'll come back here and listen to some things I have to say."

Lily didn't want to agree, but it would give her a reason to escape the dizzying masculinity of his presence and let her collect her wits again.

"Fine."

When he released her, she escaped and took every second of those ten minutes in the bathroom, plus another few to steady herself.

Finally, he pounded on the bathroom door. "Time's up. And I have coffee."

When she emerged, she found him in yesterday's clothes. He'd obviously cleaned up somewhere. Kitchen? More important, he held two mugs of steaming brew.

"Follow me." He cocked his head to the bedroom. "Sit."

Warily, she perched on the edge of the bed. He rewarded her by handing her a mug of liquid caffeine. Stone sat on the other side and sipped his coffee, staring at her over the rim.

"Did you sleep well?"

She flushed. "You know I did since it appears I slept all over you."

He frowned. "That bothers you. Why?"

"Because I don't trust you." But that wasn't entirely true. Some part of her registered him as nonthreatening to her physical safety or she would never have slept five minutes beside him, much less ten hours.

"Maybe I don't trust you, either."

"What does that mean?" She frowned. "It's not like I'm going to rape you."

He set his coffee down on the nightstand beside him. "And I'm not going to rape you. If I'd wanted to last night, it would have been damn easy," he pointed out with an acerbic smile. "But as it happens, I don't want you any way except willing, panting, and begging."

A wave of heat rolled through her body at his words. She'd say he was thinking wishfully, but when she had awakened all plastered against him, her rational mind had nearly panicked while her body hadn't wanted to let go. If she didn't steel herself against him, would all that needing and whimpering he'd described come next?

Trashing the thought, she shook her head. "You keep dreaming big."

Stone sent her a smile of supreme confidence.

His expression set her off. "Wipe that smarmy look off your face.

Or are you so convinced you're god's gift to women and that, of course, I'm going to fall all over myself to get your pants off and jump on your penis?"

He burst out laughing. "No, baby. I'm convinced the heat between us can't be denied. But you're funny, which is a point in your favor. Because I also know you're lying to me, which isn't."

"Lying?" A chill ran through her, leaching out all the heat she'd felt only moments before. "What do you mean?"

Stone reached behind him. She thought he meant to grab his mug and swig the coffee, but he turned back around with an all-too-familiar black tome in hand and dumped it on the bed between them.

She gasped. "You had no right . . ."

When she reached for her yearbook, he grabbed her wrist. "Lily Alexandra Taylor. That's who you really are. You lied to me, Thorpe, Axel . . . everyone. And you did it for years. Don't deny it. Once I saw this name embossed on the front of the cover, I looked up the corresponding picture. Imagine my surprise to find out that Misty isn't your name at all. A few Internet searches gave me a whole lot of information about you, like the fact that you're considered a teen runaway."

Lily shook her head, already trying to spin more tales to throw Stone off track. But his dark stare ripped away her composure, warning her that he already knew every story she'd concoct now would be bullshit.

"You're getting yourself into something you don't understand. Please don't do this."

"You think I don't get a man like Timothy Canton?" He scoffed.

Hearing Stone say that monster's name made Lily freeze from head to toe. She gaped at him. "You . . ."

"Figured out the name of the guy tormenting you? Not too tough. The police questioned you about him. You disappeared less than a week later. I can put two and two together. He's just a thug who put a little spit and polish on his street cred and figured out how to morph his drug money into political power. He's not hard to understand."

Stone had guessed the truth so quickly and accurately. If he could figure out all that in a night, what else could he divine during the next few days? Weeks?

"So now that your big secret is out, why don't you tell me what happened so we can start working together to take him down?"

She scrambled off the bed, shoving her mug on the little nightstand and shaking her head frantically. "There is no taking him down. You're insane."

Stone climbed off the bed and blocked her path to the door. "You're insane if you'd rather keep running than try."

"I know what he's capable of. There's no way I can stop him."

"If not you, then who? You make him sound bigger than Godzilla, like he's defeated everyone else who's ever come up against him."

"Yes!" She didn't know how else to make him understand.

"Unless you want him to keep destroying other innocent lives and killing, it sounds as if you're the only one who can make sure he gets what he deserves."

That gave Lily pause. She'd considered that before, but she lacked the deviousness and the might to vanquish him alone. Yet if she died, some of his worst secrets died with her. Then no one would ever know the terrible truth. The thought of doing nothing to stop him from killing someone else's loved ones and destroying their families slashed her more than a vague sense of shame.

She dropped her face in her hands. Tears didn't come. Of course, it couldn't be that easy. Why should she be allowed to purge all this grief and guilt and move on?

"So let's start at the beginning." His voice had gone gentle, but she didn't mistake the steel beneath. "How did you come into contact with this fucker?"

Was she going to answer that question and put him at risk, too?

But if she didn't, wouldn't she be leaving other unsuspecting people in danger? God, she didn't see a right answer.

"I need time to think about this."

Stone shook his head before she even finished speaking. "That's one thing we don't have. We have to shut Canton down now. He's about to declare his candidacy for governor of California. So unless you want him in charge of the whole state and its population . . ."

Shock pelted Lily. She couldn't breathe. Her feet almost went numb beneath her. "That can't be. Everyone from the neighborhood knows he's a violent drug dealer and a crook."

"Well, he's never been convicted of anything, so with the right spin doctors, his past looks like police bullying and smear tactics from his opponents, both political and otherwise." He sent her a cynical smile.

Feeling dizzy and cold, she clapped a hand over her mouth at the thought of someone like Timothy Canton being in charge of laws, taxes . . . and children.

As she reached out to steady herself, she stumbled. Stone was right there to catch her. "Together, we can put him down."

She turned to him, incredulity dropping her jaw. "Why are you bothering?"

"You've asked me this question."

"I still don't understand the answer."

"Let me make myself clear."

Stone pulled her body against his and grabbed her cheeks. He stared, his expression delving deep. She felt the zing and jolt of their connection. With his gaze, it seemed as if he willed her to understand that he wanted her in every way and refused to accept anything less.

Lily's heart began to thrum. Her blood heated and charged through her veins. Her breasts tightened, and she really didn't want to think about why she could feel the soft ache blooming lower again. She waited, suspended, anticipation racing over her skin. Yes, she should push him away.

Somehow, she couldn't.

He bent to her, swooping down, looming closer. Right or wrong, good or bad—it didn't matter. Lily rose to meet him, clutching his hard shoulders with desperate fingers and pressing herself against him with a gasp as he captured her lips.

Just like the first time, he didn't hesitate or test his welcome. No, he cupped her jaw in his big hands and tilted her head to his satisfaction before he devoured her as if he'd been dying for her taste.

Their breaths mingled, and she sank against his solid warmth. What was this chemical reaction to him that she couldn't seem to fight? Why did her will to resist always evaporate as soon as he touched her? In that moment, he felt not only like someone who could protect her from everything bad in the world but like the man who could bring her body—maybe even her soul—to life.

Lily clung to the taut bulges of his biceps and opened to him eagerly. Later she'd worry about what she'd do if Stone wasn't all he claimed. She'd had so little pleasure in her life, and Lily wanted to drown in the bliss he gave her now.

Suddenly, he wrenched away, breathing hard and staring, as if he needed to affirm that she found their kiss every bit as mind-blowing as he did. She didn't answer with words, just gripped him tighter, unable to hide the desire jetting through her in a hot whirl. The rush of it was scary as hell but new, exhilarating. A white-knuckled thrill. She wasn't ready to let him go.

"Lily," he breathed before he cocked his head and descended again. Their lips fused together once more. Their tongues collided. And she melted in his arms. No, she unraveled completely as he took her mouth in an urgent press, claiming her while utterly dismantling her resistance.

When she felt limp and breathless and willing to do anything for more, he backed away. "Are we on the same page now?"

"You can have sex with anyone," she blurted.

"But when I'm with someone else, I can't have sex with you.

Besides, it's about more than that. I don't like to see you hurt or afraid. When you smile, I find myself doing the same. I have a crazy, maybe irrational need to pursue you. I'm not fighting it, and I wish like hell you wouldn't."

Weirdly, she understood exactly what he meant. Her need to be with him seemed crazy and irrational to her, too. But that didn't make it any less real.

She slumped against him. "I don't understand."

"I'm not sure we're meant to understand, baby. Just deal."

Maybe he was right. Whatever she felt wasn't something she could analyze or control but . . .

"It's all happening too fast. Us, this thing with Canton . . ."

"If you drag your feet, you may be too late to save yourself or anyone else. Haven't you kept his secrets long enough? Why should you bear everything alone? I can help you." He brushed his knuckles along her cheek. "I want to help you. You just have to let me."

Lily blinked back at him. How many times had she felt the weight of the ugly past pressing down on her chest until she couldn't breathe? How often had she wished that she could share all the fears and wretched guilt with at least one person who would understand?

"If I tell you what you want to know, I don't have any proof. How could we possibly take him down?"

"If I know where to look through his records, I can unearth his secrets. We can turn them over to the police. Jack would help. So would the Edgington brothers. I'll bet Sean Mackenzie would use his resources, too."

"The FBI?" The thought of getting tangled up with the feds scared the hell out of Lily. Would they punish her for withholding the truth for so long?

On the other hand, hadn't she earned it?

Stone nodded. "Some branch of law enforcement with teeth is going to have to go after him."

She frowned. Somehow she'd imagined that an ex-con would

advocate a more vigilante form of justice, like flat-out killing Canton himself, but if he wasn't a violent criminal, she supposed his involving cops or agents made sense.

"I'm scared," she whispered, barely hearing herself over the *whoosh* of the air conditioner kicking in to combat the heat.

"I know." He reached for her hand and squeezed it. "I'm going to help you, but I need more details. How did you come into contact with Canton?"

* * *

LILY bowed her head and looked as if she was gathering her courage. Stone didn't think she intended to say anything for a long moment, and he tried to sort through other arguments he might use to persuade her.

"Canton was the local drug lord," she began hesitantly. "He ran an entire neighborhood with a tightfisted rule and enforced it with absolute violence. He tried to appear upstanding, but everyone who knew him knew the truth. My friend Erin—her brother, Corey, was one of his street dealers. Their dad had run off and left them with no money. Their mom was a binge drinker. Corey was just trying to feed himself and his younger sister, keep a roof over their heads. They had it rough. But then, the whole neighborhood did."

"So what happened?"

She dragged in a jagged breath. "Corey got arrested. At the time, his mom was in jail for driving while intoxicated. He was worried about his sister. Erin was my best friend, only fifteen. I'm guessing he didn't want child protective services coming to get her. I'm sure he didn't like jail, either. For whatever reason, he gave the police information about Canton's operations. They dragged the scum in for questioning but could never prove anything, so he got off. While my bestie's big brother was trying to lie low, Canton decided he'd make an example of Corey's family." Wringing her hands, she paused, shutting her eyes as she gathered her fortitude. "He and some of his thugs raped and killed Erin."

"A fifteen-year-old girl?" *Motherfucker*. Stone had known that, but hearing the anguish in her voice somehow made it more real. "And you saw?"

She nodded, tears pooling in her eyes. "Yeah. He did it simply because Corey was trying to be brave and escape his life of crime."

"Canton knows you saw the incident?"

"Yes."

"He let you go afterward?"

She hesitated. "Yes."

Her answer didn't make sense.

"Why?" Stone scowled and tried to dissect her with a glance.

When Lily shrugged and bowed her head, unable to look at him, it confirmed his instincts and made his guts clench. He needed to keep digging.

"Why would a careful bastard like Canton let someone who could both identify him and turn witness walk free after a crime so heinous?"

"I-I don't know."

Stone didn't believe her for an instant. "I'm not stupid. Try again."

"I guess Canton wanted me to tell Corey everything that happened so that he'd know better than to testify."

Maybe, but that still sounded off. "Why didn't Canton just kill Corey? Why would he leave you to tell the guy and potentially create another enemy?"

"I don't know why Canton didn't just off him. I can't read his mind. Maybe because no one could find Corey."

"No one? Not even you?"

Lily shook her head. "I never saw or heard from him again."

"So you never had the chance to tell Corey what happened to his sister?"

"No."

Stone heard a wealth of guilt in that one word. She'd been tearing herself up about this for years. Because she hadn't been able to save Erin Gutierrez? Because Lily had survived and her friend hadn't? "Did you tell the police anything after you witnessed your friend's murder?"

"I wanted to, but I didn't dare." Lily had gone ghostly white and he sensed her terror, even after all these years. "But somehow, the cops found out I saw or knew something. They dragged me in and asked me a lot of questions." She stopped and wrapped her arms around her middle, staring resolutely at the far wall and looking so fragile. "I can't talk about this anymore right now."

Stone studied her and scrubbed a hand over his chin. He suspected this was when Canton had killed her mother and little brother. As badly as he wanted to press her for details, Stone feared she would break. What she'd endured had been a lot for anyone to handle, much less a child. "We'll leave it here for now."

She closed her eyes wearily. "I'm even scared to talk about it. When I was a teenager, Canton had eyes and ears all over the neighborhood. Just like then, I'm afraid he's lurking around a corner now, waiting to kill me. For the past few days, I'd been feeling as if someone was watching me. Now I know I was right."

Stone jolted. "Who did you think was watching you?"

"I don't know. I ran into this guy a couple of times around town over the past few days. I only noticed him because he stared a lot."

"You're sexy, baby."

She dismissed that immediately. "He didn't look at me like he wanted me. He stared a hole through me."

That set off Stone's protective instincts. "Had you seen him anywhere before?"

"Not that I remember."

"Did you get a good look at him? How tall? Race? Distinguishing marks or tattoos?"

"He was probably five foot ten. White or light Hispanic. He wore a baseball cap, so I really didn't get a good look at his face." She shrugged. "The first time I saw him I just thought he was creepy. When I spotted him the next day, I wanted to flee."

Unfortunately, her description sounded like a lot of men and wasn't enough to help him narrow down an identity. "Did you tell anyone?"

"No."

Of course not. She'd been believing for years that she was trapped in this hell alone.

"From now on, you tell me."

"Stone . . ." She glanced his way, her chocolate eyes pleading with him to drop the questioning.

"No arguing about this. I'm going to take care of you. Together, we're going to fix this."

"But—"

He cut her off with a gentle press of his lips to hers. No matter how badly he wanted to, Stone didn't nudge her mouth open and taste her again. He didn't try to peel her clothes away and lower her to the bed. He merely told her without words that he was there for her.

Slowly, she stopped trembling. Their breathing synced up. She relaxed against him with a sigh. "You know, you confuse me."

"How's that?"

Lily frowned, looking as if she was having a tough time putting her thoughts into words. "A lot of crap happened when I was sixteen. People I'd known my whole life backed away from me. They didn't want to get involved because they were terrified of Canton. My mother threw me out of the house. One of the janitors let me sleep at school for a while, but eventually he told me I couldn't stay. Neighbors wouldn't take me in. My boyfriend broke up with me. I'd been working at a diner, but when I missed a few days, they fired me. Overnight, everyone I'd ever relied on was gone."

What had that done to her trust in people? Stone could only imagine how a girl would have processed such violence followed by that kind of betrayal.

"Baby, I'm here."

"It seems that way." Her eyes looked suspiciously full with tears, but they never spilled. He wouldn't have blamed her if she boohooed her eyes out after that tale. Instead, she sucked it up. "I barely know you, and you've been understanding and helpful and kind of perfect every time I've turned around. Thanks."

Stone knew damn well that if she had any idea that he needed her to testify, she'd take every one of those words back. But after hearing her story—at least the parts she wanted to tell him—how could he not want to help her get her life back?

"You're welcome." He tried to swallow his guilt and turn on the charm. "I know one way you can repay me."

"I'm not having sex with you as a way of saying thanks. Trust me, I'm doing you a favor," she assured.

He wanted to tell her that she must be completely wrong. With her hair gathered into a ponytail away from her naked face, she looked so earnest and innocent, yet still sexy. Sure, he liked the mysterious cat eyes she created with all that black eyeliner and her bloodred lips, the stockings that showcased her slender legs, and the figure-hugging clothes she wore that were often decorated with polka dots or bows. But who she was under all that intrigued him even more.

When he'd first met her, Stone thought she'd been a pretty mouse, too shy to come out of her hole and too afraid to testify, even though justice really needed to be served. Now he saw how incredibly strong she was to simply have survived all that as a teenager and then start her life over again.

"No, you're going to have sex with me eventually because we both want it and you don't want to say no anymore. And I'm going to prove to you that you're an incredible woman both in and out of bed." He kissed her forehead and released her. He didn't want to do anything that would press Lily for more before she was ready. "What I want now is something I can't do for myself. So you see, I'm not perfect, kind of or otherwise. So would you put me out of my misery and make me some breakfast?"

Chapter Eight

THE day passed. After a dinner of simple chicken and rice, Stone did the dishes while Lily filled the tub in the bathroom on the other side of the kitchen wall. As he stuck his hands in sudsy water, he tried to focus on cleaning plates. That was like trying to think of Grandma during sex to stave off orgasm—annoying and ineffectual.

After he'd slipped back into bed that morning with Lily and waited for her to wake, she'd curled up against him, one thigh thrown over his. It had felt like the longest hour of his life. Warm and soft and smelling so female, she'd driven him crazy. It had been all Stone could do to resist finding out for himself whether she was wearing underwear. But he'd been a good boy and hadn't copped a cheap feel to answer his question.

When he'd confronted her with her true identity, Lily had retreated into her shell, obviously trying to get her bearings again. Besides tidying up the cabin, she had read a book from the shelf in the living room about Cajun history. The place didn't have any TV, so she'd watched a movie on his phone and caught up on her favorite pop culture sites. Dinner had been almost silent. He'd willed her to say something when he'd tried to engage her. She'd only spoken once.

"Who else knows my real name?" she'd asked as she picked at her rice.

"Thorpe and Sean."

"Which means Callie knows." A flash of anger crossed her face. "You're putting them in danger."

"Don't you think they have a right to know who they're harboring so they can be prepared in case Canton shows up?"

Her guilty expression told him that she saw his point and hadn't considered it in that light.

"They won't cast you out," he reassured, taking her hand. "Jack Cole knows, too. He's helping me. We're trying to track down Canton's whereabouts now and see if we can figure out where he's been and what he's been up to lately. I hacked into his system. All I can see is that he doesn't like to do much on his computer besides play fantasy football and watch porn. If I didn't know better, his Google searches would convince me he's a fourteen-year-old."

"I didn't say he was smart or sophisticated," she drawled. "Just that he had a sharp criminal mind."

"I'll start looking at his staff and buddies next."

She nodded absently, then withdrew her hand. "Did Thorpe tell Axel about me?"

That possibility seemed to disturb her to the core. Stone tried to understand that her former protector had been her pillar, and she would have an abiding instinct not to disappoint the man. But Stone wished like hell that she wouldn't dwell on her former lover and his feelings.

That would stop tonight, as soon as he could understand her attachment to Axel well enough to discern how to work around it.

Stone wasn't stupid enough to fixate on his urge to slide Lily's naked body against his and fill her with his aching cock when they had important catch-a-killer things to do. But while he waited on Jack and others to investigate Canton's location and plots, he and Lily had so little diversion in the swamp. He found it hard to think about much other than her. Besides, Axel was due to land in Dallas in a few hours. If the guy was flying home from another continent because he worried about "his" Sweet Pea, Stone doubted that Axel was going to let little things like a long ride in the car or a state line stop him from reaching Lily.

Stone knew damn well he had to figure out how to become important to her—tonight—or he'd probably lose her the second Axel walked in.

That damn key Jack had given him earlier still burned a hole in his pocket. After he stacked the last of the clean dishes on the towel on the counter beside him, he crept down the hall to the locked door adjacent to the surveillance room.

After a turn of the key, Stone stopped. A padded table in the center of the room took up most of the space. Besides that, a couple of what looked like exercise mats had been spread across the floor. Shelves were filled with plastic shoe box–size containers, each storing its own toy. A wall of pegboard held whips, floggers, restraints. It wasn't fancy or elegant, but it was effective.

He walked the perimeter of the room, staring, his footsteps loud in the relative silence. He needed a game plan and he needed it fast. According to what Jack and Logan had told him via Thorpe, Lily had never allowed anyone at Dominion to touch her except Axel. As far as they knew, the man had never punished her with pain or humiliation. Stone understood why, knowing what she'd witnessed as a girl. Axel hadn't rewarded her with sex, though everyone suspected that he and Lily had sometimes had it. And still, she claimed she didn't enjoy it and wasn't any good at it.

So Axel had both punished and rewarded Lily with his words. Stone knew he had to be different without crossing too many of her boundaries.

Tall fucking order when, as Sean pointed out, his knowledge was all theoretical. But there was a first time for everything and his was now. He'd finally top Lily tonight.

Stone drew in a deep breath and centered himself. That Dominant part he increasingly identified with filled him, expanding his lungs, making his blood race. He had to keep his cool, focus on her, and not lose his head to the needs of his dick.

Before she made it out of the tub, he found a few implements he hoped would interest her and spread them out on a narrow table under a row of shelves. He dimmed the lights in the room, then shut the door.

As she emerged from the bathroom, dressed in that splotchy, ugly-ass T-shirt he suspected she wore to turn him off, he blocked her path before she headed back to the living room.

"I have more questions for you."

She sighed and sent him an expression that said she'd rather endure some crazy Chinese fingernail torture than talk about her past.

"They're not about Canton," he assured.

"Oh." She looked relieved. "Okay."

"It also isn't a request."

As soon as his words were out, she froze. The awareness on her face told him that she understood the command in his tone. "I don't know if I can do this with you."

"Do what?" He wanted to be perfectly clear that she understood.

"Submit." She dropped her gaze and bowed her head.

Lily wasn't sure she could submit to him? Unconsciously, she just had.

Stone lifted his palm and stroked her crown, then bent to kiss the top of her head. "You don't know until you try." He held out his hand. "I think you can. Come with me."

She hesitated, her gaze torn and fixed on his outstretched hand. She debated so long, Stone felt sure she'd refuse. Something in his chest wrenched. How the fuck could he persuade this bruised, wounded woman to put her faith in him?

Before he could devise some other idea to win her over, Lily slid her hand into his. "I'll do my best."

It wasn't a promise, and he'd wanted one. Logically, Stone knew she could simply break it, so maybe her honesty was better.

He led her to the playroom and eased the door open. As he stepped in, she got her first eyeful and gasped.

"You didn't expect this?"

"No." She shook her head. "Wow . . . I would never have imagined a place with a refrigerator built around the same year my grandma was born to come equipped like this."

Stone laughed. He liked her slightly offbeat observations and sense of humor. She had a lot to be serious about, but somehow she made him laugh when he least expected it.

"I'm full of surprises tonight. Kneel on the mat over there, and we'll negotiate."

Her smile faded, and he would have lamented its loss if a pretty blush hadn't taken its place. "Yes, Stone."

The way she said his name, with the same reverence she'd say "Sir," made him hard and more determined than ever to win her over, body and soul, tonight.

Without a word, she approached the mats. Suddenly, she stopped. "Um, I've only ever done this with Axel. When we were alone, I usually wore . . . something different."

Stone would rather see her wear something other than the garments she'd enticed Axel with, but this wasn't about him. "Do you need to wear that tonight to be comfortable?"

Lily hesitated. "I think so. It's part of my ritual, gives me comfort."

Since she had every shred of clothing she owned with her, Stone cocked his head in the direction of the hall. "Go ahead."

"I'll just be a minute."

The woman was true to her word, but it seemed like a damn long minute. Curiosity was killing Stone. He imagined everything from a body stocking to complete nudity. And he started to sweat. If she showed up wearing absolutely nothing, would he be able to use his brain and stay on top of the scene?

When she returned, he spun around to see her tiptoe into the room—and lost his jaw when it dropped somewhere around his knees.

She all but floated in wearing a white baby doll nightgown with ruffled straps over her shoulders, almost-transparent flowers over the pert swells of her breasts, a wide band around the waist that tied into a big bow at the back, and sheer fabric that brushed her thighs with every step, clearly revealing that she wore tiny lacy panties beneath.

How the fuck was he supposed to use his brain if all the blood he needed to power it fled south to his cock?

"Is this all right?" she asked softly.

He could accuse her of trying to torture him, but she already looked so uncertain that he didn't dare put her off-balance—at least not yet.

"You look . . ." Stone blew out a breath. "I'm probably never going to forget how sexy you are right now."

A tremulous little smile broke out across her face. Her sweet blush followed. "Thank you."

"Just being honest."

As she sank to her knees and settled herself on the mat, she lifted big eyes to him. "Before we start, can I ask you a question?"

That gave him pause, but he couldn't exactly say no if he wanted to win her trust. "Sure."

"Why do we need to be in here doing something so personal if you're just going to ask me questions?"

Stone had anticipated her wanting an answer for that. He pulled over a rolling stool from the corner and sat in front of her, focusing utterly on her and her alone. "Because the questions are personal and we're going to build trust while we're doing it. What's going on, both with Canton and with us, is too important to have anything less."

The little bit of challenge he'd seen on her face slipped off. "You're right. It's just . . . everything is happening so fast. I usually take more time to think about things."

"If I could slow it down for you, I would." Because he couldn't not touch her, he filtered his fingers through the soft hair at her nape. "I'll bear as much for you as I can, but that's another reason you need to trust me. If you don't, you'll try to handle everything yourself, the way you have for years. And you'll have no one to turn to if you get overwhelmed."

As soon as the words were out of his mouth, he worried she'd point out that she had Axel. God, the thought even made Stone want to grit his teeth.

Instead, she nodded. "You're right. What do you want to ask me?"

He breathed a sigh of relief.

"First, we need a safe word. Think of one for me. I'd prefer something you've never used before." It might be a bit selfish, but he'd rather she chose one solely for them and their time together.

"How about . . . 'lunar'?" She glanced at the moon rising outside the window as the sun set.

"'Lunar' it is. If you say that, I'll stop everything, and we'll decide together whether to proceed differently or not at all. What are your hard limits?"

"I found out that I'm not good with pain. I tried it a few times. The sensations temporarily blocked out everything in my head and made me live strictly in the moment. That was nice at first. But it also left me raw and alone with all my thoughts once they came rushing back. Ultimately, I felt worse afterward, not better. I didn't have the heart to tell Axel after he'd gone to so much trouble to find a sadist. By then, he was getting involved with Mystery, so it didn't matter anyway. Oh, I'm afraid of blindfolds. And definitely nothing with knives or needles." She shuddered.

"Anywhere I can't touch you?"

She sent him an apologetic gaze, looking a bit like a sad angel surrounded by her platinum hair and frothy white garment. "I never really know until that moment. It took Axel a long time before I was mostly good with him touching me whenever and wherever."

In other words, once she'd trusted the guy. Had that taken weeks? Months? Stone finally decided he'd be better off not knowing. He had tonight to make this work.

"I want to understand your experience and where you are emotionally," he told her. "How long were you under Axel's protection?"

"Almost three years. Thorpe asked him to look after me. He tried himself." She smiled. "I think he was too distracted by Callie even then. His heart wasn't in it. Axel and I got along, so it was a natural pairing."

"Why did Thorpe think you needed someone to look after you?"

"It started as a protection measure. When I first came to Dominion, some of the Doms wanted to play with me. I refused everyone. When Thorpe asked why, I told him I wasn't ready. Floating the story around the club that I belonged to Axel precluded others from propositioning me."

So it hadn't been any grand love she'd felt for Axel—at least not at first. "You trusted Axel and relied on him. You were friends, right?"

"Yes."

"How much more than friends?"

She bowed her head, finally breaking their eye contact. Stone felt the loss acutely and realized that when he couldn't see her, he couldn't read her. And he couldn't handle that.

"He did his best to take care of me."

"You mean sexually?"

"Yes," she said so softly.

Stone had known it, but hearing that still bugged the piss out of him. "And he topped you, too?"

"Yes."

"Did he spank, flog, whip, or otherwise engage in impact play with you?"

"Not much. He's not any sort of sadist."

Pain seemed to push her buttons in the wrong way, and Stone could easily live without it. "Did he restrain you?"

"Sometimes. After I came to trust him, that got easier. I even liked it every so often."

"How often did you have sex with him?"

"Occasionally."

What did that mean? Stone crooked a finger under her chin and lifted her gaze again. "How occasionally? Once a month?"

She gave him a self-conscious shrug. "More like once or twice a year."

Her answer shocked the hell out of him. The math meant she'd had sex with Axel a mere handful of times? That stunned him all over again. Why?

Stone frowned, mentally debating which of the three questions pelting his brain would best serve his needs next. He finally chose the most pressing. "Because he didn't want it more often or you didn't?"

Lily took a long time answering. "Both."

That stunned Stone silent for a long moment. In one sense, it probably shouldn't have surprised him because Lily claimed she didn't enjoy sex. But why hadn't Axel wanted her more? Was that the reason she believed she wasn't any good at sex?

"I think he usually had someone else he enjoyed sex with more," she volunteered. And she sounded really shamed by that. "He never talked about it with me but . . ."

"Who usually initiated the sex when you had it?"

Her eyes filled with moisture and her lower lip trembled. "Can we talk about something else?"

"No. I asked you a question, Lily."

"That's not my name anymore." She sniffled, but her tears didn't fall.

"Yes, it is," he shot back. "It always has been. It will be again. You're not Misty."

"I prefer Sweet Pea."

Stone's first instinct was to shut her down but he checked it. Finally, he knew something she wanted that he could give her. "If you answer my questions to my satisfaction, I'll call you that for the rest of the night."

She pondered his words for a tense moment. "I initiated. Always." She slumped her shoulders. "Axel never . . . He helped me but he didn't really want me, not like that. I only asked him when I needed to be held or got some crazy-ass idea that I could be a normal woman with a normal sex drive. And every time, the whole exercise would remind me for another six months or more that that wasn't true."

Swallowing in shock, Stone stared at her. When she turned her face away, he dropped his finger and let her have a moment of peace without him staring down at her. Without him drilling into her soul.

Deep inside, Lily seemed to feel every bit as broken as she sounded. He saw that on her face. Heard it in the catch of her voice. *Damn it . . .*

"Did he ever give you an orgasm?"

"Sometimes. When I could get out of my head enough, and we had a few hours to devote to the cause. Like I said, I'm not very good at it." She sounded both shamed and depressed by that, too.

Stone had a suspicion that though Axel hadn't intended it, the guy had made her feel more like a burden than a woman. No wonder orgasm had been difficult and rare.

"Do you love him?"

"Yes."

Her quick answer slapped him. Stone clenched his fists.

"As more than a friend?" he clarified.

Lily didn't answer right away. "Maybe. He's the only man I've had any sort of relationship with as an adult. He's talked me through so many of my fears. I'm sure you think I'm still a head case, but I'm way better now than I used to be."

She probably did see it that way, and maybe it was true. But that wasn't love. Stone simply had to prove that to her. And that urge was way more about his own feelings for Lily than his need to persuade her to take the stand.

"When we first got together, I couldn't tolerate sex at all. He's helped me with some coping mechanisms," she added.

Stone wasn't sure whether to shake Axel's hand or punch him in the face. Maybe both. And maybe he'd had other reasons for being intimate with Lily only when she'd asked for it. Whatever. That was done and over. Now Stone intended to do everything different without triggering her fears.

"Thank you for your honesty. I know it wasn't easy."

"Being dishonest about my feelings and needs ultimately hurts me more than you," she said, almost as if she were reciting something that had been drummed into her head.

While Stone supposed the statement was true, he suspected he had Axel to thank for that, too.

"It hurts both of us," he corrected. "Look, I'm not trying to get laid right now; I want to help and understand you. I'm doing my best to make you like me within the context of our larger, more dangerous situation with your past. I have a feeling that trust between us will be important if we both want to defeat Canton and come out of this alive. So before we go any further, do you need to say something? Ask me anything?"

She blinked, then dropped her gaze again. "Did you think of me when I didn't take your calls these last few months?"

"Every fucking day."

She frowned. "Why? It was one kiss."

The shaking in her voice tugged at him. He didn't want her to be worried or afraid, but the fact that she wanted to know if she'd been on his mind was pretty damn endearing.

"Hell if I understand it."

"Have you . . . been with anyone since you got out of prison?"

"Yep." He hoped that didn't upset her too much but he wasn't going to lie. "I'm not a saint."

"Since we met?"

"I've had opportunities but . . . no."

Her head snapped up again. So that got her attention.

"D-did you really like kissing me that much?"

Axel hadn't? Stone scowled. Her raw, vulnerable questions confused him. Most women protected their hearts and feelings with way more sophisticated mirrors and smoke screens. Lily simply asked.

Stone slid off the stool and got to his knees in front of her. Yeah, it probably upset the D/s psychological balance or whatever, but Lily needed the touch of a man right now way more than she needed the authority of a Dom.

He cupped her face in his hands, thumbs caressing her cheeks. "Baby, I kissed you . . . and that was it for me. I hardly think of anything else, except imagining what it will feel like when I do a lot more than kiss you."

She tried not to smile. And she didn't reply, but he was damn happy that his admission hadn't freaked her out. In fact, he had a better understanding of the state of Lily's heart and mind. Now he had to put that information to good use.

His father used to complain jokingly that women didn't come with user manuals. Stone had never really understood his dad's complaint until now. He couldn't help but feel as if he had only one shot to bind Lily to him. Tomorrow the rest of the world would probably invade. If he fucked up, he might not get the opportunity to sway her in his direction again. So he had to pull out all the stops right fucking now.

"When you had sex with Axel, where did he usually take you? Bed?"

She shook her head. "Sofa."

Lily didn't elaborate, and Stone found that odd but didn't press. Instead, he stood and peeled off his shirt, hiding a grin when she stared raptly.

"Wait here." He left and found his phone in the bedroom, then flipped through the screens to find the music streaming service he subscribed to. When he found a channel of sexy electronic instrumentals, he launched the first song and reentered the playroom.

"That okay?" he asked.

"Yeah. Music helps me relax."

Exactly what he'd been hoping. "Close your eyes."

She hesitated, closed them, and opened them quickly again. "I have trouble with that. I need to see what's happening."

He would remind her that she needed to trust him to take care of her during a scene, but he understood that fear drove her. On the other hand, he'd bet that when she was too aware of what was happening around her, she couldn't shut off her brain enough to let pleasure take over. Axel may have let Lily have her way. Stone couldn't afford to. On some things, he had to be aware not to push her too far past her limits too fast. But right now, she would never unravel for him if he didn't.

"I'm here. I've got you. We're in a secure house in the middle of a swamp. There's no one out here but us. Put yourself in my care. I'll talk you through everything."

Lily seemed to wrestle with herself, biting her lip and staring at him, silently asking if he would harm her when she couldn't see. That face hurt him, deep down where he wanted to make her happy. But he didn't rush her.

Finally, she came to the right conclusion and slid her eyes shut again.

In reward, he stroked the crown of her head. "Good job, Sweet Pea."

"I know I asked you to call me that, but could you . . ." She sighed. "I like it better when you call me 'baby.' No one has ever called me that. It makes me feel sexy."

And Axel had probably called her Sweet Pea or Misty all the time. Stone took it as a good sign that she wanted things between the two of them to be different.

"Baby, it would be my pleasure."

She gave a happy little sigh.

He walked behind her and knelt so he could whisper in her ear. "I'm going to give you pleasure now. Ready?"

"I'm nervous."

Stone placed his hands on her shoulders and stroked his way down her arms. "Nothing but goodness from here on out. I promise."

"Yes, Stone."

She barely breathed the words and trembled under his touch. Fuck, if that didn't arouse the hell out of him. Most of the women he'd taken to bed had been jaded, afraid to be vulnerable with the man inside them. But Lily seemed not to have much of a filter when it came to shielding her reactions. She laid herself bare more often than she realized, and he wouldn't want to change that for anything.

"Move the hair off the back of your neck," he whispered against her nape.

He heard her breath catch; then she raised both hands to lift the shimmering, pale mass and push it to one side, exposing the narrow column and that delicate sweep of flesh into her other shoulder.

"Good," he praised, then followed that up by pressing his lips against her sensitive skin there in reward. Fuck, she smelled good, sugary-sweet with a hint of something spicy.

He breathed her in—and his dick went harder. How the fuck was he going to restrain himself from throwing her to the mat and shoving his way inside her? He had to; she wasn't ready for that, Stone knew. But damn if he didn't burn to take her in every way known to man.

"Tell me how you're feeling."

"A little restless." She squirmed as she sat back, butt on her heels. "A little achy."

"Aroused?" he prodded.

"Yes, Stone."

God, he loved hearing his name from her lips, especially in that slightly breathy tone.

He stroked her shoulder, peeling away the frilly little strap. His lips followed his hand, setting a slow trail of kisses all the way over the slope. Lily's breath caught as he made his way back up, adding a nip of his teeth, followed by a soothing lick of his tongue.

When he reached her neck again, he moaned in her ear. "You taste sweet."

She shuddered in his arms.

"Are your eyes still closed?" he asked.

"Yes."

"Do you feel safe?"

This time she took a bit longer in answering. "Having my eyes closed may never be comfortable for me, but it's not a reflection of you."

So something about having her eyes closed must remind her of a bad experience. Her friend's rape and murder? He had to keep her from falling into her own memories and fears and failing to reach orgasm.

"Picture the playroom we're in. Remember the soft lighting. Feel the mat under your knees. Can you do that?"

She nodded.

"Are you uncomfortable beyond what you can bear?"

"No," she assured softly.

"That's what I want to hear. Now, keep that image firmly planted in your mind. Don't let your thoughts usurp that visual with anything else. If you start to drift, bring back the hardwood floors and play equipment. Picture me right here with you."

"Yes, Stone."

The sensual song ended then slid into another, this one with some chanting and panting and a seriously sexual vibe.

"Focus on the music," he instructed. "You hear that? You like it?"

She nodded.

"Tilt your head back. More. Yes, all the way."

Once she complied, Stone trailed a fingertip from the tip of her chin, down her throat, into the hollow beneath, and descended slowly toward the swells of her breasts. "Can you feel me behind you?"

She nodded. "You put off so much heat. Your skin is soft but everything beneath is muscled and hard. Every time I take a breath, I smell that you're a man." She let out a shaky breath. "I like it."

That was more honesty than Stone had expected, and he decided to reward her again with another kiss to her neck, another murmur in her ear. "You're so delicate under my hands." He caressed her arms again, then let his palms drift down to her waist. "So tender under my lips. Tell me, baby . . . are your nipples hard?"

"I think so."

But she didn't know for sure? That told him that her brain and her body might not be syncing up yet. "Touch yourself and find out for me."

Lily didn't move right away. Was she wondering why he didn't check himself? She didn't ask, simply placed her fingertips over the baby doll's wispy fabric where it covered her breast, then yanked her hand away quickly. "Yes."

He smiled. "Are you sure? Check again. Be really thorough."

"You just want to watch me touch myself," she accused breathlessly.

"Damn straight."

She didn't obey right away. Stone felt the second she went up in her head and thought too much about the mechanics of what he'd asked. Then he'd bet she weighed how she would look to him or if arousing herself more while he watched would earn her praise or make her feel ashamed.

"You're taking too long," he warned.

"I can't stop thinking that you're going to be looking over my shoulder and watching me."

"Let's make that worry go away. I'll just ease around you and plant myself right here," he said inches from her face. "So now, I'm not looking over your shoulder anymore. I'm just looking."

Her cheeks turned a pretty rosy shade and she opened her eyes, focusing in on him. "You're going to leer at me while I touch myself?"

He chuckled, liking the dreamy expression in her eyes, her slightly dilated pupils. "Pretty much. Unless that bothers you for some reason."

"No. It's just not what I'm used to."

"I know. Right now, there's only us and whatever we want." He cupped her cheek. "You got that? I'm not judging anything. I just want you to be all right. I want you to feel pleasure."

Lily nodded. "Being with you . . . it's so different."

"I'm not Axel." And though he understood why she still had the man on her mind, it pissed Stone off that she couldn't think about him when he was in front of her, half-naked and wanting.

"Obviously," she agreed.

He grabbed for his patience. "Different isn't bad."

"It isn't," she acknowledged, and he let out a sigh of relief. "What I meant was that everything feels so different when the purpose of the play is to feel good, not simply to screw my head on straight. It's . . . nice to be wanted."

Her words took him aback. He should have put two and two together earlier and realized she wasn't really used to indulging a man's desire. On the other hand, if Thorpe was right, she had the heart of a submissive. She wanted to please. It had been one thing to obey Axel when he'd merely been trying to lead her down a path to help her grow. It was another for her to actually satisfy a man she would kneel for and eventually give herself to. She'd want that.

And Stone intended to give it to her.

"I'm still waiting—and not very patiently. Touch your nipple. Take your breast out of your nightgown and caress that hard nub. Right where I can see everything."

Lily's breathing turned choppy. She trembled a bit as she lifted her hands from her lap and pulled the side of her baby doll down with one hand and lifted her sweet breast above the fabric with the other. The sight of the gentle swell in her hand aroused the hell out of him, but when she dragged her thumb across the turgid pink peak and sucked in a little gasp, Stone nearly lost his fucking mind.

"That's it. Again."

When she complied and looked at him with the big eyes seeking approval, he couldn't resist cupping his hand around her shoulder and coming closer.

"Did that feel good?" His words came out rough and low, and he hoped that wouldn't scare her.

The brave girl gave him a little nod. "Knowing that you're watching and liking what you see is its own pleasure."

Just her tone made it clear she hadn't expected that.

"Do you ever touch yourself when you're alone, make yourself come?"

At that question, she frowned. "Not so much. I feel awkward, weird, touching myself when I'm alone. I never got the chance to before I left home as a kid since I shared a bedroom with my little brother. I know toys exist so that it's more expedient and less messy, but I don't like hearing things buzz. I don't like plastic. And then there's the whole feeling-too-alone thing. Masturbation just isn't for me."

Stone would bet she just hadn't had the right impetus. In the past, she'd probably tried doing it for the same reason she tried sex with Axel, to feel normal. When she figured out how to tune her brain to pleasure and simply indulged, he suspected she'd feel very differently about the subject. And if having him watch turned her on, then he was totally game. Because seeing her touch herself even now was about to make his cock bust through his zipper.

"Keep touching that nipple for me," he coaxed. "Just flick it back and forth . . . Yeah."

Her eyes slid shut. Despite the fact that he'd told her earlier to close them and focus, now Stone felt shut out of her experience, and that he wouldn't tolerate.

"Look at me, baby."

Lily was slow to comply. She lifted her thumb away from her breast before her lashes fluttered open. "Am I doing something wrong?"

"No. I want you to touch yourself again but look at me. Right at me. Don't look away."

"You really want to watch me?"

"Fuck, yeah."

A nervous little smile crept up her face, but she didn't refuse. Instead, she dragged her thumb over the hard point again. At the flick of her digit, Stone watched her peak bend, bounce back, then harden even more. She was so close that he could nearly touch it himself. Hell, he could nearly taste it. His mouth watered just thinking about working the stiff bud with his lips and tongue, giving her a slight sting with his teeth.

He groaned. At the sound, her eyes widened. She blinked, then looked down his body, right where his hard cock fought to escape his pants.

Stone grabbed at his bulge. "This is for you, baby. This is what you do to me. Watching you is excruciating torture, and yet I can't stop. Pinch your nipple. Squeeze it. Just like that," he encouraged. "Does it feel good? Can you feel the blood filling it? Do you like the tingle and bite?"

Her breath wasn't quite steady as she nodded and tried to close her eyes again. "Yes."

"Open those pretty eyes. Look at me. Don't look away."

With a flutter of her lashes, she did as he demanded. Her eyes had darkened from the color of melted chocolate to sultry midnight. Stone couldn't help himself. He had to touch her, stake a claim.

"Do it again. Don't stop until I tell you," he murmured across her skin as he brushed his knuckles along her collarbone.

Her eyes widened. She rewarded him with gooseflesh and a little whimper. Then she did exactly as he'd instructed, taking the hard nub between her thumb and finger and giving it a squeeze.

Her whimper became a moan.

"Harder," he commanded. "Do it now."

To his satisfaction, Lily obeyed readily, almost viciously; then she rasped the edge of her fingernail across the sensitive peak. It tightened, turning rosy as it filled with more blood. Stone watched in utter fascination. And when her moan became a high-pitched keening, he smiled.

"That's fucking pretty, baby. Can you do that to the other breast?" he asked as he tucked his fingers under the other strap of her baby doll and lifted it off her shoulder, letting it fall uselessly down her arm. "Show me. Tease your nipple."

Lily didn't hesitate to lift her other breast from the nightgown and reveal the perfect swell along with its tight berry tip.

"Damn," he choked out. "So fucking beautiful. Look at you." He trailed his fingertips in a light caress down the side of her breast, then withdrew quickly in case she objected. But he shouldn't have worried. Lily's eyes softened in thanks.

As she let out a sigh, she first brushed the newly exposed kernel gently with her thumb, then frowned as if the sensation displeased her.

She blinked at him in confusion.

"You want more now," he supplied. "You're sensitive and you want to feel. Pinch, tug, twist. Make that nipple come alive. Show me how you want them touched."

With a shaky bob of her head, Lily clamped her fingers around the barely touched peak and gave it a hard yank, a vise of a pinch, then a scrape with her nail. Her whole body seemed to melt as she tossed her head back with a shiver.

Stone thought he might crawl out of his skin with wanting her. He curled a hand around her nape and forced her stare back to his. Her not-quite-focused eyes and pleading glance began to unhinge his restraint.

"That's the way I like to see you. You like it, too. I can tell." He leaned closer, whispering against her lips. "Do it again, but tease both your nipples at once. Right now."

The moment she clenched her nipples between her thumbs and forefingers, she yelped. Then she groaned as sensation hit her. Stone swallowed the sound by covering her mouth with his own and surging deep inside. In this moment, he owned her. And he craved more. He loved the idea of having every part of her belong to him, spread out for his viewing pleasure, ready whenever he wanted her. Which would be always. But with such a beauty, who could blame him?

She keened out and he drank in her need, itching to touch those sweet nipples himself. As he changed the angle of the kiss and rose on his knees above her, bringing her closer, he let his fingers trail from her shoulders, down to the swells of her pouty breasts. He covered her hand with his palm, helping her support the drawn-up curve while he caressed her so-soft skin and itched to put his fingers right where hers worked.

The moment she released the reddening tips, he moved in, dragging his thumb over what had to be her supersensitive flesh.

Lily tore her lips from his. "Stone!"

"You like it when I do that to you? Do you like my fingers tugging on your nipples, baby?"

"Yes." She stared, looking somewhere between pleading and helpless.

"You're asking for more with that expression," he warned. "Just begging me for the answer to the gnawing ache growing between your legs. You're wet, right?"

"I am," she said with such tortured honesty.

"Have you ever felt this need?"

"Not this sharply. You can't leave me . . ."

"I won't," he assured, brushing her right hand from her breast and taking over. "You like your nipples toyed with and you like it rough. I love touching you, baby. I'll take care of it." When she flushed all over at his words and her little candy peaks hardened again, he groaned. "Look at you. God, I don't ever remember anything sexier. You want more?"

She nodded adamantly, demanding without a word.

"You want more of my fingers?" He pinched, teased, toyed, twisted, enjoying her gasps and the way she wriggled as if the ache of her cunt was becoming too much to fight. "Or do you want something more? Do you want me to suck you?"

When he bent to her breast, he tested both her arousal and her fear by drawing her nipple into his mouth and rolling it around on his tongue. Lily gave an animal cry of desperation and wrapped her arms around his head, clutching him closer.

With a pop, he eased her bud from his mouth and smiled. "Would you like it if I did that to your other breast? Let's see . . ."

He didn't hear anything that resembled her safe word, so he kissed a path from the hollow of her throat, his lips coasting down velvet skin, all the way down to the hard crest stabbing the air as if silently demanding attention. Gently, he surrounded the nub with his lips, then laved it, his tongue prodding it back and forth over her aroused flesh, just barely there.

"That enough?" he teased.

"No." She clung to his shoulders. "More. Please. I'm . . . lost."

Something about the way she begged told him that she'd never done that in her life. Satisfaction and a desire to own her slammed him. Stone wanted to be the only man who ever heard her in true need. He wanted to be the only man who sated it, too.

"Lost?" He gave her a mock frown. "Oh, baby. I'll help you find exactly where you should be. Lie back."

Stone worried she would refuse or demur, but after a moment's hesitation, she nearly melted into the mat, the delicate swells of her breasts pointing toward the sky, the tips calling his name in a siren song he couldn't resist.

Lily flung one arm over her head. The other she draped across her middle. She looked like a seductive goddess finally waking to the power of her own body and sensuality. "Like this?"

He took her in, the gauzy white giving her fair skin a luminescent quality. She looked like a fucking pearl, all glowing. Stone couldn't take his eyes off her. "Almost. Now bend your knees."

With a furrow of confusion wrinkling her brow, Lily planted her feet flat on the ground. Gravity caused the handkerchief hem of the baby doll to slide down her thighs, revealing a creamy length of leg and a hint of lace underneath.

"That's nice, baby. Really nice. You would look even prettier if you spread your legs for me." When she hesitated, looking uncertain, Stone backpedaled. "Just a little more. That's all. Get comfortable."

She swallowed. "You won't hurt me?"

As aroused as he was, Stone stopped everything and caressed her cheek. When she peered up at him, fear and uncertainty creeping back into her expression, he murmured a soothing sound. "Never. Whatever happens between us, I'll never do anything but protect and pleasure you." He caressed his way down to her breast and filled his palm with it, his thumb taking a slow slide over the sensitive tip again. "Ever. Do you have any idea how good I want to make you feel?"

Exactly as he'd hoped, that turned Lily's thoughts away from whatever disturbed her and turned her back toward bliss.

Lily arched into his touch, her eyes drifting shut for the barest of moments as she groaned. And she spread her legs wider.

When he bent and took her nipple into his mouth and fondled the other, her eyes flew open wide. "Stone!"

"You like that?"

"Yes," she panted. "It's . . . I ache everywhere. It's too big. Can't fight it."

"Don't try. I ache, too, baby. I'm absolutely dying to see you give in to pleasure. Do you want that? Do you want to come?"

As he continued to lick and pinch her nipples, he stared, his gaze delving into hers until she scratched at the mats and nodded fever-ishly. "I don't know what's happening."

"Just pleasure. Follow me and I'll make sure you get to orgasm. Do that for me, baby. We both want you to reach it."

She panted, her face softening with need. Her voice thinned with desperation. "How?"

"Let me touch your pussy."

Chapter Nine

TOUCH her . . . there? Lily had never used the word Stone had just uttered in her life. Truthfully, only Axel had ever touched between her legs. Somewhere in the back of her head, she'd never been able to forget that he had done it to be helpful, out of far more pity than desire.

But the sexual heat in Stone's eyes, the flush of red slashing down his cheeks, the seduction of his words—they all promised that sympathy was the last thing he felt for her. He'd been so patient, so encouraging. With him, she felt free and sexy. Not like a burden but a woman.

She'd been desperate to feel this way for the past three years.

"If you want me to touch you and make you feel even better, all you have to do is relax and let me slip my hand under those lacy panties," he muttered gruffly. His edge of impatience turned her on. "I'll do the rest."

The pull of his mouth on her nipple again electrified her. She wanted to feel him everywhere, wanted to know just how much pleasure he could give her. But as badly as she ached, the flashes of the past simply wouldn't be banished. Horrific images of Erin's last hour on this earth pelted her, those moments Canton had ripped away her jeans and her innocence with a terrible glee before he ended her life. She still heard the screams, still smelled the blood . . .

"I-I can't," Lily sobbed as she tried to push him away, shoving at his hands and clamping her legs together again. "It's too much. I don't—"

"Shh. Okay." Stone shifted all his attention from her body back to her face. Their gazes connected. He stroked her hair so gently, she almost cried. "It's all right. Do you need your safe word? Or can I keep kissing you? Touching your breasts?"

He wasn't angry or impatient? He wasn't annoyed that despite the slow way he'd prepared her body, she was freaking out?

Those damn tears she'd never been able to shed welled in her eyes again. Just a few moments without his touch and already she was missing it. Maybe . . . Could it really hurt to let him continue a little? Yeah, she'd never reach orgasm from kisses and caresses to her breasts, but the moments of indulging her sensuality like a normal woman, of feeling wanton and lovely and connected to him? She couldn't pass that up.

"Please. Yes," she cried out. "Are you mad at me?"

"Mad?" He sent her a look of such exquisite understanding. It utterly dismissed her anxiety and vowed she'd never have to worry. "Why would I be mad? I'm trying to make you feel good, not uncomfortable or defensive. If you're comfortable here for now, we'll stay here."

His assurances made her want to try more. So did the ache between her legs. She didn't want to give up without seeing if she could let loose enough to enjoy pleasure with a man who aroused rather than coddled her.

"I don't want to stop," she sobbed.

"That's good." He tongued his way up the side of her breast and plucked at the nipple with his fingers until a little shudder ran under her skin. "If you're not ready for me to touch your pussy, you'll have to do it. I'll help by talking you through it, Lily. Can you do that?"

Talk her through it? That sounded shocking, sensual, and intimate all at once. "Can I keep my panties on?"

"If you need to."

Lily nodded. Removing them would make her feel too vulnerable and reveal too much of her body. Not that Stone wasn't perfectly capable of ripping them off himself if he wanted to take advantage of her. She took comfort in knowing that if he did, the line to detach his balls from his body would form behind Axel, and it would be long. "What should I do?"

"Don't tense up, baby," he coaxed. "This is the good stuff. All you have to do is slide your hand between your legs and look at me."

That might be all she had to do in his mind but since she'd never really masturbated successfully, much less in front of a man, it seemed like a tall order. Still, she wanted to share pleasure with Stone so badly—and wanted him to be pleased, too. Heck, she wanted him enough to push past her discomfort and try.

Dragging in a steadying breath, she slid her hand down her stomach, under the elastic of her waistband, over the smooth mound Axel had instructed her to keep bare, and between the plump folds. Problem was, she didn't know what to do next. Lily choked back a cry of frustration. What grown woman knew so little about the way her body worked?

One who'd been afraid of sex since age sixteen.

"Where are your fingers, baby?"

"On my vagina."

He flicked his tongue across her nipple. "'Vagina' is something you say when you visit the gynecologist. That's your pussy. Are your fingers on it, playing with your clit? If not, that's where they should be."

Right. She knew where to find that. Axel had introduced her to that part of her anatomy.

When she touched the bundle of nerves between her legs, she yelped, shocked by its surprising sensitivity. Every so often, Axel touched her there. She didn't feel much at first. The sensations took time to build. Then again, they'd never been to bed with passion in mind. Apparently that made everything different.

"You can feel that, huh?" He smiled. "Do it again—drag your finger right over the top. Then make sure it's wet before you rub it in small circles."

Lily shoved her self-conscious thoughts aside and pursued the sharp jolt of pleasure she'd felt just moments ago. Stone seemed to know how a woman's body worked. She disregarded the jealousy that stung her. The fact that he had clearly had a mountain of sexual experience worked in her favor right now. Since he didn't mind sharing his knowledge, she intended to savor how juicy these moments felt.

She slid her finger between her folds and drew more moisture up to her aching button. When she touched it, pleasure jabbed her again, bright and shocking. Almost against her will, she gasped and arched, jerking her gaze to Stone. She fixed there, blinking, panting.

"Yeah, you can feel that. I see it on your face, baby. Hmm, I can't even tell you how sexy it is to watch you the first time you learn how much pleasure you can give yourself. It's, like, the biggest deposit in my spank bank ever."

Despite the edge of need gouging her, Lily couldn't help but laugh. The worries that had been building in the back of her head evaporated, leaving behind a comforting warmth to go with the heat permeating her entire body. This man totally got to her.

She tsked at him. "Are you serious?"

"Absolutely. You know you're sexy, right?"

Lily had never truly felt sexy before today. But Stone changed everything with an ease that surprised her. "I like that you think I am."

"Believe it, baby." He cupped her breast, thumb teasing, as he bent to whisper in her ear. "When I came into this room tonight, I already wanted you like mad, but now that I've seen just how damn much you turn me on, I'm going to be after you morning, noon, and night. You're free to say no and I'll listen. But I'm not giving up. Now get busy and come for me."

He made it sound so easy, as if it was perfectly natural for her to engage in self-pleasure. And that, of course, he would watch. How badly she wanted to be normal. How much she wanted to please him. How desperately she needed this climax.

She spread her legs a bit wider and set her fingers over her slippery clit, then started rubbing gently. Electric tingles slid through her body. The ache turned so vicious she could feel the walls of her sex tighten and clamp down. Once they did, she felt so empty, as if she needed someone—Stone—to fill her.

With her free hand, she reached out to him. He took it in his own. His dark, focused stare pinned her, slammed down her spine, the impact making her suck in a rough breath and clutch him harder.

As she rubbed the nubbin a little slower, with a bit more brush and tease, the need surged again. The muscles of her thighs tensed. Her sex clenched. A hot flush rolled through her body. Then suddenly, her heartbeat roared in her ears. Lily swore she could hear her blood pumping.

This was big and thick and encompassing. Whatever sensation gathered wasn't like the orgasms she'd had in the past. When all this pent-up fire burst, it would burn her alive.

"Stone," she keened.

"Oh, fuck. You're so beautiful. You need this now, don't you? Yeah," he agreed when she nodded frantically. "Let it take you under. Let me hear you scream."

Lily couldn't think of anything she wanted more. As she circled her hyperaware nerve endings again, her body jerked. Desire surged. When Stone bent to take her nipple in his mouth, she clasped the back of his head and anchored him to her. Not that he'd do anything except help her drown. But this time nothing would be sweeter.

He dragged a hand up to her other nipple and tangled his fingers with her own. Together, they manipulated the tip of that breast while he sucked the other hard bud and scraped the very tip with his teeth.

Sensations mounted again. She felt like a vessel filling up with blood, with need, with an imminent explosion. It was right there . . .

Her legs shook. Her hips jerked. She whimpered, strained for it. She tasted need.

But she couldn't seem to fall over the sweetly sharp edge.

Lily pressed harder against her clit, narrowing her circles, focusing on just how good this was going to be. The seconds ticked off in her head, slowly becoming minutes. The exquisite need was its own form of hell, and she couldn't seem to escape.

The torture dragged on, and she saw no way out. She squeezed her eyes shut, feeling defeat begin to creep in.

Stone sprang into action, popping her nipple from between his lips and grazing her ear with his lips. "You got this, baby. Focus on my voice and close your eyes. Yeah, I know that's hard, but I've got you."

Oddly, she already believed that.

"Picture yourself naked and me standing over you, stroking my cock. You know I'm going to tell you how sexy you are and how much I want you. Imagine that I'd fall to my knees between those pretty thighs. When you hold your arms open to me, I'll go right into them. Then I'm going to kiss you, touch every lush, tingling curve of your body, and when you're begging, that's when I'll slide inside you. Deep. That's when I'll stroke you slowly and thoroughly and make you claw my back as you come."

As he spoke, her desire and racing blood clashed, merged. Everything inside her roared to a screaming crescendo. The wall she'd been slamming into, preventing her from falling over, disintegrated. She envisioned exactly what Stone told her to picture. She saw herself being not just perfectly able but eager to lie back and welcome him inside her as he gave her mind-blowing pleasure and she surrendered herself completely.

With a guttural scream, she careened into a thick thrall of pleasure, her fingers still working with a gentle firmness that prolonged the agony for seemingly endless moments. The climax didn't merely embrace her but sent her soaring into a breathtaking realm of dizzying euphoria. The rapture she'd been avoiding? Amazing. Knowing her body was capable of all this? Astonishing.

As she crested, the crush of sensations was suddenly cushioned in a lovely velvet embrace. The tight grip of climax loosened with a sigh. Everything once sharp now felt golden, meant to be. Perfect.

No wonder people enjoy orgasm so much.

The grip of pleasure finally began to release its hold. Of its own volition, her body shuddered and twitched with the last vestiges of bliss.

Then she sighed and melted into the mat.

"Lily, baby . . ." Stone groaned above her.

Lazy and sated, she cracked her eyes open to find him staring at her with both pride and reverence. He wasn't smiling as if he was relieved that, after dredging up his patience, he'd managed to do his good deed for the day. Axel would be horrified if he ever figured out that she'd read him so clearly. Instead, Stone was proud of *her* for taking steps forward and taking charge of her sexuality. He looked at her as if only she alone existed for him. Nothing and no one else mattered.

"You just tilted my world on its axis," he murmured.

It took her a few moments to process his words. She frowned. "I think that's what I'm supposed to say to you since you worked so hard to help me."

"You always had the ability inside you. I just nudged until you saw it. You're a whole, normal woman, Lily. You were a kid when Canton did something appalling that terrified the hell out of you and bruised your psyche. He bent you but he didn't break you. I needed you to see that. And you did. It's *your* job well done."

She knew she could never have given herself such an experience if he hadn't been right there, helping her along. But the point wasn't worth disputing. In fact, she didn't feel like arguing about anything just now.

Instead, she gave him a heavy-eyed smile. "I'm still patting you on the back."

"I was hoping for something a little lower." He winked her way.

Lily froze. She'd managed to find ecstasy, sure. And she'd left him in blue-ball hell. "Okay. I-I should warn you though. I'm not sure what to do—"

"I'm teasing, baby."

"I can . . ." *What?* The few times she and Axel had progressed this far, they usually had sex. She'd once offered to relieve him with her mouth or hand. He'd told her that he didn't want her to confuse the issue—whatever that meant—so she'd still never gotten a man off without penetration. "I can try to give you a blow job."

She could hear the hesitation in her own voice and winced.

Stone eased down on top of her, caressing the hair back from her face. Lily felt his weight pressing on her, the hard column of his erection jabbing her mound. Panic began to creep in. She sucked in air, tried to tell herself to stay calm, that Stone wouldn't hurt her. She focused on the pleasure she'd just experienced, the tenderness of his expression.

All she could see in her head was Erin fighting as Timothy Canton held her down with his superior size and strength and raped her.

Lily couldn't help it. She lost her calm, fighting and bucking and shoving, screaming all the way.

Stone jumped off of her instantly and scrambled to his feet, putting distance between them. "It's all right. I'm backing off."

But he looked worried. She sat up, realized how crazy she probably looked, and hung her face in her hands. Damn it. She was worried, too. After tonight, she would have sworn she'd broken through some mental barrier.

"It might take more than one night, you know?" He crooked a finger under her chin. Even as she tried to resist, he gave her his quiet resolve and patience. "I'm not giving up. Neither are you."

"It's been years." She wanted to cry, and the fucking tears still wouldn't come.

"But not with me. We've tried this once. Tomorrow is another day, huh? Smile for me."

"I can't leave you like this, wanting and aching and . . ."

"Without relief? Baby, that self-pleasure thing is a breeze for me. I mastered it at twelve. I can spend a few minutes in the shower and be fine. Would I like it as much as sex in any form with you? Fuck, no. You have *no* idea how much I'd give up—one eye, a nut, and my entire *Star Wars* collection. But I won't give you up. We'll get there, if that's what you want."

"Isn't sex supposed to be about give and take? I only took." That devastated her. So much for normal.

"You gave, too. Besides great spank-bank material, seeing you in pleasure will linger longer than any fleeting climax of my own. I'll remember that moment and replay it over and over in my head."

She chewed on her lip, trying to hear what he said. Guilt and disappointment stifled her. "But—"

"Shh, I'm good with tonight being about you."

Even as Lily wondered if he was right and she wasn't ready for sex, oral or otherwise, she felt almost disappointed that he wasn't insisting on more. "Can't it be about you, too?"

"I hope it will be soon. But don't sweat it now."

Before she could argue again, his phone buzzed insistently, cutting off the music that had filled the background and added to their mood.

Stone jumped to his feet and grabbed it. "Just a minute," he said into the device, then held out his free hand to her. "Baby, why don't you go to bed? You look exhausted."

In other words, their time together was over and the real world was calling. Why couldn't she have kept her shit together and opened her arms and body? He'd done nothing to freak her out or make her wary. Once she'd gotten over her violent-ex-con misunderstanding and realized she'd never met a gentler man, she really should have been able to share herself with him.

Was she even more broken than she'd thought?

Lily ignored his outstretched hand. On shaky legs, she got to her feet and headed for the door, feeling somewhere between embarrassed and broken. "Good night."

* * *

STONE watched Lily walk out of the playroom with her head hanging and her shoulders slumped. It fucking hurt his heart, but she always said she needed time to think. Maybe some of that now would do her good. He wasn't sure how she would have handled it if he had tried to . . . What would he have done, given the chance? He wanted to do more than have sex with or fuck her. He didn't merely want to mount and take her. No, he wanted to make love to Lily. Shit, he'd never really done more than scratch an itch with a woman before, and now he wanted to use his body to tell Lily Taylor how crazy he was about her.

Oh, hell. A) He had it bad. B) It would crush him if he tried to make love to her again and she freaked. And C) What the fuck should he do next?

All of the above was swirling through his head when he heard the familiar male voice call from the phone in his hand. "Hello?"

Stone jerked the device to his ear and shut the door so Lily couldn't hear. "Here. Sorry. What's up?"

He hoped it was quick because he really didn't want to leave her alone and dejected for long.

"Lots, and none of it good," Jack Cole said, his tone almost apologetic.

Motherfucking son of a bitch. "Lay it on me."

"I'll give you the 'good' news first. We can't find Canton. No one has seen him near Galveston, at least not camping. We took his picture to every state park and campground within a fifty-mile radius. Nothing. I think Hunter really wanted to pound someone's face because the baby's still not sleeping and he's grouchy, but we couldn't find anyone who seemed remotely suspicious."

If that was the good news, Stone wasn't sure he wanted to hear how terrible the bad was. "So Canton is out in the wind somewhere?"

"Yeah. I had my buddy Tyler call a few contacts back in Los Angeles from his LAPD days. There's definitely no one at the house except a maid and a pet sitter. His car is still in the garage. He's locked his phone and I haven't been able to trace it. You might try." Jack rattled off the number and the e-mail address associated with the device.

Stone didn't want to know how the other man had gotten the info and he didn't care. "Depending on the phone, I might be able to hack and track it. Some have operating systems designed to enable a full lockdown unless you have the password, but I'll see what I can do."

"Since we don't know where Canton is, he could be anywhere. It's possible he's nowhere near Lily."

But Jack didn't sound as if he believed that. Stone didn't, either.

"What else?" he prompted.

"The bomb that blew up Lily's car was grade-A professional stuff. None of this homemade shit thrown together with PVC pipe and household chemicals. My guess is that whoever he's employing had some military training—the elite kind. Hunter said he saw the pictures of what was left. It looked like something he would have learned in advanced demolitions training after becoming a SEAL. It was also programmed to detonate via remote control, not a simple timer. Which means that whoever pressed the button was probably watching her."

Stone replayed the sequence of events in his head and frowned. "If he had eyes on her, he waited too late and missed his window of opportunity. She'd just climbed out of the car a minute before it exploded. Why wait?"

"Malfunction? Fuckup?" Jack sighed. "Don't know. We should count ourselves lucky and move on. Do you remember seeing anyone hanging around outside at her apartment complex? Anyone who might have been watching her?"

Not really. He hadn't been thinking about anything except reaching Lily before she fled for good. Pacing, he mentally replayed his drive to her complex and into the parking lot. "I remember seeing gardeners and thinking I felt sorry for the poor bastards out there in the middle of the day because it's August. But they all had lawn mowers and edgers in their hands. Nothing that could detonate a bomb."

"Yeah. I'm not surprised you didn't see anyone who looked suspicious. It is fucking hot out there, and the guy who blew up her car wouldn't want anyone to notice—"

"Wait! I did see someone else." Stone suddenly remembered. "A guy on one of the balconies. I didn't get a good look at his face since he was wearing a ball cap. Dodgers, I think. I remember him holding an iPad. When I drove in, he looked up and saw me. I didn't think anything of it at the time because I was driving like a maniac. But now I'm wondering . . ."

"Where in the complex did you see him? Can you describe which balcony?"

Stone reconstructed the drive in his mind again, mentally slowing down the sequence of events. Doing his best to explain what he saw and where, he told Jack everything he recalled. "Sorry it's not more detailed. That wasn't my focus."

"I'll send Sean over there to check it out, see if he can lay eyes on this guy, maybe figure out what he saw or where he's gone. Maybe he was a random resident out there enjoying the choking, wet heat while he played his solitaire or whatever."

But probably not.

"That would be great. Keep me posted. This whole fucking mess gives me a bad feeling."

"Can't say I blame you." Jack sighed. "Now for the really crappy news."

What? "Because you've been a bundle of cheer so far?"

"Oh, yeah. That was my happy voice."

He sounded anything but. Stone shook his head. "Well, if you're going to piss in my cornflakes, then let it all out."

"Axel landed in Dallas an hour ago. He wanted to drive out there tonight and see Sweet Pea. I mean Lily. After talking to him, we realized how much he really didn't know about her past. Out of respect for their . . . friendship, we wanted to give her the opportunity to tell him everything, but he'd guessed enough to punch holes in our cover story. After that, we had to give up the rest of the truth. So Axel is up to speed now. He knows exactly who Lily is and about our plans to coax her to testify—and he's pissed."

"At her for not confessing all of her past?" Sure, the guy might have wanted to know it, but Lily didn't owe shit to the man who hadn't loved her. "Or at us?"

"At *you* for using her to get out of jail."

Stone didn't care what the ex thought. "That's not why I saved her or why I'm with her."

He might have started this because he'd wanted out of prison. Now he only wanted Lily to be happy and free. When had that change happened?

"Axel doesn't see it that way. But his first priority is reassuring himself that she's all right. Thorpe talked him out of driving the five hours to you by convincing him that he'd never find the cabin at night. Sean is trying now to persuade Axel that they need boots on the ground to help ferret Canton out more than that girl needs her former overprotective mentor to watch over her. I don't know if the argument is working."

"Axel is that determined?" Stone had hoped that the guy would merely call or want to be close by in case Lily needed him. He could picture Axel demanding that Stone bring her back to Dallas, in which case he was more than happy to tell the ex to fuck off. But Axel coming to this cabin and getting in Lily's personal space would only mess with her head.

"More," Jack murmured. "If I were you, I'd prepare for incoming. We'll do our best to hold him, but don't expect that we can keep him away from her for long."

How the fuck was he supposed to surpass nearly three years of the trust and loyalty Axel had built with Lily and become her number one in a couple of days? With a psycho on the loose who knew a shitload about making bombs?

"Son of a bitch. You got any good news?"

"The sun will come up tomorrow . . ." Jack mimicked the song from that musical about the redheaded orphan.

"Shut the fuck up, Annie."

Jack barked out a laugh, then sobered. "I'll keep working here. Thorpe, Sean, and the Edgingtons are on your side, too, man. If that's any consolation."

Not really. Helpful, maybe. But he didn't care as much about suddenly having brofriends as he did about keeping Lily safe.

"Keep me posted. Thanks."

"Will do."

Jack ended the call, and Stone marched out of the playroom and into the hall. His gaze was immediately drawn to the bedroom door. Lily had left it slightly ajar. She'd killed the lights. When he stuck his head in, it looked as if she'd already fallen asleep.

Out in the living room, he hunted up her phone, which he'd temporarily hidden in an empty cookie tin in the back of one of the cabinets. He turned it on. Sure enough, Axel had texted about ten million times and called nearly that many in the last twenty hours—with a nine-hour gap in the middle for his flight.

Stone could hack into her phone and listen to her messages, but she'd see it as a betrayal of trust, and he could guess what Axel had said. He was just surprised that the guy hadn't actually called him.

Right on cue, Stone's phone began to buzz. Axel. The number on his display matched what Lily had in her contacts. His first instinct was to answer so he could growl into the phone and cuss out the son of a bitch for so obviously not loving Lily and for abandoning her, leaving her uncertain of her own future and appeal. He also wanted to chastise the bastard and tell him not to drive the fuck to Louisiana. He would get in Lily's face—and mess with her head. She'd backtrack. And admittedly, Stone didn't need her attention on the other man when he was trying so hard to reach her.

But he stopped himself. Stone didn't know Axel well but from everything he'd gleaned, probably nothing he said or did would keep the big bruiser away. If the guy had flown back from Europe, he was clearly determined to set eyes on Lily. Whatever. Stone would rather spend his time and energy on a cause that did matter—cementing his bond with her.

Declining the call, Stone pocketed the phone and headed back to the bedroom. If he had forty-eight hours or less to earn Lily's trust and a place in her heart before Axel crashed in, then he intended to put every moment to good use.

Chapter Ten

LILY woke in Stone's arms again. This time, she wasn't nearly as rattled by finding herself plastered to his side, her nose filled with his scent, as she had been yesterday morning.

In fact, now she found it almost comforting.

From high in the sky the sun slanted through the windows, telling her that she'd slept long and soundly again.

Because on some level she felt safe with Stone.

Gently, she rolled away so she didn't wake him, then stretched. The muscles of her thighs were slightly sore from all the tensing and trembling she'd done last night while chasing orgasm. But she savored the sensation. His words, the pleasure, the intimacy they'd shared all crashed through her head. She slanted a glance back across the bed to his powerful torso and rugged face relaxed in slumber. With just his words and a few touches, he'd given her amazing bliss. Why did this particular man have such a magical effect on her body? On her psyche?

Slowly she crawled out of bed and made use of the bathroom,

including a gloriously hot shower. Leaving behind a cloud of steam, she dressed in a pair of short shorts with shiny buttons lining her hips from thigh to waist and a bright red blouse. After black liner, two coats of mascara, and crimson lipstick, she blinked into the mirror. Close enough. With a simple roll of her bangs, she secured them back with a polka-dot bow, then tiptoed into the kitchen and made herself a cup of coffee and sat, sipping at the table.

Usually this was her favorite time of day. The quiet before the rush started, a time of reflection when she could organize her thoughts without being disturbed. Right now, she felt jumbled. And terribly alone. Though Stone lay in the next room, she missed him. Oddly, as attached as she had long been to Axel, she'd never pined for him in quite this way. She'd never wanted him as deeply.

Lily nibbled on her lip. What did that mean? Was she falling for Stone?

Probably.

At the realization, she bolted from her seat and paced. But she couldn't run from the truth.

Falling for someone wasn't part of her plan. On the other hand, she didn't know how to stop it. Logically she asked where they could possibly go from here. It was one thing to have a screwed-up sex life when the man you shared it with didn't actually want it. Stone, on the other hand, seemed to crave whatever she could give him. For as long as they remained together, Lily ached to give him all he sought. He deserved nothing less.

As limited as her comfort zone was, could she even begin to satisfy him?

She swallowed. Of that, she was less sure.

A moment later, she heard his footsteps cross the hall. The bathroom door shut. Lily wasn't ready to see him, to talk. She headed outside, slinking onto the wraparound porch to gather her thoughts.

An overhang jutted out on the side of the cabin to provide welcome shade this time of year. Someone had built a bench under the railing. She sat, pulling her knees to her chest, and glanced out over the sultry heat of the swamp, just this side of bearable before noon. What the hell was she going to do?

Normally, when doubts or insecurities began eating away at her composure, she called Axel. But not only was he in England living his new life, she'd left everything behind. Everyone. If she didn't have any intention of returning to Dallas, she couldn't lean on those friends anymore. It didn't even matter where she'd set her phone, because she wasn't calling them. She had to stand on her own two feet.

Make a decision. Carry it out. Stop being afraid.

Before she could listen to her own advice, she turned and found Stone in the portal, watching her.

Freshly showered and shirtless, he gleamed, his skin bronzed and tight over all those rough-carved, ink-covered muscles. He wore jeans. His feet were bare. At the sight of him, a thrill zipped through her.

"You good?" he asked. "When I couldn't find you, I worried. I wanted to make sure you were all right."

Not because she was a responsibility to him but because she mattered.

His words touched her way more than she wanted.

She couldn't stop herself from running to him, throwing herself in his arms, feeling his strength, his warmth, his caring. In her head, Lily realized she should be putting distance between them. In her heart, she feared that was no longer possible.

Her stomach twisted with nerves as she reached Stone and flung herself against him. He grunted and stumbled a step back as he absorbed her impact. Then he planted, held firm. His arms closed around her, enclosing her tight against his chest.

"Baby?" he murmured in her ear, his voice low with concern.

Lily didn't know how to answer him. She just clung tighter. "Tell me it's all right."

"Don't worry. We're doing everything we can to locate Canton and put a stop to him. No one has seen or heard from him lately. I talked to Jack last night. But whatever the asshole does next, I don't want you to worry. I'll take care of you."

Shaking her head, she looked up, drinking in the sincerity of his dark eyes. Yeah, she should probably be worried about her personal safety. Truth was, out here she felt a million miles away from danger. And as crazy as it might seem, she trusted Stone to keep her safe.

"I know. I have no doubt you're calling in favors and doing everything you can. It's more than you should have to do." Especially because she'd likely end up leaving to start a new life soon.

"Protecting you is my first and only priority now."

"I believe you, but that's not what I meant." Suddenly she couldn't quite look him in the eye. She felt a flush crawl up her face. "Are we all right after last night? I left you hanging without . . ."

"Finishing me off?" He smiled dryly. "I'm fine. I'm more than fine because I got to see *you* in pleasure. Like I said, great spank-bank material." He winked.

"You don't have to sugarcoat it." She dared to touch his cheek, trailing a finger down the hard, slashing plane, feeling the remnants of dark stubble. "I know I'm not easy to be with. Last night if you'd been with another woman, you would have had sex with her and—"

"I'm not fifteen anymore, so my life goal is no longer to get laid. C'mon." He took her hand. "It's barely nine a.m., but if we don't find the air-conditioned comfort, I'm pretty sure we'll roast out here soon."

He was probably right, and she allowed him to lead her inside. Once he shut the door behind them, he sat her at the kitchen table and poured them both fresh cups of coffee before he took the chair beside her. He stared as if he was working hard to figure her out.

Lily didn't think it was that difficult. His unwavering attention unnerved her a bit. "Where's your shirt?"

Not that she was complaining he'd gone without one.

"I don't have any luggage. I found a few extra toiletries and a fresh toothbrush, but this is day three wearing these pants. I figure by tomorrow they'll be dirty enough for me to justify spending the day naked." He winked.

The thought that he'd spend the whole day without a stitch on made her feel tingly, fluttery—alive. The sight of his bare shoulders with the intricate ink distracted her. What would having all that power under her hands and body, intently focused on pleasure, do to her? What would it be like to feel as if she had become one with him? God, she wanted to know.

She screwed up her courage and met his gaze. "Maybe sex isn't your life goal anymore, but . . . it's kind of mine right now. I want to do more of what we did last night. I'm feeling things I'm not used to, things I've never felt. Things I think normal women experience. If we try again, maybe I'll respond like I should."

"Baby, I'm all for that, but however you respond is how you're supposed to," he argued.

"No, I need to be like other women."

"I'm not interested in them." Stone scowled. "Listen to me. There's no 'normal.'" When she sent him a skeptical stare, he went on. "You like Thorpe, right? Think he's a good guy?"

The question surprised her. "Yeah, the best. I mean, he pisses some people off by being a hard-ass, especially when he's right—which is most of the time. But nearly everyone likes him. Even if they don't, they respect him."

"Right. But by most of society's standards, he's a freak. Legally he fucks another man's wife, and her husband not only lets him but participates. Together, he and Sean tie her up and spank her and . . . who knows what else? Do you think less of him for not being 'normal'?"

She pondered that. "No. Thorpe does what's right for him. And Callie and Sean, of course. That's just them." She sighed. "I get it. You're telling me that however I behave, sexually speaking, that's just me."

"Pretty much. Our experiences all shape us, right? Mine were pretty common. Look, I don't have anything traumatic in my past, except the shit I brought on myself. I can only imagine what you went through watching your friend be brutalized and killed. Has it contributed to the way you react to sex? The way you react to me? Yeah. Does that make it bad or wrong? No. You cope however you need to. I'll play along and just be happy to touch you."

Lily caught her breath. She'd hoped he would say something like that. It went hand in hand with pretty much every other answer he'd ever given her—kind, understanding, accommodating. Lily almost pinched herself because she kept thinking he must be too good to be true. Why on earth had she been avoiding him all summer long? Yeah, her fears. The ones she was determined to overcome now.

Heart racing like a jet engine, she stood and held out her hand. "Will you come touch me now? Will you let me try to give you more?"

Stone zeroed in on her hand; then his gaze zoomed up to her face. He stood so fast that his chair scraped across the old hardwood. A glance down proved he was already erect. "You sure?"

She nodded. "You were my first thought this morning. I fixated on you in the shower. I pondered you when I sat outside, when—"

"Baby, I fixated on you in the shower, too," he assured her with a sly grin.

Lily knew he meant to lighten the mood and smiled. "Yes, but I wasn't touching myself."

"That's a shame. But the day is young. And maybe that means I get to watch again."

"Actually, I was hoping you would touch me instead. And that we could . . . have sex. Or try."

His face softened. "You don't have to hope. We'll try whatever you want. You'll find I'm a persistent bastard. I have no doubt we'll get there."

When she smiled at him, he whooped loudly and scooped her up in his arms.

"Stone!" she protested, holding in a giggle.

Everything about being with him felt so different. She and Axel had never laughed when they'd decided to be intimate. He always asked her questions, kept track of her mental and emotional state. Depending on her answers, he'd try something different. She would respond. Or not. Then the process started all over. When they'd been together, she'd sometimes felt as if they were engaged in a medical exam, not sex.

Being with Stone was more like being in the middle of a parade— always something new and bright and amazing every time she took a breath.

"Hold on, baby. We're gonna take our crazy chemistry out for a test drive." He strode to the bedroom, laid her across the bed, then set his phone on the nightstand. "One minute." He dashed back up the hall, leaving her frowning in his wake. Where was he going? When he returned, he gripped a box in his hand, which he plopped next to his cell.

Condoms.

"You on birth control?" he asked.

She shook her head. She hadn't been sexually active enough to bother. But as an adult, she'd always been careful.

"Then it's a good thing Jack is prepared. I found these yesterday when I first checked out the playroom. Sex might not be my goal but I sure as hell want it, so I remembered where to find them." He swayed closer with a grin. "Can't help it if I'm an optimist."

Just like last night, his obvious desire for her was both a balm and a turn-on. "You have a lot to be optimistic about. I'm feeling strong. I want this."

He sauntered to the side of the bed and shucked his pants, leaving himself clad in only his briefs. They outlined his rigid cock, which looked a little intimidating now that she was paying attention. Without thinking, she trailed her fingers down the valley that bisected his washboard abs and disappeared into his waistband. This man clearly believed in a good workout and had massive amounts of core strength.

As she fondled him, he sucked in a breath. "Touching me like that could be dangerous. You nervous?"

"Excited," she corrected. Anticipation jumped inside her, revving her heart. But mostly the desire to feel him everywhere, touching her, filling her, did that. "You?"

"Both. Don't get me wrong. I'm looking forward to this, baby. But I want it to be a good experience for you, not a scary one."

Lily knew that, and it was one of the things she most liked about Stone. "Me, too. I'm hoping we'll both be satisfied this time."

"You're overdressed," he pointed out. "Can I help you fix that?"

A warm flush swept through her body and heated her cheeks. But nerves crept in, too. Would he like what he saw? Would he ask questions? "In a minute. First, I want to explore."

Lily sat on her knees, balancing on the mattress. She hovered so close it made her breathless. She reached out, skimmed his shoulder with the tips of her fingers.

His steely muscles lay just under his soft skin. Just touching him made her blood churn. Her breathing wasn't quite steady. With his perceptive dark gaze, he studied her every move. No doubt he saw her pulse pounding. She placed her palm on his chest, over his heart. It raced, too. She smiled.

"You get to me," he assured.

"That makes me feel better. I shouldn't be the only one affected."

He shook his head. "You're not, but you really are overdressed for the occasion. Let me look at you, baby."

"Last night was all about me." She deflected. "Let me make right now about you."

A big smile broke across his face. "How can I say no to that?"

Now that she had such an expanse of man spread out for her taking, Lily almost couldn't decide where to start. She caressed her way up his chest, encompassed his massive shoulders, her fingers trembling as they skated over his skin. Axel had been ripped and masculine, too. But Stone affected her in a way she couldn't explain. And she didn't want to sit around dissecting it. She merely wanted to enjoy.

Leaning closer, Lily pressed her lips to the hard stretch of his pectorals just below his collarbone. She followed the trail of ink there before flitting up to his neck. He swallowed. The muscles of his throat worked. His Adam's apple bobbed. His jaw tightened as she pressed more gossamer kisses along the hard line.

Finally, she feathered her lips just below his ear. "Just touching you turns me on."

Lily could hear the trembling of her own voice. No way he'd miss that.

"Baby, when I touch you, I get so fucking excited." He caressed her arm, his palm, warm and arousing, drifting down her back to rest on her hip. "The second I put a hand on you, I just want to feel you everywhere."

She might have disputed that or chided him for overstating his arousal but when she caressed her way down the wide expanse of his chest, her fingers grazed his male nipple. It puckered tight. She felt a fine shudder roll through him.

His palm trekked lower until he cupped her ass.

"Baby, I need to get these clothes off you and—"

"You're being impatient," she chided with a sassy wink.

The truth was, she wished the room were darker. Why hadn't she waited to start this until the sun had set? Sex would be more romantic in the moonlight. And he wouldn't be able to see the rest of her body.

"I was impatient to be inside you the moment I laid eyes on you," he admitted.

Lily really had no idea why but she wasn't going to argue. She was, however, going to distract him.

Letting her fingers drift down his torso, she brushed her body against his, then retreated a step, looking his way with a bat of her lashes. Being this near him was such a thrill.

She wet her suddenly dry lips with a swipe of her tongue. "Kiss me?"

He groaned. "You're teasing me."

"A little."

"A lot. There will be consequences, Lily."

If it involved sensual torment and pleasure, yes. Despite her nerves and worries, she was game. "Kiss me."

Stone slid his fingers into her hair and tilted her head precisely where he wanted it. Then he dove into her mouth. She knew better than to expect a mere brush of his lips over hers or a peck. He went for total possession, fingers tangling in her tresses, lips nudging hers apart as his tongue swept deep and demanded her response. Melting against him, she glided her fingers up his arm, drifted a barely there touch up the side of his neck, all while opening wide and surrendering to his kiss.

In retaliation, he climbed onto the mattress and flattened her to the bed. The weight of him pressed in on her, startling her and inciting a curl of fear. Lily forced herself to breathe through it and ignore her apprehension. She did her best to give in to him.

I'm clothed. My legs are free. I'm fine. This is Stone.

She concentrated on his musky scent, the hard rasp of his stubble, his urgent moan as she closed her eyes and slowly drowned in his kiss, opening her senses to him. He wasn't hurting or forcing her, just making her dizzy and tingly. How did he do that by merely melding his mouth to hers?

When he rolled between her thighs and pressed against her female flesh already dampening and softening for him, he gripped her hips. His chest eclipsed hers. He buried his face into the crook of her neck. His hot, heavy breaths heated her skin. Biting her lip, Lily tried to find a little wiggle room or daylight.

None.

Stone thrust, shoving his unyielding cock roughly against her mound. Suddenly, she couldn't move. Couldn't take a breath. She felt too pinned, too confined. Even with clothing separating them, his touch overwhelmed. Panic rose. She tried to breathe past it and keep calm. God, she didn't want to stop him because she was a head case.

Despite her snap judgment of him when they'd first met, he was a good guy.

Last night, he'd been such a giving lover. He could say that her hesitation and fear didn't matter, but Lily knew better. They were never going to make it if she couldn't give back to him sexually in any sort of reciprocal way.

Wrapping her thigh around his hips, she gave him a shove and urged him to roll to his back. He complied, breaking their kiss, then settled her on top as she straddled his hips.

The relief she felt was instant.

"Oh, you look pretty up there." He clasped her hips with firm fingers, gyrating her down on his iron-hard erection. "I'm going to enjoy watching you ride me."

That's exactly what she wanted. She laid her palms flat on his bulging pectorals, sighing at the way he tensed, flexed, and rippled under her hands. "I want to do that. Right now."

When she reached for the waistband of his briefs, he grabbed her wrists. "You're nowhere near ready. What's going on? You're in a big hurry to get on with it."

She hadn't fooled him at all. Lily sighed and closed her eyes. "I'm just unsteady with . . . weight on top of me, with not being able to move." *Or get away.* "But I want you. I need to believe we can do this."

"I'm so sorry, baby. All you had to do was say so. We'll work with it. We'll get there. It's fine."

"But I'm frustrated! How many accommodations should you have to make for me? It's been years. I wasn't the one raped."

"Physically, no. Mentally, you were. You saw something really ugly when you were still a kid and it lingered. It disturbed you. It affected you. I don't blame you for that. You shouldn't blame yourself."

Maybe not, but blaming Canton didn't make her feel any less frightened or more normal.

Lily cast the thought aside. "You're so patient."

That almost made her feel more guilty. Tears pooled in her eyes.

One or two even hit her cheek. As usual, though, she couldn't seem to have a gut-deep, heartfelt sobfest. That frustrated her as well.

"I have a feeling you're going to be worth it." He sneaked a hand up under her shirt, caressing the curve of her waist and wrapping his arm around her. "Where were we? Wasn't I kissing you?"

Slowly, Lily nodded. Obviously Stone didn't see the point of dwelling on what she couldn't change right this instant. He would never enjoy sex with her if she kept worrying and whining about it, too.

She forced a smile. "I think so."

Lowering herself against his chest, she took his big face in her small hands, her pale skin a sharp contrast to his bronzed cheeks, and layered her mouth over his.

Unlike the way he kissed, she hesitated, at first barely more than a sharing of breaths. It wasn't enough—not even close. So she tilted her head and laid her lips over his, pressing her breasts against him, reveling in the way he cradled her against his more powerful body and moaned.

"Open to me, baby."

Lily didn't think twice about complying. She felt safe now, so she parted her lips to him with abandon, seducing him with a slight curl of her tongue and a coy retreat. He surged deeper, stalking her, forcing his way into her mouth as he grabbed handfuls of her shirt, ensuring she couldn't pull away this time.

Beneath her, he bent his knees, spread them apart, and surged up. His thick erection prodded her slickening flesh, causing her to gasp.

"That's it." He trailed his lips down her neck, making her shiver. "I want to see you come apart for me. I want you unraveled and tousled and out of your mind with desire."

"I'm halfway there," she panted.

"Good. Now let's get to the other half." His fingers snaked around her back. A couple of strokes later, the band of her bra loosened. The garment fell away from her body.

"How did you do that with one hand?"

Stone grinned. "Determination. I'm going to touch you every-where, baby. You tell me when it's too much."

He didn't wait for her to say anything more before he sat her up straight again and reached into the short sleeve of her blouse, then pulled one bra strap over her elbow and off her arm. He did the same with the other, his dark stare focused on her, watching carefully. When he eased his fingers under her shirt and up her abdomen, he pulled her bra away and tossed it across the room. She gasped at the sudden freedom, at the friction of her nipples against the starched cotton.

Through the fabric, Stone cradled her breast in his hand, lightly pinching her nipple. "This sore?"

She panted and arched into his hand. "A little. But it feels so good."

"Want to add to the sensations?"

"Yeah." She nodded, losing herself in his touch, in the mounting bliss.

"That's a good girl. Hmm . . ." He withdrew his hand from her breast. Before she could protest, he unfastened the first two buttons of her blouse.

When he reached for the third, she gripped his thick wrist to stay him. Damn, she could even feel his muscles flex and bunch there. "Can you leave this on for now?"

He didn't hesitate. "Absolutely. But I want to see those breasts. I want to take those nipples in my mouth and hear you whimper."

Even if he left her shirt on, she didn't think whimpering would be any problem. "Please."

Stone tugged the two halves of her shirt as far apart as he could without busting the buttons. Lily looked down to see her breasts entirely exposed. He stared raptly.

"They're not big," she said in apology.

He scowled at her self-criticism, then pounced on the twin mounds. Cupping them as if riveted, he dove in, his thumbs capturing and pin-ning the twin points against his thick fingers.

"They're perfect," he muttered. Then he took one of the tight buds in his mouth.

Lightning hissed down Lily's spine. She arched and balanced herself as best she could for his onslaught. She'd barely absorbed those sensations before he switched to the other breast, tonguing her taut bud, nipping at it with his teeth.

"Stone," she moaned. "Oh my god . . . Yes!"

Though she knew he could be capable of great tenderness, he ate at her as if he were starved, as if he couldn't wait another moment to taste everything she offered. Over her flesh, his lips dragged, tongue swirling. He sucked, tugged, moaned.

Curling her hand around his neck, she drew him closer, holding him against her as if she couldn't stand for him not to have her sensitive tip in his mouth. Then she tossed her head back and felt her caution begin to break.

With a growl, he switched to the other peak. She felt every one of the muscles in his arms and chest bunch with effort as he pulled her in tighter, dragging her down on top of him.

Her nipples tingled as they drew up tighter than she'd ever felt them. As he left one to torment the other, the tip he'd just abandoned throbbed and ached. She could get used to this every day. In fact, she wondered how she'd live without this heaven if he didn't want to touch her again tomorrow.

He released her breast, panting wildly. "Fuck, Lily. I've got to touch your pussy."

She whimpered at his words. But Stone was a man of action. He used all his brute strength to roll her over. He leapt to the side of the bed and tugged her to the edge, then tore her shorts from her body, yanking them down her thighs. Her panties didn't fare any better. He all but shredded them in his hands.

Stone stared at her bare mound, his chest rising and falling as he dragged in deep breaths. "Oh, I need that."

Even with her heart pounding against her chest and an anxious ball knotting her belly, Lily wanted to give it to him.

Slowly, she parted her thighs. As he pulled her drenched folds apart with his thumbs, she hissed at the feel of his hands on her. He was touching her right *there*.

Discreetly, she tugged her blouse down to her hips and anchored it in place. It might look like a nervous reaction to him—if he even considered it. As focused as that melting chocolate stare of his was, she didn't think it crossed his mind at all.

"This is mine."

That had to be the most caveman thing any guy had ever said to her. What had sparked so much possessiveness on his part? "What do you mean?"

"Your pussy." His nostrils flared as he dragged her scent in. "That fucking delicious scent."

"You can . . . smell me?" The thought horrified her.

"Oh, yeah. You don't understand, do you?" When she shook her head, he just grinned. "Baby, sex isn't polite or sanitary. Done right, it should be dirty and intimate. That scent serves a purpose. It tells me that you're aroused. And it only makes me ache for you more. So don't you dare wish I couldn't breathe you in. Ever."

"Really?" If he enjoyed it, then she wanted to give him more.

Lily spread her thighs a bit wider.

"Yes," he groaned. "Those pretty, pouting lips. That tight clasp I know I'll feel once I work inside you. That pussy may be between your legs, but make no mistake. It's mine."

An irrational zip of thrill whisked through her. She should correct him since they would probably only be together until the danger died down or he got bored, whichever came first. But she didn't want to refute him. She liked the idea of being his.

"Yours."

Triumph lit his face. "Give it to me. Hold it open so I can take it."

A voice in the back of her head shouted that this was too intense, happening too fast. The woman inside Lily didn't care. She wasn't listening to fear anymore. She was sinking into ecstasy. Stone would take care of her.

With her elbows, she pressed the fabric of the shirt down to cover her abdomen. Then she lowered her trembling fingers to her flesh and held herself open for Stone.

His stare felt like an inspection, as if he was cataloging everything about her. Desperately, she waited for his next move, finding it hard to breathe without gasping, to lie still without shaking.

Then Stone lowered his head and kissed her thigh. As she moaned, he swiped a pair of fingers right over her most sensitive spot. Her body jerked. Heat scalded her veins. The ache under his touch tightened viciously, gripping her in a thrall she never wanted to escape.

"You like it." He slanted an arrogant stare up her body, sounding proud. "Tell me."

He didn't touch her again until she complied.

"I like it," she whispered.

"You want more."

She gave him a shaky nod. "I want a lot more."

"Remind me who your pussy belongs to. Who *you* belong to."

"You." *For now.*

He smiled in satisfaction. "Yes, you do."

Then he said nothing else, just rubbed her sensitive nubbin in small, lazy circles, ogling her. She couldn't look away from his eyes, falling under his spell as she writhed under his talented fingers while he slowly dismantled her composure and restraint.

Pleasure swirled and gathered, coiling, tightening. The familiar grip of need made her body tense, her breath hitch and catch. She ached for him to hurry her to orgasm. Ironically, she wanted this slide of bliss to go on forever. For so long, the delicious build to an explosion of desire had been a rarity. If she stayed with Stone for long, Lily suspected she'd be regularly bucking and keening and crying out his name.

"Touch your nipples. Keep them nice and hard for me. Good . . . The moment you come, I'm going to get inside you, baby. And I'm going to suck those pretty peaks while I slide deep. It's going to feel so fucking good."

Lily had no doubt about that.

As he dragged those ruthless fingers over her swelling bud, her folds grew slicker. They plumped. Sensations mounted. Her nipples stood at rigid attention, and every time she touched them, heat suffused her, lingered, spread. She nearly crawled out of her skin with need.

When she shifted her hips restlessly, he pinned her to the bed with his free hand and resumed his unrelenting torment. "There you are. Your clit is hard, baby. Waiting and pouting and desperate. I love to watch your skin turn rosy for me. God, you're fucking gorgeous."

She'd always felt like the "cute" friend. Callie was a striking beauty, so of course she'd found love. Axel had taken one look at Mystery's exotic features and fallen hard. Even playboy Xander, whom she'd never pictured settling down, had surrendered his heart to a curvy siren of a blonde. Together with his brother, the threesome now had the most precious bow-lipped baby girl.

Until Stone, no one had really looked her way and seen a desirable woman. Of all females on the planet, why her?

"No. I'm just me," she gasped out.

"Yeah, gorgeous. You're delicate at first glance. Petite. Your lipstick and stockings and tiny waist sitting on top of those stacked hips made me hard the minute I saw you. A man who isn't looking closely would think that sweet high-pitched voice belongs to a little girl. But underneath, you're a woman. And a survivor. You may be quiet, and I think you fool a lot of people, but you've got gumption, baby. I can only imagine what you were thinking when you pulled a gun on an ex-con. I dig a chick who can hold her own, and you definitely can."

The hand anchoring her to the bed glided down her hip and stole across the inside of her thigh.

Without warning, he eased two fingers inside her, filling her up completely. And he groaned. "Jesus, you're so fucking tight. And crap, you're begging me for this orgasm with those fuck-me eyes. Your whole body is shaking, working for it. You're right there, aren't you?"

Lily nodded frantically. The way he talked to her turned her inside out. Axel had always coached and encouraged, ever helpful and gentle. He'd never verbally seduced her or made her feel as if he couldn't wait to get inside her. Even when he'd given her climax, she'd felt more like a science experiment than a siren unleashing her sexuality.

Stone's fingers inside her felt intimate. He stretched her flesh with a gentle burn. The thumb still working her clit ramped up the sweet ache even more. It climbed, overtaking and overwhelming her. This orgasm, even though it hadn't crested yet, blew yesterday's away. Up, up, she soared until the cataclysm seized her entire body. She no longer belonged to herself but entirely to him. He toyed with her flesh, wielded it against her, then manipulated her until she jolted, froze, and wailed in startling, sparkling bliss.

She stopped breathing, thinking—bathed only in feeling—as the deluge of ecstasy encompassed her, sweeping her up in its path, tossing her around in a dizzying swirl, before sending her tumbling back down.

Lily dragged in air as she melted into the mattress with a moan. Her eyes drifted shut as Stone bent to press a kiss to the expanse between her breasts as he slid his fingers free. A moment later, she heard cardboard ripping, then a tear of something with a slightly metallic sound.

When she cracked her eyes open, she found Stone standing between her legs, rolling the condom slowly over his impressive girth and length. Axel had probably been big but she hadn't really looked, just reacted, mostly focusing in on her thoughts when he'd asked questions.

The way Stone stroked his erection, he clearly wanted her eyes on him. He was obviously aroused by touching himself while she watched his every move.

Finally, he rolled the condom in place. "You still good to do this?"

After that monster orgasm? Eager was more like it. "Yes."

He smiled and it brightened his entire expression. But nothing would erase the dark fire of his stare penetrating her as surely as he intended to with his body. "How do you want to do this, baby?"

"Can I be on top?"

"That sounds perfect." He laid his big body across the rumpled bed, and Lily was amazed at how much of the space he consumed. He looked all bulging arms and rock-hard thighs as he stretched his wide torso across the mattress.

As she began to climb on the bed, he picked her up, plopping her down on top of him until she straddled his hips. Beneath her slick sex, his steely erection prodded her, a silent demand. After the climax she'd just had, she shouldn't be able to feel arousal for weeks, maybe months. She was certainly used to going without. Anxiety should be returning. Sanity, too. But no. The moment she felt him hard and ready and impatient underneath her, she wanted him.

"Hurry," she implored.

"Yeah, I want it, too, baby. One question before I go any further. How long has it been for you?"

Chapter Eleven

AT his question, Lily shrank back. Stone clamped down the urge to damn the consequences and start pounding her deep. Instead, he gripped her hips, forced himself from one rough breath to the next, and waited.

"Um . . . A few months."

With that vague tone, he didn't believe her for an instant. And that pissed him off. "How many is a few?"

She wouldn't meet his gaze. "I don't remember exactly."

More bullshit. She might be sitting above him now, but he didn't want her forgetting who was on top.

He grabbed her chin and forced her to look at him. "Give me a ballpark. Was it over the summer?"

The idea made his gut grind, his jealousy flare. While he'd been refusing perfectly easy hookups because he couldn't forget a certain petite pinup girl, had she been "working through her issues" with Axel? Had she been giving the man her pussy?

"No. Axel has been with Mystery all summer."

Right. Good. Stone dialed back on his homicidal thoughts of the other man. "Spring?"

Lily frowned as if she couldn't quite remember. She closed her eyes to avoid his gaze. "It was colder, as I recall."

"Give me the goddamn truth. I don't know why you're hiding this from me, but I'm dying to be inside this sweet cunt, making you mine. I don't want to hurt you by fucking you too hard. Give. Me. An. Answer."

His growl obviously startled her. Stone didn't want to scare her but he was at the end of his restraint, damn it. He'd done his level best to be gentle and patient, putting his needs on the back burner, and she gave him lies in return? When all he wanted to do was take her thoroughly, stake his claim, and make her feel so damn good.

"It was just after New Year's. I was feeling stupidly optimistic and hopeful and . . ." She sighed with defeat, tugging her blouse down.

It wasn't the first time he'd noticed the gesture.

Making a mental note to pursue that soon, he prompted, "And?"

"And we got through it. Axel . . ." She shook her head. "Let's not talk about it now. You've waited. I want you. I'm sorry. It feels awkward to talk about him when we're about to . . . you know."

"Yeah, I know." But Stone hated that her last experience—hell, pretty much every experience—had been less than sublimely thrilling. He dragged in a deep breath, forcing himself to find some patience. "We're going to do more than 'get through' this."

Lily nodded, her platinum curls caressing her shoulders. But she looked uncertain, as if she were already preparing herself to be somewhere between disappointed and miserable.

More than anything, Stone wanted to roll on top of her, take charge, show her what it felt like to be well and thoroughly pleasured by a man who didn't want to be anywhere else or with anyone else. But she wasn't ready to relinquish that sort of control. If he hadn't already wanted to slit Canton from throat to testicles, he was certainly itching to now. At the moment, he wasn't a huge fan of Axel's either.

"Do you need me to touch or stroke you first?" she asked shyly.

Did she think he was having trouble getting hard? He grunted and shoved up from under her, pressing against her pussy to dispel that notion. All she had to do was breathe, and he was ready to take her.

"Just lift up onto your knees, baby." He waited until she complied, then urged her down until the head of his cock rested against her sweet, snug opening. "Ease down at a pace you're comfortable with. You're in control for now. I'm not going to force or hurry you."

As much as allowing her that power might drag him to the brink of insanity, she needed it. Stone knew that as well as he knew his own name.

Lily sent him a grateful stare, then slowly began to lower herself, easing the swollen head of his cock inside her.

God, she felt like hot silk. He glided through the tight clasp of her flesh, inch by mind-blowing inch. She started and stopped as she breathed, wincing and readjusting. Then she began coasting down again—and stared as if her world began and ended with him. A fresh bolt of thrill zipped through Stone's veins. He clasped her closer. Damn, he could get used to seeing that expression on her sweet face. He could come to crave it.

For now, he gritted his teeth and resisted the urge to clasp her hips and shove his cock high and hard inside her. "That's good, baby. Keep going."

She gave him a shaky nod, along with a cry that sounded like a cross between a gasp and a whimper.

"Does it hurt?"

Lily paused, rose again, then wriggled her hips. A groan tore from his chest. He needed inside her so badly, and not being completely submerged in her tight clasp was killing him.

As he bit back his protest, she began seating him inside her again. Holy fuck, the tingles screaming under his skin and up the length of his dick astounded him. She was still inching her way down, and the feel of her supercharged his bloodstream. Lily wasn't like anything he'd experienced in his life.

As her body swallowed up another inch, Stone knew beyond a doubt that he would forever be addicted to her. Making her stay and give him his fix was going to be one uphill fucking battle. It started with making sure he didn't spook or hurt her now.

"Does it?" he urged. "Hurt?"

"No," she breathed out, tossing her head back as she sank down a bit more.

Damn, she looked pretty, even with that damn blouse blocking his view of most of her torso. More than anything, he'd love to see her body completely bared to him, all her ivory flesh shimmering in the sunlight.

Stone gritted his teeth. She was going to make him lose his fucking mind before she was done. Tension knotted in his gut. His balls felt as if they were about to burst. He had to hold his shit together . . . somehow.

"Want help?"

She must have heard the strain in his voice. "I've got it."

Finally, she pushed down on his cock, sucking the last few inches inside her snug, sultry clasp. Sensations soared through him with a spike of heat. She let out a groan. He did the same, and their sounds melded together as perfectly as their bodies.

Stone gripped her thighs, willing her to move her hips and stroke them both to ecstasy. "Baby . . ."

"Yeah," she promised as if she understood, then raised herself to his tip before she lowered down in a slow, torturous slide.

"Shit." He blew out a breath as the tingles screamed across his skin.

Every instinct inside him roared that he should roll her over and pound her deep until she couldn't remember her own damn name, much less a tragedy she'd witnessed years ago. Stone knew that wasn't possible, so he checked himself and let her set the pace.

Experimentally and excruciatingly, Lily wriggled her way up his shaft, then glided down again, inflicting maximum damage to his self-control.

"Does that feel okay?" she asked hesitantly.

Okay? "Oh, Jesus, baby. You're killing me."

But for all the torment of her slow slide, experiencing every nuance of each sensation made Stone marvel. He was finally inside this woman he wanted more than his next damn sunrise. Now he was filling her up, knew exactly what she felt like closing around him. Lily was finally, truly his. Possession was nine-tenths of the law, so he intended to possess her well and often.

She gave him a hesitant smile and picked up the pace just enough to deliver a new level of torture. Every glide of her walls dragged over his cock, giving him more friction than his unhinged brain could handle.

When she leaned forward and dug her nails into his shoulders, her shirt gaped, exposing the delicate mounds of her breasts and the berry-sweet nipples topping them. And whatever train of thought he'd had fucking evaporated.

Lily picked up speed and steam, tossing back her head and breathing hard. She clamped him with her thighs and the walls of her cunt. He reached under that blouse he wanted to rip away and clutched her hips, finally giving over to the need to pull her into every stroke as he shoved up deeper. He surged faster, harder inside her. Lily cried out, her cheeks flushing, her body writhing in graceful abandon.

With a hiss, Stone decided to shove her closer to ecstasy.

He worked one hand down to the plump flesh of her mound and settled his thumb over her clit. Slick, hard, ripe. *Fuck, yes.*

At his touch, she turned frenzied, thrashing on top of him, slamming him deeper inside her stroke after stroke. Stone held on for dear life. The need swelled and jerked and hacked at his self-control.

Her nails dug deeper. Her breathing turned uneven. She fixed her stare on his digits as her cunt clamped down and every stroke became labored. She lost her rhythm entirely. Her eyes turned slightly wide and panicked. "Stone!"

Relief and primal need took over as he lifted her by the hips and slammed her down on his cock while he arched up, hitting some sensitive spot inside her that had her keening out in a wailing cry of pleasure, spasming around him in quick, tight pulses.

With a growl, he gritted his teeth. He needed to see her. All of her.

Stone didn't ask permission, didn't wait, just tore her blouse open. Buttons pinged, fabric parted, and he clapped eyes on her flat belly. His brain registered the uneven skin and slightly silver stripes low on her belly with shock.

Then nothing mattered. The need to be one with Lily and mark her as his hit hard. He didn't have time to argue, so he braced himself by clasping her wrists in an unyielding grip and anchoring them at her sides as he surged inside her, one animal stroke after another until the dam inside him unleashed the torrent of cataclysmic need. The spike of ecstasy had him shouting, gripping at her, going deeper than ever, and coming as if he hadn't taken care of himself barely an hour ago. Hell, as if he hadn't come in months.

The rush seemed to go on forever, and his body jerked uncontrollably as he emptied himself utterly inside her. Even after his body had ceased shuddering with pleasure, he couldn't get control, couldn't regulate his breathing. Forget blowing her mind. What they'd just shared had been right, meant to be. Stone felt that certainty in every cell of his body. She'd changed his fucking life.

Before he could catch his breath and hold her close, tell her how much she amazed him and assure her that what he'd seen on her belly made no difference to him, she scrambled for the sides of her tattered shirt and tugged them back together, stabbing him with an accusing glare as she wrenched free. "Damn you!"

Stone reached for her again, but Lily dashed out of the bedroom and across the hall. The door slammed. He heard the *snick* of the lock and her fist pounding the hard surface with a cry.

He stared in shock, in regret. Damn. She hadn't been ready for him to see all of her and he'd fucked up. Not the first time. It probably wouldn't be the last either. The question was, could he repair the damage his curiosity had done to her trust? Or would she insist they were done?

* * *

SHAKING, Lily started the tub. As the water heated, she paced the little bathroom. Maybe Stone hadn't seen or noticed. Maybe he didn't know what those marks on her belly meant.

When she marched back toward the sink, the mirror overhead reflected her from head to hips. Even at a distance, she could see those silvery paths up her lower belly that neither cocoa butter nor time had totally erased.

Out of the corner of her eyes, she caught sight of steam rising from the tub. She whirled away and plugged up the drain with an old-fashioned stopper and held in a shocked sob.

Why had he done that?

What was he thinking now?

What would he say when she had the courage to leave the bathroom?

Lily grabbed her ponytail holder off the counter and shoved her tresses up in a haphazard bun around her crown, then sank into the tub, curling her knees to her chest and rocking.

She had no idea what to do.

Behind her the click of the lock sounded, followed by the squeak of the hinges as the door opened.

Shrieking, she jerked her gaze over her shoulder, keeping her knees pressed to her chest. "How did you get in? I locked that door."

"That's the downside of being involved with an ex-con, baby. I still know how to get into shit I shouldn't. I'm sorry I upset you. Tell me what's going on."

She sent him a rapid shake of her head. "Go. I need a few minutes to myself."

Stone peered at her with narrowed eyes and perched himself on the edge of the tub. "I don't think you do. See, when I give you 'time,' you tend to burrow back behind your defenses and think you need to handle everything yourself. You convict yourself of terrible 'crimes' you have almost no fault in, and close yourself off from everyone who wants to help you."

"You don't understand. That's not—"

"True? Yeah, it is. This time, we're going to try dealing with your feelings my way. Head-on." He looked as if he had to hold down his temper. "When did you have a baby?"

His words were like a fist to the stomach. With their impact, her belly button sank back into her spine. Her shoulders rolled forward. She couldn't breathe. "Don't."

"I thought we were in this together and that you'd told me the truth about everything."

The damn tears that wouldn't fall welled in her eyes again. "Everything about Canton. Everything that's important to stopping him."

"I've been as deep inside your head and body as a man can go, Lily. I have been straight up with you every moment of every day we've been together. I have put my life on pause to protect you. Doesn't that, anywhere in your head, entitle me to hear the whole goddamn truth?"

With every word, his volume increased. When he finished, he stood, stared, waited. She wanted to lash out at his anger, but he merely looked hurt.

Lily shook her head. She couldn't talk to him about this. She couldn't talk to anyone. She never had. The pain cut too deep. Telling him would only carve another notch in her soul.

He clenched his fists. "I'm fucking in love with you. Does that mean anything? Will you try to give me a chance to help you?"

His admission only made her ache more. Lily didn't know what to say. Stone couldn't love her. She was a mirage of vintage style and shy flirtation. The girl underneath was distraught and messed up and wouldn't be good for anyone.

"Whatever you're feeling will pass," she managed to choke out.

That only pissed him off more. He took hold of her arms, lifting her out of the tub. Water sloshed around her as he displaced it with one yank of her body. She dripped and gleamed. But with sunlight streaming in, there was no way she could hide the stretch marks shooting from her lower belly, ending a couple of inches below her navel. He zeroed in on them. His jaw clenched; then he fused their gazes together, willing her to understand.

"It fucking won't. You might have a hundred ways to fool yourself, but I don't bother with that shit. I know better. You're it for me, and what we just did in that bed together proved it. I'm smitten. Gone. And I can't stand it that you don't trust me enough with the truth."

Lily gasped. He wasn't upset that she'd given birth, just that he believed she lacked faith in him? "That's not the problem."

"Then tell me what is."

"Talking about what happened, it's . . . agony." She turned her face away. God, she really couldn't look at him and think about all the lives she'd destroyed. And she didn't want his to be next.

"I want to know you. I want to hear everything about you. I know it hurts, but if you purge it, it might get easier. Tell me."

She'd been so judgmental when they'd first met. He was an ex-con. Dangerous. Not good for her. So no matter how she'd wanted him, Lily had shut Stone out. Now that she knew the man? She'd never known one better. Certainly not her sperm donor of a father. Thorpe was a great guy . . . but unyielding and remote. She suspected that he only bent and smiled for Callie. Axel had moved mountains to help her. He cared, but he couldn't fake love—nor would she want him to. He'd been a good mentor. Though they hadn't shared anything real or deep, even he knew this truth. There'd been no way to avoid it.

After all she'd been through with Stone in the past few days, didn't he deserve to know, too?

With a sigh, Lily nodded. "Give me a chance to get dressed, and I'll tell you."

"You don't need to cover up your boobs to explain what's bothering you. I'm naked, too. Let's do this together."

She paused. He was right. What good would hiding behind clothes do? He wasn't trying to shield himself. Maybe having a naked body while she bared her soul would help her finally feel as if she'd really purged this part of her sadness.

Drawing in a calming breath, she focused on the facts. She could start her story with those. "When I was fifteen, the cutest guy in school showed interest in me. He played football. I was a cheerleader. We went to homecoming together and held hands in the hall. It sounds so cliché now. When we'd been dating a few months, he started pressuring me to have sex and told me that if I didn't, he knew plenty of girls who would."

"He sounds like a self-centered, immature little bastard."

"Completely. But I couldn't imagine losing my boyfriend because I refused to 'prove I loved him.' I would be a laughingstock. Girls would whisper about me behind my back. Besides, I'd eventually have sex anyway, so it didn't matter who I did it with first, right? I liked him well enough." She rolled her eyes. "These were the things I told myself. I was young and stupid, and my mother worked three jobs to try to feed me and my little brother, so she wasn't really around to give me advice."

"So you had sex with him and you got pregnant."

She nodded. "I found out two days before my sixteenth birthday. He'd planned to take me out for dinner and a movie that night to celebrate, like on a real date. I was so excited. I'd bought a new dress with money I didn't really have. I told myself that, of course, he loved me and I loved him. But that home pregnancy test changed everything. The day I found out, I told him. He dumped me, called me stupid for getting knocked up, and said he knew I'd been screwing around behind his back. Which wasn't true."

Stone nodded. "Asshole. That was how he absolved himself of any responsibility."

"And he spent the night of my sixteenth birthday with another girl, one he knew I didn't like. I heard he knocked her up just before graduation and they eventually got married."

"Did he not know how to put on a condom?" He scowled.

"He didn't like them. They were 'unnatural.' He swore that if we timed it right with my cycle, I couldn't get pregnant. What I didn't understand was that I'd never had a normal cycle, so I didn't know when I might be ovulating." She sighed. "I didn't understand a lot of things, actually."

"You were a kid. And without parents to guide you . . ."

"I didn't know what to do. Once I found out I was pregnant, I knew my mom would freak. I hid it as long as I could, but she eventually figured it out. She kicked me out of the house."

"At sixteen?" He gaped as if he could scarcely believe what she was saying. "You may have screwed up, but she had a responsibility to finish raising you. Where did she think you and the baby were going to go?"

"She didn't care. I'd been a glorified babysitter for a long time anyway. She favored my little brother. By then, he'd gotten old enough to take care of himself after school and cook his own meals if she couldn't be there. I was just another mouth to feed and a teenage problem to deal with." Lily tried to shrug those facts off, but deep down, they still hurt deeply.

Stone gritted his teeth and shook his head as if he didn't understand at all. That was a balm to Lily's heart, especially when he took her hands in his and gentled his voice. "What did you do next? What happened to the baby?"

Now the conversation got difficult. She tried to wrap her arms around herself, but Stone wasn't having any of that. He hugged her to his chest and pressed a kiss to her forehead. Instead of feeling intrusive, his touch gave her strength.

"I went to my friend Erin's house. Her mom had gotten pregnant with Erin's older brother, Corey, when she was sixteen. She understood and took me in. I moved into Erin's room with her and kept going to school. I found a county clinic that gave me cheap prenatal care. I was working part-time and planning to finish high school. I had the future mapped out. Or so I thought. But nothing worked out that way. Erin was killed."

"Did Canton spare you because you were pregnant?"

She tried hard to hold herself together. "I think so. I was thirty-eight weeks along. He told me if I said a word to the police about what I'd seen, he'd hunt me down and cut my baby from my belly and laugh while he killed us both."

More horrific glimpses from the past began to bombard her, the most terrifying times and faces. Images that haunted her to this day. The sounds of ripping fabric, the smell of blood, even too much male laughter still sometimes set her off.

"Then?" he prompted.

She clenched her fists and slammed her eyes shut. *Just get the words out.* "The baby was a girl. Regina Rose. Stillborn."

He froze. "Your baby was . . . dead?"

"Yeah. The cord wrapped around her neck." Lily's nose tingled as the tears welled again. She tried to sob, tried to grieve. Her expression collapsed. She could almost cry. Almost . . . but not quite.

God, when would she be able to put her terrible past behind her and have a decent future?

"In less than a year, you got pregnant, you lost your boyfriend, your family cast you out, you watched your best friend be raped and murdered, and then your baby died?" He looked at her as if it was a wonder she'd survived. "Lily?"

That wasn't all, and as long as she'd come this far, she might as well tell Stone the rest of Canton's sins. "All that, yes. About a week after Erin was killed, I gave birth alone. I left the hospital alone. I went back to my mom's house, hoping she could spare a little empathy for me. When I got there, she made it clear I wasn't welcome by calling the police. They came and picked me up and asked me questions about Erin's murder."

Less than twelve hours after her daughter's death, she'd been in a station house being interrogated until exhaustion set in. She'd still been bleeding, hungry, reeling.

Stone gripped her tighter, holding her closer. "Let it out, baby. I'm here."

Lily looked down to realize she was holding him so tightly, her body was shaking. "I was weak and I wanted the interrogation over. I wanted justice for Erin. So I told the police I would testify. They set me up in a safe house and found me a doctor." She sobbed—a dry sound without tears, a grief without healing. "While they pumped my IV full of antibiotics and fed me soup, Canton sent his goons over to my house to kill my mother and little brother. She had the merciful death. They slit her throat quickly. My brother, they tortured. He had over a hundred cuts on his body. He called 911 after they left and was able to tell the police that 'one of Erin's friends' was looking for me, but it was too late for him. He died an hour later. He was twelve."

The guilt of so many deaths sat on her chest like an anvil, slowly crushing her. She wanted so badly to move on with her life, be happy. Every time she revisited that year, Lily remembered all the reasons she didn't deserve peace or joy and never would.

"Oh, Jesus, baby." He stroked her crown and kissed her forehead. "I don't know how you got through all that without crumbling."

"I did crumble." She pulled away from him. "Don't you get it? That's why I can't be normal. That's why no one can really love me."

He took her face in his hands, forcing her to look into his dark eyes. "You are worthy of love and *I* love you. Canton took your family, your friends, and years of your life away. Don't let him take your heart and soul, too."

Lily wanted to heed his words so badly but . . .

"So many people died because of me. Because I was stupid. Because—"

Stone didn't let her finish that sentence. He captured her mouth with his own and stole inside. It wasn't a kiss of passion. He filled her with tenderness and comfort. He held her with shaking hands and told her without words that he wouldn't let her suffer alone anymore.

Confusion and yearning wracked her. Let him soothe and ease her? Or take the self-punishment she deserved? Give this man all the love she could muster in her scarred heart? Or leave him because Canton would find and kill him, too?

She wrenched away from Stone, staring, breathing hard, shaking her head. "I . . . I don't know—"

"You don't have to know right now, baby. I'm here. I'll fix it. I'll wipe this fucking dirtbag off the face of the earth."

Lily sent him a rapid shake of her head in denial. "You can't. You just got out of prison. I'm not worth you risking your freedom."

"You are to me. I would move mountains to give you happiness and peace."

"Then don't go after him. I couldn't stand it if anything happened to you." Her fingers bit into his shoulders. Her tears crept ever closer to her lash line. One rolled down her cheek, then nothing more. "I couldn't live with myself if I lost you. After I left Los Angeles, I spent so many years existing but not being important to anyone. By design. If no one cared, no one would mourn if Canton found me or if I had to leave abruptly. If I didn't invest my heart in anyone, then I wouldn't really miss anyone once I was gone." She hugged him close, trembling against his body. "Then came you."

"Fuck this." He held her in his arms and cradled her against his chest as he darted across the hall with her.

Lily didn't fight him as he laid her on the bed and tumbled down after her, wrapping her in the sheets that smelled like Stone and comfort and the sex they'd shared. She grabbed on tightly, never wanting to let him go.

"Baby, you can't stay afraid and running forever," he murmured in her ear.

He spoke the truth, and she didn't know how to hear it. "I don't have many choices. He found me in Dallas. Those flowers had to be from him. The car bomb . . . He wants to finally silence me forever. That would give him a clear path to become governor. If you let me leave and I run—"

"You'd be alone, and it will take him anywhere from days to years to find you again. But that kind of guy? He *will* find you. Why not take a stand? Stay? Fight him finally? I'll help you."

She stroked the steely curve of his shoulder. "I would never want you in danger."

"And I'd never leave you to face it alone. If you don't want me to kill the son of a bitch, then let's do this the right way. Let's contact the authorities. Testify, baby. Put him behind bars. End this for good."

That sounded so wonderful and noble . . . and so unrealistic. "If I agree to do that, the police can't protect me."

"But I can. Jack and Sean and the Edgington brothers, too. They're the best, baby. Governments hire them to protect and defend. I can track Canton's movements via his computer or phone. They can give you a fortress until the trial is over. We can make this work. If he goes away, you're free." He brushed her hair from her face and thumbed her cheek, making everything inside her melt. "You can have a future with me."

In some ways, what he said made sense. If Canton was behind bars, he couldn't simply hop in his car or get on a plane and hunt her down. Yeah, he probably had underlings more than happy to do his bidding, but if she testified, if she lopped the head off that snake, maybe it would die. The others in his organization didn't have a personal beef with her. It was possible they'd let it go.

Maybe.

And maybe she was fooling herself.

It wasn't as if she'd never considered testifying before. But she'd always held back. Lily had been tied to a chair while she watched Erin lose the fight for her innocence and existence. She'd been the one to identify her mother's and brother's bodies. She'd seen firsthand what Canton could do.

But Stone was right. What sort of life would she have if she didn't do something to end his reign of terror?

Not long after leaving Los Angeles, she'd roamed around, hitchhiking, looking for someplace that could be home. One dark night in Bakersfield, she'd thought of stepping out in front of a speeding semi. She'd been standing on the side of the freeway at night in the cold, starving and wondering where her next meal would come from. It would have been so easy to end the pain with one impact.

She hadn't been able to put that driver through the guilt and hell to end her life. Instead, she'd stepped back and marched down the freeway, eventually making her way east through Vegas, Phoenix, Albuquerque, Amarillo, and eventually Dallas, where Thorpe had seen her in a diner. She'd sat down to a plate of eggs and a cup of coffee she couldn't afford because she hadn't eaten in three days. The waitress had disappeared into the kitchen, and she'd been looking for the exit when Thorpe had offered to pay her bill if he could have ten minutes of her time. She'd shrugged and figured that nothing terrible could happen to her in public. At the end of their chat, he'd offered her a job and a place to crash. Finally, she'd had a steady roof and people who felt like friends. It was the most normalcy she'd had in years. But she never let anyone so close that she couldn't bear to leave.

Until Stone.

"A future? I don't know. I hear you about Canton always hanging over my head if I don't do something. But—"

"You don't want to put anyone else in danger. I get it. But you don't have to be brave alone anymore. Think about it, okay?"

"I will." She owed him that much. She owed it to any sort of future they might have because she loved him, too. And she didn't know how she would ever live without him again.

Chapter Twelve

AFTER their eventful morning, Stone watched Lily cook in silence. They ate, then she lost herself by trolling through her favorite pop culture websites and another book she'd found at the cottage before she opted for a nap. He tucked her in with a kiss and told her to rest up. If he felt gutted by everything she'd admitted to him today, she must be fucking exhausted.

Once he knew she'd drifted off, he rang Jack, who picked up almost immediately. "What's going on there?"

Tons, but nothing Jack needed to know. "Not much. You have something to report?"

"I talked to Thorpe an hour ago. Axel is still sleeping. Sean gave him a little something to help that along so he'd stay out of your hair for a while. Sean told me to say 'You're welcome.'"

"I owe him big."

"He's going to head over to Lily's old apartment soon. He has to let the police presence over there die down. And the press are crawling everywhere, speculating about the reason for the car bomb. I've heard them say the cause was everything from a vengeful ex-lover to al-Qaeda."

Stone sighed. "But nothing about Canton?"

"Thankfully, no," Jack assured.

"Still can't find the bastard?"

"It's as if he's dropped off the face of the earth. I don't like it."

Stone didn't either. Anyone capable of raping a girl or torturing a little boy deserved to be gone from the face of the earth—and not on his own terms. But he squashed his homicidal leanings—for now—and prayed they could figure out how to end this nightmare for Lily. He'd ten times rather meet the guy in a dark alley and dust him without having to involve her at all. But she was right; he'd probably end up doing more hard time. Scuttling his urge for vigilante justice sucked, but going through legal channels was the only way he saw for him to have any sort of future with her. Besides, he couldn't deny that going back to prison was the last fucking thing he ever wanted to do.

"Keep looking and tell me how I can help. Please," Stone said. "Lily has been through even more than you know, man. She needs this nightmare to be over."

"You're in love with her."

Jack didn't ask, and Stone didn't bother to deny. "I think I always was. These last couple of days have made that really fucking clear for me. She comes first, period."

"That's how it is, you know. You find that perfect woman and *bam*. You'd do or say anything to make her happy and keep her safe."

Absolutely. When they got out of this shit, he was going to call his father, make up for the past, then put a ring on Lily's finger and live a life so wonderful she couldn't do anything except be happy.

Until then, he had to tie up every single loose end. "Exactly. So why was Canton never arrested in connection with the murders of Lily's mom and brother?"

"Canton himself had an airtight alibi. The kid didn't live long enough to ID anyone. The crime scene didn't produce any physical evidence or witnesses. It happened fast. Based on what I read, I'd bet they took the family by surprise and subdued them within seconds because there didn't appear to be much of a struggle."

"But the kid managed to tell the cops that his killer claimed to be one of Erin's friends who was looking for Lily, right?"

"Sure, but he didn't know the guy's name. The police suspected that Lily might know who the assailant was, but they never could find her. She'd already fled."

Shit. As much as Stone didn't like the truth, it made sense. "Did you ever track down the rest of Erin Gutierrez's family? Maybe they could shed some light. The girl had a mom and an older brother who took Lily in when she was a teenager. They must have been devastated by what happened to Erin and wanted justice."

"I just started looking for them yesterday. Here's what I know so far: Renee Gutierrez left Los Angeles. She got picked up for DUI in Seattle about four years ago. She skipped bail. I've heard rumors she crossed into Canada, but they're unconfirmed. Corey found himself in and out of juvie for a bit. Someone made an attempt on his life, and they transferred him out. I'm double-checking some facts but I think he wound up enlisting and fought in Afghanistan. He's currently listed as MIA, but I'm trying to track down the details. I'll let you know."

"That would be great. Thanks. I need one more favor." Stone swallowed, trying to choke down the lump of grief on Lily's behalf that clogged his throat.

"What's that?" Jack asked.

Stone hated having to ask anyone for anything but he couldn't protect Lily if he was focused on too many other things besides keeping her safe. "Can you look for a burial place for Regina Rose Taylor? She would have died as an infant."

Jack didn't say anything for a long moment. "Lily didn't have a baby sister, did she?"

"No."

"Fuck, man. I'm so sorry for her. As a parent, I can only imagine what that poor girl must have gone through."

"She's . . . an amazing fighter. But everything that happened damn near ruined her. I'm determined to give that woman some happiness." And babies. They would get married and raise children and live happily ever after, damn it. "But the baby died as the child of an indigent single mother. At best, she got a pauper's burial, most likely courtesy of Los Angeles County. For Lily's sake, I'd like to give Regina Rose something more."

"Yeah. I'll get right on it."

"I know that's not your usual thing. You'd rather knock heads together than scan the Internet, but I've got a lot going on here, so thanks."

"You're welcome. While I'm doing that, you want to know how you can help? We can't find Canton, so you need to stop tiptoeing around Lily and ask," Jack insisted. "Point-blank find out what she knows about this guy."

Stone gripped the phone tight. He'd rather hunt down the violent shit stain without involving Lily. "Whatever information she has about the man and his running buddies or habits is seven years old."

"But it's still knowledge we don't have. It may be helpful. It's certainly better than nothing."

The idea of shoving more upset and upheaval on her right now bugged the hell out of Stone. "Damn it . . ."

"I know. I get it. Sometimes, protecting your woman from the bad guys lurking outside her door is much easier than shielding her from what's hurting her on the inside."

Stone couldn't have summed up his concerns any better.

They rang off, and he mulled over Jack's suggestion. The guy was probably right. Tracking down the enemy would be so much easier with insider information. And as much as he wanted to protect Lily from more emotional pain, he had to prioritize her safety first. *Fuck.*

Determined to see if he could find Canton first, Stone grabbed her computer. He would have preferred his own. He had it all set up just the way he wanted with software and tools that hers lacked. Her hard shell of a pink case with the matching keyboard overlay certainly didn't say "badass." But he found a beautiful irony in using Lily's computer to try to bring down her tormentor.

Unfortunately, nothing he tried panned out. The guy hadn't used his credit cards in almost a week. He hadn't flown on a commercial airline or rented a car. He hadn't even used an ATM. No hit on his license plate. His phone had been upgraded to a software version that made it virtually impossible to access without the password. Anyone that paranoid would have taken steps to ensure that if someone tried to change his password, he'd receive not just an e-mail but a text, too. Stone didn't want to tip his hand and send Canton scampering into hiding, so that was a dead end.

He discerned Canton's cell phone carrier and tried to ping a database of towers but only received back a signal that told him the device was turned off and hadn't been active in days. More than likely he was using burner phones. No fucking way to trace those.

With a curse, he sighed and tried another tactic. Canton had social media accounts, but they all made him look like a family man and a hometown hero who'd avoided street gangs as a kid and put himself through college. Since graduating and opening his first dry cleaner's, he'd been using his business for good in their lower-class neighborhood and taking his own profits and time to open teen centers and after-school care for children whose parents had to work long, hard hours to make ends meet. He'd received awards at the community and state level for standing against violence and drugs.

Stone shook his head. This guy sounded like a fucking saint. He'd fooled pretty much everyone around him. Canton was wily and knew how to hire the right people to spin some good PR. He'd especially stepped up his game in the past twelve months, probably about the time he had decided to make a run at the state's top office.

Stone closed out the open windows on those dead ends and tried police reports next. He made a mental note to let the LAPD know later that they really needed to upgrade their cybersecurity. First, he prowled through their e-mail servers and available incident reports. The police had been called out to Canton's home and business multiple times, and he'd always managed to spin everything to make himself appear like the victim of unsavory elements in the neighborhood who wanted crime to flourish. Reports from more than five years back appeared to be archived elsewhere, which made Stone curse. But he did manage to collect a list of Canton's known associates. Unfortunately, running them up didn't prove to be any more useful. Just a bunch of garbage, none of which Stone believed.

There had to be some avenue or clue he was missing. Resolving that he wouldn't give up, he made another cup of coffee and combed through all the details again. Still, he came up empty-handed. As much as he hated it, answers probably lingered in some long-forgotten corner of Lily's head. Like Jack had said, he had to persuade her to dredge them up and give them over—then pick up the pieces if she fell apart.

* * *

THAT night, Lily said almost nothing. She'd withdrawn into herself, and Stone suspected she was still thinking about whether or not she would testify. A part of him wanted to sit her down and make her see that might be her only option if she wanted a future. Another part of him understood she had to come to this decision on her own—no matter how much waiting and gritting his teeth he had to do.

Until then, he had to figure out what she knew about Canton. He hated to add to her mental burden, but they were running out of options.

He pushed his empty plate away and turned to her. "I need to ask you some questions."

Lily straightened in her chair. He could almost see her gathering her defenses, raising her walls. "About what?"

"Canton. His habits. His associates. Where he might run and

who might help him. We're not having a lot of luck. What do you remember about him?"

"Besides him being a terrible, violent sociopath?" She sighed as she pondered. "I don't know."

Stone hated feeling as if he were plowing through her psyche with a screwdriver. "You said Erin was gang-raped. Who was with Canton that day?"

"Um . . . a guy he referred to as Killer Mo. Another he called Reaper or just Reap. The last guy answered to Mafia. I didn't get real names, so I don't know if that's even helpful."

It was more information than they'd had. Stone jumped up from the table and retrieved her laptop, tapping on the keys and accessing the Internet in seconds.

"Hey, how did you get into my computer?" She frowned. "Oh, yeah. You're a hacker."

Slanting her a glance that suggested she get serious, Stone scoffed. "Baby, I can do that in a blink." He dug around a bit more for the identities of Killer Mo, Reaper, and Mafia. He narrowed his search, adding places, dates, details he knew. He came back with a trio of suspects and pictures. Then he turned the screen around to Lily. "They look anything like these guys?"

Color leached out of her face. She turned the same shade as a slab of cold marble. "That's them."

Stone squeezed her hand before he turned the computer screen back in his direction. "I'm doing this to give Jack and the other guys some information. I'm not dredging up the past to upset you."

"I know." Lily nodded, trying to hold it together. "I can still see their faces. Killer Mo and Mafia held Erin down while . . ." She fell silent, shaking her head and holding up a hand as if she couldn't say more.

"It's okay. You've given me some information to work with." Stone performed a slightly different search, waited for results, hacked back into the LAPD, trolled through its database, then ultimately scrolled through some county and state records. Finally, he found what he needed.

"Killer Mo died at the ripe age of twenty in a drug-related shoot-out about six months after you left LA. Mafia was twenty-two when he went down for twenty-five to life after the rape-murders of a pair of sisters, fourteen and twelve, who lived down the street. Reaper got caught dealing just before he turned eighteen. He was put on probation and his parents moved him to Iowa. Apparently he's been 'born again' since then and is now a youth minister at a local church."

Lily absorbed that information with a thoughtful nod. "So . . . none of those thugs run around with Canton anymore?"

"No. From what I can tell, he's distanced himself from everyone who's got a record so he can look like an upstanding citizen with a slightly checkered past who's risen above, blah, blah, blah. He's married now with three fancy cars, two kids, and a partridge in a pear tree." Her face wasn't giving away much, and he was dying to know if she was all right. "I'll send all this information to Jack so he and some of the others can track the surviving dudes down. Do you feel better, knowing they won't come back for you?"

She shrugged. "They only helped destroy Erin. They didn't plan or instigate. Canton is still out there."

"Yeah." Stone rubbed at the back of his neck. "Since he's dropped off the grid, we have to find him. Can you think of anything else that would help us? Habits? Places he liked? People he'd reach out to?"

"One of the things that disturbed me most after Erin's murder was Canton's dogs. He had these two puppies, and he took them with him everywhere. He was always walking them. I remember Erin screaming and fighting . . . and the dogs scratching at the door of the warehouse to get in. As soon as Erin lay bleeding out and dead, Canton opened the door and the puppies loped in. He bent and petted them, smiling as they licked his face, as if he was the best guy in the world and the dead girl in the corner meant nothing. He probably still has those dogs."

As she talked, Stone sent a text with the information to Jack, who wrote back quickly that they would query the campgrounds and state parks again looking for a guy with a pair of mutts.

"He also had this habit . . . According to Corey, who used to deal for him, when Canton was nervous or excited, he'd suck on a Tootsie Pop. He liked the grape." She shrugged. "He was sucking on one when he entered the warehouse that day."

Lily closed her eyes as if she didn't want to remember more. She clenched her fists, fighting to hold it together.

Stone threw his arm around her. "It's a lot to remember, I know. Everything you can recall is helpful. I'm here if you need someone to lean on."

She clutched him. "Thanks."

When she broke away, Stone texted the rest of the information she'd given him to Jack. It might not be a lot but every bit helped.

"Oh," she added. "He has a son by a former girlfriend. Matt, Mike, Mark—something with an 'M'. The kid's mom went by the name Sherra. The boy would probably be about eight now. But back in the day, Canton was a devoted daddy. Went out of his way to buy him cool stuff and give him the best of everything. Maybe he still sees the kid?"

"That's great, baby. We'll definitely use that information to try to track down this asswipe. If you think of anything else—"

"I'll let you know." She stood. "I think I'd like a few minutes on the patio alone. I'm sure the mosquitoes will eat me up but I'm starting to find the swamp surprisingly peaceful. It's definitely quiet. I can think out here. And no one will find me."

After she let herself out, Stone cleaned up their simple dinner of hamburger steaks and potatoes, totally secure that she wasn't going anywhere. She knew the gators and the outside world were too dangerous for her to flee.

Ten minutes later when Lily slipped back in, gnawing her lip, she looked a million miles away. No, she looked as if she were still in that warehouse, reliving the horror of Erin's death. He wished like hell he could calm and divert her mind. He'd tried to give her an ear . . . If she truly trusted him and wanted him as more than a protector, wouldn't she be telling him her thoughts, her fears? Hell, right now she wasn't even looking at him.

As he rinsed off the last of the dishes and set them on the rack to dry, he watched her as she paced the room, arms crossed protectively over her body. When she stared at a spot on the far wall and frowned, hugging herself tighter, Stone had seen enough. Even if Lily couldn't—or didn't want to—share her feelings with him, she was too far up in her head, burying her past and worrying about the future.

Talking to the woman only went so far. Time to try something new. Stone suspected he knew how to fix her while working on their trust.

He turned off the faucet and dried his hands, then snagged her when she crossed the room again. "Get ready."

She blinked, her dark eyes finally focusing on him. "For what?"

"We're going to the playroom. You have five minutes. Come naked."

As he turned away to make preparations, she grabbed hold of his arm. "Stone . . . I'm not in a good place tonight."

"You're not. We'll fix that."

"I can't focus on sex now."

If she imagined for one minute that he couldn't redirect her gloomy thoughts into something more pleasurable, she was sorely underestimating him. "Who said anything about sex?"

She flushed a pretty rosy shade. "Well, if you want me naked in a room designed for sex—"

"A playroom isn't always about sex." He sent her a chiding glance. "After working at Dominion, you know that."

With a nod, she conceded the point. "True. But you—"

"Have no idea what I'm thinking, baby." He slanted a commanding gaze her way. "Do you?"

"I assumed it was sex," she murmured, dropping her gaze. "Sorry."

And there was her pretty, submissive side.

Stone couldn't call her wrong precisely. He did want sex. With her, he always wanted it. But he was capable of thinking about more . . . mostly.

"Have I given you any reason not to trust me?"

"No," she admitted, her voice approaching a whisper.

He crooked a finger under her chin and lifted her gaze. "I'm not bringing this up to make you feel guilty. I want to talk about what you're thinking and feeling. I want you to open up. You don't have to do anything about Canton tonight. You also don't have to do anything about him without help. So don't think about him now. Five minutes."

With that reminder, he left and headed to the playroom, scooping up some items he might need along the way. At the moment, he wanted to thank Jack and Logan for his last three months of BDSM training because he had ideas running through his head that he couldn't wait to test.

Stone took a few minutes to prepare the room. As he finished, he glanced at the time on his phone. Lily's five minutes were up.

Before he could haul out to hunt her down, she appeared in the portal, looking uncertain and sexy as hell. She hadn't heeded him exactly, but she'd added more kittenish black liner to her eyes, refreshed her siren lipstick, then donned a pair of white thigh-high stockings with lacy bands and a pair of chunky red heels. She wasn't wearing a single stitch anywhere else on her body.

Oh, holy shit. He'd never seen a woman look hotter in his life.

"You're on time," Stone forced himself to praise. And even though he didn't want to chide her, he couldn't let her choice to rebel pass. "But you didn't follow instructions. I said naked."

She opened her mouth to argue, closed it. Then frowned. "You don't like it?"

"I do but that isn't the point. You disobeyed, and that comes with consequences." He narrowed his eyes at her, a litany of all the possible reasons she might have disregarded his instructions flipping through his head. "Did you hope to distract me so we wouldn't talk about your past or the fact that you've been letting it stand in the way of your future? Would you rather give me your pussy than your truth?"

Lily's face flamed with a guilty flush. "I've told you pretty much everything."

Stone turned those words over in his head. "Except what you're thinking right now."

"I'm trying not to think about anything but you."

"But I know there's more rolling through your head." He quirked a brow at her, daring her to deny it. She didn't. "Either kneel here and face me or leave the room. If you choose the latter, I'll know you're not ready to trust me. If you stay, I'll want to test that you're serious, and I won't make it easy."

"Why?" She looked torn, confused.

"I've done everything I know to prove that I'm here for you in every way, yet you keep me on the outside looking in. I need to know if you're with me."

Lily's expression crumpled. She stood frozen for a tense moment before she crossed the room and lowered herself to the mat and knelt. "I only put on the stockings to please you. I never meant to make you feel as if I don't want to be here or don't want to be with you. I'm just so used to thinking through my problems alone. I've never been that great at sharing how I feel and . . . Yes, I know I'm not the only person here. I'm sorry if I've been selfish."

He softened. "You went through something way harder than I can imagine. You haven't worked through your trauma because you don't have any resolution. I'm not implying that you're selfish. I'm asking you to work *with* me. Let's put your life back on track together."

She bowed her head and drew in a shuddering breath. He could practically feel her thinking. Stone clenched his fist, itching to lend his support by stroking her crown and caressing her jaw. But she had to reach some conclusions alone.

"You want me to testify." Lily looked as if the idea terrified her. "I understand why. I know I probably don't have a future unless I do. I get that you want me to talk to you about it. I just . . . For seven years, I've tried to do everything myself. I let Axel understand my feelings as long as I didn't involve him too deeply in my past. That was my burden to bear." When Stone prepared to launch into his argument, Lily held up a hand to stop him. "I know you want to help. And I'm more touched than you know. But I'd be lying if I said that changing my mind and facing Canton after all these years is simple. I'm still thinking about this. It's not a quick decision. Can we talk again tomorrow?"

Tomorrow wasn't good. Tomorrow, Axel might be rolling down the highway to get in the middle of this shit in the name of protecting his former sub. Tomorrow might be too late.

But Stone couldn't exactly force her to make a decision right now. He could only keep working on their trust and hoping that their future was important to her, too.

"All right. We will be talking at first light. Understood?"

"Yes," she murmured.

"That gives us hours to play, baby."

Her gaze snapped up, meeting his. Then a surprising coy feminine power transformed her expression. It was as if knowing that tonight she didn't have to think about the past anymore flipped a switch inside her. Suddenly Stone understood. She'd become a pro at deferring the tough decisions ahead because she'd been doing it for years.

That would definitely stop tomorrow.

Lily smiled at him and sat back on her heels, thrusting her breasts up. "That's good to know. Do you see something you want?"

Oh, she wanted to toy with him? Stone couldn't help a rueful smile at her sensual, playful tone. He enjoyed this side of her. *Game on.*

He took a step closer and anchored one palm on her head so she had nowhere to look but his zipper and his throbbing cock imprisoned behind it. "Look straight ahead, right at me. What do you think?"

"You're hard." She almost sounded proud.

"Damn straight. But you know what, baby? When you look at me, I think you see something you want, too."

Lily licked her lips nervously, staring at his cock straining against his jeans. "I do."

To his shock, she leaned forward and nuzzled her cheek against the fold covering his zipper, nudging his bulge. The contact was like an electric bolt firing his blood. It shot straight to his dick. Crap, the woman was driving him out of his mind. He had to take control of the situation.

Fighting for a steadying breath, Stone stepped away. "Stand up."

"You didn't like the way I touched you?" She batted her lashes.

"I think you know better," he pointed out. "And we'll get back to that, but I have an agenda tonight. I'm going to give you instructions. You're going to comply without question. If you need clarification, I'll provide it. Otherwise, I expect immediate obedience."

As his tone changed, so did her demeanor, and she lowered her gaze. "Yes, Stone."

Even her voice sounded submissive, and it did something to the man in him.

Since direct confrontation wasn't loosening her up, Stone had chosen a form of communication Lily was familiar with. According to Thorpe, Axel had used it to make completely different points with her, but she knew this game was serious. Stone intended for her to listen and obey. When she slipped into submissive mode, she didn't want to disappoint. Right now, Stone would use whatever he could to make her see he was right.

"Good. Before we get started, let's cover a few reminders. What's your safe word?"

"Lunar."

"That's it. I *will* push your boundaries. But you're free to use your safe word *if* I'm actually hurting you or you feel as if you cannot handle what I'm doing. Make sense?"

"Yes, Stone."

"Good." He couldn't stop himself from caressing the crown of her head, letting her know that he both heard and appreciated her compliance. "Have I ever done anything to actually hurt or endanger you?"

"No, Stone."

"Will I?" The question came out automatically because he knew the answer: never. But how hurt would she be if she heard about the deal the feds had tried to cut him? Very. She'd feel utterly betrayed. He wished he didn't have to accept it to have a future with her. But with trust so tenuous between them, if he tried to explain the situation to her right now, every bridge he'd tried to build with her would crumble. He'd tell her soon; he had to. After tonight, when he hoped they'd be stronger.

Then Stone realized Lily was still silent. It only reinforced all his worries about their trust. She'd given him all her other answers quickly, almost as if instinct had provided her replies. This one she thought about a few moments longer. While he understood, waiting for her to weigh her trust nearly ripped his guts out.

"I don't think so." She lifted her gaze to him, her lower lip trembling. "I'm just being honest. Remember, I'm slow to trust. This is the fastest I've ever just . . . believed in anyone."

On the surface, it didn't seem as if she had put much faith in him. But given what she'd been through and what he knew about her habits with Axel, he realized she'd put a lot of trust in him already. He needed to be worthy of it and be patient. She was staying with him in an unfamiliar place she couldn't easily escape. She slept in his arms every night, too. Then . . . there was the sex. Thorpe had hinted that Axel hadn't reached that point with Lily for months. Even more, Stone realized, she'd trusted him with her whole tragic, terrible story. She'd shared shame and danger and helplessness. Even now, she knelt in front of him with big eyes that pleaded with him to understand that she was giving her best.

"I know, baby. Just like I'm trying to be patient. Being a pushy bastard is in my nature, but I'll keep trying to stifle that side of me and be reasonable." He caressed her cheek. "To be totally clear, I will never hurt or endanger you. I want you to remember that tonight."

"A-all right." She sounded worried but didn't argue . . . yet.

With a satisfied nod, he pulled out his phone and launched the app to stream radio, choosing a mellow station that played ballads. He wanted her relaxed, calm. What he planned wasn't romantic but held gravity. Stone needed her to feel it.

"Put your hands in front of you, palms up, shoulder width apart."

Instantly, she complied, and he couldn't miss the shudder that went through her. Yeah, she liked complex, adult Simon Says–type games. According to Thorpe, she enjoyed the challenge and played to win.

Stone turned and retrieved a pair of cuffs, then stopped in front of her again. "I'm putting these on your wrists. Don't flinch. If they're too tight, say so."

"Yes, Stone," she replied in a breathy whisper.

Without hesitation, he buckled the leather cuffs, one around each wrist, and checked to make sure he could still fit a finger—but no more—under the wide strap.

"Turn your palms down."

Again, she obeyed. The O-rings on top of the cuffs winked in the overhead light. Stone whirled around to the table behind him and reached for a long snap hook.

He closed the little metallic device up in his fist. "Hands behind your back."

A bare hesitation later and she complied, winding her arms around her and grabbing the fingers of her left hand with her right. "Like this?"

With slow steps intended to drum up her heartbeat, Stone circled behind her, pretending to consider whether to give his praise. "That's correct. Hold still."

"Yes, Stone." Her voice sounded a little lower, a little more remote, as if she were beginning to feel more and think less.

Exactly what he wanted.

He fastened the two-headed hook to her cuffs, one end to each of the O-rings. Then he rounded her again, staring down at the way the position thrust her breasts out. He wouldn't be a heterosexual man if that didn't get to him. But he couldn't let her know that the very sight of her beat the shit out of his self-control, so he kept his groan of appreciation to himself.

"Do your shoulders hurt?"

"No."

"Good to hear. Tell me about the tattoo on your shoulder blade."

She dragged in a shuddering breath then spoke in the softest whisper. "The wren flying from its cage symbolizes Regina leaving the pain of this earth to be free. The rose in its beak is both for her middle name and because I wanted to give her a token of my love as she left me."

So simple and poignant. Something hot stung the back of his eyes. Tears. Shit, both her grief and her tribute moved him. How amazing that she'd chosen to honor the little girl's memory this way. "It's perfect. Now close your eyes. You don't need to control anything here. I've got you."

He would remind her again if that would ease her along, but right now she needed to hear the assurance and the authority in his voice.

With a little nod, Lily snapped her eyes shut. "Yes, Stone. Sorry."

He circled to her front again and grazed a fingertip over her cheekbone. "You're forgiven."

And now it was time to put this game into overdrive.

With a few clicks of a button on his phone, he turned up the music. On bare feet, he crossed the floor, exiting the playroom. He dashed down the hall, grabbed a few things from the fridge, then headed back.

He sneaked up on the portal and stuck his head around the corner, trying to catch her peeking or otherwise giving him a sign that she didn't trust him. But he found Lily exactly as he'd left her—head bowed, shoulders back, the long line of her spine an enticing view above the heart-shaped ass sitting on those fuck-me red heels.

Sucking in a breath, he grabbed a refrigerated can and shook it, stopping before her again. "Open your mouth, tongue out."

Lily pressed her lips together for a moment. Thinking it over? Gathering her courage? Before he could bark at her about trust and compliance, she did as he'd bidden. Stone stood back and stared.

Like a child sticking her tongue out to catch the rain, she waited. The way she sat back on her heels, eyes closed, awaiting his next move, undid him. She was fighting for this composure, but Stone had no doubt she did it because she wanted to please him.

That realization was heady shit.

He flipped off the top of the can and turned it upside down, right over her outstretched tongue. Then he pushed his finger against the red plastic dispenser. A soft *whoosh* filled the air. Whipped cream piled on her tongue.

She managed to curl her tongue up in a little smile.

Stone bit back a curse. Wouldn't he like to put his cock right there?

"Swallow," he instructed.

He didn't have to tell her twice. She closed her mouth and sucked, smacking her lips with a widening grin.

"Tongue out again."

Happily, she complied, almost comically eager for more.

Stone couldn't take his eyes off Lily, looking ready, breath held, anticipation rolling off her. Her nipples peaked. Her skin looked so damn luminous in the light. Goddamn it, he wanted to fuck all the games and make love to her.

But she needed to trust him. She needed to feel the comfort of something familiar with him. She needed levity and joy in her life.

What he wanted right now didn't matter two shits.

Stone approached the bench with his goodies again and set the whipped cream aside. He grabbed a couple of things that made him grin. He couldn't wait to see what she made of this.

He broke off part of a strip of bacon left over from breakfast and placed it on her tongue. She smelled it before she tasted it and started moaning impatiently.

"Wait," he demanded.

She wriggled as if she had ants in her pants . . . despite the fact that she wore no pants at all.

Popping off another plastic top and lifting the spout, Stone squeezed the bottle. As he watched honey coat her tongue, his cock got harder by the second. "Taste it, then swallow."

Lily drew her tongue past her lips and almost instantly started moaning. "Bacon and honey? You are a genius. Oh my god . . ."

Stone grinned. "When I was a kid, my grandma made this casserole every Christmas morning with those two ingredients. It was always my favorite."

"It's to die for. What's next?" She sounded completely eager.

"Not food. Hold still."

Her breathing stuttered. Awareness crept across her face once more as she remembered they were playing a game.

He grabbed the next item he'd set aside from the table, then approached her from behind. That gorgeous ass bracketed by her red patent pumps and almost innocent white stockings turned him the fuck on. He bit back a moan and focused.

"You've done really well so far. Keep your eyes closed and remember I'm here to protect and guide you."

She swallowed as if she knew he intended to challenge her boundaries. "You know I'll try."

"Nope. In the immortal words of Yoda, 'Do or do not; there is no try.' And yes, I grew up a *Star Wars* nerd, so no talking smack." Stone hoped his teasing would set her at ease.

Lily gave him a shaky nod, then slid her eyes shut. Stone braced himself for the worst, even as he hoped for the best.

Then he dropped the blindfold in front of her face, settling it over her eyes, and waited.

She stiffened and sucked in calming breaths, clearly fighting her instinct to panic. Though she did well, Stone sensed she was losing the struggle and redirected her.

He quickly tied the scarf off, then laid his palms on her shoulders and bent to murmur in her ear. "This is no different than having your eyes closed. You have a safe word, remember?"

"But with my hands restrained, I can't take the blindfold off."

"If you need to see, communicate with me."

"Blindfolds make me panic. I was never able to handle one with Axel." She sounded anxious.

Stone got the feeling that something terrible had once happened to her while she was blindfolded. If that was the case, he would try to erase that torment for her, make some good memories to counter the bad. "We will, you and I. Just stay with me."

Lily hesitated for a long moment. She trembled and struggled for air. Stone watched and worried and waited. Finally, she nodded. "Okay."

"I've got you. Now open your mouth."

She was familiar with this exercise, now comfortable giving him this access. Quickly, she stuck out her tongue, almost as if she'd decided that the faster she complied, the faster he'd remove her blindfold.

He unwrapped a square of chocolate he'd found in the groceries Jack brought and set it directly on her taste buds. It began to melt almost immediately. She inhaled, taking in the scent, and gave him a groan of delight.

"You can eat it." He smiled at her excitement.

Still licking her lips, she moaned. "Do you have more?"

"Little glutton," he teased. "No."

He had something else ready for her, and he was dying to know how Lily would take it and if she would enjoy it.

"Open your mouth. Wide," he demanded, reaching for the button of his jeans.

Chapter Thirteen

LILY'S heart flipped in her chest at Stone's command. Whatever he meant to feed her now wouldn't be whipped cream or chocolate. She heard the dare in his voice.

Gathering her courage and fighting the residual apprehension from her blindfold, she did as he bid and waited. She would not cave in. She would not let anything Canton had ever said or done ruin this moment for her and Stone. Because when this man touched her, she shivered. When he commanded her, as he was doing right now, she realized how badly she wanted to rise to his challenge. She ached to trust him, submit with grace, and show him how much he was rapidly coming to mean to her.

He trailed his finger from the middle of her tongue to the tip, then rimmed her lower lip. He tasted of salt and man and strength. Lily liked everything about him. The gentle alpha way he handled her, helped her, settled her—even as he excited the hell out of her—was like a fantasy. But when he touched her . . . she'd never felt bliss like it.

Playfully, she sucked his digit back in her mouth, wrapping her lips around it, cradling it with her tongue, mimicking what she wanted. He so often touched her for her enjoyment and pleasure. In that moment, Lily yearned to please him in return . . .

Suddenly he withdrew his finger and nudged her lips apart again. "Open wide. Wider."

As she complied, Lily heard the hiss of his zipper as he lowered it.

Her heart raced. Her insides jumped with a jolt of thrill. Would she finally have the opportunity to return some of the ecstasy he'd given her?

"I want you to suck my cock, Lily." His voice sounded gruff and raspy as he looped a hand around the back of her neck and urged her forward.

A fire flashed directly between her legs.

"Yes, Stone." She couldn't say the words fast enough. She couldn't wait to take in his flavor, savor his taste, saturate him with her need, take him to the edge. At least she hoped she could. "I've never done this before."

"Never?"

She shook her head, wishing she could see his expression. Was he intrigued? Weirded out? Annoyed that she'd be a novice?

He let go of her neck and gripped her chin. "How is that possible?"

Though he'd barked the question, Lily still didn't really know how he felt about her admission and gave him an uncertain shrug. "My high school boyfriend was way more interested in straight intercourse, probably because he was one of the first of his pals to be 'getting some,' I found out later. And Axel . . . he never wanted to make the sex we had about him. He was always trying to help me deal with my triggers so I could move forward. You know, mentally. Our relationship wasn't romantic. We were friends, but we had a Dom/sub dynamic. And the first rule of any Dominant—"

"Is to give the sub what she needs." Stone clearly understood.

Since he also didn't seem to like Axel much or want to talk about him more than necessary, Lily cut short her explanation. "I'll do my best."

Because she ached to satisfy him. Yes, she felt the yearnings of a sub who'd been stuck on some training treadmill and never allowed to give in to her natural instinct to please. But she wanted it more because he was Stone and she was quickly realizing that he held her heart.

"I don't have any doubt you're going to drive me out of my ever-loving mind, baby. Tongue out."

Lily thrust it out farther than before, breathing audibly, shaking.

"That's good. You look so fucking pretty waiting for my cock. Take it."

He came closer, and Lily could smell the musk rising from between his legs. The ache gathering between her thighs drew up, tight and sharp. Then he slid his erection directly on her tongue, its weight foreign, heavy, and intoxicating. As the silken-smooth head glided over her taste buds, she licked something salty. She wanted more time to explore that, swipe her tongue over the slit and tease the ridge, but he kept easing in, inch after steely inch. The groan that came from his chest sounded somewhere between tortured and ecstatic.

For a moment, Lily was glad she couldn't see. Now she had to simply let herself go and feel.

"Oh, yeah. That's it. That's so fucking . . . wow. Now close your lips around it and suck me."

She balanced on her heels as she leaned closer to take more of him inside her mouth. Once she felt steady, she drew his length toward the back of her throat with a whimper of pleasure.

"That's it. Oh, damn. Baby . . ."

Twirling her tongue around his shaft, she tried to map every inch of him, did her best to take all of him into her mouth, pushing her head down and swallowing deep until he poked the back of her throat. The animal sounds of need he made aroused her. She'd never felt so alluring, enticing, so filled with this heady brand of feminine power. And she basked in it, eased down farther, trying to close her lips around his root. Instead, she began to choke.

"Lily . . ." He pulled back. "I love your mouth. God, it's like heaven. But you're attempting penetration that looks like something out of the Oral Olympics. You're not ready for that."

He might be right, but that frustrated her. It felt as if she'd never been ready for anything. People always worried she wasn't strong enough or prepared enough or experienced enough. And damn it, she couldn't fix that without doing and feeling and practicing.

She groaned in protest, lunging forward to suck him back deep. When she lost her balance, he caught her.

"Baby, you can't—"

She yanked away and he withdrew from her lips with a pop. "I can. I'm doing this. I need to give this to you. Don't stop me. Please . . ."

He paused for a silent moment, and Lily had to believe that he was trying to figure her out. Because he couldn't see her eyes with the blindfold covering them, she had to hope her voice conveyed her passion.

"You sure?"

"Are you going to hurt me?"

"Of course not."

"Then what's the harm? I'm a big girl. I should be able to handle this. You. Us. Being together." She was nearly ready to scream. "I don't just want more togetherness. I think *we* need it."

"You're right." He thrust his hand in her hair and drew her closer. "You're goddamn right. Open for me. Remember, you don't have to rush and you don't have to prove anything."

Lily let his words sink in as he filled her mouth again with his slick, steely hardness. If there was such a thing as smiling on the inside, she was doing it. As she sucked on his thick staff and moaned, Stone gripped her hair and pulled just enough to soak her senses with his musk and gruff tenderness, to make her head buzz with desire.

She curled her lips around him, lapping at him with her tongue again, finding new spots to taste and delighting in the sounds of his ragged breaths, hisses of pleasure, and guttural groans. The little divide at the bottom of the head tempted her tongue over and over. And every time she lashed at it, he shuddered and pulled her hair tighter before he quickened his pace, shuttling in and out of her mouth.

"Baby . . . Oh, shit. I can't even tell you how amazing that feels. Hmm . . ."

She redoubled her efforts to give him every shred of her earnest need to serve, along with a delicious pleasure he wouldn't forget.

He ramped up his rhythm, thrusting into her mouth with long strokes that demonstrated his utter control and mastery. Around him, she moaned and shook her head to take more of his length into her mouth. She couldn't quite put her face against his abdomen but the closer she drew to his root, the stronger his masculine scent rose to fill her nose. It intoxicated her senses like a drug. She could easily crave this intimacy all the time just for the sheer pleasure of breathing him in.

Lily pulled back as he tugged her away again. She resisted, but he forced her to break their connection, proving that he was the Dom and had command of both the situation and her.

"Stop," he growled.

She panted hard, wishing she could read his expression. Then it dawned on her that, not once while she'd had him so close and tasted his flesh had she been panicked about being unable to see. Not once had she replayed that harrowing time leading up to Erin's death.

Yes, it was probably weird to feel a sense of accomplishment from sucking a man's cock while blindfolded, but engaging in "firsts" and pushing through fears absolutely made her want to celebrate. She'd conquered one of her hang-ups with Stone and felt a bit more whole because of it. Which made him even more amazing to her.

When they'd first met, he'd been like a powerful star, glimmering so bright and so hot that she'd been afraid to touch him. Now he seemed like all that *and* a hundred feet tall. But she wasn't afraid around him anymore.

"If that's what you want, Stone."

He was breathing hard, too. "Not really. Would I love to stay in that silken mouth and ride it until the ecstasy turns me inside out? Hell, yeah. But I've got other plans. Tonight isn't simply about me getting off."

"But can't it be?"

"When our trust is stronger, when I know I've satisfied you first, sure. But I've got other ideas at the moment."

With that, she heard the rustling of cloth. Was he pulling his pants up . . . or taking them off?

Lily didn't have an answer to her question when Stone helped her to her feet and led her across the room. Then he unhooked her wrists.

Slowly, she brought her arms to her sides again. They tingled slightly as blood rushed back in. "Are you . . . Are we done?"

She couldn't help the disappointment slashing through her.

Stone massaged her shoulders. "Not unless you're giving me your safe word."

"No." She shook her head vigorously. Her nipples were tight and her clit burned with need. The only thing she wanted was more. "No."

"Good. Then bend over."

He guided her down and nudged her torso over the padded dungeon table. She trembled as he pressed her breasts down into the cool, cushioned surface.

"Now raise your arms. Lay them above your head and stay still."

Lily yielded and lifted her arms straight up, draping them on the table. Stone stepped behind her and leaned over her body, every inch of his hard frame covering her as he caressed his way up her waist, over the exposed side of her breast, before he veered to the vulnerable underside of her arm, eventually gliding his way down to her wrist.

He clipped the O-ring to one of the bondage points on the side, near her head, rendering that arm immobile.

Slowly, carefully, he reached for her other wrist, his fingertips prowling up her body again, inciting the kind of shiver that raised goose bumps and made her suck in a sharp breath. Despite her dizzying arousal, Lily nearly resisted as he pulled her wrist inexorably closer to the next bondage point. Instead, she breathed through the anxiety and forced herself to give over to him.

"That's beautiful, baby. So pliant and perfect." Stone stepped back and moaned. "And you look amazing stretched out for me, all pale skin and sweet ass." He rubbed one palm down her exposed cheek. "It's right here, so vulnerable and untouched and mine."

Lily tensed again. What did he have in mind? Not that he would hurt her. She believed now that he wouldn't. But she was completely at whatever mercy he possessed—or didn't.

"Stone?" She needed to hear his voice, needed him to reassure and ground her.

"Right here. Not going anywhere. Just contemplating the punishment I should dish out for your disobedience. I still haven't repaid you for disregarding my instructions and making my cock ache with those stockings and shoes."

She hadn't thought he was serious. Clearly, she'd been wrong.

"Nothing to say about that?" he urged.

Lily's thoughts raced. She could defend herself or ask what punishment he had in mind. But after her years of working at Dominion and dealing with Axel, she knew better. Querying a Dom about his punishments was a punishable offense in itself. And while Stone hadn't been topping for long, and she wasn't afraid of what he would do to her, she wasn't the sort of brat who went out of her way to earn "funishments."

"No, Stone."

"Hmm. Good girl." He massaged the back of her neck, his hand engulfing the fragile column and her shoulders before he slowly slid his palm down her spine in a silken glide.

Lily shivered. Every callus, every drag of his fingertips, all the heat of his body she could feel in that one touch. She arched, head tossed back, lifting her ass and weeping sex to him. Wherever and however he wanted to touch her now, she urged him to hurry in silent supplication.

As he reached the small of her back, his touch grew even softer, the skate of his fingertips slower down her flesh. Then he lifted his hand away, leaving behind a trail of tingles. Her breathing picked up speed, then became a gasp when he reached between her legs and cupped her wet sex.

"I want this."

"Take it," she whimpered.

"I will." He pulled his hand away. "As soon as I finish your punishment."

That would only delay what they both really wanted. "I know you're disappointed, but I promise I won't do it again."

Behind her, he froze, then braced a palm at the base of her spine. "I'm not disappointed in your appearance. I want to be clear about that. You're all kinds of sexy, and it's only by sheer strength of will that I haven't decided to shrug off your disobedience and fuck you. I'm punishing you for three reasons. First, I don't want you to forget who's in charge. Second, don't think I'm not paying attention to every single thing you say and do, baby. I always am. Last—and most important—we're growing the trust between us. After this, you'll know that if I say it, I mean it. Maybe then, if push comes to shove and Canton finds us, I'll be able to direct you in the escape route I already have planned and you will obey without hesitation or question. All that make sense?"

The independent part of her that had lived alone for years and taken care of herself through the darkest days of her life wanted to bristle. Her head told her that maybe she should. But Lily couldn't deny that—politically correct or not—his attention to her and his unyielding dominance made her feel special, cared for. Loved.

"Yes, Stone."

"Again, just to be clear, you are submitting to this punishment with the understanding that I'm doing this for our good, and you have a safe word if it becomes too much?"

She nodded. "I am."

"That's what I wanted to hear, baby."

Before she'd even processed the words, she felt his big hand *thwack* her ass. The surprising sting burned into her. She clutched the edge of the table with a gasp. The sensations startled her, not good . . . but not bad, either. More like a shock of tingles, a flurry of heat, a lingering awareness of her skin. Lily wasn't sure how to process all that at once and still take in Stone's masculine scent and his long moan. Everything about him intoxicated her. The soft, pliant leather beneath her, along with the sultry heaviness of the swamp air, wrapped her in a warm cocoon. Time seemed to stop. Right now, only the two of them existed.

Lily closed her eyes and savored the odd peace. "More, please?"

At her whisper, Stone rubbed his palm across her prickling backside and heat seeped under the top layers of her skin, down into her very muscles and bones. "Oh, I wasn't anywhere near done."

Closing her eyes, Lily smiled. Until now, she'd never been a fan of spankings. Axel had doled out a few punishments during their time together. The sadist he'd brought in from Houston once or twice had immediately tested her pain threshold with a hard-core paddling. She hadn't hated or loved it then. But that act also hadn't possessed any emotional context for her. Both of those men had been trying to pry her open or draw out her pain. By contrast, Stone simply wanted to align her with him, get them in sync. He wanted to show her another way they could be right for each other.

"Good," she breathed.

It probably sounded unfeminist or backward or some other negative that she would consider changing anything about herself to suit a man. Lily didn't see it that way. Compromising a little so that Stone would also have what he needed made sense. Weren't relationships give and take? Yes, and he'd already done so much to make her feel adored as he helped her heal from the past. This spanking was an unspoken outline of his expectations. The way he explained it, he wanted her to understand his desires because he intended for them to have a tomorrow. And unlike with any twisted abuse or heinous act Canton had inflicted on Erin, Lily could make everything stop by uttering a single word.

Stone lifted his hand, and she held her breath, tensing. Her heart pounded. Her skin sprang to life as she anticipated his impact. Where would he spank her? How hard? How good would it feel?

He didn't smack her again right away. Instead, he caressed his way down her cool, untouched cheek, his fingers slipping between her legs. Her slickness coated him as he explored her all the way from her empty, clenching opening already aching for him to the nub of nerves throbbing for more of his gliding fingers and teasing touches.

"This is how I want you." His dark, deep voice filled her ear—and her head. "Wet. Eager. You're aching, aren't you?"

"Yes, Stone."

"Hang on to this feeling," he instructed as he slowly rubbed at her clit, making her tense and moan and quiver. "Remember how delicious this is."

Before she could ask why, he withdrew; then he smacked the unoffended cheek of her ass. He lit it up like the first one, until it danced and shimmered, heating bone-deep. She'd barely had time to drink in the sensations before he did it again. Then again. And again.

He alternated cheeks, smoothing the fire under her skin, before sparking a new blaze in another spot. The array of sensations smarted, both stunning and dazzling Lily. They confused her because she wasn't quite sure how to feel. Each impact hurt, no denying. Stone wasn't holding back. And yet the hurt came with a warmth she could barely comprehend. It spread with every audible impact. He took care with her, not striking the same place twice, not imparting more punishment than she could bear.

Lily wasn't sure how much time passed before she dissolved onto the table. If she hadn't locked her knees, she might have hung from the restraints at her wrists. Her bones felt like softened butter, her muscles like pudding, her mind like melted chocolate. Stone could probably put her back together and create a confection much better than she'd been before. That realization allowed Lily to disengage from her concerns and sink into the experience.

"I think you like this, baby," he murmured against her ear. "Besides a red ass, your skin is flushed the most beautiful rosy shade and"— he parted her slick folds with his blunt fingers again—"you're wetter than ever. I have a paddle ready to go but I'm enjoying the stinging of my hand every bit as much as you're enjoying the smarting of your ass. It feels more like we're in this together."

Because they were. Lily knew it down to her core. And the fact that he wanted to be with her every step of the way made her sigh in bliss and trust him even more.

She relaxed every muscle and lost count as his palm made contact with her backside repeatedly until the fiery sensations overtook consciousness, until time bled away, until all she knew was Stone, his touch, and the blossoming feelings in her heart.

Lily had no idea when he lifted his hand from her throbbing flesh. She only knew that he kissed a line up her spine, the most tender brush of his lips worshipping her back, before he nuzzled her neck.

"You with me?"

"Yes," she managed to whisper.

"You all right?"

"Feeling a little floaty."

"Not in too much pain?" He sounded concerned.

A little smile crept across her face. "Yes and no. My butt is on fire. But I'm good with that."

He chuckled in her ear and unlatched the first of her cuffs. "All right, then. Let's try something else I think you'll like."

She could have asked what but she trusted him too much to waste the words. "Hmm . . ."

"You're amazing." Stone unlatched the second cuff and caught her as her legs gave way beneath her. "The trust you've shown me . . . I know it's not easy for you and I know why. Thank you for giving me a chance."

When he removed the blindfold and lifted her in his arms, he held her against his chest. Lily could barely find the strength to hold her neck up but she did it so she could look into his eyes. She ached to stay there, drown there, die there. If she did, she'd be completely content.

She sighed and admitted what she'd been suspecting for a while. "I love you."

Emotion ripped across his face. Lily saw the impact of her words in the way he tightened his eyes and furrowed his brow, in the way his mouth flattened and the tendons in his neck bulged before he swallowed hard. "Baby, I love you, too. I know it's fast. I know most everyone would think we're crazy. But they aren't us and they can't feel what we do. I saw you across Dominion that first time and I swear, mentally I felt this click, like we fit together."

In all honesty, Lily had experienced it, too. The minute they'd met, their eyes had locked and he'd spoken to her, a jolt of something she couldn't describe had rumbled through her. In retrospect, it had been an intuition that she'd found her missing half. Of course, Zeb had imparted Stone's past then, and logic had taken over, convincing her of all the reasons she must be incorrect, so she'd shut Stone out.

How much did she regret that now? How much better would her life be if she'd listened to her gut then and learned to trust him sooner?

As he stepped into the bedroom and lay her down across the mattress, he shucked everything he wore, revealing miles of bronzed, inked skin, ridged muscle, and a thick cock she wanted to touch and pleasure again. Then he grabbed a condom out of the drawer, sheathed himself, and crawled onto the mattress.

She watched, unblinking, unmoving, unconcerned.

Then he lay directly on top of her.

The weight of him flattened and pinned her down. She knee-jerked. Cold panic laced her veins, obliterating all the peace she'd been feeling moments ago. She flailed, screaming, shoving, and bucking in a desperate bid for freedom.

"Shh." His voice soothed, even as he wrapped his arms around her and loosely held her. "It's me. We're hugging. Nothing more. I'm not threatening you."

Lily heard the words. Somewhere in her head, she knew he was right. She needed to be more rational, less of a head case. But she kept remembering Erin's struggle. She couldn't forget that her bestie hadn't left that bed in which she'd fought—and failed—to stay alive.

Stone braced himself on his elbows and cupped her face in his hands. "Look at me. Right. At. Me."

He tugged on her hair just enough to snag her attention, and Lily blinked up at him, her whole body shivering despite his heat.

"Can't you get off me? I'm scared. Please."

"I could," he murmured. "But how long are you going to let this fear limit you? Us? Are we going to spend the rest of our lives not being as close as two people can get? Won't Canton have taken even more from you then? Try for me. If it's too much, you have a safe word. Otherwise, I want to make love to you, Lily."

Logic warred with instinct. He was right, and she knew it. But she had to fight every urge in her body not to scream that one word rolling through her head.

Deep breaths. You know Stone and how gentle he can be. Stop wimping out and woman up. Don't blame him for Canton's crime and don't put them in the same league.

Lily dragged air in through her nose and out of her mouth until her thoughts stopped pinging all over her brain and her heartbeat approached something normal. The adrenaline slowly seeped away. She let go of the sheets tightly curled in her fists.

"That's it. I'm still on top of you. Nothing bad has happened. Nothing bad ever will," he swore.

"I-I know that in my head. I'm reminding myself of that."

He brushed hair from her face and pressed a kiss to her forehead. "We'll conquer this together."

Through the residual panic, she looked into his dark eyes and wondered where Stone had come from and how he'd gotten so perfect. "Why are you so patient with me?"

"Because you're worth it."

This man had said a lot of nice things to her, but that unraveled her most. She teared up. As usual, the drops didn't fall, and Lily often thought she would benefit from a good cry. But for the moment, it was enough to look into his eyes and feel total acceptance.

He had no idea that she didn't really deserve it. "No."

"Yes," he insisted, staring her down as if he could push that belief into her soul. "You are. What you witnessed wasn't your fault, and you couldn't have helped Erin. I know you think you could have or should have, but you have to cut yourself slack. If anyone should regret their past, it's me. I threw away an upbringing of upper-middle-class privilege because I arrogantly thought I could make a few bucks and the law didn't pertain to me. My parents had me take out student loans and work part-time during college so I'd learn the value of money and hard work in school. I disappointed them in the worst way possible and I can never mend that fence with my mom. On the other hand, I'm not that person anymore. You're not either. Put the past behind you and look forward with me."

His words calmed and soothed, like the rhythmic strokes of his hand through her hair. He brought reason and light.

Lily needed that more than she could express. And maybe he was right.

"I want to."

"Then let me in." He parted her legs with a nudge of his thighs and pressed his erection to her opening. "We'll do it together."

How badly she wanted to replace those atrocious memories with good. How much she'd love to associate having a man on top of her with arousal and love, rather than absolute terror.

"Together." She lifted her head and kissed him, layering her mouth over his and clinging for a timeless moment.

He met her halfway, welcoming her lips with a crush of his own. It quickly caught fire, and she opened to Stone, lips parted as he rushed inside with a heady melding of mouths that soon had her breathing hard and surrendering.

He backed away, switched angles, dove deeper, nestling her into the mattress and nudging at the very depths of her mental boundaries. Just when she thought she couldn't handle more, he found some new way to revere her with his lips. Lily didn't feel threatened but totally worshipped. The gravity of the moment astounded her.

Somehow she knew that if she allowed him the closeness he sought, it would change her forever.

Lily dragged in a deep breath, resolved to jettison the past, and grabbed onto Stone as she parted her legs wider. Wonder spread across his face as she bent her knees and fitted him into the cradle of her thighs.

He caressed his way down her body until he reached her hips and held firm, rooting around for her opening. "That's my baby. Now who's ready for an orgasm?"

When Stone winked at her, her tension broke. Lily smiled. That probably wasn't possible, but she loved his enthusiasm.

Then he began to probe inside her, every inch sliding deeper until the two of them seemed to become one.

As he filled her up, she gasped at the slight sting of her flesh stretching to accommodate him. His hot breath fanned across her mouth as he drilled down into her body, into her eyes, taking her sex and her soul at once. The tingles she'd thought were impossible moments ago erupted, along with a shiver that ran through her entire being. This desire came from a whole new place because it wasn't just that he roused her body; he moved her heart.

Lily glanced at him in wonder. "Kiss me."

"I'd love that," he murmured as he took her lips with his own, parting them and plunging inside with the same solemnity with which he would make a vow.

He mimicked the same movements with her body, lighting her up with every stroke. His hard cock scraped against her sensitive nerves, as if he could read her, knew exactly how to kindle the desire now humming through her blood.

His fingers bit into her hips as he pistoned deeper, faster. He groaned. And Lily felt the sound of his agonized need reverberate through her body as she reached for the peak right in front of her.

She pressed her fingers into his shoulders and raised her knees around his hips, welcoming him even deeper. The angle of his thrusts, the intimacy of their bodies, the connection of the face-to-face contact felt completely new to Lily. Her boyfriend in high school had climbed on top of her and screwed. Vaguely, she recalled it. But what Stone did now wasn't that at all. He paid attention to her body and adjusted every time she gasped or tensed or whimpered for more. The experience wasn't just about him, the way it had been with Rick. It wasn't only about her, either. The lovemaking they shared was for them both. They joined and melded. She could almost feel their bond fusing even more tightly together.

A few days ago, she'd started her morning by buying a gun because she felt alone and unprotected. Now she'd cast off all her barriers simply to be with Stone because she felt treasured and surrounded and safe by his side. And so amazingly loved.

His breathing ramped up. His skin flushed with effort as sweat gathered at his temples. With every push inside her, the muscles of

Stone's body flexed and worked. He gave his all for her pleasure, to be closer to her than ever.

The burn behind her clit grew hotter, the need sharper. Lily thrust up at him, grinding. He hooked one of her knees into the crook of his elbow and leaned forward as he shoved his way inside her once more. With the head of his cock, he rubbed a spot that had her back arching and nearly set her reeling.

"Stone!" She needed more. Needed him now.

Lily bit into the fleshy part of his shoulder, her hips gyrating and matching his rhythm. He threw his head back and let out a guttural rumble deep in his chest. He grew longer, got thicker, pumped faster, gave her more.

"Are you with me?" He barely managed to get the words out.

"Yes," she wailed as the intensity torqued between her legs and the urge to surrender all of herself to him grew.

"Together," he muttered as he picked up the pace to something unrestrained and breakneck that made her catch her breath and hurtle toward explosion.

In the next breath, her body seized up. Her heart nearly beat out of her chest as blood pumped, her skin charged with life, and she flew straight into ecstasy with a clawing scream. Stone's long moan of satisfaction rang in her ears, and she clung to him as if she'd never let go again.

Chapter Fourteen

WRAPPED in Stone's arms, Lily felt a sense of contentment that she hadn't felt in . . . ever. Living hand to mouth with a mother who had regarded her as a problem child in a neighborhood where violence had been shrugged off hadn't provided the framework for many happy moments in life. The few she'd cherished, the times with Erin, had ended in horror. Her years with Axel had been helpful, but not particularly joyful.

Then Stone had come along.

He reached her on every level. From the beginning, he'd made butterflies dance in her stomach and tugged on her libido. But her feelings had gone so much further so fast. As she lay, her arms and legs tangled with his, he enveloped her in the comfort of a warm velvet hug where nothing could touch her now except the love they shared.

"After an orgasm that should have short-circuited your brain, you're thinking too hard," he murmured and kissed the top of her head.

Lily laughed. "About how happy I am, yes." She planted her hands on his chest and stared into his eyes. Nothing, no one, existed except the two of them right now. "It's all your fault."

"I'll take full responsibility." He winked. "But we should share the blame, you know. I pried you open so you'd confide in me, but you reached out in return. You overcame your fears to take the lifeline I tossed you. You've been so beautifully honest, baby."

Mostly. Almost . . . but not entirely. "I've been lucky that you cared enough to be patient. Most men would have given up. But you're not most men."

She couldn't help but stare. He'd changed her life in a few short days. He'd given her everything. She needed to give him her all, too.

"You keep talking like that, and more than my ego will be big." He grinned.

"I'm counting on it." She didn't want to squash the levity of the moment but she wanted to give him her total truth. "The blindfold thing was major for me. If you hadn't challenged me on that . . ."

"Well, to most couples a fear of blindfolds wouldn't be a deal breaker. But we might be a little kinkier than most."

"It meant way more than that." He needed to understand. "Being okay with the blindfold was life changing." She paused, gathered herself. He'd been deeply understanding so far, and she had to believe he always would be. "I-I was wearing one just before everything went so wrong with Erin."

That made Stone pause, and he sent her a dissecting stare. "I suspected something like that when the blindfold fear first cropped up. You want to tell me what happened?"

Not really. The thought made Lily sick. But she had to get this off her chest. She needed the man she loved to understand. "I told you that after Corey got arrested, he talked to the police, right? Once he went free, Canton and his goons started looking for him, and he disappeared, went totally underground. Mafia approached me one day as I walked home from school and told me that he wanted to talk to Corey. I told them I didn't know anything, that I was just house-sitting while they'd gone away for a while. He told me to let him know if I saw Corey because Canton wanted to call a truce. He said Corey was one of his best street dealers, and he hadn't meant to leave him in jail for two days. Mafia said Canton and Corey needed to iron their shit out. I didn't really believe him but . . . I wanted Corey to be the one to decide if he wanted to talk to Canton or not. But he wasn't answering his phone.

"I waited a while. Then I walked to the abandoned warehouse where Corey told Erin to squat inside and hide. Canton's goons followed and when I approached the building, they came up behind me, blindfolded me, and shoved me inside. After the doors opened, I heard a girl scream and I knew it was Erin. I tried to get free but I was too pregnant to move fast. They trapped her inside. As they tied me to a chair, I heard scuffling. When they ripped the blindfold from my eyes, they already had Erin gagged and pinned to the blow-up mattress she'd been sleeping on. Then like in a perfectly timed movie, Canton walked in. He told me that I needed to watch what came next so that I could tell Corey that he'd brought this on himself and could understand the consequences of crossing him." She shuddered. "You know the rest."

Stone's expression filled with empathy for her pain and loss. "Baby, if I could take that ache from you, I would. I know you've blamed yourself—"

"Who else could I blame? I led them to my best friend, who died horrifically. I never thought that Canton's goons would follow me. I was too busy wondering how I was going to raise my baby. Hell, I didn't even know where my next meal was coming from. Erin's mom had taken most of the food from the house when they fled, and I didn't have much money. I was hungry and stressed. And I wasn't fucking thinking about the fact that Canton wasn't the sort to make amends. He just slit throats and tore apart lives."

"Shh." He stroked her hair and kissed her forehead as he murmured the low, reassuring sound. "You didn't think like a criminal. That's not your fault. You had so much else on your plate. Why didn't Erin's mom take you with her into hiding?"

Her eyes welled up with tears but they didn't fall. "She offered to. I wanted my high school diploma. I knew I'd need it to get a better job once Regina was born. I still had two years left but I had a plan for tackling those with some online classes and babysitting help. I'd pretty much passed all my sophomore stuff. I just had two more exams. If I didn't take them, I had to repeat the whole year again." She clenched her hands together and stared as agony and misery ripped through her. "I never did get to take them. And I never got my diploma, just a GED. I went into hiding that night. Less than two weeks later, I left LA and never looked back."

Stone blew out a breath. The story was a lot to take, and she wouldn't blame him if he didn't want to be with someone so naive, who'd left nothing but death and destruction behind her, even if unwittingly.

"Now I can understand why seeing the lilies in the front seat of your car freaked you out. The note I assume was from Canton telling you to bury the past—"

"Yeah, that's not going to happen. Maybe I should be a bigger person but I won't forgive him. And I can't forgive myself."

"Is that why you don't cry?" he asked.

Lily froze. He'd noticed? "I tried to cry after Erin's death but I couldn't. I wept dry tears after Regina died. I felt the urge to sob my first night as a homeless girl, the first time I had to steal to eat, when I finally left California. But the tears remained trapped inside me. I tried too hard after the first time I had sex with Axel. I wanted to feel better, healed. Something. But I still felt broken. And empty. I keep hoping that someday I'll figure out how to let it all go."

"You will. *We* will because we'll do it together. We will talk or laugh or make love or whatever you need, Lily. Whatever it takes. I'll be right beside you."

"I know what it's going to take." Lily swallowed.

There was no avoiding the reality anymore that the only way she'd have a future with this man was if she confronted the past in a court of law. Once, she'd been able to pretend that maybe Canton had moved on and didn't care about her now. She'd been cautious but hopeful that as long as she stayed quiet, she wouldn't meet the same terrible fate Erin had. Now she knew better. She could keep running and never have anything to look forward to. Or she could face her fears, tell the truth, and make him pay for what he'd done. Make sure he could never hurt anyone else again.

Even the thought of facing that man across a courtroom terrified her. Her palms were already sweating. Her heart started thumping furiously. A knot of anxiety balled in her stomach. Once, those symptoms would have been enough to convince her that she wasn't ready to be anyone's crusader.

But now she had something to fight for, someone worth the risk. She had Stone.

"I'll do it." She closed her eyes. "I'll testify."

Beside her, Stone froze. Then he lunged at her and took her face in his hands, scanning her expression. "You sure?"

Lily hesitated, checking her thinking again. But she came to the same conclusion. "Yeah. I'm stronger now. It's time. He should pay for what he's done, and I'm the only one who can make that happen."

"Exactly. That's great, baby. I'm proud of you."

"You'll stay with me?" Lily hated being needy but she already knew she would need him to get through what was sure to be a long and terrifying ordeal.

"Every second. I'm here for you."

She melted against him. Stone would keep her safe. "I don't know what I ever did to deserve someone as wonderful as you. How did I get so lucky?" She caressed his face, her heart brimming with devotion.

She could look at this man and pour her heart out to him forever.

He had changed everything for her. He'd filled her when she felt empty. He'd understood when she felt confused. He'd made her believe she was a good person when she felt unworthy. It sounded cliché, but he completed her.

"You did, didn't you?" He winked, then sobered. "It's going to be fine. You've made a good decision. You'll testify, this mess will be over, and then we can get on being happy together."

That sounded perfect. "I love you, Stone Sutter."

"I love you, too, baby. You feel like sleeping . . . or are you ready for round two?"

Lily bit her lip and smiled with her eyes. She could barely contain the joy inside her.

"Tough decision. Wow, let me think." She tapped a finger to her cheek in mock consideration. "I think I'll take round two."

Without prompting, she rolled to her back and spread her legs, arms open to him. Bliss and euphoria rolled over her in a rapturous mix, all stirred up with an undying love she would always feel for this man.

Then he grabbed a condom, rolled on top of her, and took her to heaven.

* * *

STONE lay sleeping all curled up with Lily, spooning her with his back to the door, as if he intended to protect her with his own body if Canton or anyone found them. Because he did. Nothing—no one—would come between them.

A buzzing jolted him from sleep, and he turned to find his phone lit up and vibrating on the nightstand. Jack.

He rolled away, grabbed it as he landed on the hardwood and walked out of the bedroom. "Talk to me."

"I'm afraid I'm the bad-news fairy again. Sean got into Lily's apartment. Apparently after the police removed the crime-scene tape, the landlord sent a cleaning lady to spic-and-span the place up.

When he hadn't heard from her in a few hours, he let himself into the apartment and found the woman spread out on the bed. She'd been restrained, sexually violated, and stabbed twenty-four times. The killer wrote 'BITCH' in big letters on the wall in her blood."

Groping for the nearest chair, Stone sank down at the kitchen table, his whole body shaking. "Fuck."

"It gets worse, man. The victim was the same age as Lily. Same height, similar build. She even had brown eyes. I don't think it's a coincidence. I'd bet Canton mistook this woman for Sweet Pea and ended her."

Stone didn't disagree. But maybe that could work to their advantage. "This will sound terrible, but if Canton thinks he's won, maybe he'll go home. If you guys can persuade the police to tell the press that Lily was the victim—"

"It's too late. The evening news already interviewed a few witnesses who live in the building and knew the dead woman wasn't Lily."

If the press knew, then so did Canton. "Damn it."

"I'm not done," Jack warned.

"Jesus! Every time you open your mouth, you have new crap to unload and I want to punch the shit out of you," Stone snarled in frustration.

"I'm just the messenger, man. Here are the bigger issues: Mafia got shanked in prison two days ago. He tangled with another inmate about who ruled the Aryan Brotherhood in their house. Looks like he lost. Other witnesses say these two hadn't had a beef with each other in years. But their fight suddenly morphed into murder."

Stone closed his eyes as cold dread rolled through him. "Or maybe Canton is emptying his closet of all the skeletons. Anyone who could open their mouth and put him away is on his hit list. So what about Reaper?"

"He's missing. His wife reported this morning that she hadn't seen him in nearly twenty-four hours. According to police, she told them that he'd been acting strange over the last few weeks, but then he just disappeared."

"Jack . . ." Stone gripped the phone. He didn't have to be a genius to do the math. "Two dead bodies and a missing guy all within a few days? Canton is coming after Lily."

"And coming hard. In your shoes, I'd be reaching the same conclusion. You have to convince her to go to the feds now and testify. They can lock her down and protect her."

Maybe. But sometimes that didn't work out. Given how far Canton had already reached, Stone couldn't deny that the douchebag was connected and powerful. He probably knew exactly who to pay off so he could find and dust the last witness alive who could keep him from the governor's chair.

A plan started to form in his head. It was the least smelly pile in a field of shit, but it would keep Lily safe.

"But federal protection isn't foolproof or a guarantee," Stone argued.

"It's not," Jack agreed.

Stone rolled the thoughts in his head around some more and came to one conclusion. "You wouldn't take that option, would you?"

"As a law-abiding citizen, I would try like hell to choose it first. But if I had to leave the protection of my woman to someone who could be bribed not to do the job right, then no. I would only put her safety in hands I could damn well trust. Then . . . well, if the problem isn't going to go away, I know how to deal with it."

Stone did, too. "True that."

"If it helps, if you decide that you need to handle the problem personally, I'll do whatever you need to help keep Lily safe."

That was exactly what Stone needed to hear. "Thanks, man. That's good to know."

"It's what friends do for one another."

Stone hadn't really had one he trusted in years and never one as solid as Jack.

"I'd do the same for you. And as much as I didn't like the info you imparted, I appreciate you keeping me posted. Sorry to bite your head off. I'll be in touch."

They rang off, and Stone heaved a giant sigh. He had decisions to make—and fast. But really, how much choice did he have? He'd never risk Lily. Ever. Time to try door number two.

With a shaking hand, he texted Logan for One-Mile's phone number. The younger Edgington sent it back with a quick Can I help? Stone replied that he was cool. Hopefully, that gave Logan plausible deniability since the man had a wife and twin girls to consider.

As soon as the number he'd requested appeared in his display, he clicked the link with an unsteady finger. Yeah, this could put him away for a long time.

But Lily and her safety were way more important than his freedom.

One-Mile answered on the first ring. "Who the fuck is this?"

"Stone. Logan introduced us earlier this week." *Just before you fought with Cutter about the girl you both want.*

He didn't think reminding Pierce of that incident would be wise.

"Yeah." The sniper sounded only slightly less hostile. "I remember."

"I have a question for you, straight up."

The guy growled. "If this has anything to do with Brea—"

"No. That's between you, her, and Cutter. I called to ask for help with a dirtbag capable of raping young girls and torturing children. His murder quotient is high."

"Is this personal?" Now the sniper sounded way more interested.

"Yep." He cleared his throat. "And I have money."

One-Mile didn't say anything for a long time. "The cops?"

"It's a federal matter now. This asshole has disposed of most of the witnesses. I think he's coming after the one I'm protecting next."

"And you can't handle him?"

"The feds won't leave me here to protect her much longer."

"That's right, you're the ex-con."

Stone gritted his teeth. "Current. They want me to persuade this woman to testify. If I do, they'll commute my sentence because this murdering douche is a huge fish and someone will get a nice feather in their political cap if they can put him behind bars. But she won't be alive long enough to testify. And he'll make her death as ugly as he's made the rest of her life. Me? I could live with going back to the big house if this guy got planted six feet under. That's as straight up as I can put it."

"To be clear, are you asking me to kill him for money?"

Stone didn't have a huge morality problem with permanently stopping someone who intended to cut down the woman he loved. But the tone of One-Mile's question told him the answer better not be yes. Oh, that's right. Jack and all his buddies were heroes, not killers. It might have sounded as if Jack would be ruthless enough to shoot Canton but he wouldn't take the criminal way out. None of them would.

That's why Stone knew he would never fit in.

"I'm asking if you would assist Jack in protecting her and use your skills if he comes within ten feet of this woman once I'm gone," Stone clarified.

One-Mile let out a long breath, not so much a release of tension as a sound of satisfaction. "That's the kind of shit I like. You think he's planning to make a move soon?"

"Any day now. He's already tried."

"Keeping my trigger finger ready day and night will cost you ten grand a month. I get a ten grand bonus if I have to 'act' because the hassle and paperwork are a bitch. And that's the friend discount."

"Done." Stone had some money saved. He'd spend every dime to make sure Lily stayed safe.

"When? I'll have to talk to the three stooges—I mean, my esteemed bosses—and clear everything."

"I hope I have another day or two before this shit blows up. That give you enough time to take care of your business?"

"Plenty."

"Then I'll be in touch."

One-Mile hung up before he could say another word, and Stone stared at the phone, exhaling a nervous breath. Now came the hardest phone call of all. He toyed with the device, tapping it on the table from corner to corner. Once he did this, it couldn't be undone. He would be giving up his future for another few years, maybe more depending on how much he pissed off the feds.

Slowly he rose and made his way down the hall, toward the bedroom. Lily lay there, her slender curves barely concealed under the white sheets they'd tangled up less than an hour ago. He'd wrap her up there again tonight and hold her in his arms until the sun rose.

Tomorrow . . . he had no idea exactly what would happen but he knew he would be gone. And he'd done everything he could to ensure that Lily would be safe.

Nothing else mattered.

Back in the kitchen, he picked up his phone again. Oddly, his hands no longer shook.

Bankhead, his FBI handler, picked up on the third ring, sounding slightly groggy. "You got something for me, Sutter?"

"Yeah." Stone dragged in a deep breath and pissed away what was left of his future. "I'm out."

Chapter Fifteen

THE next morning, the sound of boots on the pier in front of the cabin broke the swamp's silence. Stone's eyes flew open. Dawn slanted through the bedroom window. Lily lay sound asleep, naked and warm, beside him.

Someone uninvited had come.

Stone rolled out of bed and jumped into his pants, then grabbed his phone and rummaged around for Lily's gun. Who the fuck knew where he and Lily had hidden? Jack hadn't advised that he was coming out with more groceries this morning. Could Canton possibly have found them? If so, then goddamn it, they had a mole somewhere in the inner circle. Who? Jack would never sell him out. Neither would Thorpe or Sean.

Maybe you shouldn't have opened your mouth to One-Mile, fidiot.

Gritting his teeth, Stone stepped out of the bedroom and crept down the hall. The sounds of footsteps outside grew louder as they approached the front door. He heard low conversation, so more than one guy waited out there. *Shit!*

Stone braced himself against the wall at the end of the hall. In the wide-open space inside, he couldn't find decent cover between there and the door. Judging from the sound of the boots, it was too late to slip out the side entrance and intercept them out front. He hoped that whoever had staged their attack out there didn't have the key code to open the door, but that probably wouldn't stop them from busting it down or smashing in a window.

The door handle jiggled. When it didn't give, whoever stood outside pounded on the door.

What the fuck? Were these intruders so cocky that they no longer bothered with stealth?

He needed backup—and he needed it fast.

Yanking his phone from his pocket, Stone tapped in the security code with his free thumb, still gripping the semiautomatic subcompact nine millimeter with his other hand. Before he could even call Jack, a message from Thorpe jumped out at him.

Axel woke in the middle of the night and started driving your way. Sorry. I didn't realize he was gone until now.

Dominion's owner had sent the message thirty-eight minutes ago. So Axel was probably one of the men on the porch. Who had come with him?

"Sutter, I know you're in there. Open the fuck up."

Yep, that was Axel.

Letting out a breath, he pocketed the phone again but left the firearm in hand. It was better to have Axel creep up to his door than Canton, but not by much. No doubt, shit was going to hit the fan—and splatter back hard.

As Stone tiptoed closer, he calculated the odds that he could wake Lily and, with her, sneak out the bedroom window, then make their way back to his truck while Axel and his buddy barged in the front of the cabin. Before he could decide whether it would work, Axel squashed the idea.

"C'mon, Sutter. I didn't come alone. We've got the place surrounded. Open up and let me see Sweet Pea."

Son of a bitch.

Wanting to pound in the asshole's head, Stone stomped to the door and yanked it open. "Her name is Lily. I'm taking care of her from now on, and she's fine. Why the fuck are you here?"

Axel stood about three inches taller and outweighed him by thirty pounds. Despite the fact that the big guy could assuredly beat the pulp out of almost anyone, Stone stood his ground. This was his plan, damn it. She was his woman.

"I say she's okay once I've seen and talked to her and I'm convinced, not before."

Stone's entire body clenched with a surge of fury. "She doesn't belong to you anymore."

Axel raised a skeptical brow. "And you think she belongs to you now?"

"Yeah." Stone stared him down. "In fact, I don't think. I know."

The guy scoffed. "You're a con man who has a hard-on for her. She is never going to choose a criminal with a record."

That comment dug under Stone's skin, mostly because he worried that Axel was ultimately right. Lily might trust him with her body and she might let him give her pleasure. But if they could ever live that normal life he'd fantasized about just yesterday, would she really choose a man whose every job application would read 'felon'?

Probably not, but Stone refused to let Axel take her without a fight. "You didn't even know her real name, asshole. You didn't know all the details about her past." *You didn't get to blindfold her or make love to her on top.*

"She kept secrets to protect me. I've always known that. I dug enough to be sure she was all right but not enough to invade her privacy. Where the fuck do you get off trying to keep me at arm's length from a sub under my protection?"

"You released her," Stone reminded Axel, who had conveniently forgotten.

The big guy's jaw worked with anger. "I will always care about her and her well-being. I don't give a shit whether she's formally my responsibility or not. So unless you've slapped a collar on her or an engagement ring on her finger, your 'claim' isn't more important than the nearly three years I spent with her, and you can fuck off."

When Axel shouldered his way through the front door, Stone scrambled back and pointed the gun in his face. "No. You will not upset her. You don't get to hurt her anymore."

"What does that mean? Everything I ever did for Misty—Lily—I did to help her."

"You made her feel like a science experiment, like a broken fragment of a woman. She needed love, not training. She needed a friend more than a Dom."

"Fuck you," Axel spat back. "I love that girl. Maybe not romantically, but I've always loved her. She's one of my best friends. I held her when she seemed down. I listened when she felt like opening up. I gave her vanilla sex when she wanted to feel 'normal.' I couldn't force myself to *be* in love with her but I tried to anticipate her needs and provide her with whatever I could to help her feel whole. Who the hell are you to judge me for it?"

"Because she was still broken and bottled up when I took her away. She—"

"Yeah, that's something else I want to talk to you about. You took her—abducted her—without consulting Thorpe or Sean or—"

"Oh, excuse the hell out of me for deciding to get her away from the car bomb rather than stop and ask everyone's permission like some pansy ass. I think Canton was watching her that day. That moment. If I hadn't tossed her in the car, I really don't know what would have happened. If the guy could see her, did he have a high-powered scope zeroed in on her too, in case the explosion failed? I didn't know, and

I didn't hang around to find out. Besides, Lily isn't a wilting flower. She pulled a gun on me."

That made Axel grin with pride. "I never said she was weak. I said you didn't have permission to take off with her. If you hadn't saved her ass, I would have you drummed up on kidnapping—"

"Why do you hate me? I thought you were happy with your fiancée." Stone's eyes narrowed. "But you sound like a jealous prick."

Axel reared back. "Fuck, no."

"He's an overprotective older brother—and a wanker at that," said another guy who walked around the corner and entered the cabin, then stuck out his hand. He looked to be a few years older than Axel. He sounded very British. "Heath."

Yeah, Stone remembered seeing the guy's face the night he'd first met Lily. At least he sounded more reasonable.

"Stone." He shook the man's hand.

"Trust me when I tell you that Axel and Mystery are quite happy. Every time I stay near them, I inevitably hear precisely how happy they are from the next room. He makes sure of it. I'm a bit surprised he doesn't simply piss on her."

Axel turned to Heath with a scowl. "Don't make me regret bringing you along. You wanted something to do? Help me get Sweet Pea away from this dude and out of here."

* * *

AWAKENED by shouting, Lily rolled over to find Stone gone. His side of the bed was still slightly warm. She frowned, bleary-eyed. He'd kept her awake half the night making love to her over and over. He'd never let her far from his side, always wanting to touch her somewhere, in some way. He'd melted the rest of her defenses last night. But now she was wishing she'd gotten more sleep because she couldn't remember if Stone had been expecting company, nor could she think of anyone who would want to shout at him.

The decibel level of the voices outside the solid bedroom door increased but she couldn't make out the words. Lily frowned.

What if someone had come to threaten them? What if that someone was dangerous?

What if Timothy Canton had found them?

The last vestiges of her sleepiness fell away. She shoved the blankets off, eased to the floor, and tiptoed across the room. The old cottage had beautiful original hardwood floors, but they creaked. Doing her best to ignore the squeaky floorboards, she crept closer to the door. A quick search revealed that her gun was gone, and she already knew that nothing in the bedroom would make an effective weapon.

Instead, she paused, trying to detect the threat level, and pressed her ear to the door. That voice, the loud one, sounded like Axel's. Shock pinged her. Wasn't he in London with Mystery?

With a frown, she donned a pair of yoga pants and an old oversize T-shirt, then eased the door open. Not that anyone could possibly hear the slight squeak of the door over their shouting. Then a vaguely familiar voice reached her ears, this one British. Heath? Had he come from the UK with Axel? What the heck was happening?

". . . help me get Sweet Pea away from this dude and out of here." *Axel?* Lily frowned. Who was he talking to and why did he think she needed to leave Stone?

"Don't be a fuckwit. He loves her." That voice belonged to Heath.

"I don't believe that for a second." Yes, that *was* Axel. When had the two men flown to the States? And why did he sound so pissed off?

"Then you're an idiot." Lily smiled at Stone's voice. He sounded honest and a bit snarky, but she heard the tenderness under it all. Maybe that made her sappy and lovesick, but that man did it for her. "You set me up with that first meeting—"

"Because you extorted it from me. If I hadn't needed that information, I would never—"

"But you used me to get it because you wanted to find Mystery," Stone cut in.

Lily was shocked. That's why Axel had allowed them to meet? So he could pursue another woman? She tried not to feel hurt . . . and she mostly succeeded. But she did feel a bit second-class.

"And you knew I was hot to meet Lily." She heard the accusation in Stone's tone, as if he was angry with Axel for using his desire against him. It warmed her heart a little. "So are we going to stand here and argue about what's best for her? Or do you want to help me protect her?"

Okay, that warmed her heart even more. Stone wanted her. He always had. And he was willing to mend fences with Axel for her sake.

"I won't argue about what's best for her because I already know," Axel shot back.

"Bullshit."

And now the two of them were going to make this a pissing match? She started to exit the bedroom, shaking her head. Then Axel scoffed and spoke again.

"You think you know her but you only know the information you've managed to worm out of her. I know that woman deep down, all the way to her soul. I know how she thinks. I know what she enjoys doing in her spare time. I know her quirky habits. And I know how she's going to react when she finds out you schemed to romance her so you could exchange her testimony for your freedom."

At Axel's accusation, Lily froze. A chill spread through her blood. Stone had made a deal to get out of prison if he persuaded her to testify? Was that true? Could he have lied that terribly?

She pushed out of the bedroom and stood in the hallway, her gaze finding Stone. He zipped around and stared back. She knew her face must be begging him to defend himself and refute Axel, to rewrite that insidious version of events with some other story. Instead, Stone winced.

Lily's stomach dropped to her knees and she clutched herself, fighting the urge to throw up. "Is Axel telling the truth?"

The other men swiveled in her direction.

Heath rolled his eyes. "And now you've unleashed the kraken."

"Baby . . ." Stone tucked the gun into the small of his back, then took hesitant steps in her direction, clearly uncertain of his welcome.

"Don't 'baby' me. I want answers."

Stone cursed under his breath. A guilty flush ran up his face. A hundred alarm bells pealed inside her head.

Axel started plowing across the room in her direction, looking grim and determined and furious. "Every word is true."

She took a step back and held up her hands to ward both men off, her gaze bouncing back and forth between them. "Stop there."

They halted, glanced at each other to ensure each intended to honor her request, then turned their gazes back to her.

"It's not what you think." Stone sent her an imploring expression.

He wasn't denying Axel's claim. He wasn't insisting on his innocence.

Stone was guilty as hell. That realization hit her like a physical pang.

"Don't let him tell you any more lies," Axel reasoned. "He sought you out because the feds offered him a chance to commute his sentence. All he had to do was get you to agree to testify against Canton before the dude runs for governor."

Lily had already pieced that together but when she heard the words, they stabbed her in the heart. They made her curl her arms around herself and want to fall to her knees in agony.

Stone hadn't loved her; he'd used her. Everything between them had been a lie.

"How did you find out?" she asked, hoping that Axel had gotten it wrong or misunderstood or somehow twisted the facts.

But in her heart, she already knew that wasn't the case.

"Thorpe. He knew. Sean knew. Jack, Logan, Hunter—they all knew." Axel gritted his teeth. "Hell, they all helped him prepare for this con job. And no one told me because they knew I'd object like hell. You're not a pawn, goddamn it."

So nearly everyone in her life had betrayed her? Nearly everyone she'd ever trusted had played a part in manipulating her to testify and hadn't cared if Stone broke her heart or Canton ended her life? Why?

"Is this all true? I want to hear it from you." She turned to Stone, feeling as if she were breaking apart inside. Her composure was cracking with every labored breath. Her chest hurt more with each second. The silence was terrible.

"The feds offered me this deal after I'd begun working for Jack because Canton had no reason to associate me with you, and if he managed to somehow connect the dots and wanted to take out a threat to his organization, I'd be expendable. No one cares if a convict dies and—"

"Answer the question! Did you seduce me with all your bullshit tenderness and lies so you could get out of prison?" She managed to shout the question, but she had no idea where the energy had come from. She really wanted to curl up into a ball and rock back and forth while trying to understand why everyone she loved, especially Stone, had so completely betrayed her.

Maybe this was karma repaying her for what she'd done to Erin.

Stone opened his mouth, like he intended to say something, but he didn't speak. Worry crossed his face. Then regret.

Lily felt as if her world tilted, threw her off balance, then dropped out from beneath her. She was in free fall, her stomach sickly tense and unsettled. Pain lanced through every vein. Her heart felt ready to explode.

Oh god. "So it's true. I shouldn't be surprised. You're a nobody and I don't deserve love. Of course you know all the reasons why."

"Baby . . ." Stone started toward her. "I care about you, not the deal."

God, how stupid did he think she was?

"Don't touch me," Lily hissed. "You must really have been fist-pumping and mentally high-fiving yourself when I said last night that I would testify." She shook her head in self-loathing at her own idiocy. "You were damn good. I didn't just reluctantly agree, no. I *volunteered*. So cunning and clever, I'll give you that. You mentioned it, pointed out all the reasons it made sense, then let me stew on the idea while you plied my body and unhinged my mind with pleasure. You're a brilliant man. I wish I'd listened to my logic in the first place and stayed away from you."

"Baby, I turned the deal down last night," he swore.

Stone looked so earnest. Then again, he must be one hell of an actor if he could sleep with her to earn his freedom.

He'd been lying to her from the start. Why should she just believe him? "So you can prove that to me right now?"

"Not this instant. I called my FBI contact, Bob Bankhead, and I expect he'll come after—"

"If you can't prove it, I don't believe it."

"Let me call him." He patted his pockets. Finding them empty, he looked around the room for his cell. "I can prove it if you let me call him again."

"You know what? Forget it. I don't believe anything you say anymore."

Axel reached out, coming toward her again, his big face full of empathy. No, pity. "Come here. I've got you."

Stone whirled on Axel, blocking her former mentor's progress with his own body. "Stop trying to come between us, you meddling prick. Leave her alone."

"Oh, I have a feeling she'd ten times rather come with me now than be anywhere near you."

Lily stared, dry-eyed and stunned. Her entire world was falling apart, and they were sniping at each other?

"I'm not a thing or a possession. Or a trophy," she hurled at them. "I'm a woman with a heart that used to beat." She pressed a fist to her chest. "And now . . ."

"Sweet Pea," Axel called softly.

Lily shook her head. She wasn't that woman anymore. "Why did you come here?"

"Because I worried about you after Thorpe told me someone had rigged your car with a bomb. As soon as I found out you were hunkered down with a convict you barely know and I heard about his scheme, I came to rescue you."

"Why? You agreed to introduce us in the first place. Oh, but you only did that so you could get together with Mystery. I was a good bargaining chip, but you didn't care enough to tell me that you weren't actually sanctioning Stone for me. And now you're going to throw him under the bus for using me, too."

Axel flushed, and Lily couldn't think of a time she'd actually seen him rattled. "It wasn't like that. I never said Stone was good for you. I intended to stay around that night Stone came to meet you, but Mystery ran off from Dominion and—"

"You left me to him. But suddenly I matter now?" She cocked a fist on her hip, disillusion wiping away everything except the worst pain and a resolution to shove them both from her life.

"Thorpe told me you'd refused to see him all summer. I didn't think—"

"About me? You didn't. In my book, you're guilty of the same sin as Stone. Go back to your fiancée, Axel. Leave me be."

"I left Zeb to monitor you that night because I knew he would bust Stone's balls if the bastard did anything untoward. I left you in a protected environment and I came back. That's totally different than you jumping into a car with a convict, crossing state lines, and shacking up with him."

"Don't call me that again," Stone warned. "And don't make her feel stupid for trying to stay safe when you weren't around to do the job. She's an adult with a good head on her shoulders and she did what she thought was best in the situation. Why don't you back the fuck off?"

"Are you hoping that if you suck up to her enough or sound like you're on her side she won't refuse to testify and dump your ass back in prison?"

"Shut up!" she shouted, her vocal cords rattling in a growl. "Just shut up. I'm leaving now. Don't stop me. Don't try to find me. Don't say another fucking word to me. I'm done." She turned to Heath. "Will you get me out of here?"

"No!" Stone and Axel both yelled at once.

Then they looked at each other as if they were shocked they finally agreed on something.

"You're not leaving." Stone crossed his arms over his chest and blocked her path to the door with a challenging glare.

Axel stood beside him, their poses almost identical. "What he said."

It would have been funny if her heart weren't breaking into a million pieces. "Neither of you own me. I'm not a child. I'm not a burden." She cast a pointed glare at Axel, then sent a deadly glower to Stone. "And I'm not a fool."

"Of course you're not," Axel said in his "patient" voice. "No one said you were."

He didn't mean it to sound condescending, she knew. But it felt that way and it made her want to grit her teeth and punch him. After nearly three years, she'd thought they were friends at least. She'd believed that he cared. Yeah, he'd traveled here from London to see her but now she wondered if he'd done it more to assuage his over-developed sense of guilt than because of any real attachment.

"Baby, you can't leave. It's too dangerous." Stone clenched his hands into fists. Anguish furrowed his brow, and she would have sworn he was swallowing down pain. "I don't want to lose you at all but I especially don't want to lose you to Canton. If you leave when you're unprepared and emotional—"

"Don't say another word, either of you," she hissed. "You both lost that right when you deceived me. Axel, I'll probably forgive you someday because you sold me out to follow your heart. In a weird way, I get that." She turned to Stone and shook her head, the tears she felt desperate to shed clinging to the edge of her lashes. She'd almost be amazed if she weren't so crushed. "But you . . . you used me. And it had nothing to do with your heart."

"That's not true," he swore. "You stopped being about my freedom a long time ago. I took one look—"

"And fell in love?" she scoffed. "The me of thirty minutes ago would have believed that and thought it was so damn sweet. That girl would have thanked her lucky stars that someone so kind could love her. God, I was stupid. But I know better now. I just wish I hadn't told you every single one of my secrets."

Axel sidled closer. Wisely, he didn't touch her. "You're angry. I completely understand. I'm so damn sorry if I hurt you. But don't risk your life because you're pissed off. Canton is out there. Two minutes before I walked in the door, I got a text that police in Iowa found Reaper's body overnight. Someone put a bullet right between his eyes about eight hours ago."

Lily wasn't shocked at all, but knowing that told her one important fact. "If Canton was in Iowa eight hours ago, he can't be in the swamp right now. Give me my phone and gun," she said to Stone. "I'm taking my belongings and going."

Axel cursed and looked ready to break the furniture. Stone paced, then roared as he approached a wall and punched it. He shook his hand, and Lily winced. That must have hurt. Already she could see that his knuckles were bleeding. But damn it, he didn't care about her pain. She shouldn't care about his.

"I'll take you into town, if you like," Heath offered. "We'll talk about your plans from there."

"I don't need a babysitter." She marched toward the bedroom to gather the clothes and the personal items she'd scattered around.

"So you know where you're heading?" Heath called after her.

"No," she admitted. "But anywhere is better than here, and Canton should have no idea how to find me. So I think I'll be safe."

"You have money, then?"

"Some." She did a quick mental calculation and realized it wasn't much but it was loads more than she'd left California with at sixteen. "I'll get by."

Just before she rounded the corner into the bedroom, she cut a glare back into the living room. The men all exchanged glances. None of them wanted to let her leave, and they were speaking that silent man language and communicating a plan. No idea what, and she didn't care. She was going to live her life on her own from this moment forward. When she'd first arrived in Dallas, she'd let Thorpe take her in, a bit like an adoptive father. He'd passed her to Axel, who'd been like an arranged husband. He'd taken care of her, but his heart hadn't really been in it.

Stone . . . Well, he'd come at her like a lothario, preying on her desire for love and acceptance for his own gain. Lily wasn't sure what hurt worse, that he'd done it intentionally or that she'd been naive enough to let him.

"Lily, baby." Stone shook his head. "Don't risk yourself. Please."

She swallowed back her anger. He pretended to care because if she walked out the door, there went his meal ticket. Fuck him.

Still, she saw how this was going to work. They were three strapping men, all protectors by nature. They could—and would—physically hold her here unless she pretended to concede that they were right, she was wrong, and of course, she was helpless without them.

"I'll have Heath with me," she reminded. "On the way to town, he can help me figure out how to slip away from Louisiana undetected. I'll start over. I'll be fine."

Stone barreled toward her. And he wasn't stopping. Lily retreated with every step he took, scrambling away until her back hit the doorjamb. Without preamble, he wrapped strong fingers around her nape and tilted her head, crushing her lips beneath his.

The feel of him taking her mouth, plunging inside to claim her, was a shock. Her senses registered pleasure and safety and love. Her heart wanted to throw her arms around him, melt into his solid warmth, and hold on forever. Her head knew better and revolted.

Lily shoved him away. "Don't."

"I will fight for you," he vowed. "I will do everything in my power to keep you. I love you and I don't want to let you go."

His dark eyes pinned her in place with conviction and sincerity and devotion. He really should win awards for his performance.

In the back of her head, she wondered if, by chance, he was serious. Lily grimaced. Nope. No more of this giving-him-the-benefit-of-the-doubt shit. She refused to be gullible again.

"You're wasting your breath, Stone. I'm done. It's over. See, you— and everyone in my former life in Dallas—decided I was weak. They coddled and deceived me. None of you realized that I don't have to be loud to be strong. I have survived more in a few years than many do in a lifetime. I admit I have feelings for you. I believed I was in love with the man you pretended to be. He was a mirage. Yeah, my heart is broken. But it won't break *me*. I refuse to be a victim again. Now give me the goddamn gun."

No one said anything for a long moment. Lily could almost feel the moment he realized that he couldn't prevent her from leaving.

"I'll watch over her," Heath promised.

Which was, no doubt, code for "Heath wouldn't let her out of his sight until she either saw reason or Stone found a way to persuade her back into his arms and bed."

Fat fucking chance of that. But Lily played along to get away from the million memories of Stone's seeming tenderness—all a lie.

"Let go," she demanded in a hoarse whisper.

Slowly, Stone released her and stepped back. Reluctance stamped itself all over his face, and he looked as if he wanted to grab her, caveman-carry her to the bedroom, and screw her until she was too sated to care. What did it say about her feelings that she was a little bit tempted?

Before her hormones and her heart took over, she held out her hand for her weapon. With a sigh, he pulled it from the small of his back, checked the safety, and set it in her palm.

"You never took the gun-safety class. If you don't know what you're doing, at least let me take you out this afternoon and we can practice—"

"No." Because that sounded as if he was stalling for a way to keep her there so she could cool down while he used his masculine wiles on her. "Please get out of my way."

Stone made a great show of agony and regret as she marched down the hall and back to the living room with a growled curse. As she gathered up her belongings and tossed them back in the suitcase, she could hear the men talking among themselves in low tones. Scheming bastards. Still, a fresh cleaver of pain threatened to split her chest in two. How could any part of her still love a man who had deceived and used her? Who had plotted to do whatever it took to turn her into a lovestruck idiot, willing to risk her life so he wouldn't have to return to prison?

Lily knew that if she testified, Canton might finally pay for what he'd done to Erin and her family. She'd love to see that sick sociopath put away for good. But would her testimony be enough? What if Canton went free? She would have gained nothing. And even if she got on the stand and held her hand to a Bible, it wouldn't bring back anyone she loved. It might curb any potential future violence, true. But it would sure as hell benefit Stone most of all right now.

She refused to stay another minute so he could find a new vulnerability in her soft underbelly to use against her again. Time to finally let go of the past, both distant and recent, and start over—this time alone and standing on her own two feet.

Chapter Sixteen

IT'S quite eerie out here. But peaceful," Heath remarked as he rowed away from Stone's skiff and through the swamp, toward the waiting dirt lot of parked cars on the other side of the water.

Lily wondered if he simply couldn't stand the silence or he wanted to drag her into a conversation so he could convince her she was making a big mistake. As if Axel's regret and Stone's anxiety weren't hint enough that they both thought her leaving now was as safe as bathing in chum before swimming through shark-infested waters . . .

She refused to get involved in his conversation. "Hmm."

Heath shot her a glance. "All right, I'll skip the chitchat then. They're worried."

What was she supposed to say to that? *Thank you, Captain Obvious.* "They're not my problem. I know they only allowed me to leave because they thought you would make sure I didn't do anything stupid and that the big bad wolf couldn't get me. But realistically, you can't watch over me for the rest of your life, so you tell me what it will take to convince you that I'm safe enough. What do you need to leave me in peace?"

"I'd rather hoped you would cool off and . . ." He stopped there and sighed. "But that seems unlikely, so what are your plans? I can help. Once I think you're secure and I'm assured Canton isn't on your trail, I'll back off."

Maybe. But Lily didn't believe any of these guys anymore. Yes, they sought to keep her safe, but each and every one of them was cut from the same cloth—convinced they were right, determined to protect, and certain that the ends justified the means. Whether they meant to or not, they made her feel incapable and dependent. She'd been that for far too long.

Lily didn't voice any of this to Heath. If she did, he would only stick to her like superglue.

"I have a few hundred dollars and waitressing skills. They're rusty, but if you can get me to New Orleans, I can find a job. I'm a pro at dyeing my hair. I'll splurge on a pixie cut. I've got some blue contacts in my tote bag leftover from my Halloween costume last year. I know how to change my name and disappear."

Heath was already shaking his head. "Canton found you once. He has resources at his disposal you can't even imagine. Jack Cole told us that it looks as if Canton had Mafia shanked in prison days ago and Reaper shot between the eyes only last night."

Lily recoiled in horror. After years away from that man's violence she'd forgotten how swift and cruel it could be.

"Testify." Heath drilled her with a dark stare. "That's the only way this mess ends."

Of course he'd say that. And she'd agreed to it last night when she'd been sated, wrapped in Stone's arms, believing they had a future together. In today's cold light, she saw clearly they had nothing, especially not honesty. "I'm not doing it simply to keep your pal out of jail."

"Stone is no friend of mine. I scarcely know him. And before you imagine that I have any allegiance to Axel, remember that I knew and loved Mystery first. I stopped fighting for her because I could plainly see that her heart was otherwise engaged. It's actually in my best interest to have you in Axel's life, causing friction between the two of them. But I'm getting older, and I suppose I have a bit of a sentimental streak. I want what's best for people since life so rarely gives that to anyone without some finagling or a shove. Testifying and finally closing this chapter of your life would benefit you most of all. I don't know the details but I know you've had a difficult road. Get on the stand and tell the truth. Get closure. Make certain Canton can't harm anyone else. *Then* start over however and with whomever you fancy."

Heath had some good points. But right now she was too disillusioned to sort through her thoughts and too heartsick to make any decisions. The idea of entering a courtroom alone and dredging up every bit of the excruciating past to a jury of twelve strangers both made her sick and filled her with terror. Of course, that assumed she would live long enough to testify at all. The minute Canton learned what she planned, he'd come after her with everything he had and he would take her down without mercy.

The easiest path would be to start over as a new person with a new life, hopefully one Canton would never find. Forget Lily Taylor ever existed.

Could she live with that?

Lily said nothing to Heath because engaging him in conversation only meant he would try to influence her more.

The sounds of nature broke the silence as they reached the dock beside the dirt parking lot. Callie's pretty new Audi SUV sat beside Stone's black truck. Axel must have borrowed it since he only owned a motorcycle. Heath was "visiting" so he didn't have a car, either.

Lily eyed the vehicles and the road beyond. Then she turned back. The sun slanted in shimmering beams through the cypress trees and over the still waters that, despite looking dead, she knew teemed with life. She couldn't see Jack's cabin or Stone and Axel standing on the porch watching Heath row her away anymore.

She literally had come to a turning point in her life. Keep running to stay alive or risk death to tell her truth in a court of law?

Heath tied off the boat, then clambered out, lifting her suitcase and duffel out of the little skiff. On wobbly legs, she stood and clutched her tote and the box of her most personal items.

"Let's talk this through, shall we?" he suggested. "I can be the voice of reason—"

"I have plenty of reason on my own. Can you just let me think for ten minutes?" She sighed.

Holding out a hand, Heath helped her onto land, then withdrew the keys to Callie's car from his pocket. "Of course."

Lily winced at his clipped tones. She hated to be rude but tried not to worry about the feelings of a man doing her betrayers' bidding. On the other hand, she had no doubt that Heath, a former MI5 agent, would keep her safe if Canton managed to track her down before she made her great escape.

But at the end of the day, she didn't want to exchange one keeper for another.

"Thanks," she murmured as he carried most of her luggage to the vehicle and stowed it inside.

He merely nodded at her as he opened her door and started up the car.

So now what? Lily didn't have an answer.

Inside the leather interior of the SUV filled with that luscious new-car smell, Lily settled beside Heath and tried to decide her next move. Regardless of whether she testified or not, she had to stay off Canton's radar. It would be smarter if she kept off everyone else's, too. That meant she had to scrap her plan to head to the Keys. Stone knew all about it—and he might not be the only one. No going to New Orleans, either. Now that she'd mentioned it on a whim to Heath, they'd look there as well.

At the first possible moment, she would have to ditch her phone and computer. If Stone wasn't tracking both, Axel might be. Or Thorpe. She'd thought they were all such concerned protectors. Instead, they were deceiving bastards. But every one of them was a control freak, and she had a suspicion they wouldn't simply let her go. For the life of her, she couldn't figure out why.

Lily tried to think through her options. She didn't really have money for new gadgets, but she could buy a new burner phone this afternoon and leave the other two devices behind somewhere. The batteries would run out soon enough; then her trail would be cold unless she did something stupid.

Heath navigated the seemingly long drive to central Lafayette. Traffic bustled during the lunch hour as he stopped the sleek white SUV in the parking lot of a Walmart. "If you're leaving, you'll need a few items from here, right?" He looked up at the facade of the building. "I loathe this place."

Despite the really crappy day she'd had, Lily had to grin. "Me, too. But yeah. I should grab a few things."

"I'll help." He reached for the handle to open the door.

She grabbed his arm and pulled him back. "You can leave me here. I'm a big girl. I'll manage on my own. *If* I decide to testify, who do I contact?"

Lily thought it wise to keep her options open, just in case.

Heath shrugged. "Keep your mobile handy. One of us will text you shortly."

Seriously, her patience was coming to an end. "Don't treat me like an idiot. You know I'm ditching the phone as soon as I can. I need an answer now."

With a sigh, Heath pulled his phone from his pocket and fired off a text. Within moments, the device dinged, signaling that he'd received an answer. "Special Agent Bob Bankhead. He's out of the Los Angeles office. Stone is texting you the man's phone number."

She'd just bet her sneaky Casanova was. Would he love it if she saved his ass? "Fantastic. Now ask him to leave me the hell alone for good."

Lily wasn't sure why she'd made such a demand. No, that wasn't true. Some foolish part of her hoped that he'd disregard her wish, come riding up on his white horse, and choose her after all.

So stupid.

"I can already tell you he won't agree," Heath supplied. "Ever."

Heath must be wrong. Stone would totally let her go as if she meant absolutely nothing to him because she didn't. Still, maybe she was better off not hearing Stone's answer. It would only hurt more, and she didn't need the added pain.

Damn it, she had to stop with the self-pity. She'd closed the chapter on her existence once at sixteen. She would simply do it again.

"You think I'm wrong. I can tell." Heath shook his head. "I've seen far too many men in love lately. I know what one looks like."

"Maybe. But I don't think you're very good at spotting a con man, and I wish you well with the future. Sounds like you'll need it." She hopped out of the car, not surprised when Heath followed. She ignored him and retrieved a shopping cart from a nearby corral, then opened the hatch in back and dumped her luggage in the cart. "Thank you for the ride. I hope you're able to get over Mystery and move on. Good-bye."

Just like she hoped to recover from Stone someday. Realistically, that was probably far in the future.

Heath shifted his weight, looking reluctant to go. "Lily, how will you leave town? You don't have a car. As a target, you're too easy to take out all alone like this. You'll want privacy soon. Night will fall. Don't make this easy for Canton. He might not have been the one to shoot Reaper in Iowa. It's quite likely he still has violent men in his employ willing to do his bidding. He could be waiting for you around the next corner."

In her head, Lily knew that. She didn't want to put her stubbornness over her personal safety but she was going to have to make do without these guys for the rest of her life. Why not start now? "I'm no longer your problem. Consider yourself relieved of duty or whatever. In less than three hours, I'll be a completely new woman and long gone. Thanks for the lift."

With that, she headed into the store, only glancing back once to ensure that Heath hadn't followed her. She'd half-expected him to, but to her surprise, he stood unmoving next to Callie's sleek white vehicle, the hot wind ruffling his dark hair.

Inside, Lily tried not to feel completely alone. She was surrounded by people, after all, some of whom would make for great social media posts.

She hurried through the cool air of the big-box store and picked up a prepaid cell phone, along with a few other necessities, then hightailed it to the hair-care aisle. She scanned the dyes, trying to decide on a color. Red tended to attract attention and bleed out quickly. Most shades of dark blond washed her out because they contained too much gold for her pink skin tone.

Why had Stone pretended to love and care for her, listened to her secrets, worshipped her body, and become her everything if all he'd wanted her to do was testify? Why hadn't he just flat-out asked her? He'd barely tried to appeal to her logic. Maybe because he didn't credit her with any. Right now, she was questioning that herself. She didn't understand how he could look at her with such naked feeling, slide deep inside her, all the while convincing her of a love he didn't feel.

No. She wouldn't think about him anymore. Stone wasn't important to her future. Getting out of this town was. A medium brown color would help with that. She'd done it before. Not her favorite, but she would blend in.

She grabbed the box, scanned it, and threw it in the shopping cart beside her.

"Lily Taylor," a masculine voice called from directly behind her.

She froze. She hadn't heard that voice since she was a teenager, not since one of the darkest days of her life.

Timothy Canton.

She turned slowly, hoping like hell her ears had deceived her. But no. There he stood. Despite his looking a few years older and a few pounds heavier, she recognized him. He definitely appeared more respectable in a pair of casual shorts and a crisp golf shirt with a cap low over his face. Anyone who saw him would imagine he'd just come off the course.

How had he found her and crept up behind her?

"It's been a long time," he murmured in a low, almost secretive voice.

Fear froze the blood in her veins. Her eyes flared wide. Panic sliced through her like a physical pain. She backed up a step, rattling into boxes of hair color and shampoo. "You can't kill me here. My murder will be on security cameras."

"Murder?" He gave her the same fake laugh she'd heard when he'd pretended surprise at finding Erin at the warehouse. It sent chills down her spine. "I came to Louisiana to talk to you, nothing more."

Sure, he had. Next, he'd try to sell her a bridge. Before he offed her and buried the evidence, of course.

Timothy Canton didn't compromise or give anything in return. He simply smashed everyone in his path with an iron fist. And because he wanted to be governor, they both knew she stood in his way.

"I have nothing to say." She fumbled for her purse and shoved her hand inside, rummaging around for her gun. "Go away."

"If you're reaching for a firearm, I wouldn't do that. The store management will have the police here in three minutes, and you'll go to jail for carrying a weapon without a permit in Louisiana. If you point it at me, it would be natural for them to assume you mean to rob or kill me. And maybe everyone else in the store."

Canton was right, and Lily's next instinct was to drop him to his knees with a swift kick to the balls, then start running. But the moment she left the store, she would no longer be in a public place, and she'd be so much easier for him or one of his thugs to eliminate.

"I also feel compelled to point out that if you touch me in any other way, I can press assault charges." He gave her an empty, almost benign smile.

A politician's smile, she realized. It promised benevolence and delivered whatever served him best. Though he looked more suited to the country club than to the mean streets these days, she couldn't forget that he raped and killed without remorse. He'd taken her mother, her brother, and her best friend from her without blinking.

Heart racing, thoughts whirling, she tried to decide what to do next. "What the hell do you want?"

"Just to talk to you. I approached you in public, hoping that wouldn't scare or intimidate you. Toward the front of the store there's a sandwich shop. Let me buy you a soda. We'll sit. I'd like you to hear me out."

"No."

"I suggest you reconsider." His tone was silky, almost casual, but she heard the underlying threat. "It's in our mutual best interest. I need your silence. And I have a lot of money, which you'll need now that you have no job, no car, no friends, no home . . ."

Lily felt as if he'd just punched her in the stomach. "H-how did you know all that? How did you find me?"

"Come to the sandwich shop and I'll explain." He gestured to the end of the aisle.

She looked for a way out of the situation. The last thing she wanted to do was sit across a table from Timothy Canton and pretend to have a civilized conversation. Under his new veneer, she had to believe he was still the same old criminal and sociopath. Still, the minute she left the store she was probably dead. Maybe she could play along, then tip off someone in the restaurant or an employee that she was in trouble. But what if she got an innocent bystander killed? Maybe she could escape to the women's bathroom to call . . . who? She couldn't ring anyone she'd left behind. Even if they came, she couldn't trust them. And if she called the police, what could she say? A man from her past had accosted her in Walmart and forced her to have a carbonated beverage with him?

No, but she had Bob Bankhead's number on her phone. The fed might be able to get her out of this bind. True, but to secure his help, she'd have to agree to testify. Looking at Canton now, she wasn't sure that was a smart idea.

Lily forced herself to exhale and think. Canton wouldn't hurt her in a public place with so many cameras on them. Maybe if she heard him out, she could find some way to escape this mess, hopefully for good.

She prayed for calm as she pushed the cart filled with all her worldly belongings. As she walked up the aisle and turned left toward the sub shop she'd noticed when she first walked in, she passed row after row of shoppers and employees. No one seemed to notice anything unusual. That was good . . . and bad.

When they reached the sub shop, Canton ushered her in and grabbed hold of her arm, ensuring she stood right beside him. His fingers bit into her arm with just enough force to remind her how dangerous he could be. But the smile he sent her, blankly kind, made her want to cringe. Its deceitful emptiness scared her most of all.

"What would you like to drink?" he asked as if he didn't have a care in the world.

Nothing. She felt sure if she tried to swallow anything, she would throw up. But she already knew he wouldn't accept that answer. "S-sprite."

When he reached the cashier, he ordered her soda and an iced tea for himself. She didn't dare look at the girl behind the counter. She looked every bit as young as Erin had the day Canton had killed her. Lily didn't want to be responsible for another young girl's torture and death because she still remembered how much the barbarian had enjoyed taking Erin's innocence before he'd taken her life. So she clutched the handle of her shopping cart and looked anywhere else.

As soon as they had their cups, Canton led her to a square booth with a sticky wood laminate tabletop in the corner. He parked her cart behind it and set her cup down and shooed her into her seat before he planted himself across from her.

"I have nothing to say to you." She glared his way.

"I think you'll want to hear this." He paused and sent her a considering stare. "You left Dallas quickly. Did that brute you used to sleep with break your heart when he started shacking up with the famous director's daughter?"

He knew about Axel? "How long have you been watching me?"

"Years," he assured her. "Keep your friends close . . ."

And your enemies closer.

Lily swallowed. And Canton hadn't tried to kill her in all that time? Of course, since he was running for governor, that meant he had to rid all the ghosts from his past. "Why the hell bother with chitchat now that you've blown up my car and my life?"

He scowled. Even though his golden brown hair didn't move, his face appeared to turn down into something that looked almost like a real expression. "I heard about that incident. I didn't plant that bomb. I merely left you flowers in your car at work, telling you exactly what I wanted. I was waiting across the street for you, watching for the moment you found the bouquet so I could approach you. But you weren't alone. That ex-con who wanted you so badly followed you to the parking lot. When you left Dominion, you did it so quickly, I didn't have the opportunity to follow. The bomb was unexpected."

"Meaning one of your goons did it?" She sneered.

"No." He managed to grit his teeth yet still flash her that terrible smile again. "Meaning I have no idea how or why it happened. Let's try to be pleasant, all right?"

She leaned in and scowled. It didn't matter if she was a bitch to Canton because he was probably going to kill her. "I can't sit across from the animal who murdered so many people I loved and not want to both vomit and stab you myself."

He gave her a nod of seeming regret that she didn't believe for a second. "Ancient history, Ms. Taylor. That was a different time, and I'm a different man now."

Bullshit. "Yeah? Then why did you rape and kill a woman in my apartment who looks suspiciously like me? Or are you going to tell me that wasn't your handiwork, either?"

"I had nothing to do with that." He shook his head, doing his best to look innocent.

"Then one of your thugs did."

"I no longer have thugs. I'm a businessman these days, nothing more. And following you has been a full-time job. When you disappeared into the swamp, I kept trying to figure out how to explore the area and pinpoint your location. You had your phone off for days and—"

"You were tracking my phone?"

"How else did you imagine I could find you? Once I figured out your alias, I had an associate who works for your wireless provider keep an eye on you. If you veered more than fifty miles from home or work, he alerted me. Thankfully, you rarely did."

"Cut the crap," she growled at him. "You're no humanitarian. You had Mafia shanked in prison a few days ago. You had someone put a bullet between Reaper's eyes last night. You're going to off me, too."

She wasn't sure she would be brave enough to confront him if she weren't surrounded by people coming and going in the little eatery. An elderly couple sat in the middle of the area, both talking loudly to each other. A pair of teenage boys stared at the girl behind the counter, one openly flirting. A blond woman bounced a baby girl on her lap and picked at a sub. Lily thanked god she wasn't alone with this savage psycho. He might kill her, but she'd get to speak her mind first.

"Mafia met with an unfortunate event during his incarceration," Canton advised. "Such a shame that he made enemies behind bars. I guess he'll never get that deal for a reduced sentence in exchange for his testimony about our past . . . dealings." He shook his head in mock sympathy. "Not my fault at all."

Which meant he'd totally been behind Mafia's murder. The thought made her sick.

"But Reaper?" He frowned, looking genuinely puzzled. "Someone killed him last night."

"How did you hear? Didn't he live in Idaho?"

"Iowa."

"Ah, yes. He'd found God. I remember. Well, hopefully he's at the pearly gates now being welcomed with open arms. But I had nothing to do with that. Truly." He leaned forward and dropped his voice so that even the bored blonde trying to eavesdrop over her baby's squeals couldn't pick up their conversation. "Look, I've done some things in the past that don't match the image I'd prefer to convey now. You've been a quiet, unobtrusive girl for years. That tells me you're reasonable. So I'm willing to compensate you for continued good behavior. I have some paperwork in my motel room, a fairly detailed nondisclosure agreement. Come with me to look it over."

Was he crazy? "Go to hell. I won't follow you anywhere. I won't sign anything. And I especially won't go to your motel room."

"It's worth half a million dollars to you."

"It could be half a trillion but if I'm dead, I can't spend it." And she had little doubt the money was a ruse to lure her someplace he could kill her. Besides, what kind of price tag could she possibly put on the lives of her loved ones? Five hundred thousand dollars was probably more money than she'd ever see in her lifetime but that amount for three of the most precious people on the planet to her seemed awfully cheap.

"I'm hurt." He pouted, and she didn't buy it for a minute. Canton didn't actually have feelings, just ruthlessness, greed, and ambition. "I'm trying to engage in simple commerce. You're being difficult."

"What happens if I refuse?"

He gave her what he probably thought was his most concerned

smile. "I'd hate for a serious, maybe even fatal, accident to befall you. But these unfortunate things sometimes happen. So sad."

Of course. To be honest, she was surprised he'd offered to pay her anything, but she was pretty sure he merely meant to scam her.

"Before you reply, I've learned over time that money can contribute to a much higher quality of life. You might enjoy the windfall."

No. She'd feel terrible every moment of every day she had the blood money with all those zeros in her bank account. As far as Lily was concerned, she'd heard enough. She needed to grab her stuff and get out of the store before Canton caught up to her. "Fuck you."

She stood and grabbed her cart from behind the table, then darted around the maze of tables in the little place. A glance back at Canton told her that he watched, shaking his head. "We're not done, Lily."

The blonde with the baby shot her a concerned glance, then stood, anchoring the little girl to her hip. Lily didn't wait to see what the bystander would do. She needed to escape before Canton or his goons grabbed her.

She dashed to the checkout with her box of dye, burner phone, and other assorted goodies. When she reached the front of the line, Lily used some of her precious cash to pay for her items. As she did, she scanned for Canton or his thugs—anyone who looked as if they were watching her too closely and waiting for a chance to pounce. But she saw no one suspicious inside the store.

Now she just had to get outside, through the parking lot, and escape. Obviously, if Canton was going to run for governor, he wasn't going to shoot her himself in a place teeming with cameras. She didn't have the time to wait for a taxi or the money to pay for one. It was a thousand freaking degrees out there. She had everything she owned in her luggage, and she needed to move fast. To do that and make a clean getaway, she needed to make sure Canton couldn't follow her.

As she hustled to the exit, the store manager stood next to a big guy wearing a name tag pinned to his vest. "Excuse me. I'm hoping you can help. I was accosted by a man in the store earlier. He's about five foot ten, midthirties, wearing a white golf shirt." Lily turned and spotted Canton lurking around a nearby impulse aisle, pretending to be engrossed. She pointed. "Can you help me? Just keep him here until I can get to my car and leave?"

The store manager, a fortysomething African-American man, looked pissed off on her behalf. So did his bodybuilding pal. He nodded. "Go. We'll take care of him, ma'am."

"Thank you. I was scared." And that wasn't a lie at all. "I appreciate it. So much."

They waved her out the door and stood blocking it as Canton started in her direction.

Outside, she sighed in relief, then ventured away from the building cautiously, scanning the half-empty parking lot for anyone who might be on Canton's payroll with a mission to finish her off. She saw an elderly woman driving away. A guy with dark hair and sunglasses, rocking out in his Jeep. He glanced her way once, then apparently lost interest. He didn't seem threatening, simply as if he were waiting for his buddy or girlfriend to come out of the store.

And no sign of Heath. Well, the British bodyguard had sworn he was leaving. She didn't see any sign of Callie's car. It was just as well. She needed to find some quiet way to carry all her stuff down the road and rent a motel room long enough to dye her hair, change clothes, wipe her devices clean of all data and software, and trash everything she didn't intend to take with her. She still had a few hundred dollars left. Maybe she could buy a bus ticket and be somewhere else by nightfall.

Knowing it was now or never, Lily strode away from the store. The craggy asphalt radiated heat, and a mirage cropped up across the half-full lot. The twentysomething blonde with the baby she'd seen earlier approached her, pushing her shopping cart of groceries.

"You need help? I saw that man talking to you. You looked scared." Empathy softened the woman's face.

Lily really did need help but she didn't want to involve anyone else in her problems, especially someone with a baby who didn't look older than six months. Out of the blue, she wondered how the woman felt about motherhood. She'd dressed her precious daughter in frills and pink. It reminded Lily of the one outfit she'd scraped her money together to buy Regina before . . . Well, before everything. She shoved the thoughts away.

"I'm good." She tried to smile, aware her hands were shaking. "Thanks. Your daughter is adorable."

The woman smiled and stroked the little one's head. "She's such a good baby, too. I'm lucky. Have a nice day."

"You, too." Lily saw the woman stop at a blue compact, then load the baby and her plastic bags in the backseat before she slid behind the wheel. Someday, if she could ever put the Canton mess to bed, maybe she'd find a man who truly loved her and have the blessings that woman seemed to possess.

But first she had to escape.

Lily glanced over her shoulder as she rolled everything she owned in the shopping cart and headed toward the far end of the lot. The young mom backed out of her parking spot. The guy with midnight hair still sat in a big gray Jeep with the windows rolled down. When he looked at her again, his dark stare didn't seem quite so disinterested. She pushed her cart across the blacktop faster.

"Lily!" a male voice shouted across the lot.

She turned and spotted Canton running after her between the parked cars. Instantly, her heart revved up and terror juiced her bloodstream. He'd probably smooth-talked his way out of her distraction. And he'd caught her alone. God knew what he'd do now, but she expected he'd have some plan to get her away from here and make her death more horrific than she could imagine. No one crossed Canton and lived. Besides utter terror, the only thing Lily could feel was regret. She'd failed Erin, her mom, and her brother. Her secrets would die with her. And their killer would win.

"You can't do this!" But Lily was painfully aware he could do whatever he wanted. She'd been stupid to send Heath away, even if she hadn't thought Canton could possibly find her this quickly. She'd only needed three hours alone to transform herself, damn it.

But that was clearly three hours too many. Canton was obviously every bit as devious and determined as he'd always been.

"Three quarters of a million," he shouted, charging after her. "Cash, if you sign today."

Not that she believed he'd ever give her money for silence, but where would he get that much liquid money?

"No. Leave me alone." At the edge of the lot, she picked up all her belongings and tried to run for the sidewalk off the main drag ahead. With cars passing to and fro, Canton couldn't shoot or abduct her in broad daylight, could he? There would be witnesses or sidewalk cams— something. Right?

Just then, a car weaved up beside her, stopping between her and Canton. A blue compact.

The tinted window on the driver's side slid down, and the woman with the baby turned to her with a worried expression. "Can I give you a lift someplace?" Lily started to refuse, but the woman glanced in her rearview mirror at Canton, who'd now halted. "When I was younger, I once found myself stranded in the heat, carrying most of what I owned on my shoulders, too. A kind soul helped me out. I'd love to pay it back. I could use some good karma about now. And I would feel terrible leaving you with that guy."

Lily looked at Canton barely twenty feet away, just waiting for the opportunity to pounce, then to the woman's earnest face. The baby cooed and shook its rattle in the backseat. Surely a woman carting her infant around wouldn't be a crazy ax murderer. And the blonde had to be safer than Canton. Besides, the sooner she got to a motel, the sooner she could wipe her phone clean, transform herself, and leave this town.

"I'm Emma and this is Isabel. I promise, we don't bite. Well, she's teething but . . ."

Lily cocked her head. The sun beat down on her, and she was beginning to sweat. She hated snap decisions, but Canton would catch up to her in the next ten seconds. Still . . .

"This man is dangerous. You're taking a big risk with your safety and your baby's."

Emma nodded. "Yes, and my husband would kill me. But I know that look on your face, like you've lost everything and don't know where to go. That man is harassing you and you're afraid. I was in a similar place two years ago. I'll get you away from here, hon."

It was either get in the car with the woman or wait for Canton to wrap his hands around her throat and squeeze.

"That would be great. Thanks." Lily wanted to hug the woman and hoped Canton didn't make the stranger pay for her kindness.

Everything that had happened the past few hours was catching up with Lily. She hadn't eaten yet today and didn't know where she'd be in eight hours. She had no idea where she'd lay her head to sleep tonight. No idea how she would keep herself alive. The thought was enough to make her want to break down and give up. But she was strong and resourceful. She had some money, a gun in her purse, and experience on her side.

Emma shoved the car in park. "I'll help with your gear."

Together the two women tossed her luggage into the trunk and barely managed to get it slammed shut. A glance back proved Canton stood beside a huge brown pickup encased in mud and stared, wearing a furious glare on his face. Clearly, he hadn't expected a bystander to help her. But he also wasn't going to harass her with a witness.

Once she slammed the trunk, Emma hurried toward the driver's side of the car. Lily watched and noticed the car had California license plates. She paused, unease trickling through her.

"What's wrong?"

"You're a long way from California."

Emma gave Canton a nervous glance, then nodded. "My husband started his own company recently. He can work from anywhere, so we decided to move closer to my family for Isabel's sake. The cost of living is cheaper, which is important right now. I'll miss San Diego but I think here will be all right, too."

Emma slipped back into the car and cooed at her baby. Lily hesitated. Not every one of the thirty-something million people from California were involved with Canton.

Taking a deep breath, she slipped into the blessed air-conditioned comfort of the car. "Good luck with everything."

"Thanks."

As the woman pulled out of the lot, Lily powered down her cell phone. As soon as she got to a motel room, she would wipe it clean and set up the burner.

Emma smiled and drove to the main road. "Where to?"

"There's a little motel down the road off to the left here." Lily pointed. "It's not far."

"Oh, we're staying there too until we find a house to rent." With that, Emma pulled out onto the road.

One last glance back told Lily Canton still watched. She didn't think for one minute that she'd seen the last of him.

Two minutes later, they pulled into the lot, and Emma put the car in park. "Here we are." She twisted around for her purse on the floorboard behind her and dragged it into her lap. "Let me give you something before you go." Lily was already wording her refusal to accept money if that's what the woman intended. Instead, Emma whipped out a syringe and shoved the needle into her arm. "Sorry. I know Timothy Canton is dangerous." Her expression melted into something that looked like hate. "But my husband and I are far worse."

Chapter Seventeen

I CAN'T fucking stand this." Stone paced the floor of Jack's cabin, nearly ready to crawl out of his skin. "I have no idea what's going on. Is Lily okay? Is she safe? Where the hell is Heath with a report?"

He hadn't liked any of this, especially letting her walk out the door. But she didn't trust him now, not after the damage Axel had wrought. Lily would have only hated him if he'd refused to let her go or he'd followed. At the time, that had seemed important. Now, he didn't care. He just wanted to know that she was all right.

To be on the safe side, he'd texted One-Mile the moment the skiff had disappeared into the swamp and given the sniper her position. As soon as Heath had advised Axel that he'd taken her to Walmart, he'd texted that information, too. But the bastard had never answered, and now Stone worried she didn't have enough protection. He felt as if someone had shoved a hot poker in his chest, as if his guts were now twisted around a ball of anxiety.

He wanted to throw his phone that wasn't buzzing with information across the room. No, he wanted to go find Lily and convince her that the only thing he'd ever wanted from her was her love.

Instead, Axel and his big mouth had persuaded her that Stone had only been using her.

"You think I'm going to let anything happen to her?" Axel scowled. "Hell, no. Heath is watching over her. He knows exactly—"

"Why the fuck did you show up and undo everything I'd built with Lily?" he growled. "She'd been making so much progress. We'd been growing our trust."

"Based on what? A huge fucking lie?"

Stone shook his head and tensed every muscle in his body. It was the only way he could restrain the urge to rip Axel's head off. "Nothing and no one is more important to me than Lily, you holier-than-thou asshole. You made a lot of assumptions about my motives without actually knowing me. I have done nothing but try to get that woman's attention and persuade her to believe in me since the day we first talked about her. I used the FBI's offer to get close to her because Thorpe and Sean and Jack wanted to hear that I could help her actually have a real future by persuading her to testify. At first, I was in favor, too. I admit that I didn't want to go back to prison. But now I want her to be safe way more than I care about anything else."

Axel rolled his eyes. "Pretty speech but I don't believe a word of it. You have no way to back that up."

He didn't. Stone gritted his teeth and cursed under his breath. Then something occurred to him. "Actually, I do."

He whipped his phone out again and texted Bankhead. I told you yesterday that I wanted out of your scheme since it's too dangerous to make Lily testify. When can I expect to go back to the big house?

Bankhead wrote back almost instantly. Tomorrow, you stupid prick. You were lucky to have this opportunity and you pissed it away. It won't come again.

Stone didn't feel lucky, but at least he had proof of his intentions.

He shoved his phone in Axel's face. "Read this. I'm done wasting my time here with you. I'm leaving to talk to Lily. Before I go back behind bars, I want her to know that I loved her and never betrayed her. I've already got a plan in motion to make her safe while I'm gone. So go back to your fiancée and get the fuck out of my way."

With a frown of concentration, Axel mulled over the texts. "You really tried to bow out?"

"Yes. I also tried to hire someone to kill Canton. I'm already going back to prison, so I really didn't care if I got hit with solicitation of murder, too. Fucker wouldn't take the job but he agreed to watch over her and put a bullet between Canton's eyes if necessary."

Axel cocked his head. "Seriously?"

"Yeah. You obviously thought me finagling that first meeting with Lily showed my true mercenary colors or whatever, but I really did just want to meet her. And I want to spend my life with her—" He sighed. "Why the fuck am I explaining myself to you? I don't care if Heath has an eye on her. I'm done. Letting her cool off was a bad idea. I'd rather have her be with me and pissed off than gone and in any possible danger."

"Sorry." Axel swallowed, looking contrite. "I had no idea you actually had feelings for her. I didn't come here with anything in mind except to provide her protection and—"

"Save it. I'm going to find her." But when he used the app he'd installed on his phone to track hers, it told him the device was offline. Cold dread sliced him in two. He had to get to town before she changed her appearance and got away for good.

As he made for the door, Axel's phone dinged. "Wait. We have an issue."

Stone froze. "What?"

"Heath says Canton was inside the Walmart where he dropped Lily off. She looked shaken when she came out. He followed her."

Stone couldn't breathe. He'd failed her, totally fucking blown it by letting anyone come between them. He'd wanted her to calm down; then he'd hoped to explain the situation to her again and that she would choose him. Or at least forgive him. He'd thought for sure Canton couldn't find her that quickly or easily, that she'd be all right for an hour or two. The risk had been too big, and now he regretted it like hell.

"I have to go right fucking now." Stone grabbed his keys and left everything else behind.

"But wait. Heath says now that a Good Samaritan gave her a lift. A woman with a baby."

That news cut through a bit of his panic, unwinding some of the knots in his gut. "So she's safe?"

"It looks that way for now. Heath said the woman drove away too quickly for him to follow, though. I'll ask him about a license plate."

Before he could finish tapping out the text, Stone's phone dinged. One-Mile finally responded. The only message was a picture of a license plate. Text followed. Your girl got away from the dirtbag and escaped in this car. I'm following them now.

"I've got the plate." Stone told Axel. "I don't have a goddamn computer here. We need to run this number. It's from California."

Axel froze. "A coincidence?"

That bugged the shit out of him. "I don't believe in them. Fuck."

His head raced. Who the hell could he call? Who would know . . . He prowled through his contacts and hit Logan's number.

"Hey, fucker, I'm still not talking to you after that Dilbert thing," the former SEAL grumbled after one ring.

Stone didn't bother with the banter. "Lily left the cabin and jumped into an unfamiliar car. I need to know who it's registered to before she disappears."

"I'm not good with—"

"I'm calling to ask for your wife. I didn't know how to contact Tara directly."

"Send me the info. I'll find her and call you right back when I've got something."

Relief poured through Stone. Maybe all wasn't lost. One-Mile was still trailing her. They might be able to quickly identify whether this woman in the blue car was friend or foe.

"Texting it right now."

Stone forwarded One-Mile's picture, then gripped the device and waited.

"We should head out, I think," Axel suggested.

It might have been one of the few times the big bruiser hadn't tried to boss him around. "I don't give a fuck what you do but I know where I'm going. So if you don't want to be stranded here until Jack comes to fetch your ass, let's go."

Axel nodded, and they headed to the boat, Stone locking up behind him. He'd turn all the generators and breakers off later. If he even had that much of a later before heading back to prison. If not . . . Jack could handle it.

They settled into the skiff in silence, he and Axel rowing quickly through the thick, still water. It wasn't fast enough for Stone, who needed to move, to do something to find Lily faster—climb out, swim, run, whatever worked. But logic told him they were moving faster now than he could do any of those things, and he simply had to put a lid on his worry and impatience.

A minute later, Logan popped up with a message that didn't make sense at first. The name of the man to whom the vehicle was registered seemed familiar and Stone couldn't recall why.

"What?" Axel asked.

"Thinking . . . Something about this is wrong."

All of a sudden, the name made sense. The puzzle pieces slammed into place. A cold, sick dread assailed him. He felt as if someone had ripped his heart from his chest. Lily was in much more danger than he'd even imagined.

"I don't think Canton is the one trying to kill her."

Chapter Eighteen

LILY awoke, feeling dazed. As her head lolled around on her slack neck, she pried her eyes open. Sunlight pierced the sliver of space between the curtains and stabbed her eyes. She shut them, recoiled. Where was she? Why had she fallen asleep in the middle of the day?

She moaned and forced herself to look around the other side of the room. A cheap motel. Gold walls. Gray patterned bedspreads on the two double beds. A cracked plastic light fixture on the wall above them. A baby cried behind her and Lily tried to whirl around to the sound.

But she couldn't move. A startled glance down proved that she'd been restrained at the wrists and ankles to a chair with zip ties. Fear cut through the vestiges of sleep and jolted her wide-awake. Adrenaline surged through her racing blood and pumping heart.

The last time she'd been tied to a chair, everything had ended badly.

Lily sat up, blinked. This couldn't be happening. How? Why? But as she tugged and pulled, trying to loosen the restraints at her wrists and ankles, she couldn't deny that her ordeal was all too real—and terrifying. If she couldn't wriggle free, maybe she could get on her feet, chair and all, and walk out. But when she tried to stand, the clunky chair felt bulky. Drugs still weighed down every muscle and surged through her veins. She managed to wobble upright for a few seconds before her quivering muscles gave out. Exhausted and clammy, she sagged back down.

Who would do this to her? No one she knew would be irresponsible enough to restrain a sub and leave her unsupervised. Any good Dominant knew—

Suddenly she remembered the Walmart. Canton. The woman with the baby. That was the fussy infant she'd heard moments ago.

The afternoon's events rushed back to her, especially the blonde— a stranger—saying that she and her husband were worse than Timothy Canton.

Panic gripped her chest, stole her breath. What the hell had she gotten into? In trying to escape one evil, she'd fallen prey to another. Lily wasn't precisely sure what this woman and her husband had planned, but they probably intended to end their day with her horrific death.

A door behind her opened. To the bathroom? The faucet turned on, and a female voice called to the baby. "Pretty Isabel. No crying, little love. Mommy will be right there."

The water turned off. A moment later, the baby's fussy groans quieted to a staccato pout; then Emma—if that was really her name— appeared in Lily's line of vision with the baby on her hip and a sneer on her pretty face. "I'm glad you're awake. My husband just texted. He'll be here soon."

"How do you know about Canton? What do you want with me?"

"No." She shook her head. "I'm not telling you anything. I promised my husband I would let him explain. He's waited for this day for years. I won't take the joy of his vengeance from him, you traitorous whore."

Lily blinked at the woman, trying to figure her out. She'd never seen Emma in her life. Was she just crazy? Had they mistaken her for someone else?

"You must have the wrong person. I haven't slept with anyone you should be angry about. I don't think—"

"I know who you are, Lily Taylor. And you're going to get what's coming to you. Finally." She kissed the top of her daughter's head and soothed her with a brush of her fingers. "I'm hoping that my husband will finally have some peace. He's had nightmares for years. You drove him to violence and rage. He's got PTSD. And a gaping hole in his life—because of you."

What the hell was this woman talking about? "Do I know your husband?"

"And you're stupid, too," Emma scoffed. "I'd love to unload all my anger on you. He has the potential to be such a good man and you've just . . . reduced him to depression and anxiety. I came up with this plan, hoping that it will help to cure him. Nothing else has. Counseling? Ha. A waste of time and money. He didn't need to talk about his feelings; he needs to act on them. That's how men are, you know?"

No, Lily really had no idea what Emma referred to. "There has to be some mistake. I've never willingly hurt anyone in my life."

"Oh, look at you, all doe-eyed and sad-faced. You can't sway me, bitch. Canton may think that paying you off is the way to make the past disappear, and he'll get his comeuppance shortly. He's definitely earned it. But you're going to pay for your treachery first. And we're going to make you an example of why he should be very, very afraid." Emma's evil smile flashed wide, transmitting her obvious anticipation for whatever torture they had planned.

"How do you know Canton?"

She shook her head. "Oh, I've never met him, but I've heard plenty. If any man deserves to die horribly, it's him."

"So . . . your husband is upset about something he thinks I did as a teenager?"

If it had to do with Canton, her "misdeed" must have been then. She hadn't had dealings with the man since. And the most terrible contact she'd ever had with him had been the deaths of everyone she loved.

"Upset?" she shrieked. "Upset? No, upset is what happens when someone takes the last toothpick at a diner or steals your cab in the rain. What Canton did *ruined* my poor husband. It destroyed him."

Lily couldn't deny that Canton had run the neighborhood without mercy and made a lot of enemies, so Emma's rant didn't narrow things down for her much. A lot of people hated the man. But she had no idea what that had to do with her. "I'm sorry to hear that. If you can help me understand who your husband is and what happened, I'll do my best to talk to him when he gets here. Maybe we can find a way to heal him together."

Emma looked as if she was itching to spew another tirade, but she clamped her mouth shut. "I'm not saying another word, and you can't talk your way out of this. Don't ask me questions. I'm already plenty annoyed that I had to wait around for days for you to crawl out of that swamp. I thought we were never going to get you away from all those big, protective guys you spread your legs for. But then you strolled through Walmart like you thought you were untouchable." The woman's laugh chilled her with its malicious fervor. "I can't wait for you to find out how wrong you were."

So yet another person knew she'd been in the swamp. As for the men she'd spread her legs for, Emma must be alluding to Stone and Axel. *Or,* Lily wondered, *am I trying in vain to decipher a crazy woman's ramblings?* Maybe, but Emma didn't sound insane as much as righteously mad.

"How did you know where I fled after I left California?"

"Please." Emma rolled her eyes. "We'd already narrowed down that you were somewhere in Texas, but my husband found you the minute you bought that gun. He has friends. Really dangerous ones. You'll meet them soon." She grinned. "The second you decided that you needed to protect yourself, he was all over you. We've been following you, more or less, ever since."

If she had stayed in the swamp, she would have been safe. True, she couldn't have lived there forever, but leaving abruptly, without being certain of her safety, should be a good life lesson for her about acting emotionally. She'd simply wanted to flee the pain and hadn't thought the situation through. Lily already knew she would probably pay the price for letting her heartbreak rule her brain. At the time, the thought of being forced to look at—not to mention share a bed with—a man who thought nothing of digging into her soul while he stabbed her in the back had been unfathomable. Now she wanted so desperately to see Stone and tell him that, despite everything, she still had feelings for him that ran heart-deep.

Whatever else he'd done, Stone had done his best to heal her so she could go on. He'd tried hard to repair the damage to her psyche, her backbone, and her sexuality. Until this morning, she'd believed he had the most beautiful soul she'd ever encountered. He'd certainly reached her on a level no other human being in her life ever had.

Was that why his betrayal hurt her more than anyone else's?

Irrelevant now. She had to focus on getting out of these binds and escaping before Emma's husband put in an appearance. Clearly, she was safe until he arrived because the woman wasn't going to steal the glee of hurting and killing her from the man.

Lily's thoughts raced, and she tried to think of something to say that might lure the woman into giving her information that could help her out of this danger or enable her to confront the husband when he arrived, but she heard a pounding on the door.

Startled, she gasped. Please god, let that be a miracle—someone come to save her. Because she had no idea how she was going to get out of this mess herself.

Emma walked past her with a wide, sinister smile and headed for the front of the room. "I'll bet that's the party arriving." She opened the door a crack, then gave a little squeal of delight, unlatched the chain, and threw the portal open wide. "Hi, Dan. So glad you're here!"

The tall, tatted guy sporting ink sleeves on both arms and more signs on his neck and shaved skull hugged her in return and grinned. "Hi, little sis."

Sis? Lily stared. So Dan wasn't Emma's husband? Apparently not. Maybe this guy was one of the "dangerous friends" the blonde had mentioned earlier.

The big guy went on. "I drove the rest of the trek from Cali last night. Your earlier text said the guest of honor was here, and I came running." Then he turned on Lily a startlingly pale pair of eyes that stared through her while conveying a terrifying love of violence. That expression shook her to her core. "Look, she's already afraid. This should be fun." He turned when he saw the motel room's door gaping open. "Shut that. You don't want anyone seeing what we're up to."

"Oh, right." Emma gave him a dizzy little smile. "I'm just so excited."

"Me, too. I found a hardware store in this Podunk town and brought some of the things you said you needed."

"Good. Walmart was picked over. Thanks."

"No sweat." When he held up a plastic bag Lily hadn't previously noticed, Emma grabbed it out of his hands and shifted the baby into his arms. "And, of course, I had to come see my little Isabel. Hi, pumpkin girl. Did you miss Uncle Danny?" He cooed, gently stroking the baby's cheek and making her flash a smile that showed off her two bottom teeth. "I think you did."

Lily took the sight in. If he could be that warm and gentle with a baby, there might be hope for her, right? She really prayed that whatever plot these people had in mind wasn't half as bad as her imaginings.

Then Emma began to pull items from the hardware store bag. "You remembered the tarp! That's one of the most important items. I can't believe I forgot it."

"And I got you the big one because I know this is going to get messy, and we don't want to risk stains." Dan swiveled his gaze in Lily's direction and sent her a chilling grin.

She shuddered. Oh god. His gentleness with the baby definitely did not extend to her. Lily had an inkling that whatever they had planned was far worse than anything she could conceive. She had to swallow down a lump of fear. What the hell did they plan to do to her that required a layer of plastic? Did she even want to know?

"Good thinking," Emma quipped. "And it's clear, too. You're awesome."

"I figured you wouldn't want anything to obscure the color of her blood."

"No, totally. That's going to be the best part, right? The pools of it?"

Another wave of terror shuddered through her, stealing her breath. She bit her lip to hold in a scream. They sounded eager to make whatever they did as gory as possible.

Oh, dear god.

"So, what else . . ." Emma reached into the bag again and pulled out more items. "Heavy-duty scissors, pliers, handheld pruning shears. And they're titanium!"

"Superstrong. Only the best for my baby sister." He smiled fondly.

Lily watched in horror. They meant to carve her up, let her bleed out. She swallowed against a rising tide of panic and tried to keep thinking of ways out.

"This could be the start of a whole new life for you, Em. Thanks for inviting me to be a part of it. I'm happy to help."

"Aww . . ." She kissed his stubbled cheek. "I can't imagine anyone I trust more."

Lily watched, utterly stunned. As if torture and murder were somehow happy occasions, like a marriage or birth? Nausea whirled in her stomach. Discreetly, she tugged at her bonds again. But they still held firm.

"We're just waiting on the others now," Emma told her brother. "Should we get set up?"

"Yeah, we can do that. Kev isn't far behind me." He frowned, and Lily wondered if that was Emma's husband's name. It didn't ring a bell. "What are you going to do with Isabel?"

"She's nearly due for her afternoon nap, so I'm planning to move her carrier into the bathroom and shut the door. I'll put on the playlist of lullabies she likes. I think she'll sleep right through it."

"Excellent." Dan nodded his approval. "Why don't you get her settled, and I'll work on these preparations?"

This room would get more crowded once another man showed up. Her ability to escape would dwindle. Lily had no idea whether Stone was trying to find her now. After everything that had happened, would he? The man had a wide protective streak but now that she'd refused to testify, did he really care what happened to her? Maybe Axel still had a bead on her phone, but since she'd turned it off back in the Walmart parking lot, he wouldn't be able to locate her. If he checked, he would see her last location but have no idea she was barely half a mile up the road, surrounded by bloodthirsty savages.

Emma moved to the back of the cheap, stale space, ostensibly taking the baby with her. The bathroom door clicked shut. The air-conditioning unit below the window rattled, but the faint strains of "Brahms' Lullaby" bleeding through the thin walls rose above it. Then Dan added his own sounds as he shook out the plastic tarp designed to catch her blood.

Lily scanned her surroundings again. What could she do? Say? Offer? Would anything persuade the man currently tearing the stiff sheets and threadbare blanket off the bed to let her go? As she watched him cover the stained mattress with the new tarp, she highly doubted it.

"Don't do this." The pleading words slipped past her lips. "I never hurt your sister. I don't even know her. I'll give you anything."

He swiveled his head around to pierce her with that eerie gaze, colorless brows raised in challenge. "You've taken more away from Emma than you could possibly know, you selfish cunt. And there's nothing you can give me that I won't just take for the fun of it." He leered, looking her up and down with a cruel half smile. "I hope you're a screamer."

Terror exploded in her belly. He didn't plan to simply kill her. No, he intended to extract a pound of flesh first by forcing himself on her. Lily swallowed bile. God, she knew what rape looked like, had a terrible suspicion how horrific the experience would be. She'd never forgotten the unspeakable violation Erin had endured before Canton and his goons had ended her life.

In some ways, Lily wished Dan and whoever else Emma was waiting for would skip ahead to the quick death. At least then she'd find relief from the pain and humiliation her attackers plotted to heap on her while they forced themselves on her body, her mind. But death meant she would have lost her dignity and her battle with these animals. Lily refused to be a quitter.

She wanted to live.

Another pounding on the door sounded through the little room, and Dan straightened up from the bed with a jump in his step. He weaved around her chair and whapped her cheek with a mocking slap. It stung more than a little as he sprinted for the door and opened it a crack. "Kev!"

He pulled the door wide, and the newcomer laughed. "Danny Boy, let me in. I'm ready to get this party started. Where is she?"

Dan stepped back, and Lily got her first view of Kev. Toweringly tall, the guy had muscles on top of his muscles. His olive complexion and nearly black eyes made him appear Hispanic or Italian. He wore denim loose around his hips and a leather jacket with lots of zippers.

"I also brought my favorite toy." He pulled a blade from his back pocket, something wicked and serrated and capable of slicing flesh with frightening ease. Then he turned to her and held it up in her face. "What do you think, little girl?"

Lily shrank back and couldn't stop the whimpers that escaped her throat.

Kev shut the door and pocketed the blade again, then rubbed his hands together as if he couldn't wait. "You look pretty when you're scared."

"She does," Dan agreed as he came closer and dragged his fingertips over her chest, down the valley between her breasts, before he landed a surprisingly harsh slap on her mound. Despite his striking her through her clothing, the sting reverberated through her body and turned her blood to ice.

Against her will, she cried out. She desperately sought to close her legs and cover her chest with her arms but Emma had restrained her well. Lily couldn't move, couldn't do anything to protect herself at all.

The blonde poked her head out of the bathroom, hand on hip, expression annoyed. "Hey, no starting early. And try to keep it down for another ten minutes. Isabel is settling down."

Dan held up his hands. "Sure, sis. Sorry. But Lily is going to be loud. Did you say you booked the rooms on either side of this one?"

"Yep. And the one directly below, too. Thankfully, a flash of cleavage and cash kept the old guy behind the desk from asking many questions. Finish getting ready and let me get the baby to sleep. Hi, Kev. Good to see you. It's been a while."

"Yes, ma'am. You, too."

So Kev wasn't Emma's husband, either. Which meant they were expecting a third man to join their "party."

When the bathroom door shut again, Kev ignored her. Dan checked the tarp on the bed, smoothing it flat and tucking it under. Then he stripped off his tank top, exposing an expanse of pale skin riddled with scars, some from a blade, others round and symmetrical like bullet wounds. Along one side of his back, the texture of his skin was uneven and lined, as if he'd been in a motorcycle accident. He'd tried to cover most of the marks with ink.

Beside him, Kev peeled off his jacket, revealing a fair number of open scabs. His teeth looked as if they were beginning to rot. She'd bet anything he was addicted to meth.

Lily shrank back in her seat. She wanted to close her eyes and divorce herself from reality. She wanted to release her consciousness and soul from her body so she didn't have to be aware of the awful end as it came. But to do that would be to accept that death was inevitable, and she refused to concede that. She might not have a lot to look forward to right now, but she had so much life left to live. She had laughter to share, love to give, things to learn, mistakes to make. She had heart and wit and compassion.

Someday she would find a man who would truly want to share all those with her. Deep down, past her hurt, she wished it would be Stone.

But in order to have that, Lily couldn't bury her head in the sand now. She had to wage the battle of her life. Maybe she didn't deserve a future, but she would fight for hers until her very last breath. If Stone had taught her anything over these past few days, it was that fear of something was actually more terrifying than the thing itself. She had to stop being afraid of everyone and everything—even death—if she wanted to live.

And if she somehow managed to escape, she would confront Stone. She would visit Regina's grave. She would see every one of these people willing to torture her put behind bars, and she would testify against Canton, too. She would avenge Erin, her mom, and her little brother. She would be unwavering and fierce.

The resolve gave Lily something to look forward to and made her feel stronger.

The two men swept everything off the nightstand and began to line up the implements of torture on the dark laminate surface. A shiver rolled through Lily, but she focused on her breathing and shoved her terror into a compartment she'd open later. It would do her no good now. At the moment, she had to use her head.

There was no way to escape this chair until they unfastened her restraints. If they were preparing the bed for the next phase of their plan, they would free her at some point. She'd have to make a run for it then. Yes, they had a row of sharp objects nearby, but Lily could grab one. She also spotted her purse strewn haphazardly on the chair near the door. If she could grab it and get to her gun, maybe she could shoot her way outside. Maybe someone would hear or see her and call for help. Or she could turn on her phone, dial 911, and hope that someone willing to help her was still tracking the device.

If she could get her hands and feet free, she'd surprise them and fight to the death.

A soft click at the back of the room sounded like the bathroom door. The faint sounds of classical music still filtered through the walls. Lily heard a feminine sigh of satisfaction.

"Isabel is asleep. Since she missed her morning nap, I'm thinking we'll have a good two or three hours with this bitch."

"Oh, a lot of fun, then." Dan whooped with excitement as a big smile spread across his face. "Did you get booze?"

"I did. Drink?" She bustled around in the background, then headed toward the two men, bottle in hand.

Dan grabbed it from his sister, and Kev crowded in to wrench the cap off. Emma darted away again, then returned, this time with murky lowball-style glasses in hand.

"Ice?" Kev asked.

"I didn't get any," Emma said. "I was too busy with this whore. She was a lot of trouble to wrestle up the stairs, even half-conscious."

Lily had no memory of that and wished like hell that she'd had the presence of mind to struggle or run or cry for help. But everything was blank after the needle in her arm.

"No big deal. I'll drink it as is. It still burns going down, right?" Kev grinned.

The men both poured liquid from the bottle, then set it down. Wild Turkey, according to the label. Lily only had the vaguest idea what kind of liquor it was, but it looked smoky and hard and more than capable of intoxicating a person. It would dim what few inhibitions these lunatics had.

They both jumped when Kev's phone buzzed.

"Oh, shit, bro," Dan guffawed. "That startled me."

"Right?" Kev pulled the device from his pocket and read whatever was on the screen. "Oh, sweet! My neighbor's kid just got out of juvie. It's probably his last trip since he turns eighteen in a few weeks, but Emma said she needed one more and this kid loves a piece of unwilling ass and some blood. So I invited him."

"Good job, man. The symmetry is perfect." Dan clapped him on the back.

Symmetry? Lily wracked her brain, but that comment didn't make sense. All she knew was that the juvenile wasn't Emma's husband, either. She would be tied and helpless while four men, one just shy of eighteen, meant to rape and kill her.

Just like Erin.

The truth slammed into her just as the whoosh of the key card in the lock sounded and the door opened. A face from the past appeared, almost obscured under the blue bill of a Dodgers cap. His dark eyes zeroed in on her with a glaring smile of evil.

Corey Gutierrez. Erin's older brother. A guy she had once considered her friend.

Now he was her enemy come to exact revenge.

"There you are!" Emma said, shutting the portal behind her, then leaned toward Corey for a kiss. "Hi, baby. How was your trip to Iowa?"

He was Emma's husband. He supposedly suffered rage, PTSD, depression, and fits of violence. Because of Erin's murder?

"Successful." He grinned. "Turns out Reaper was cheating on his wife when I found him. What an asshole. So I sent him to meet his Maker with a bullet between the eyes. Mom drove out to see me afterward so I could let her know about the progress I'm making with our plans. She sends her love, by the way. She wants to come down for Thanksgiving."

Renee knew about Corey's murders and condoned them? Lily blinked, horrified.

"Great." Emma gave him a proud smile. "So how did it feel?"

"To shoot Reaper? To see his shock and watch the life leave his eyes? Amazing. I can't even describe . . . But this one will feel even better, more personal." He glared at Lily, then took his wife's hand. "You have the best ideas. Is the baby okay?"

"She's fine. Sleeping in the bathroom. We were just getting ready for the . . . festivities." Emma giggled. "And waiting for you."

"Well, I'm here and ready to get this party started." Corey's smirk turned vicious. "Hello, Lily. This has been a long time coming. Ready to experience everything my sister did when you brought those killers to her bed?"

Chapter Nineteen

As Stone raced toward Lafayette, he gripped the wheel tightly. He had been so focused on Timothy Canton that he hadn't seen Corey Gutierrez coming. Hell, Erin's brother being her tormentor had never occurred to Stone. But revenge made perfect sense. An eye for an eye. And since Lily knew precisely what Erin's death had been like, she must be utterly terrified right now.

He thought of all the times he'd held her as she trembled, as she struggled over mental obstacles, fighting assailants who hadn't touched her and she could no longer see, but had scarred her psyche all the same. Now those men would be all too real. For years, Lily had been the sort to flee, not fight. She'd crawled into her shell, as if atoning for having survived that day. She'd let those monsters rob her of what might have been a bright future. Stone prayed she didn't do that now. He hoped like hell that she clawed and bit and screamed—whatever it took to survive.

If he'd helped her realize her mental strength and it gave her the confidence to retaliate so she could take another breath, Stone would count himself blessed. Even if she couldn't forgive him for ever considering Bankhead's deal. Even if she never spoke to him again. Even if he spent the rest of his life pining for her, he'd still be eternally grateful.

At his side, Axel looked tense, staring out the window. "How much longer?"

"Fifteen minutes."

In the taut silence, it was terribly clear that both men knew that fifteen minutes could be fourteen minutes and fifty-nine seconds too long. Stone pressed a little harder on the gas pedal.

"I can't sit here and do nothing." Axel picked up his phone and began dialing. "Jack!" he barked when Cole's voice sounded over the speaker. "Emergency. Lily has been taken. Get me everything you know about Corey Gutierrez. He's probably somewhere here in Lafayette. Or he was less than an hour ago."

"He's the one after her?"

"Yeah. Heath and One-Mile both saw Canton leave her untouched and watched as a woman they've never seen drove away with Lily. The car was registered to Gutierrez. Heath was on foot and lost them. One-Mile followed, but we haven't heard from him in a while. He isn't answering his phone, and I hope that's not bad news. We need another way to catch this asshole before it's too late."

"I'm still on it. I poked around at his background a couple of days ago but I'll focus there now. Hang on." Jack tapped a few keys. "I should hear something soon on that inquiry. The guy owes me a favor."

"I'll send you the plate number. It's from California. We've got to track that car down. It's our best hope of finding her in time. Can you call the cops there in Lafayette?"

Anxiety bit into Stone's gut. He counted himself lucky that he knew people willing to help find Lily and bring her home alive. But he didn't want to have to wait for Jack or anyone else to rescue Lily. He just wanted her safe and sound—preferably in his arms.

Before Jack could answer, Stone's phone on the console beside him buzzed. As he swerved around an elderly couple taking a leisurely drive, he scooped it up, heart racing. He hoped to fuck it was Lily.

A glance at the screen dashed that hope. "One-Mile says he followed a woman with a baby taking Lily, who looked sleepy or drugged, into a motel room. He's been trying to get the sitch since. Three men have entered in the last few minutes, the first with a bulging bag from a hardware store." That made Stone's guts knot up. "The second one sauntered in waving a knife in her face. Jesus! The third wore a Dodgers cap." The guy on the balcony at Lily's apartment building? Again, Stone didn't believe in coincidences. "Why the fuck didn't One-Mile barge into the room or shoot everyone on their way in?"

"It's a public motel." Axel scowled. "First, you don't know what room someone is entering until they've actually gone inside. There's all kinds of hell to pay for shooting an innocent bystander. Second, if they're smart, they've drawn the drapes. If that's the case, One-Mile can't see inside to shoot the bad guys. And he can't barge into a motel room without knowing who's there and lacking backup or any idea what he should be prepared for. It could get both him and Lily killed quickly."

Stone didn't like it but he grasped the concept. "One-Mile has taken up position on the roof of the Philadelphia Christian Church off of 167."

Axel frowned. "If he's on the roof, he's reconnoitering from his sniper position and is waiting to take them out as they exit. What's near that church?"

Stone hadn't paid that much attention to the places of worship since he'd come to town. It sounded familiar, but he couldn't place it.

"It's right next door to the Royal Inn, a scuzzy little motel with a name that's way loftier than its reputation," Jack informed them.

"Taking Lily to a no-tell motel would make sense." Stone snapped in the direction of Axel's phone, despite being worried out of his fucking mind. Still, he had to focus and stay calm for her sake. "Gutierrez isn't from around here. He'd need someplace to take Lily where people could come and go in a pretty transient fashion without raising too many questions. He'd want a bed." And a place to restrain her so he could do his worst. "And he won't be alone."

Do you have any way to reach her? he tapped back to One-Mile with one hand on the wheel.

To his shock, One-Mile actually began to respond. The three tiny dots in the text bubble said he would get an answer, but it seemed to take forever while anxiety gnawed at Stone's composure.

If I did, would I be wasting my time texting you?

"What is he saying?" Axel asked.

Stone gritted his teeth and shoved the phone in Axel's face so he could read for himself.

"Ask One-Mile if he knows anything else pertinent to the sitrep," Axel insisted. "We don't have a minute to waste."

"No shit. You think I'm not entirely fucking aware of that? That knowing every passing moment could be Lily's last isn't utterly dismantling me?" Stone snarled. "Hold the wheel."

Once his big passenger had a firm grip, Stone pulled up the text message and replied. There in less than 10. Do you have Lily's exact position? What else do you see?

Again, One-Mile answered promptly. Royal Inn on 167. Facing church. Second floor. Can't see anything. Drapes drawn. Looks dangerous. Get here.

At the man's reply, Stone tried to stay calm. At least he knew where to find Lily. They couldn't leave the room without One-Mile seeing. Problem was, Stone wasn't worried about them escorting Lily from the building. He was concerned that when they opened the door again, it would be to dump her body somewhere. One-Mile might be a great sniper, but he couldn't start shooting through a covered window without potentially hitting Lily. And if Gutierrez's wife was still inside, it was possible the baby was in the room, too.

How long has she been in there? Stone typed back to One-Mile.

10. No more texting unless emergency. Concentrating.

No doubt about it, One-Mile was a douche—exactly like Stone thought when he'd first met the guy. But he also couldn't argue. As much as he wanted information that might help him understand what Lily was enduring and how he might best rescue her, he didn't want to distract the sniper from such a critical task.

Raking a hand over the stubble covering his scalp, he blew out a breath and turned to Axel, who shouted into his phone as he relayed One-Mile's information.

"Got it," Jack said. "I've got some cop friends. I'll call them. If you get there first, do what you need to do and they'll help you out. I'm on my way. I'll see if I can ping the Edgington brothers for backup."

Stone didn't bother commenting, and he heard the call end. Beside him, Axel cursed.

"This shit is going to be over in fifteen minutes," Dominion's security officer said, concern darkening his voice.

One way or the other. "Yeah."

Axel reached for his phone again. "We need a plan. No one is better at that shit than Heath."

Had Axel come fucking unhinged? "He lost her!"

"She was on foot, so he ditched the flashy white SUV to follow. He didn't expect her to get in someone's car." Axel sighed. "And don't you ever tell the fucker I defended him."

Stone didn't want to argue or joke. He just wanted Lily back. Axel was right about the fact that they needed a plan. His head started whirling with possibilities. He discarded as many as he considered almost as quickly as they popped into his head. How could they get into that room without startling Corey and his posse? He didn't want them to panic and ice her before he could get close enough to pull her out alive.

In the near silence of his truck's cab, Stone heard the ringing as Axel called Heath. The Brit answered almost immediately, his voice sounding clipped over the speakerphone. "I'm still looking. I know she left the parking lot with that woman and her baby."

"The Royal Inn," Axel supplied.

"Brilliant. Popular place today. A woman approached Canton in the parking lot and flirted. I'm guessing she gave him a sex invite and they headed there as well."

Stone heard every word. That seemed awfully coincidental. He didn't believe it for an instant.

"At least if Canton is getting his jollies with a stranger, he can't be hurting Lily," Heath offered.

Axel gave the Brit the lay of the land, explaining that the woman in the Walmart was probably Corey Gutierrez's wife, who was apparently helping him mastermind and execute his revenge against everyone who had anything to do with his sister's death. In fact, he'd bet the woman who picked Canton up was a plant, too. And that Corey intended to dust the gubernatorial hopeful ASAP.

The internal *ticktock* of each passing second pounded Stone's chest like the blow of a hammer. He didn't want to think about what would happen if he didn't get there in time, but as the miles between the swamp and town whipped past, that was all he could focus on. How fucking meaningless would his life be if he couldn't save Lily? Then it really wouldn't matter if he went back to prison or they put him six feet under. Somehow she'd become his one reason to live. If Corey Gutierrez took her away, Stone would waste the asshole on the spot— gladly and with joy in his heart. Even knowing he'd go down for murder one didn't bother him. The scum who had robbed him of Lily's light and her of a promising future had to go.

Stone finally turned onto 167 from I-10. Only a couple of miles to go.

Hang on, baby. I'm coming for you . . .

"We need a fucking plan now." And this was where Stone felt at a distinct disadvantage. He'd never been a battlefield hero. Everyone around him had risked life and limb for their country, their loved ones, their pride. He'd stupidly decided to con some assholes out of money because his student loans had seemed daunting, and why would rich people miss a few bucks? "Should we have the motel management send housekeeping up there to knock on the door and stall them?"

Even as he spoke the words, he knew it was a bad idea.

"No!" Axel and Jack, via phone, said almost instantly.

"They could panic and kill Lily," Axel explained.

"Or whoever knocks on the door. Or both," Jack added.

Axel nodded. "We don't want to spook Corey and his cohorts. We don't want to give them any reason to be suspicious. It needs to be a clean takedown."

"It sure would help if we could find some way to persuade them to open that fucking curtain so One-Mile could get a shot in there and disrupt them, maybe pick off one or two," Jack said just before Stone heard a ding over the line and the rough Cajun swore. "We're in deep fucking shit. Corey Gutierrez was MARSOC."

"What?" Stone asked, worry tightening every muscle because Jack made that sound bad. "What does that mean?"

Axel winced. "Marine Corps Special Operations Command. It means he's a determined motherfucker with ice water in his veins and he's probably done some nasty-ass missions in his time."

"What he said," Jack agreed. "It means he's not some street thug without serious skills. He's going to be well-prepared and thorough."

That worry in Stone's belly turned to acid as it rolled and pitched, eating away at his insides. "We have to be better."

No one argued that point as he passed the Dollar Tree on the right.

"But according to the report I just received, Gutierrez was discharged a few months ago for 'adjustment disorders,' which is the military way of saying he has psychological problems, and they wanted him gone. That fact and his special ops background explains why it took me a while to track his service down."

It sucked but none of that mattered now. Stone could see the ugly blue sign for the Royal Inn up ahead. He didn't want to have hauled ass the last thirty-five fucking miles to get here, then dither about what to do.

"Plan, guys?" he shouted. "We need one now, or I'm parking this sucker and busting in that door, guns blazing."

"Then you'll get dead," Axel pointed out in annoyance.

Stone shrugged. "If it saves Lily, I don't really give a shit."

* * *

LILY couldn't imagine a worse nightmare. A guy she'd always thought of as a friend and big brother meant to kill her. No, not just kill her. Violate her in every possible way, then cut her into tiny ribbons and let her bleed out while he reveled.

"I didn't know they were following me when I went to the warehouse that day, Corey. I tried to call you and ask you what you wanted me to do but—"

The sharp rebuke on Corey's face told Lily that casting any blame on him would only make her death more harsh.

Did he feel terrible guilt about his sister dying because he'd been stupid and desperate enough to get into dealing drugs for Canton? Because he'd talked to the police? Was he unable to handle the reality that he'd also been at fault? Likely, which was why he found it easier to cast blame on the girl who'd inadvertently given away Erin's hiding place.

Corey had always had a weak side, enjoyed using drugs more than facing reality. He'd left his mom and sister to fend for themselves once the police had released him after his arrest. He must have known when he talked to the cops about Canton's operation that it would get back to the vicious street boss. No way Corey couldn't know that punishment would come, swift and severe.

"Erin was perfectly safe until you came along. I'll bet they threatened to cut that baby out of your belly and kill you, you dumb whore. I heard later that you had a stillborn." Corey's lips stretched wide, something big and ugly that celebrated her total devastation. "Couldn't happen to a more deserving bitch. And when the pigs came looking for you because you knew something about Erin's murder? I reminded one of Canton's underlings that your mom and little brother were just waiting at home and that you should be taught a valuable lesson about silence."

Lily shrank back in her chair and stared at Corey with absolute horror. At one time, she would have trusted him implicitly. She'd shared meals with him. When she'd been pregnant and scared, he'd promised to hold her hand in the delivery room. Heck, he'd once even given her the shirt off his back after her ex-boyfriend had ripped hers during a fight.

And now he meant to kill her.

The shock of that rippled through her. For years, she'd been imagining that Corey, like her, struggled with grief. She'd always hoped she would see him someday, when she got the courage to go back to California, visit everyone's graves, and make peace with the past. She'd pictured running into Corey and finally sharing her sorrow with the only other person she'd been close to who'd also loved Erin unconditionally.

"They were innocent!" she protested.

"So was my sister. In every sense of the word. I made sure no one touched Erin and knocked her up, like you. The one person I trusted, the girl I thought would always have her back. You cunt. You sacrificed her to save your own skin." He loomed over her menacingly and raised the back of his hand to her face. "I should have seen you for the cowardly traitor you are."

Though she knew it was futile, Lily couldn't help herself. Even if Corey never believed her and it didn't save her life, he needed to hear the words. She had to tell her truth.

"I didn't trade my safety for hers," she insisted. But he'd clearly expected her to choose her best friend's life over her own and her baby's. Would she have made that choice? Could she? Even before going into labor, her instinct to protect Regina had been unshakable. But Corey blamed her when he hadn't stayed around to protect those most vulnerable in his life. He'd gone into hiding and saved himself.

"You're a fucking liar," he growled.

Lily shook her head. "Mafia followed me after school. I told him I didn't know anything but Erin was like my sister, too. Maybe I should have guessed that they wouldn't believe me. But you didn't hang around to protect her. You left her at their mercy. You left her to die." Tears trembled at her lash line, threatening to spill.

"Shut the fuck up," Corey snarled, looking ready to commit murder right now.

"No." If she was going to die anyway, she was going to get everything out in the open. "I loved Erin. I mourned. I still miss her every day, along with the rest of my family. Having them taken from me left a hole in my chest I can never fill. The last conversation I had with my mom was an ugly fight, and now I will never be able to repair it. You took that from me."

Even if her mom had washed her hands of her only daughter and hadn't known how to mother a headstrong girl, the woman had given birth to her, fed her, probably even loved her at some point. She and her brother had been super close. And they were both lost to her forever because of this man.

"I can't believe you suggested their murder to Canton." She stared at him like the monster he'd become. "What happened to you?"

"I *said*, shut the fuck up." Corey flushed with fury before he backhanded her across the face.

Lily's head snapped to one side. Her cheek exploded. Pain bloomed. She tasted blood on her tongue.

None of that was going to stop her.

"No. You fucking listen," she shot back. "Not only did I lose Erin, you took what was left of my family. Then my baby girl died. Imagine Isabel slipping away before you'd even gotten to hold her. I clutched Regina's corpse wrapped in a pink blanket for five minutes before they took her from me. I already loved her so much and I cried because she would never know me at all. So how dare you think you were the only one to suffer?"

Anguish and terror steamrolled Lily, crushing her heart already bruised by the seeming betrayal she'd endured from Stone and everyone she'd met since moving to Dallas. The tears she'd shoved down inside her for too many years stung her eyes, nearly closed her throat. They rose, refusing to be denied, and began to fall. Corey would see them as a weakness or a plea, and she didn't care. They were her tribute to those she'd loved, the proof she was still human and cared. They were healing.

Even if she didn't have the chance to shed any more tears before death and no one else saw them, she'd know she'd finally let go of the pain and grief and fear that had held her back for seven bleak years. She released it all and sobbed. The hot tears lashing her face felt like the most lovely, delicate pain. With her hands bound, she couldn't wipe them away—and she didn't want to. She let them flow, felt the dam of so much latent grief release. Terrible time for this emotional breakthrough. But then again, despite her best efforts, she might not have a tomorrow.

As she tasted the salt of her tears, she wished Stone could see her now. Even if he didn't love her, he'd cared at least a little, right? He'd looked after her in so many ways. He'd be proud that she'd finally freed her anguish.

"The heartbreak I felt over her loss almost killed me," Lily choked.

"In a week, everyone I had ever cared about died or disappeared. I was shocked and alone. And yet I still worried about *you*. I even tried to find you. And all the while, you were indicting me in your mind, deciding that I'd committed something like treason and I deserved torture and death. All of this—Erin's death, your misery, *my* misery—it's your doing."

This was the real betrayal in her life, Lily realized. Not Stone's. Corey befriending her, seeming to care about her, being close enough to share a past and secrets—then plotting to harm her *after* they'd established trust and affection. What Stone had done, agreed to a deal that exchanged her testimony for his freedom, he'd done before he truly knew her. People sometimes found themselves forced to make difficult choices. Those decisions defined who they were as people, the moral makeup of their character. Corey had proven his was every inch rotten. He blamed everyone else for the misfortune he'd begun. Lily didn't completely blame him for dealing drugs. He'd had so few choices as a kid trying to keep a roof over his family's head and food in their mouths. But for leaving them to fend for themselves when Canton had turned his vengeful heat on them? Yeah, no one else was to blame more in this situation than Corey.

"Oh, boohoo," Kev mocked.

"Shut the fuck up," Dan sneered.

"I can't listen to you whine anymore," Corey growled. "We're getting started now. And the first thing I'm cutting out is your tongue."

"Sweetheart," Emma ventured. "Before you get too busy, Jacinda has Canton in the room downstairs. I think she's currently blowing him, but if you want to drug him so we can have fun with him later . . ."

"You didn't do it?"

"You said you wanted to."

Corey sighed with impatience and shoved a fall of dark hair out of his face. "Damn it. All right."

"Hey, I'll go," Kev volunteered, his brows waggling in a leer. "I want to see how hot my woman looks giving this dude head. Maybe she'd be willing to do us both before we cut his dick off and blow his brains out."

"Good thinking." Corey nodded. "While you're gone, we'll get this slut stripped and tied down to the bed. She needs to start paying."

"I'll knock when I'm back." Kev crossed the room.

Emma followed him, opening the door for him. Lily looked at the blue sky and the beckoning golden sun for those few precious seconds. The other woman dead-bolted the door behind him, shutting Lily in the dark again with a roomful of psychos.

Her tears had slowed. She felt cleansed. And ready to fight. If she didn't succeed . . . well, she was also ready to face whatever came next.

As Emma crossed the room, she lifted her face to Corey for a kiss. He slipped off his shoes and absently brushed a peck on his waiting wife's lips, like today was a normal day for an average married couple.

He and Dan would soon detach her from the chair to move her to the mattress, and Lily knew that might be her only opportunity to escape. She studied the room again. The door was a good six or seven steps away. Kev had longer legs and it had taken him four to reach the handle. Her purse fell into a similar category. A bit closer, but maybe too far to run before someone caught her. That meant she was going to have to fight her way out of this room with her bare hands if she wanted to survive.

And she did—so very much. Not just because the imperative to live beat strong in her chest and raced fast through her veins. She wanted more from life. To laugh and cry and love. She wanted to see Stone, tell him she forgave him. And she hoped he understood. She wanted to see if they could have something real if she gave him her all. Could he ever love her, as he'd claimed? She ached to touch him, yearned to share tomorrow with him. And someday, god willing, she wanted to have another baby.

As Emma sat on the other bed, she stared raptly, ready to watch the live rape and murder as if it were a pay-per-view event. Corey came at Lily with the shears. He snipped them a few times in her face, laughing when she shrank back involuntarily. Then she forced herself to stop reacting, start planning.

The nightstand with the rest of those gleaming sharp implements was maybe three steps away. Still far but her best bet. She'd have to find some vulnerable spot on Corey's body and hit him before they got her to the bed. The juvenile hadn't arrived yet. Kev and his considerable muscle would only be gone a few minutes. She couldn't assume that Stone or anyone else could find her here, no matter how hard they might try.

It was now or never.

Lily swallowed as Corey cut through the zip tie securing her left ankle to the chair. He made quick work of the restraint holding her left wrist, then tossed the shears to Dan, who did the same on her right side. Together, they hoisted her to her feet.

Corey wrenched her arm behind her back, until she gasped and stood on her tiptoes to prevent him from dislocating her shoulder or breaking her arm. "Don't try anything."

Or what? He already meant to rape and kill her. Frankly, he couldn't threaten her with much worse. She might as well risk it all.

Squeezing her eyes shut and saying a prayer, she pretended to lose her balance and toppled forward. Corey automatically reached out to catch her. Before he could shove her back to her feet, Lily bit the fleshy inside of his biceps and clamped down with her teeth as hard as she possibly could. Almost instantly, she tasted his coppery blood.

He snapped his arm back to dislodge her hold and glanced at the red indentations of his wound. "Bitch."

But she wasn't listening to him. She was lunging for the nightstand, trying not to stumble. She barely managed to snatch up Kev's big serrated blade. Lily knew she only had a fraction of a second to whirl to her left and hopefully plant this blade in Corey's belly. But she'd fallen too far forward and couldn't quite get her balance quick enough to turn and defend herself. Instead, when she arced the blade through the air, she missed Corey altogether.

On her right, Dan leapt onto the bed and came at her in a full tackle. Lily screamed and managed to sidestep him at the last instant, gratified when he fell between the two beds and hit his knee on the base of the nightstand with a thud. In feinting, she ran right into Emma, who shrieked and tried to scramble away.

Corey latched onto Lily's left wrist and started tugging. This time, she was ready, twisting around to slash the blade down at him. She sliced through his forearm. A deep wound opened. Blood welled quickly and flowed from the gash.

"What the fuck?" he roared and released her to clap his hand over the wound, glaring at her as if she had done the unthinkable. "Oh, that's it, bitch. If Kev doesn't get here in the next two minutes he's going to miss your last gasp."

Lily didn't doubt that he meant every word.

When he lunged for her again, she went for the weak link, rolling onto the bed and scrambling behind Emma. The woman looked over her shoulder left and right, screeching wildly, as she tried to see the threat to her safety. Dan jumped for Lily again too, and she knew she didn't have time to be polite or gentle. Emma certainly hadn't been either of those with her. Neither would these men. So Lily grabbed the woman's long ponytail and tugged hard, exposing her throat. In the next breath, she put the blade, still wet and red with Corey's blood, against it. A drop fell onto Emma's breast and rolled into her pink tank top.

Corey and Dan both froze.

"Leave her out of this. She has nothing to do with this shit," Corey grated out.

"I'm still breastfeeding!" Emma shrieked.

Lily ignored her. "I had nothing to do with any of this shit, either. Just because you don't want to pay for your sins doesn't mean

I will. Will you make your wife pay, you selfish bastard? Then mourn her loss and blame me for wielding the blade? Yeah, you're the kind of coward who would, without admitting that I wouldn't have been here to slice her throat open if you hadn't plotted your ridiculous revenge in the first place."

"Step away from my wife and I won't kill you." Corey tried to barter.

Obviously he thought she was stupid. "Not happening. Emma and I are going to back out of the room and leave. If you make a move in my direction, I'll slice her in half."

Lily wasn't sure she could actually do it, but she had to at least threaten and bluff. And if the worst happened, she would have to try. She would also have to hope that Kev wasn't on his way back up and that his juvie friend didn't show. With luck, maybe some law-abiding citizen would see her fleeing for her life and offer aid.

Neither man said anything right away, just looked at her with wary, worried eyes. Finally Dan stepped forward. "I'll take her place. Let my sister go, and you can take me hostage."

"So you can fight back and try to manhandle or overpower me? No. Stand up, *bitch*." Lily gave Emma a taste of her own medicine.

With a high-pitched whine, the blonde rose to her feet on shaking legs. "Don't hurt me."

Lily scoffed. "If I had pleaded for your mercy ten minutes ago, you would have laughed. Luckily for you, I'm not bitter or bloodthirsty. I'm also not stupid enough to love a man capable of cold-blooded rape and murder or psycho enough to encourage him. As far as I'm concerned, you get what's coming to you. But I don't have any interest in hurting you unless you force me. Now, we're walking . . ."

As Lily sidestepped toward the door, she dragged Emma and kept her back to the wall. Her hostage served as a buffer between her and the two men watching her every move.

They neared the door. Emma stumbled, her feet tripping over each other. On purpose?

Lily caught the woman with her free hand. "Be careful. This knife is awfully sharp and you wouldn't want me to cut you by accident, would you?"

"No. No. No," Emma panted, her heart beating so hard it was a wonder everyone in the room couldn't hear it.

As Lily tugged her near the door, she reached for the dead bolt and unfastened it; then she grabbed the handle to the door with shaking fingers. A nervous sweat sprang up all over her body. Anxiety stung her veins. Her heartbeat gonged in her head. Freedom was so, so close.

Before she could open the door, she heard car doors slam in the motel's parking lot. One man shouted, the sound primal and disruptive. Another yelled back an obscenity that made her jaw drop. Seconds later, someone fired a gun.

Everyone in the motel room froze, even Lily.

"Wait. Don't . . ." Corey instructed, even pleading a little. "I don't know who's shooting out there but that's no one I know. Dan, look out the window, will you?"

Lily thought about objecting but decided if Emma's brother was peering outside at whatever mayhem was going on in the parking lot, he wasn't paying attention to her. Still, she kept sharp in case this was some sort of trick.

Dan rubbed at his knee where he'd hit it as he climbed back over the bed, sending his sister a concerned glance. She whimpered. Boy, for a woman who'd been so eager to see her sexually assaulted and ripped to shreds, Emma sure had turned mousy and squeamish at the first sign that she was in danger.

"Go on," Lily ordered Dan when he edged too close to his sister. She drew the knife tighter against the woman's throat.

Corey stepped into the space between the beds and glanced out as Dan drew the drape aside and scowled. "Five guys out there fighting. Oh, that looked like a hell of a punch."

"Who are they? Can you tell why they're fighting?" Corey demanded.

"I don't know." Dan shook his head, leaning closer to the dirty glass. "They aren't punks wearing colors or anything."

"Who has the gun?" Corey asked.

Dan cocked his head and frowned as if trying to decipher the scene in the parking lot. He drew in a breath as if he meant to answer.

Something struck the window. With a loud thump, it cracked the pane. The sound of shattering glass filled the room. The shards fell. Then Dan crumbled, falling on the bed nearest the window.

With a bullet hole right between his shockingly pale eyes.

Emma screamed. "Dan. Dan! Oh my god . . ."

But Dan didn't answer. He was never going to. He was dead.

"Jesus!" Corey blinked. "What the fuck?" Then he turned an evil glare Lily's way. "You did this. Somehow. What did you do?"

"Me?" Lily's heart lurched. She had no idea who was out there, firing. That shot couldn't have been an accident. Someone must have been waiting. A sniper? Friend or foe?

At this point, did it matter? Corey absolutely meant to kill her. The men in the parking lot might or might not. Lily would take those odds.

When Corey charged toward her, she lowered the knife and shoved Emma in his direction. His wife stumbled into him, and he was forced to catch her. Lily didn't stay to watch what happened next. She wrenched the door open, the fight-or-flight response searing her veins with adrenaline. Sunlight rushed in, golden warmth and blue skies wrapping around her as she darted out of the terrible little motel room with a cry.

Over the second story railing, she spotted familiar faces in the parking lot. Hunter Edgington and Jack Cole both crouched behind the open doors of Stone's big black pickup, weapons visible through the windows. Police sirens suddenly wailed, splitting the sleepy air of small-town peace, coming closer with each second. Logan Edgington darted to the edge of the parking lot to meet them.

Axel sprinted across the expanse of blacktop toward her. "Sweet Pea!"

As he disappeared under the overhang where the stairs originated near the first-floor rooms, she ran—toward freedom, a familiar face she knew represented safety.

But she wanted the one who made her ache for love and devotion and forever. She wanted Stone. Where was he?

She heard pounding footsteps ascending the stairs in a full-out run, just about to hit the second floor. Axel couldn't have reached her that quickly. Had he called out to her because he'd been trying to warn her that the violent juvenile had arrived? Or that Kev was coming for her?

Knife in hand, Lily crouched in a fighting stance, ready to defend herself to the death. She'd just outwitted two men willing to do her in. By god, she'd take on another. She'd never be a victim again. She intended to do whatever necessary to protect herself, see justice done, and put every one of those fucking bastards in the ground or in prison.

Instead, a nearly shaved head emerged, followed by a beloved face, then the broadest shoulders and a wide chest she'd cradled her head against during some of the best nights of her life. Tight abs rippling beneath it, his gray T-shirt popped into view. He held a gun in one hand, sprinting, his legs pumping wildly to reach her. "Baby!"

Relief swelled inside her.

"Stone," she sobbed his name as she dropped the knife. It clattered to the ground as she ran down the stairs, arms outstretched, to meet him halfway.

She threw herself into his embrace, crashing into the solid cradle of his chest, against his thumping heart. Tears streamed down her face, stemming from her heart and wrenching her insides out.

"I've got you," he vowed. "I always will. I love you."

He'd come for her. And she swore to god that she'd never let anything or anyone tear them apart again.

"Fucking bitch!" Corey roared from the upper level above and behind her. "You're going to die!"

She'd barely heard the words and processed them by the time Stone had raised his gun and pulled the trigger.

Her heart lurched as she gasped and whirled to meet the threat. But Corey was already crumpling to the concrete walkway above, his gun clattering to the ground with him. Then he lay unmoving, his blood splattered wide around his still body.

"Fuck you," Stone quipped. "Who's the bitch now?"

Chapter Twenty

BOUQUET of flowers in hand, Lily pushed open the wrought iron gate to the cemetery. God, she couldn't believe she was here, finally about to see the graves of all her loved ones for the first time.

The Southern California sky winked blue and hot, but the gentle breeze carrying the air inland from the ocean made it somewhat bearable.

She'd once belonged in this city but no more. Not that she missed the sticky-hot humidity of the Texas summers, but after weeks of talking to both Bankhead and the feds about the drug-trafficking case pending against Canton, as well as the LA County District Attorney about the various murders and assorted crimes he'd committed, Lily figured he'd be going down for a long time. She'd needed to consent to testify—for Erin, her family, even for Regina in a weird way. Her daughter may not be here to realize that her mom had decided to do the right thing, but somehow Lily hoped the girl watched from above with pride.

Most especially, she needed to agree to testify for Stone.

Last night, she'd spoken to Sean on the phone. He'd explained the FBI investigation taking place and her role in it. He'd apologized for helping to orchestrate the plot to strong-arm her testimony. Thorpe had hopped on the phone next and followed suit. And since Dominion's owner and resident badass never apologized gracefully to anyone for anything, especially in such a heartfelt voice, Lily realized they were simply men who had made a mistake. Her heart welled because they'd made her feel like an important part of the club and the tight-knit community of its members.

When she'd first learned of their "perfidy," she'd been so furious at them for making decisions that affected the rest of her life without consulting her. But now that One-Mile had executed Dan from the roof of the church across from that skeevy motel, Corey was dead, his mom extradited from Canada, Emma and Kev behind bars, baby Isabel in CPS custody, and Canton potentially in for a lifelong prison sentence, Lily understood that with the past obstructing her future, she'd been going nowhere, doing nothing, committing herself to no one.

Everything had changed now that she'd made peace with her bleak teenage years. She couldn't change them or wash them away. She could only accept them, embrace them, and understand they were a part of who she'd become.

Her phone, which she'd tucked into the pocket of her polka-dot shirtwaist dress, buzzed. Axel had texted her a link, ostensibly to a story from a major news website. She clicked it and had to repress tears. It seemed as if she cried all the time now. After years of being unable to express her sorrow, now she overflowed. And god, she felt so much better.

The article popped up on her browser. More of Canton's victims were coming forward. More people he'd beaten, raped, swindled—all too terrified to say anything in the past. A tremulous smile wobbled across Lily's mouth. Once she'd been brave enough to tell the truth, others had followed suit—some with video evidence. The DA was taking all of their statements and compiling one big, long list of Canton's crimes. Gory details had been splashed across the news in every medium. He'd been denied bail by the judge because he'd been deemed both dangerous and a flight risk.

Subsequently, he had declined to run for governor of California.

Lily had been just about ready to click her phone off when it vibrated, low and rhythmic, indicating she had a call. She glanced at the display that popped up and smiled. "Hi, Axel."

"Hi, Sweet Pea. And yes, I'll probably always call you that."

She laughed. "Thorpe and Sean do, too. I kind of like it now that y'all know my real name." The nickname that used to be a means of hiding had now become a sweet endearment.

"Sorry I've been out of pocket but I've been wondering how you are. It's good to finally talk to you," he said.

Lily smiled at the sound of his voice. "I'm fine. Don't worry about me. You've got a wedding to plan."

"I'm up to my eyeballs in lace and tuxedos but it's good." He paused. "How does it feel to be you again?"

Interesting. Since Lily had come back to her old neighborhood over the past few weeks, she'd encountered so many people she'd known as a kid. Some were scraping by, trying to raise their own kids. Some were behind bars. Others had become drug addicts. A handful were already dead and buried. In some ways, Lily felt fortunate to have stepped out of the shadow of this awful barrio with its mediocre schools and parents too involved in their own jobs, addictions, or hookups to care about their kids. She'd seen a whole new way of life since leaving here. She'd experienced a whole new sort of family—the kind she chose.

"Let's say I'm not moving back. But I ran into Rick Mensell, my first boyfriend."

"The guy who knocked you up and walked out?" Axel growled.

"Yeah," she said sadly. "I actually think that kind of messed him up. He married right out of high school because his girlfriend at the time got pregnant. She had a miscarriage. They divorced. He never had more kids. He says he got a vasectomy at twenty-five because he didn't think he could go through the pain of losing a child again."

True, he hadn't been by her side for Regina's birth or death, but he said he visited her grave pretty regularly. Lily supposed everyone grieved and dealt in their own way.

"I would say he probably did the world a favor since he didn't handle his responsibilities well before but—"

"Let's not go there. It's done, buried, past. I'll always be sad, but I'm young. I'm recovering, thanks in part to you."

He sighed, his voice low and full of regret. "I tried to do my best by you."

"Oh, you did so much more than anyone should expect." He'd loved her more like a pal and had been happy to watch over her. But he hadn't been in love with her and he hadn't been interested in her sexually. But when she'd needed to be held and feel like a woman, he'd given her the sort of sex that was counter to his nature in virtually every way, just to help heal her and build her up. Most people wouldn't understand, but Lily did. And she couldn't have asked for a better protector and friend.

"I wish it had been more."

"It was plenty and then some. In part, because of you, I have hope for the future." And that was all she wanted to say about that or she'd start crying again. She sniffled and managed to hold the rest back. "Speaking of which, how much longer will you be in London?"

"For another few weeks. Marshall wants Mystery and me to attend some royal freaking ball that's being held in his honor," Axel said of his fiancée's father. "After that, we'll be back in Dallas, hopefully for good. You?"

"Soon, I think. It will take a while for all the trials to get underway here. I expect to be flying back and forth. But that's okay. Someday, it will all be over and . . . I'll put it behind me forever."

"Has Stone reached out to you?"

The one bleak spot in her life now. "No. It's been almost two weeks. Last I heard, he's still with the feds. I've left a couple of messages . . ."

But maybe he didn't want to spend his life with her after all. Maybe he'd put a bullet in Corey simply to end his miserable life and protect her. Then Stone had held her afterward because he felt sorry for her. Two weeks ago, she would have never believed that. Today, she didn't know what else to think.

"He'll come for you, Sweet Pea," Axel swore, his voice deep with gravity. "I might have stepped in the shit and given him a hard time when I raced out to the swamp that morning, but I figured out during your rescue that he loves you something fierce. The 'fight' in the parking lot of the motel? That distraction was his idea to get you out. If it didn't work, he was going to bust inside and rescue you. And probably get himself killed."

Lily didn't know what to say. "He's a good guy. He wouldn't have wanted anyone to die the way Corey had planned for me."

"Don't be stubborn," Axel chided. "Stone really had called off the deal with the feds before I'd busted into Jack's cabin all full of my righteous self, just like he claimed."

That took her by surprise. "Stone was telling the truth?"

Lily almost hated the hope his words gave her but she needed it so badly. She ached for him, yearned for the promise of those tomorrows he'd once said he wanted to share with her. She knew committing to each other was no guarantee of happiness—but it would be such a lovely start.

"Yeah." Axel sighed. "He would have put down his life for you, walked through fire, conquered hell. Whatever it took to keep you alive. You deserve that."

She teared up again and didn't hold anything back. "You're making me cry, damn it."

"Good. You've needed a real cry for a long time. But don't worry. He'll come for you. And you know I'm here anytime you need me. Just a phone call away."

"You're the best friend a girl could want. Thank you for everything. I can never repay you except by saying that I can stand on my own two feet from now on. And I'll be your rock if you ever need it."

"I know you're more than capable. Bye, Sweet Pea."

"Bye." She sniffled again and pocketed her phone.

Damn it, she needed to start carrying a purse with tissues. The Technicolor world of emotion was new, and she didn't always find it easy to process but damn . . . Life felt so much richer when she stopped wallowing in guilt and grief and tried to appreciate every day and the people in it. From now on, until she drew her last breath, she'd never stop living that way.

When she brushed the latest batch of tears dry, she approached Erin's grave and its simple headstone and placed some of her flowers in the holder. She hoped that somewhere up there Erin could forgive her for being careless. And that her bestie could forgive her brother for being mired in anguish and letting it cloud his judgment.

"I miss you," she told her best friend. "We should still be holding hands and telling secrets and laughing about stupid movies. But I won't stop thinking about you. Ever."

Lily laid her hand on the top of the headstone and caressed it, hoping that Erin could feel her regret and affection.

More tears flowed as she made her way a few rows down to her family, buried side by side. Her mother had only been thirty-eight. She'd lived terribly and died fast. She'd been a kid trying to raise a child in a bleak situation. Lily didn't blame her for her anger, desperation, choices, and coping mechanisms. She'd only been human, too. She wished she'd understood the woman better, but maybe with age and wisdom, she could. Or maybe in another life.

Lily laid down fresh flowers. "I hope I'm making you proud now. I'll always try, Mom. I hope you're up there finally resting and smiling in peace."

Then she stepped over to her brother. Brady had been so young.

He'd had no way of understanding the terrible violence that had ended his life with such frightening finality.

"Hey, Brady Boy." He hadn't wanted her to call him that in public, but at home, he'd liked it until the day he'd been taken from her. She laid down flowers, one with a fluffy teddy bear attached. It was probably something most twelve-year-olds wouldn't admit to still liking, but Brady had loved his stuffed animals. "I brought you a little something to play with. I hope you've found soccer balls and video games in heaven, too. You deserve them. I'm so sorry those terrible men hurt you and for the way you died. You can kick my butt when I get up there someday, huh? Until then, maybe you can forgive me?"

Of course, he didn't answer, but the wind blew, brushing her skin almost like a caress, as if she could feel her brother's hand on her shoulder letting her know he was all right. Maybe Lily was thinking wishfully, but Brady had been a good kid and a kind soul. She'd loved him. "You and Mom take care of each other until I can get back here to visit again, okay?"

That answering breeze kicked up once more, and she smiled, feeling more at peace than she had in over half a dozen years, maybe ever.

Now came the hard part.

Lily clutched the last of the flowers and made her way to the corner of the graveyard. She knew where to find Regina. She'd made contact with the cemetery a couple of weeks ago and received a map. She was late in visiting her loved ones but she hoped they could forgive her. She was finally learning to forgive herself.

When she reached the corner, climbing ivy and bougainvillea filled in the slats of the fence with their gorgeous greenery. A nearby willow bent protectively over her baby's grave, leaves swaying gently, almost like an eternal mobile.

She also saw an unexpected sight. A gleaming white headstone marked Regina's final resting place. Beside it stood a man so familiar, her stomach clenched. Her heart swooned. Had he arranged the big marble monument for her daughter?

"Hi, baby," Stone said quietly, turning and reaching out his hand for her.

"You found me," she said numbly, though her heart pounded in a crazy, thumping rhythm.

"I always will. Come here."

She slipped her hand in his and peered up into his dark eyes. He looked tired and nervous but so incredibly wonderful in a simple gray suit and a solemn expression. "You're really here."

"And I'm not leaving you. The feds and I are good now. Because it looks like Canton is going away for a long time and I helped, they agreed to commute my sentence. I'm a free man—and only in part because I'm not going back to prison. You gave me a whole new path in life. You showed me a love worth fighting for."

Lily shook her head, smiling at the great news. "I think you're the one who taught me how to look past my fears. I'm sorry I yelled and I accused. And I left."

"I'd help you twenty times over if I could. I'd do anything for you." He gave her a small smile. "I called my dad today. We made peace. It was . . . surreal and a little awkward but nice."

"That's fantastic. I'm really happy for you. I think you needed the closure."

"Yeah. We're going to try to talk more, maybe get together soon. See how it goes. We both have some forgiving to do."

"But that's important. Helpful. I know it's been good for me." She swallowed, nodding slowly. "What brings you here?"

He squeezed her hand and looked down at the marble headstone, engraved with Regina's name and a baby's rattle. "Do you like it?"

"It's beautiful. You did that for her?"

He nodded. "And for you."

When he raised her hand to his lips and kissed it, Lily's heart nearly exploded. The tears that were ever present these days sprang up again and spilled down her cheeks. She looked at him, completely baring her love for him in her eyes. "Thank you. That's the most amazing thing anyone has ever done for me."

"I want to do wonderful things for you for the rest of your life." He shoved his hand in his pocket and looked down, decidedly nervous. "I'm not a man of flowery words and I've fucked up a lot in my past. But every mistake has led me to you. I know what I've done wrong. I know what I want for the future. And baby, I never would have coerced you to testify just so I could get out of prison, not once—"

"Not once you knew me? I figured that out." She barely squeaked the words out past her crying. "Axel told me that you really had given up your freedom before he barged in at the cabin. But I realized that awful day when Corey plotted to kill me that I couldn't blame you for making that deal. When you did it, you didn't know me. Of course you wanted freedom. And I should have wanted to put Canton away before he could hurt anyone else."

"Knowing you changed everything I felt. I swear it."

"I believe you." She caressed his shoulder and stepped closer. "I know the kind of man you are deep down. We all make mistakes. You made yours young, like I did. Since then, you've grown into someone so wonderful."

Stone grabbed her, swept her lips under his, and held her close as they exchanged breaths and silent vows. Finally, he pulled away. "Marry me?"

She cupped his cheek, feeling both giddy and hopeful. "I never want to be with anyone else."

For the first time that day, he gave her a wide, genuine smile—and lit up her world. He showed her colors of the heart she hadn't known existed before. And she'd always be so thankful for Stone.

"That's a yes?" He looked anxious and hopeful.

"A big yes." She managed a grin, though she couldn't seem to stop crying. "A hell yes. An I-can't-wait-to-be-with-you yes."

Stone managed a deep laugh as he pressed another kiss to her lips, then pulled out a simple solitaire set in white gold from his pocket and slipped it on her finger. It fit perfectly. "For the record, I wasn't letting you get away again."

Lily looked down at the diamond winking on her finger. "I wasn't planning on walking away anymore. You're stuck with me forever."

"I like the sound of that." He wrapped his arms around her and held her close.

His heart beat against hers. Lily breathed in the man who had become her life, her hope, her future.

"How did you know I was coming to visit Regina?" she asked.

"I knew you needed to make peace." His solemn expression of support almost turned her heart inside out. "And I'm still tracking your phone."

She laughed even as more tears fell, but these felt happier. "So you're free to start a new life?"

"Yeah. But I have this boss in Lafayette. He's a cranky Cajun who's impatient to have me back. And a group of friends who apparently don't mind having a wild ex-con around and want me back in town. You?"

"I think . . . I want to get married and have another baby, this time with the man I love. What do you think?"

"I love that plan and I love you, Lily. I always have." He looked into her eyes, focused, strong—all hers. "I always will. Let's go home and start our new lives together. Preferably naked." He winked.

Lily nodded happily, gratefully, as she laid the flowers down on Regina's grave and blew her daughter a kiss. She would forever mourn the little girl, and no baby would ever replace her, but she knew she would love the children she and Stone would have someday and that Regina would smile down on them. "I'd love that."

She slipped her hand in his, and together they walked into their future.

WATCH FOR . . .

Holding on Tighter

A WICKED LOVERS NOVEL
COMING FEBRUARY 2017
(HEATH'S STORY!)

About the Author

Shayla Black is the *New York Times* and *USA Today* best-selling author of nearly fifty novels, including the Wicked Lovers series (*Wicked for You, His to Take*) and, with Lexi Blake, the Perfect Gentlemen series (*Seduction in Session, Scandal Never Sleeps*). For more than fifteen years, she's written contemporary, erotic, paranormal, and historical romances via traditional, independent, foreign, and audio publishers. Her books have sold well over a million copies and have been published in a dozen languages.

Raised as an only child, Shayla occupied herself with lots of daydreaming, much to the chagrin of her teachers. In college, she found her love of reading and realized that she could have a career publishing the stories spinning in her imagination. Though she graduated with a degree in marketing/advertising and embarked on a stint in corporate America to pay the bills, her heart has always been with her characters. She's thrilled that she has been living her dream as a full-time author for the past seven years.

Shayla currently lives in North Texas with her wonderfully supportive husband, her teenage daughter, and a very spoiled cat. In her "free" time, she enjoys reality TV, reading, listening to an eclectic blend of music, and playing Fallout 4. Connect with Shayla via her website (www.ShaylaBlack.com), Facebook (ShaylaBlackAuthor), Instagram (shaylablack), or her newsletter (http://bit.ly/SBNewsletter).